MW00657011

SOME OTHER TIME

ALSO BY ANGELA BROWN

Olivia Strauss Is Running Out of Time

SOME OTHER TIME

a novel

ANGELA BROWN

Little

a

This is a work of fiction. Names, characters, organizations, places, events, and incidents are either products of the author's imagination or are used fictitiously. Otherwise, any resemblance to actual persons, living or dead, is purely coincidental.

Text copyright © 2025 by Angela Brown
All rights reserved.

No part of this book may be reproduced, or stored in a retrieval system, or transmitted in any form or by any means, electronic, mechanical, photocopying, recording, or otherwise, without express written permission of the publisher.

Published by Little A, New York

www.apub.com

Amazon, the Amazon logo, and Little A are trademarks of Amazon.com, Inc., or its affiliates.

ISBN-13: 9781662516375 (hardcover)
ISBN-13: 9781662516368 (paperback)
ISBN-13: 9781662516382 (digital)

Cover illustration and design by Alicia Tatone

Printed in the United States of America

First edition

For my mom and for Jay—
how many days until our next trip?

Just always be waiting for me.

—J. M. Barrie, *Peter Pan*

PROLOGUE

It could have ended a hundred different ways.

She could have stayed in that mess of an apartment, seated uncomfortably on the scratchy, secondhand yellow couch, listening as the boy she thought she loved lectured her on the vast differences between emotional and physical cheating, and why what he'd done didn't fit neatly into either category.

She could have remembered to put gas in her car the night before, just like her parents always told her to do (*a little gift to your future self the next morning*) instead of driving around on fumes and then finally, moments after leaving said apartment, having to pull off the main road, wipe her tear-soaked eyes, and then ask the man in the blue coveralls to please put twenty dollars' worth of poison in her tank. Better yet, she could have asked him to fill it and then sat there breathing in fumes for five extra minutes.

Or she could have said screw it, pushed the car to its limits, ridden it out on E, and gone straight back to her apartment, with her books and her bed and that quiet little balcony, and just sulked, the way all twentysomethings do the day they learn the person they thought was *the one* is actually an enormous ass. But she didn't, because she knew her new sublet roommate, whom she hadn't quite hit it off with, would no doubt be in the living room day drinking or smoking weed or making out with her own boyfriend, all scenarios that would undoubtedly push her already-stretched-thin emotional bandwidth to its limit.

For the record, she could have opted not to get a sublet.

When she arrived at the four-way stop, gas tank half-full and ready for almost anything, rather than turn left to go home, she turned right instead and just kept going. She was heartbroken, and apparently single, and the only thing that felt good when faced with those circumstances was to put the windows down and to turn the music up and to drive and to feel the air and to cry.

Well, that. And coffee.

Which was why, a few minutes later, she turned right once again at a different intersection so she could stop at that new coffee shop across the street from the bookstore where she worked full-time and buy herself something strongly caffeinated, as well as some sort of gooey, sugary, you-definitely-earned-this-after-a-year-with-that-fool treat.

On that particular afternoon, Ellie Grace Adams, who in two years' time would become Ellie Grace Baker (though she didn't know that yet), could have made a million different decisions. She'd read once, in a book displayed near the register during an exceptionally quiet shift, that the average adult makes something like thirty-five thousand choices in a day. Ellie had wondered how researchers had come up with that number, and whether it was highly exciting or incredibly overwhelming to consider such a mind-numbing fact. As she set the book down to ring up a lone customer, she couldn't decide if that stat did more to support the idea of free will (*The choice is, quite literally, yours!*) or fate (*With all those minuscule decisions, what are the chances of, well, anything?*).

Ellie, like so many young and wanting-to-be-in-love women, believed in the latter as devoutly as if it were her faith.

Of course, Ellie wasn't thinking about any of this when, at exactly 1:11 p.m. (almost her mother's "angel" number, but not close enough for Ellie to bother making a wish), she stopped her car at a red light, both the coffee shop and the bookstore up ahead. Her car noisily idling, she looked away from the road for only a minute to adjust the wires that spewed from her car lighter and fed into her yellow Discman and then played another song from the artist she'd listened to on repeat ever since she'd left not-the-one's apartment. It was sad music, a perfect soundtrack for post-breakup, a bit of a cliché, but still it worked. Ellie clicked the Discman buttons until she reached her favorite song, which she'd already heard at least three times, then looked back up, set her hands on the wheel at ten and two, daydreaming about what hot beverage and chocolate something or other might heal her. The light turned green. Ellie released her foot from the brake, clicked the music up a few more decibels. And then—SMASH!

Years later, when people asked Ellie and Jonah how they met, they'd joke that it was thanks to a little love tap—their cute manner of describing the fender bender that had brought them together. That was when things were still good, when their marriage and their life together felt like some simmered-down fairy tale about regular, everyday people. Ellie should have known better. If there was one thing she had a grasp on in life, it was books, and as such, she was well aware from the start that all stories—even fairy tales—eventually end.

But that realization—in terms of her life, anyhow—came later. She wasn't mentally there yet.

And so, when a frazzled, midtwenties Jonah, who had just come off a breakup himself (though not quite as recently), dashed to Ellie's driver's side window and apologized to her in a thousand diverse ways, she could have made a dozen alternate choices. After they'd inspected both their cars and then exchanged names and phone numbers and insurance information, she could have said goodbye, turned her music back up, and driven away. She didn't. Rather, when the man who'd just hit her car pointed to a place in the near distance and asked if he could treat her to a coffee as one final form of apology, she wiped her tearstained face and allowed herself to laugh at the ridiculousness of her day—a breakup, a car collision, what next?—right before she said yes. *Yes.* Funny coincidence, she'd explained, but she'd actually been heading there anyway.

It wasn't until more than twenty years later, when asked about their story yet again, that Ellie finally started to change the narrative and tell people that no—no!—it wasn't because of a cute little love tap.

It was because of a crash.

Looking back, her rose-colored view of the event long gone, that seemed to her like a more accurate way to describe it.

But even that felt a little bit sugarcoated.

Which was why, in those final weeks they lived together, Ellie—a lover of words and stories and happy endings, a woman who once upon a time had believed in foolish things like fate—finally mustered up the courage and began to describe their chance encounter—the one built upon the backs of so many small, throwaway choices, and that ultimately shaped the trajectory of the rest of their lives—as something else, the thing that in all reality it had always been, even though neither of them had initially wanted to believe it.

An accident.

PART ONE

The Departure

ONE

Twenty years later . . .

Florida is hot.

It is an instant sunburn, a fever that will not break. Despite years of traveling here, zipping up and down the Eastern Seaboard for dozens of different milestones and on infinite spring breaks, Ellie has never gotten used to it. The humidity is enough to suffocate her, or to at least make her feel constantly short of breath. Ellie's parents swear the tropical dampness is good for their aging joints, like free medicine they don't need to run through Medicare. Ellie isn't so sure. But then again, her parents, both in their early eighties, still take walks most mornings, around and around their condo community as if on a carousel, the rising temperatures hardly enough to make them break a sweat. Back home in New Jersey, Ellie, on the other hand, has worked out less than a dozen times in the last year, which is probably part of the reason why her back and her chest are soaked and that delicate strip beneath the underwire of her bra is currently a damp slick.

She's dripping, and she hasn't even gotten off the plane yet.

"You can ease up on the armrests," Jonah points out while peering down at Ellie's hands, clenched for dear life on those slender plastic strips. He casually taps the porthole-like window beside him, the shade pushed up even though, due to her fear of heights, she's asked him a dozen times to keep it closed. His knuckles drum the double-paned glass (an extra layer of protection, Ellie knows, so that if it cracks, they won't all get sucked out of the plane and spit helplessly into the stratosphere). Beyond the window, the world is a diorama—strips of black pavement, patchworks of brown and tan and green, dollhouse-size houses and buildings, cars as small as insects. "You're all right, Ellie," Jonah says, even though, of course, she isn't. Neither is he. "Just look." He taps the glass again, his attempt at kindness, despite the circumstances. "You can already see the ground. We're almost there."

Great.

Ellie has always been a bad flier. Even though she's flown this exact route—Newark to Orlando, and Orlando back to Newark—innumerable times in the last two decades, she's never grown used to the experience. The too-tight quarters. The comically sized bathrooms, which seem to her to have been designed for paper dolls rather than humans with actual bodies. The sound of air rushing past the plane, like flying with a blow-dryer pointed at your ear. The blatant fact of being surrounded by more than one hundred strangers and everyone just *breathing.* To Ellie, buying a plane ticket is like purchasing a panic attack, then fastening herself into a gas-fueled bullet and self-electing to shoot herself high into the sky. *Wheeeee!* At least on all those other flights, some happy gift was always waiting for her on the opposite end. A sunny vacation. A chance to return to the comforts of her home, rested and relaxed. But this trip? It's like someone has drawn a straight line to connect destination A with destination B, and then lit the paper on fire with a thousand matches.

"*Gooood* afternoon, ladies and gentlemen, just a little message from the flight deck." A man's voice chimes through the overhead speakers. "Letting you know we've officially begun our final descent into Orlando. *Shooould* be on the ground in about another ten minutes. Weather in Orlando, clear skies, good visibility, temperature a steamy eighty-one degrees. Been a pleasure having you with us on this Friday morning. *Hoooope* to see you again on a future flight."

"Why do they always do that?" Ellie asks Jonah, her posture as straight as an arrow, her entire body stiff, as if in survival mode.

"Do what?" Jonah is seated comfortably, his gaze turned away from Ellie and cast instead on the seat-back television. He's spent the entire flight like this—his tree-trunk legs casually splayed, his fingers dipping in and out of a bag of pretzels, as if he were home hanging on the couch watching football and not being dangerously catapulted through the clouds. But then, this is part of it, isn't it? The simple fact that they've always been so different. "What did they do?"

"Make it sound like they're not sure how things will end," Ellie continues.

Jonah sets his snack in his lap, tilts his head at her as if she is a complicated math problem he struggles to understand. His yellow-flecked eyes narrow in question.

"You know," she says, "we 'should' be on the ground, or we 'hope' to see you again." The sweat erupts through her pores, like hot lava bursting from a volcano. She feels her breath quicken, her inhales and exhales happening too fast, as if someone has given her lungs the wrong batteries. "Why don't they use firmer language? We 'will' be on the ground, or we 'will' see you again."

"Come on, Ellie." Jonah reaches above her, twists her small, cylindrical air-conditioner vent open. It releases a rush of cool air. "They're not foreshadowing a crash."

Ellie drops her head back, inviting the arctic blast onto her damp skin. "Was that thing working the whole time?" she asks, rolling out her neck. "I tried it at the start of the flight. It was jammed." She lifts her face. "I'm so hot."

"You probably tried to twist it the wrong way." Jonah smiles, knowing Ellie always does things like this. Give her a book, and she can provide you with an in-depth analysis. Give her a light bulb, and suddenly she doesn't know her left from her right. "Also, you're wearing a cardigan." He turns his attention back to the TV, flips to a sports broadcast. "Probably not a great choice, right?"

Right, Ellie thinks, though not about her wardrobe. Unfortunately for her—for them both, really—right now, this seemingly basic statement can apply to just about everything.

How have they arrived here? Not to these specific airplane seats—16A and 16B, just like always—but to this precise moment in their lives, the one where, despite years of intimacy, they've begun to feel like strangers who also somehow know each other quite well. Marriage doesn't make much sense. But then again, neither does strapping yourself into a vinyl seat and spending two and a half hours racing through the air while you nervously consume crackers and an early-morning plastic cup of bad white wine, like a guest at a bizarre cocktail party. Both things, if handled the wrong way, can turn out to be reckless.

Ding. Ding.

The overhead seat belt lights flash, a reminder for them to prepare for whatever destiny awaits them on the runway. Ellie tugs the nylon strap tighter around her waist. She doesn't know what will happen down there. She only knows she isn't ready for it.

~

After wrestling with the cramped overhead compartments, and then standing elbow to elbow with a line of strangers as they inched their way up the jet's narrow center aisle, like prisoners walking some airline-sponsored plank, Ellie finally exits the plane.

She spills out of the accordion passenger bridge—the harsh humidity already sneaking in through gaps in the jet bridge—with a rush of other travelers, half of them donning Mickey ears and wide smiles and matching family shirts. *Johnson Family Vacation! Happiest Vacation on Earth! Most Expensive Vacation on Earth!* People like this sort of thing, anything to show they are a unit. Ellie always wanted to do something like this when Maggie was small—coordinated patterns at the holidays, complementary travel gear—but Jonah always rolled his eyes anytime she mentioned the idea.

Ellie navigates past the gate, already packed with other travelers ready to board the exact vessel she's just left. She races to catch up with Jonah, who is several feet ahead, oblivious to the fact that Ellie, a slower walker with shorter-than-his legs, trails behind him, weighed down by her travel book bag. Not a purse or a small duffel or even a cross-body. A book bag, like it's her first day of elementary school, or like she's suddenly taken up hiking. It's the one she started to use for trips like this years ago, when her daughter was young and required so many things, but that Ellie has never quite gotten around to swapping back out. Now, as she walks (sprints?), the navy-blue canvas rucksack bounces on her back like a fussy toddler intent on kicking her, over and over, just above her rear end. Ellie doesn't even know what is in the bag. Wallet. Snacks. A book, like she might have the clarity to read on this trip. The contents don't matter. Ellie knows the bag is a waste. So far, the only thing it's provided her with is a ripple of new muscle aches.

The underarms of her tucked-in favorite white T-shirt wet (she shoved her taupe cocoon cardigan in her backpack—at least the bag's been good for this), Ellie adjusts the straps while she walks, loosening their death grip on her shoulders and the chafing sensation they keep instigating in her armpits. Jonah's wide stride places him several paces ahead, like a Thoroughbred. This is what he's built like, anyway. Concrete muscles. Strong limbs. His body all well-placed indentations and lines. What a sham. He rarely even works out (she can't talk much on this point herself), his whole shape just false advertising. It's like he was born this way, as if he's some Greek god or charming cartoon prince. Ellie gave birth almost two decades ago, and she still has the loose pouch of skin to prove it. Infuriating.

Regardless of his body shape, Ellie follows him across the airport's patterned carpet. It's clear from his stance (sure, certain) and his pace (confident, quick) that he knows every inch of this place. Where to find coffee. Bathrooms. A bottled water. Ellie should know these things, too. She's traveled here just as frequently as him, though honestly, she's never fully paid attention. This has always been Jonah's job—to know where they're going, where to find certain things. And isn't this just marriage? One person in the driver's seat, the other person staring out the window, bouncing along, pleased to be enjoying the ride.

Ellie hustles past a stretch of glass-enclosed hallway. Jonah's head—all thick, chestnut hair accented with silver strands, like tinsel on a tree—mixes in with the heads of strangers. She keeps moving forward, thinking about how she's spent years—decades, really—just happily, obliviously, following along behind him.

~

"I talked to her," Jonah announces when Ellie walks out of the bathroom. He slides his phone into the pocket of his jeans—good denim, a medium wash, an age-appropriate cut—which he's paired with classic low-top sneakers (no socks) and a nice salmon-colored T-shirt. Jonah passes Ellie back her book bag, which he offered to hold when she joined the snaking line of other women, all desperate to pee and wash their hands and peek in the mirror (she foolishly touched up her simple makeup, like it mattered, ran a slick of bare shimmer over her lips), anything to feel human again after their respective flights. "She's meeting us at the baggage claim," he continues as Ellie slides the bag back on her body.

For a moment, they stand here, a parade of people walking past in every direction, and look at one another, the weight of the weekend ahead suddenly settling on their shoulders as uncomfortably as those backpack straps. They both inhale deeply at the same time, like a pair of synchronized swimmers dedicated to pulling off the same routine.

"Ahh!" Someone bumps into Ellie from behind, the person's head glued to his phone. "What the—" she shouts, but it's a waste of breath. He doesn't even apologize or acknowledge her—women her age really are made to feel invisible sometimes—and rushes off in the direction of his gate.

The moment between them interrupted, Jonah pulls up the handle of his sleek wheeled carry-on—the only thing he's packed—with a quick and efficient snap. "Coffee?" he asks, already turning to take a step.

A few minutes later, their plastic cups of cold brew in hand, and they are inside the airport's monorail, shoved in between strollers, crying children, stressed-out families, and the solitary business traveler who keeps looking around, perhaps considering how he's ended up here—in the vacation destination and T-shirt capital of the world—dressed in a black suit and tie. Beside Ellie, a little girl dressed in a made-in-China princess costume bounces up and down like a windup toy.

"I'm Elsa!" she keeps exclaiming to anyone who will listen, accidentally whacking everyone around her with a plastic wand.

Her mother smiles down at her daughter, snaps a quick picture on her phone. "Sorry," she says to Ellie in that way mothers sometimes apologize for their children, even when they aren't necessarily doing anything wrong. "It's her first time."

A memory. One of their first trips down with Maggie. She was a toddler—two or maybe two and a half—her pale, chubby thighs exposed from the bottom of that adorable pink dress and kicking around in all directions like a puppet as they wheeled her stroller up and into that same glass-enclosed train. They weren't heading off like all the other tourists to one of the overpriced theme park resorts, but rather to stay with Ellie's parents, who had recently sold their home in New Jersey to her and Jonah (*Too much space for us! Those winters!*) and resettled themselves in the Sunshine State. Midway through the brief, two-minute monorail ride to the next terminal, Jonah had reached out and squeezed Ellie's hand. "I'm really happy," he said, his face—more than fifteen years younger then—a wash of raw emotion, his eyes misty. "Just really, really happy." Ellie was happy—satisfied—then, too.

Back in the present, "Elsa" smacks Ellie in the thigh with her wand. *Sorry,* her mother mouths as the train comes to a stop.

"Please stand clear of doors and hold on to handrails," an automated voice announces overhead. "The doors are now closing." Through the glass, the scene is a hybrid of the tropics—palm trees, thick green grass—and industry. The train slides into the terminal. The electronic doors glide open. "Please exit and follow the signs to Baggage Claim B."

~

"Maggie!"

Ellie and Jonah both call out her name the minute they spot her. She stands near the baggage carousel, a giant slide of metal that circles around and around but as of yet remains empty. She nibbles on some snack—trail mix or dried fruit or something of the sort, Ellie assumes—her long, sun-kissed brown hair stretching down her slender back. She is a natural beauty, the type who makes people pause to take a second look. It's already May, nearly the end of her semester. Sometimes, when they go weeks or months without seeing each other—Ellie hates how long they go without seeing each other now—she forgets just how striking.

Ellie, instantly disregarding her strained muscles and her ridiculous bag, dashes across the terrazzo floor and throws her arms around her daughter. She nestles her face in the girl's—the young *woman's*—hair, breathing in her scent: rosemary shampoo, a hint of lavender lotion on her skin, and then just the scent of *her*, this musky, familiar smell she's always emitted. Ellie can't help herself. She begins to sob.

"Mom!" Maggie pulls back. She may be an adult now, a thriving college student and self-proclaimed "Vermonter" even though she's been at Middlebury for less than a year, but when face-to-face with her mother, she becomes a disgruntled, perpetually mortified teenager all over again. "Pull it together!"

Jonah walks up from behind Ellie, gives Maggie a quick hug and a kiss on her cheek. He rumples her hair, just like he did when she was five. Maggie smiles. Apparently, this sort of affection from her father is still fine. "You look good, kiddo," he tells her and picks up her bag—a patchwork number that looks like it belongs in a museum exhibit about Woodstock. "How was your flight?"

~

Naturally, Ellie's bag is lost, or at the very least caught in a battle with punctuality. Beside her, Jonah and Maggie, both of whom have their carry-on luggage, stand and impatiently wait. Apparently, Ellie is the only one who felt she required her bigger baggage (as if there isn't already enough of it to claim at the moment). She can't help it. This is just one of many symptoms of all those years she felt so responsible for everyone, always making sure the three of them had every possible thing, this forever maternal urge to overpack.

"I'll go ask someone again," Jonah decides, and Ellie can tell he's annoyed by this inconvenience, as if Ellie has planned it, like she was dying to have her things lost.

Annoyed and likely looking like a mess, Ellie watches as Jonah approaches some TSA employee whom she can already tell doesn't have a clue. Maggie follows behind her father like a shadow. She wears a long white cotton skirt, its hem trailing the ground, a faded tank top, and a tan fisherman's sweater (she must have slipped it on in a still-cold Vermont this morning) tied around her waist. Like always, as of late, her feet are covered by those ridiculous Jesus sandals. This is Maggie's look now, her *vibe* (oh, to still have the luxury of such self-indulgences as a vibe, whatever that even means), something to go along with her total protestation of eggs and gelatin. Apparently, according to her daughter, Ellie's love of fizzy grapefruit seltzer and certain baked confections is the sole reason there's a hole in the atmosphere.

"He said we should head to that window down there," Jonah says with a frown as he walks back toward Ellie. "We can fill out some paperwork. They'll call us when they find it."

Before Ellie has a chance to have a complete and utter mental breakdown over this announcement, something thuds heavily behind her. They all turn. Her black hard-shell suitcase—badly scuffed and half-unzipped—tumbles onto the conveyor belt. Jonah immediately turns back toward the TSA employee to give him a wave—*It's okay!*— like the man cares. Ellie doesn't want to wait. She bends down, grabs the handle, and tugs.

"Damn it!" she exclaims, knowing instantly that she's tweaked it, the one unruly muscle in her back, which she ruined years ago during childbirth.

"Mom!" Maggie scolds her mother as she nibbles on her dehydrated vegan snack. Her yellow-hazel eyes—*Jonah's* eyes—narrow with judgment. "Your energy!"

Jonah crouches down, helping Ellie with her suitcase, which is splayed open, half her possessions on the filthy floor. Why, of all the bags, did they need to check hers? As if she—an unremarkable suburban mother, looking like a stock character of a typical late-forties woman on a film set—might be hoarding guns or drugs or exotic animals in her luggage instead of menopause medication and a few extra light layers in case she gets chilly at night.

Jonah zips the suitcase, positions it upright. "Do you need a hand?" he finally asks.

Do you need a hand? She mimics him in her brain by way of her most sarcastic tone, not because what he's said or done is wrong but because this is modern marriage—the constant internal tug-of-war of wanting to be an independent woman and yet still longing for your husband—with all his visible muscles, like some kind of real-life Gaston—to carry your bag.

"No, I'm fine." Ellie's back is already seizing up, like she's been tased. "But thanks."

Jonah and Maggie lead, navigating toward the wall of automated doors. Near one of them, a man in a slightly wrinkled dress shirt and slacks holds up a sign. THE BAKER FAMILY, it reads.

"That's us!" Jonah shouts. He waves at the man with one hand and uses the other to slide a pair of classic black sunglasses from his T-shirt pocket and over his eyes.

Yes, Ellie thinks, hustling behind once again. *But not for long.*

From the corner of her eye, she catches a glimpse of a digital clock overhead. 11:11 a.m. There's no time left for wishes, though.

In front of Jonah and Maggie, the airport's automatic doors open and then close and then open again.

"Ready, gang?" Jonah asks over his hulking shoulder.

Ellie nods. And then, without a word—and already knowing it's too late to turn back—for the last time in her life, she walks with her family beyond the glass exit and out into the oppressive heat.

TWO

The drive from the airport to the condo is hell.

Their hired driver, who won't stop talking or playing with the radio dial (*Look up, look up, look up*) is either new to the world of driving or is training for a career in NASCAR. It's hard to say, but based on the way he swerves from lane to lane, like a child behind the wheel of an arcade game, Ellie feels confident it's one of them.

"How are we doing with the air?" Jonah asks from the front seat. The sunlight through the window catches his dark hair, all brushed with silver, like the scales of a fish. The gray only adds to his looks, which is complete garbage. Ellie pays $200 every three months so some twenty-eight-year-old can paint her head with chemicals and help fuel the cultural belief that women should not age.

"More," Ellie answers, slamming her foot on an imaginary brake pedal. The sweat keeps on pouring, like an enthusiastic bartender. "We definitely need more."

Air shoots through the vents, billowing Ellie's straight, shoulder-length (dyed and highlighted, definitely not natural) honey-brunette hair. Jonah picks up a conversation with the driver about some construction project they've driven past as naturally as if they've always been friends. Ellie once loved this trait of Jonah's—his ability to talk to almost anyone about the most mundane topics. Now it just makes her sad. They rarely talk like this together anymore.

In the early days, both of them in their midtwenties, they'd stay up late every weekend night fueled by wine and romance and youth, talking about—what, exactly? Life. Dreams. Childhood memories. Before they left for the airport this morning, they'd conversed about the carbon monoxide detectors, which they both agreed were probably due for new batteries.

Beside Ellie, Maggie stares through the window, still gnawing her way through steak-size slices of dried mango. *You know how you'd be less hungry?* Ellie thinks. *If you put aside these foolish new politics and actually ate a steak.*

Just a year earlier, Maggie would have gladly devoured a thick cut of grilled meat. Maggie, who served as the vice president of her high school class and who constantly pleaded with her mother to purchase her whatever new preppy blouses or straight-leg jeans were in the window display of the J.Crew in the downtown shopping district of their agreeable, midsize suburb. Apparently, up at Middlebury, where Ellie and Jonah are paying more than some people's annual salary for Maggie to hang out and drink locally brewed craft beers for four years, someone has convinced their daughter that her comfortable upbringing is why the world keeps catching on fire. Probably the same individual who stabbed a needle and silver stud though her nostril. Ellie imagines that this person drives a bumper sticker–marked Subaru.

When Maggie was growing up, she and Ellie were always close. Sure, they had typical mother-daughter tension, though mostly they got along well. But midway through Maggie's junior year, things quickly changed. It started on the night the high school hosted an informational college event. The gym was nothing but folding tables and fanned-out brochures. Together, their family browsed the offerings, collecting literature from every imaginable campus. Ellie just smiled and went along with things. Her whole life, Maggie had expressed her desire to stay close to home, stick with a good state school, maybe even try her luck with Princeton. Ellie had never tried to hold Maggie back. If her daughter wanted to be nearby, who was Ellie to talk her out of it? She pictured hand-delivered care packages and frequent visits home. It'd be college, yes, but not with so much distance that Ellie would completely stop being needed.

"So, California sounded cool," Maggie half mumbled once the three of them were in the hallway. "A bit far, but that's the point of college." She cleared her throat. "Right?"

Ellie stopped walking. "California?" She looked to Jonah, who appeared entirely unfazed. "You're kidding. Is she kidding?"

Jonah shrugged. "Nice weather." He'd gone out west for college, too.

Maggie and Jonah exchanged a glance. "It's just, Dad and I have been talking, and—I don't know—there's just so many choices out there. Maybe I ought to take more of a risk."

"Wh-why wasn't I included in this conversation?" Ellie stammered.

"Come on, Mom," Maggie said, her tone condescending. "I mean, you've lived here forever." She glanced at her father, something private hovering between them. "No offense, but you've never even left the East Coast."

Back in Florida, the car races forward.

"How's school, Mags?" Ellie asks, her tone intentionally even—not too high, not too low, like some maternal Goldilocks. This is a safer segue into conversation than *How are you?* or *How is life?* or anything that might unlock real emotion.

"It's fine," she says, like always. No details about friends (even though Ellie knows she has them) or a romantic interest (with a face like this, she's never struggled here, either) or classes (a hodgepodge of philosophy and botany and Eastern religion, as if she might go on to establish some particularly spiritual pot dispensary). "Finals start in two weeks."

Ellie wishes she could ask Maggie something deeper. *What are you thinking? Are you happy? Why are you so mad?* But she can't. She and Maggie aren't the same, due to reasons Ellie doesn't understand. It's something more than Maggie growing up. Ellie misses her daughter, even though she's right here. She knows this isn't logical—how can you miss someone who's seated beside you? But with the passing of time, you learn you can. And Ellie does.

At the start of Maggie's senior year, the PTA organized a breakfast for the parents—this group of adults who, ever since their children had entered their town's kindergarten program, had watched together from the sidelines as their babies learned how to read and to solve equations and to navigate heartache and puberty and friendship and a million other things. Naturally, it was mostly the mothers who showed up to the school cafeteria to eat dry pastries and talk.

The other women seemed so excited. They were thrilled their children had reached this next stage. Some had begun to plan trips with their spouses. Others had already drawn up renovation plans for the soon-to-be-empty spaces in their homes. Ellie spent most of that morning picking apart a danish and nodding along, wondering the whole time if something was wrong with her for feeling so sad about this next chapter, especially now that Maggie had decided to go somewhere—anywhere—far away.

It was Ellie's choice to stay home and raise Maggie. Not once had Jonah ever pressured or guilted her. Ellie, who'd studied English at a state school in Pennsylvania—electing to move home after graduation—left her short-lived career as a bookseller in town when Maggie was born. Early on, Ellie had felt satisfied with her choice. She loved full-time motherhood. It was exhausting, and busier than most people likely imagined, but she adored it. That morning, however, she began to consider how it might leave her feeling in the end.

Later that night, Ellie and Jonah found themselves tangled up in the first of a long string of arguments. They were in the kitchen, winding down from the day and sipping wine while Ellie sorted through an endless stack of beginning-of-the-year school forms.

"You should have heard them all, Jo." Ellie licked a finger so she could flip through the pile more efficiently. "It's like half of them can't wait for their kids to leave."

Jonah leaned back in his kitchen chair. "Do you really think that's what they meant?"

Ellie shuffled the papers into an orderly tower, placed them in Maggie's book bag. "I—I don't know." She spritzed the counter with disinfectant spray. "What do you think?"

Jonah moved across the room. "I think people are just making plans. Next steps."

"While we're on the topic, I wish you would stop trying to influence her to go to a completely different time zone instead of staying—"

"I'm not trying to influence her," Jonah interjected. "But when she comes to me and asks how I enjoyed going away for school, I'm going to tell her the truth."

Jonah was a great father, very engaged and hands on. Still, when it came to the big topics, Maggie had always come to Ellie for advice. These recent conversations—the ones Ellie was never invited to be a part of—felt like a betrayal.

"Look." Jonah set his empty wineglass in the sink. "I don't think any of the other mothers meant anything by what they said this morning. Everyone's just getting ready to let go."

A dropping feeling formed in Ellie's stomach. "So you think I'm not letting her go?"

Jonah's face morphed into an unnatural, scrunched-up expression. "I never said that."

"But you were thinking it." Ellie tossed the soiled paper towel into the trash. "I could tell by the tone of your voice. That's what you meant."

"You've been tense ever since she told us she wants to go away." He nodded at Maggie's bag, which hung from a wall hook like a piece of incriminating evidence. "I mean, you're still packing up her things for her. She's nearly eighteen."

"Of course I am," Ellie noted. "It's my job to make sure she has what she needs."

"Well, yeah, but—"

"But what?" Ellie posed, a tight feeling creeping into her throat.

"But not forever," Jonah added, then lifted a brow. "Right?"

Ellie shakes away this memory. Through the window, International Drive is a showpiece of everything terrible. Fast-food joints. Name-brand hotels. Outlet malls. Chain restaurants. To arrive at the theme parks or her parents' small community or any place else desirable, one must navigate this road first. It's like flying to a sketchy island and having to drive through its upsetting third-world section before you reach your all-inclusive resort—a visual reminder of what has been sacrificed so you and your family can relax.

"I still don't understand why we're here," Maggie probes, working hard to grind up the fibrous slices. "Why now?" Finally, she turns, looks at Ellie. Her skin is makeup-free, showcasing the pattern of pale freckles on her nose. She twirls a piece of her sandy-colored hair around her finger, all stacked with silver rings. "I know it's only one weekend, but shouldn't I be up at school studying?" Beyond Maggie's head, towering palm trees stretch toward the blue sky, like an illustration from a Dr. Seuss book. "Is Grams sick or something?"

"What?" Ellie's voice catches. She jerks—a physical reaction to Maggie's comment. Her muscle tenses up again. "No!" In the rearview, Jonah meets her eye. "We j-just . . . ," she stammers. That one stretch of her back is somehow both frozen and quivering. "Dad and I thought it would be nice to have everyone together for a few days." The car stops at a red light, idles. Beside it, another car with blackout-tinted windows vibrates with bass. The driver revs the engine, as if the whole line of cars—tourists and locals alike—is about to race. The light changes. Ellie ignores the throbbing in her back, takes a chance, reaches out, and squeezes Maggie's hand. "It's nice, right?"

~

"They're here!"

Ellie's mother, whose actual name is Rose but who for Ellie's entire life has gone by Bunny (some inside joke from before Ellie was born), stands at the edge of the terra-cotta-colored walkway outside her condo. She's waving a white dish towel above her dyed-from-a-box blond bob of hair, as if she's watching a ship come into port. Just like always since her migration to this place, Bunny wears a pair of sensible khaki shorts and a punch-colored cotton top, as well as a visor stamped with the word *Florida*, like she might forget where she now resides. When she lived in New Jersey, her entire wardrobe was black, as if she were in a constant state of mourning. Now? Every shirt she owns is the color of fruit juice, like her stylist is the mascot for Hawaiian Punch.

Jonah settles up with the driver, and their little family of three piles out of the car, clumsily pulling their own luggage from the trunk—a courtesy said driver is apparently not interested in adopting. They wheel their baggage across the parking lot. It's past lunchtime, though they didn't stop to eat, and the air is thick and damp, like the inside of a sauna. Ellie's scratched-up suitcase *clunk-clunk-clunking* behind her, she wishes she were inside a sauna—anything to help relieve the now-persistent tremble alongside her spine. Actually, come to think of it, Ellie wishes she were almost anywhere except here.

"Frank! Frank!" Bunny yells out for her husband, even though he literally stands behind her. He's dressed in his retirement wardrobe, too: golf shorts (he doesn't golf), sandals, and an aqua-colored T-shirt, a far cry from the neat collared shirts, crewneck sweaters, and tan boat shoes he favored up north. Ever since their relocation down here, Ellie has wondered if her parents buy their clothes in the tchotchke section of the local Publix supermarket. Probably. "Quick, Frank, get a picture!"

Frank fumbles with his phone, even though he's owned it for years and should absolutely know how every bell and whistle on it works. "Hang on, hang on," he's shouting while he pats the neckline of his T-shirt (*Florida!*) in search of his drugstore reading glasses. He locates them, slides them on his face. "Okay, okay, everyone huddle together!"

Ellie, Jonah, and Maggie, all glossy with perspiration, pause. Frank snaps a dozen pictures, then looks at his phone screen, confused. Without the need to see the device for herself, Ellie knows her family appears decapitated in every shot. "Later, Dad," Ellie begs and starts to move with her suitcase again. "Please. It's so hot. We all just need to sit."

~

The inside of the condo is nice. White tile floors. A decent-size kitchen. A spacious living room, wide enough to fit a sectional, as well as both Bunny's and Frank's old reading chairs. At the far end of the first-floor unit is a small sunroom that looks out onto their petite square of private grass, as well as the communal neighborhood pool beyond it. All over the walls are framed pictures of Ellie and her family, her parents' home-decorating style rooted almost entirely in memory.

"Sit! Sit!" Bunny herds everyone into the living room while she hustles into the kitchen, opening and closing every cabinet like she's concurrently hosting guests and trying out for a drumline. "You can change that!" Bunny shouts in reference to the television, which is tuned to the Game Show Network—one of her parents' favorites. On the screen, an old 1970s episode of *Family Feud* airs. A dapperly dressed Richard Dawson makes an overtly sexual comment to a female contestant. The whole studio audience laughs at the woman's expense. Things were different then. "Here." Bunny races into the living room, where Ellie, Jonah, and Maggie appear to be melting into the couch while Frank sits comfortably in his reading chair and flips through a newspaper. Bunny sets down a circular platter of rolled-up lunch meat. Maggie takes one look at it and closes her eyes. "Everyone, eat."

Seventeen years earlier, when Bunny and Frank first told Ellie and Jonah they were finally ready to pack up their belongings and move forward with their longtime retirement plan, Ellie wasn't sure they'd actually like it. It's easy to fall in love with a place when you're only visiting, but to *live* there—to go food shopping and on doctor's visits and to the drugstore to pick up your blood pressure medication—is something else. Ellie was wrong. Her parents love it. If they have their way, they'll never see an outside temperature that dips below fifty degrees again.

"You can keep Christmas!" they often say, and every December first they send Ellie a picture of the multicolored string lights they wrap around their palm tree out back, their gifts for the family arriving a week later via UPS. Ellie is happy for them. Really. She misses them all being together, though.

Bunny and Frank raised Ellie in New Jersey, in a quiet suburb right on the New York City train line. Not that her parents held jobs that required the commuter rail. Prior to her retirement, Bunny worked as a part-time administrative assistant at her church. Frank owned a small deli near the train station, a place that mostly catered to the men and women in desperate need of a coffee or a newspaper (back when they still mattered to the masses) or a breakfast sandwich before they rushed off toward the tracks.

"We want to give you both the house," Frank had said at that family meeting. They were seated around Bunny and Frank's wooden dining room table, eating spaghetti and meatballs, Maggie propped up in a high chair. "I know, I know," Frank added, already putting up his hands in his defense. His hair, a pale shade of brunette at the time—still a few years away from turning white—was neatly combed back. "I know you don't *need* it. But you're our only child, Ellie, and this has always been our plan for your inheritance."

Ellie, in her early thirties then, had set down her fork, stunned—about the house, about the move, about the fact that her parents were suddenly old enough to talk about such things as an inheritance, like they were already dead. "Dad, I—" She stuttered over her words, looked at Jonah, who appeared equally as confused. "We can't—"

"But you can," her father had insisted and placed a hand on the chest of his pressed button-down. He smiled proudly at Bunny. "We paid the house off years ago." He lifted his hand, waved it in the air. "I know we've never held glamorous jobs, but we've made good decisions," he continued, hinting at their finances. Bunny nodded her agreement, neither of them expressing an ounce of hesitation. "We've already talked to our attorney about getting the title transferred to your names. If you really don't want it—or don't want to live in it—then rent it out to a nice family, and one day you can give it to Maggie," he said, which made them all turn and look at her—a chubby baby covered in sauce and bits of ground meat—and try to imagine her ever being old enough for such a thing.

The truth, which her father had touched upon, was that Ellie and Jonah did not *need* the house. They were comfortable—not wealthy, though probably a pace ahead of middle class. Jonah, who grew up in a different part of New Jersey, was the only one of them who actually *did* work in the city, where he spent his days analyzing numbers in a way Ellie simply did not understand. They owned a small, charming house not far from her parents ("charming" being code for the fact that it was in constant need of repair), though with Maggie getting older, it was no secret to anyone that they'd soon require additional space.

While Frank talked through his offer, Ellie allowed herself to day-dream. She'd always adored her childhood home. It was spacious but not too big. It had a perfect amount of flat yard where Maggie could play. It was not cookie cutter, but also not quite so "charming" as their current money pit. The home boasted a certain quaintness: a covered porch, nostalgic black-and-white kitchen floors, a picket fence, and exterior windows arranged in such a way that it looked like the whole house smiled at you when you arrived on the front doorstep. You couldn't buy homes like that in town anymore. They'd all been bumped out or built up or refurbished in some severely time-stamped way, like someone had power washed them with the renovation equivalent of retinol. Worse, unlike when her parents had bought their home there decades earlier, every property came with a nearly heart-stopping price tag.

"What? What is it, sweetheart?" Frank had asked, observing the mixed bag of emotions on his daughter's face. "Someone say something. We didn't offend you, did we? We know you don't *need*—"

"It's—it's wonderful." Ellie smiled and turned to Jonah, who, based on his expression, shared her belief. "Everything is just—it's perfect."

Back in her parents' Floridian living room, Maggie nibbles on a sprig of parsley and some raw broccoli—accoutrements from the deli platter tray.

"What are you doing, Maggie?" Bunny asks, spearing a tube of turkey onto her paper plate. "You need to eat. You can't just have broccoli."

"I'm fine, Grams," Maggie says, setting down her parsley stem. "I'm not all that hungry."

Jonah, his gaze half-focused on his phone (likely checking a sports score or skimming some nonurgent news article), helps himself to more ham, not at all annoyed by his daughter's new dietary preferences. Not at all annoyed, it seems, by anything.

"Maggie doesn't consume meat anymore, Mom," Ellie announces. "Apparently, it's bad for the planet."

"Bad for the planet?" Bunny repeats, as if personally offended. "That's ridiculous." She drops a piece of turkey and a slice of orange cheese onto Maggie's plate. "Here, sweetie," she says. "Enough with the herbs. You're not a rabbit." She kisses Maggie's head, and, when she does, Ellie notices that her daughter does not budge or visibly scoff. "You're all skin and bones." She pats the girl's—the *woman's*—hand. "Have something real to eat."

~

After lunch, Ellie decides to take a short walk through the condo development by herself. The heat, she knows, will be awful, but she hopes the movement—the stretching that is required in order for her body to propel her feet in stride—might help to release something, both emotionally and muscularly.

Ellie slips on her brown leather sandals and oval tortoiseshell sunglasses—she's still wearing her jeans and T-shirt from the flight (she doesn't have the energy to start sifting through her damaged suitcase)—and then moves through the sunroom, the screen door slapping shut behind her as she takes a step onto the pebbled walkway.

She glides past the gate at the edge of her parents' small piece of tropical property, her forehead instantly wet. She doesn't care. The heat is the least of her concerns right now.

Ellie just walks, past the stucco community clubhouse where, once a week, her parents play cards with their retirement friends, along the winding paths near the shuffleboard court, where they participate in a round-robin-style tournament every other Tuesday evening, beyond the palm trees and neat squares of thick, blue-green blades of Florida grass. Every few feet, a lizard darts out of the lawn and onto the walkway—dinosaurs in miniature—before it scurries, confused, and disappears back into it.

The neighborhood isn't large, and so it's only a few minutes before Ellie is looping her way back to her starting point. She's not ready yet to go inside. Instead, she swings open a fence, slips off her sandals (her toenails, just like her fingernails, ballet pink, as ever), cuffs her jeans up her slender calves, and sits on the edge of the pool. The water is heaven—cool, but not too cool—the bubbling from a nearby hot tub almost enough to make her fall asleep. In the water, two senior citizens—one male and one female, both donning yellow bathing caps—are busy doing some sort of aquatic aerobics.

"You're Bunny and Frank's girl, right?" the woman shouts out, a trace of a New York accent evident in her voice. Ellie nods, drags her fingers through the water. "I'm Shelia!" the woman exclaims. "I'm new! I'm three doors down!" She smiles as she begins her underwater arm circles. "They've been excited for days!" she proclaims. "Nothing better than a last-minute visit!"

But nothing about this trip was last minute. Their frustrations with each other have been building—a slow burn—for months.

Prior to Maggie's senior year, Ellie hadn't realized it was possible to envy her husband. They were a team, a partnership, what's mine is yours, blah, blah, blah. But as their only daughter's graduation drew nearer, it turned out that was exactly what—and how—Ellie felt.

"You don't get it," she shouted at Jonah one night that autumn while they cleaned up from dinner, Maggie off at one of her many activities.

Earlier that afternoon, Ellie had had lunch with her book club, a group of other stay-at-home women whom she'd met with monthly for a decade. Over the years, they'd become friends, but in a casual way. The occasional lunch during school hours. Morning walks through the park now and again. Their relationships remained on a surface level, like swimming in the shallow end of a pool but never bothering to dive in deep. Ellie understood. Their friendships were built on convenience. They all had too many other commitments to keep.

Mostly, their relationships centered around their books. Plot. Character. Maybe a bit of fun gossip in between. That day, they'd been chatting about the historical novel in question when the conversation took an unexpected detour. What did everyone plan to do with the next chapter of her life once the kids went away? Maggie was the oldest among the women's children, and so the attention shifted to Ellie. Would she rejoin the workforce? Or volunteer? Maybe take some classes?

"What, Ellie?" Jonah spat back and slammed the dishwasher shut. They'd been fighting like this—and always about some variation of this topic—for weeks. "What don't I get now?"

"No one is asking you this," she pointed out. "Nothing about your life has to change."

Jonah moved to the sink and started to scrub a pan. "That's a little unfair, seeing as Maggie—the one who's leaving—is also my child."

But it wasn't the same. Yes, he—like Ellie—would come home to a quieter house, too. He'd miss her, of course. But everything else—his career, his day-to-day sense of purpose, his whole identity—would all remain intact.

In the pool area, a sturdy shadow emerges.

"Did you make some new friends?"

She shields her eyes with her hand before she turns and discovers Jonah positioned behind her. He waves to Shelia, who is dipping her body in and out of the water like a tea bag into a mug, and then takes a seat beside Ellie on the lip of the pool.

"Here." He hands her one of her mother's palm-leaf-stamped acrylic tumblers. "I brought you something cold to drink."

"Thanks." Ellie accepts it, then gulps down a long, refreshing sip. "This heat," she says. "I feel like I'm dead. I have no idea how my parents do it." She shrugs. "They insist it keeps them young."

Jonah smiles, nods in a knowing way. His parents, who are of a similar age, claim to like the heat now, too. But then again, who knows. Jonah hardly talks to them. After they retired and sold their home, they embarked on what Ellie has begun to gather is a never-ending river cruise. With the exception of a brief FaceTime call every few weeks, they haven't seen Jonah's parents, actually face-to-face, in over two years.

"How are you doing?" he asks, his feet swaying through the water, like he's a kid and not a forty-nine-year-old man.

He steals a look at her through his hazel eyes, and when he does it occurs to Ellie that Jonah has aged nicely. A few well-placed lines around his lips. A couple of subtle sunspots along his cheeks—enough to serve as a reminder that, *no*, he's not old, but he's also not twenty-five. Jonah is just the right amount of handsome.

Ellie has not aged poorly, either. In fact, if pressed, she'd give herself credit and admit she's aged well, too. A naturally slender waist (save for the loose pregnancy skin). No signs of a sagging neck or crease-marked décolletage yet. Still, it's not the same for women. The world views them differently, like canned pantry staples that are a few months past their expiration dates—the contents still fine, but perhaps better to toss them, just in case. Now, thanks to this new circumstance, Ellie wonders how people will view her, if they'll figuratively trash her, too. Or if she'll still hold any real worth.

"You know," Jonah continues, "just with—well, with everything, I guess."

It isn't his fault—the intentional vagueness in his words enough to make it seem like they're both new to the language. But really, what else is he—or she—supposed to say? The life they thought they knew is officially over. Well, not yet, but soon. Despite the sun and the lush vegetation and their loved ones a few feet away inside—all the elements needed for them to have an enjoyable weekend trip—they are both in distress. All they can do now is their best to be kind to each other, small gestures like a cup of water hopefully enough to get them through.

"We don't have to tell them, Ellie," Jonah says and then smacks his thick lips, already parched. A strand of his neatly trimmed hair falls across his forehead, giving in to the unrelenting humidity.

"Don't be ridiculous, Jo." Ellie hands over her glass, offering him a sip. He takes it, relieved. As he does, she pulls her (dyed) hair—already frizzing—away from her face. It catches on her classic gold huggie earring. She tugs it off, twists her highlighted strands back into a low bun with the black hair band she forever wears on her wrist. Ellie will probably be buried wearing a hair band on her joint. At the very least, there will be a deep-red indentation in her skin from it. "That's the whole reason we're here. To tell them."

"I didn't mean not at all," Jonah clarifies, handing Ellie back her cup. "I mean we don't have to tell them right away. It's not required that we do it tonight."

Nearby, Shelia wraps up her exercise routine and exits the pool. She towels off, gives Ellie a big, enthusiastic wave. "Have fun!"

Fun, Ellie thinks, waving back. *Right.*

"No, Jo," Ellie insists and finishes off her drink. "We can't stall any longer." She sighs, her breath a cloud of humidity. She is every emotion. Mad. Sad. Angry. Nostalgic. Furious. "We're telling them." She pulls her feet from the water. "Right after dinner." Ellie stands. It takes only seconds for her skin to dry. "I—no, we—can't put this off another night."

THREE

W e're getting divorced."
   Around the table, metal utensils drop onto porcelain plates, like fallen soldiers. No one moves or blinks, the meal suddenly forgotten. A blackfly, who has invited himself to the gathering by way of the open sunroom sliders, makes a home in the bread basket.

"Someone please say something," Ellie pleads, beads of sweat sliding down the back of her neck like rambunctious children on a waterslide. "Dad, can we turn down the AC?" She twists her arm at an unnatural angle, wipes her hand across her upper spine. "Honestly, I feel like I'm suffocating."

Frank, still decked out in his grocery store T-shirt, shoots Jonah a look of fury, then storms away from the table and practically punches the thermostat.

"Mom? Maggie?" Ellie wipes her hairline with a paper napkin. "Can one of you please speak?"

"Oh, Jesus, Mary, and Joseph," Bunny finally cries out and, in desperate need of a task, begins to clear the dinner plates. "I need to call Father Joe." She's frantically scraping tangles of pasta into the salad bowl, much to Maggie's disappointment. The vegetables were the only thing she could eat. "Frank! Frank!" She piles the empty dinner plates into a wobbly, oil-slicked stack. "Where's my phone, Frank?"

The air conditioner clicks. An arctic blast blows like a storm through the wall vents.

"What did you do?" Frank presses, his aging eyes dead set on Jonah's face. His head is all thin white hairs, which right now look like wisps of angry smoke. "What did you *do*?"

"Dad!" Ellie exclaims, her heartbeat like a knife stabbing her in the neck. "Please calm down!" Across the table, Maggie releases a loud sigh and then, without any comment, drifts toward the sunroom and disappears, alone, outside. "Jonah didn't do anything!" Ellie keeps her gaze cast on the sliders, hoping to get a look at Maggie. But all she sees in the glass is a reflection of the scene—the nightmare—she's currently stuck in. She turns away from the door and meets Jonah's eyes, hoping a brief glance between them will show her parents that this is a decision made in solidarity. "And, to be clear," she continues, "neither did I."

The news officially delivered—this announcement that has weighed on them as heavy as lead for weeks—Ellie and Jonah look away from each other and both tilt their heads down, like two embarrassed children who have been caught doing something bad.

"This is ridiculous," Bunny declares, her tone shifting. She swats away the fly. Her gold cross pendant sways on her chest. "You're not getting divorced," she decides, as if it is her choice.

"I don't understand, sweetheart," Frank admits, patting his shirt in search of his reading glasses, even though a second pair is propped up on his head. He slides them from his neckline and onto the bridge of his nose, like his nonprescription drugstore readers will help him see this situation more clearly. "If he didn't do anything wrong"—he offers Jonah one more threatening sneer (or as threatening as an eightysomething retiree can get)—"and neither did you, then why would you get divorced? Why now? You've been married more than twenty years."

Bunny begins to cart the plates back into the kitchen. "They're not getting divorced, Frank!" she shouts out, setting the dirtied dinnerware into the sink with a noisy *clank*.

How could she ever explain it? The invisible fractures that have slipped into their marriage.

What had started as arguments about her second act—Ellie perpetually flip-flopping and full of doubt about what she ought to do once Maggie left, and Jonah constantly frustrated with his wife ("It's not up to me! I'm not the one telling you anything needs to change!")—evolved into more significant debates when their daughter officially began to apply to colleges. Disagreements about how far was too far. Quips about how they'd fill their extra shared time and space once she was gone. Ellie, feeling embittered and adrift, found herself privately (and constantly) questioning if she'd made the right choice by dedicating herself to everyone else, only to be left feeling like she lacked real purpose in the end.

It was a few weeks before Maggie headed north that Ellie and Jonah both finally erupted. They'd been out earlier for dinner with some other couples—all their kids recent graduates of the local high school. It had started out nice. But by the time they arrived home, Ellie felt tense. She might as well have been twenty-two again, listening to everyone excitedly rattle off plans for the next decade, while she pushed a piece of chicken around her plate, feeling lost in plain sight. She took her grievances out on Jonah, choosing to snap at him about the recycling bin, of all things ("If you would just flatten the boxes!"), though, of course, that wasn't really it.

Finally, Jonah had had enough. He slammed a balled-up fist against the kitchen table. The wooden legs shook. "What is all this"—he waved a hand around the room—"these last few months, and this constant back-and-forth! What is it all really about? Whatever it is, just say it!" He squeezed the sides of his face with his hands. "What do you—what do you want, Ellie?"

"I—I don't know what I want!" she shouted, but it was a lie, and they both knew it.

"That's not true. You know what you want. And so do I." He took a breath, licked his bottom lip to buy himself a second. "But I can't give it to you, Ellie. No one can."

"I don't want to let her go," Ellie whispered.

"You're not," Jonah pointed out, and when he did, something between them shifted. "But I can feel it, Ellie."

"Feel what?"

"The fact that you're starting to let go of me instead," he said.

Back in the dining room, everyone is waiting for someone else to say something.

"Look," Jonah finally announces, and for the first time since they set foot on the plane earlier this morning, a look of real heartache washes across his sculpted, cleanly shaven face. "This isn't the way either of us thought our story would end," he explains, repeating the lines the two of them prepared back at home, their sad, poorly crafted script. He looks at Ellie, nods. "But this is what we've both decided is best."

"This isn't best!" Bunny exclaims as she rushes back to the dining table, wiping her hands on a dish towel. "What's *best* is that you uphold your vows and stay married." A devout Catholic, she quickly makes the sign of the cross over her chest.

Frank settles back into his chair, sips from his perspiring glass of iced tea. He looks at Ellie, then at Jonah, then back at Ellie, unsure where to steady his gaze. "What happened?"

Ellie and Jonah both sigh in unison. Jonah gives Ellie a look, an invitation for her to be the one to speak.

"We just—" Ellie exhales again, longer and heavier now. How is she supposed to describe it? The answer is so sad, so boring. No juicy cheating scandal. No lies. No hidden money or secret credit card accounts. "We just fell out of love, I guess."

"Oh, baloney!" Bunny starts to pull her china coffee mugs out from the hutch. She's shaking her head a hundred miles per hour. "You think marriage is about *love?*"

"Um, yes." Ellie watches her mother set the table for dessert, as if nothing has happened, like her daughter has simply made some throwaway comment about the weather and has not announced the death of her current life. She looks away from Bunny and glances down at her own hands, sweaty and shaky and, weirdly, aging (Who knew how much hands could age?). Her thin, understated gold wedding band—the one she's hardly removed since the day she first slipped it on at twenty-eight—still hugs her finger. She hasn't had the heart yet to remove it. "I'd definitely like to think that," Ellie adds.

In the period that followed Maggie's departure, their disagreements became as predictable as the sun rising. They had an empty nest, which was terrible and sorrowful, but was also meant to be freeing. They were supposed to glide gracefully into their next act, start going dancing, like one of those happy, gray-haired couples having the time of their lives in pharmaceutical ads. Instead, they fought about everything. The television volume (always too loud or too low for one of them, like characters in some dysfunctional fairy tale). The toilet seat (constantly left up) and the hair in the shower drain (constantly left behind). The groceries and their excess food waste (Did they buy the spring mix *just* to throw it away?). The way the other person drove or perpetually watched murder documentaries or never emptied the bathroom trash. The way one of them snored or chewed or breathed. Their marriage felt exhausting. It was like running a marathon, only when you reached the finish line, instead of someone handing you a medal, your spouse was there to shout about how the dishwasher was broken again.

Ellie, who no longer needed to fill her days volunteering at the high school's front desk or organizing bake sales for the varsity soccer team or helping to oversee book drives or attending dozens of morning meetings to help plan the prom, found herself with something she hadn't had in years: unstructured time, alone, to think. About her choices and contributions. About what they'd amounted to in the end. No, she hadn't cured diseases or landed rockets, but she'd made an impact. Her life—her choices—had been simple. But all those years, Ellie had been doing something important. Hadn't she?

Ellie pushes her chair away from the table. "I'll be back," she says and makes her way toward the sunroom. Before she closes the glass slider behind her, she turns back. When she does, she sees Jonah helping

Bunny slice up a yellow loaf of pound cake. Ellie swings open the screen door. "I need to go find Maggie."

And then, alone, she walks out into a blue-tinged evening.

~

Maggie is seated on the edge of the diving board, her flowy white skirt hem flirting with the pool's surface. Behind her, the tropical sun has started to set. The sky is a layer cake of colors. A band of blue. Slivers of bright orange. A thick layer of purple and another of pink. Her feet hang over, trailing through the water, just like when she was a kid, back when she was still too young and afraid to actually dive off the board, and so instead she'd perch there and imagine.

"I don't want to talk about it," she announces as soon as Ellie pushes open the pool area's safety gate. Maggie doesn't look up when she speaks, just sits and stares at the reflection of the palm trees rippling around her unpainted toenails.

"Maggie," Ellie begins, approaching her daughter from the opposite side of the pool deck. She arrives at the deep end of the water, then sits on the back of the diving board, enough for them to be close, but not so much for Maggie to feel like her mother's proximity is an invasion or emotional threat. "We wanted to tell you sooner, but this obviously isn't something we'd call and drop on you while you're up at school." Another bad script. "We thought it was important for all of us to be together so we can talk and try our best to work through this as a family."

"Ha!" The girl laughs—laughs!—but not because anything Ellie has said is funny. "A family! Great word choice, Mom."

"This isn't what your father and I had planned, Maggie!" Ellie shouts, not meaning for her voice to escalate, though she can't help it. She feels like a can of one of her planet-destroying seltzers, all shaken up and ready to burst. Nearby, she notices Shelia—sans diving cap—out on a walk with a man—Her husband? Her friend?—on the pebbled walkway. Shelia waves, craning her neck to see what's happening, as if Ellie and Maggie are an interesting news clip on TV. Ellie waves back—a courtesy—and instantly lowers her voice. This is the last thing she needs—her parents' neighbors talking. She'd never hear the end of it. "Trust me, Maggie," she whispers. "No one is more surprised by this news than your father and me."

Looking back on it, over the last two years, Ellie feels her whole life has become an onslaught of surprising news.

"So, as I'm sure you know," the high school guidance counselor had said one autumn morning early in senior year, "Maggie has edited her list from twelve down to eight schools."

Ellie and Maggie sat opposite the counselor.

"What happened to the other four?" Ellie posed.

Maggie, wearing a preppy crewneck sweater, shrugged. "I made a few changes."

Ellie waved a hand at the counselor, who passed her the sheet. "You pulled off *all* the state schools?" Her breath felt short. "You're not even going to apply to one or two, just in case?"

"In case of what?" Maggie asked, her gaze out the window.

"In case you decide—Can you look at me while I talk, please?—in case you decide to go back to your original plan," Ellie offered.

Maggie swiveled her face. "Do you mean *your* plan?"

"What?" Ellie scoffed as the counselor looked on awkwardly. "I never said you had to stay close to home. That was what you always told me you wanted."

Maggie offered an uncharacteristic eye roll. "Only because it was what I knew you wanted me to do."

The counselor stood from her desk chair. "Maybe I should—"

"Maggie, I don't understand," Ellie said. "You've always said you wanted to study someplace nearby." She peered at the paper. "Colorado isn't exactly a hop, skip, and a jump from here."

"Mom, *no one* in my class is staying around here," Maggie insisted, shooting her counselor a look.

The counselor hesitated, then lowered herself back into her chair. "Many kids are—"

"I don't care what the other kids are doing," Ellie snapped. "I care about what *you're* doing, Maggie." She glanced back at the paper. "I mean, since when are you longing to go to—to—Texas?"

"Look, *all* my friends are going away," Maggie insisted. "And I want to go away, too."

"Does your father know about these changes?" Ellie asked, already sensing the answer.

Maggie balled up her sleeves, looked at the floor. "I mean, a little."

"A little?" Ellie squeezed the bridge of her nose. "Maggie, I just don't understand why you've had such a sudden—and drastic—change of heart. Is someone telling you that staying close to home isn't a good choice?"

In the hallway, the school bell rang.

"We should probably wrap this up," the counselor suggested, standing again.

"It's not sudden, Mom," Maggie said, and Ellie couldn't tell if it was a lie. "I just don't want to get stuck here forever when there's a whole world out there. I want to get out, see things, figure out who I really am." She kicked her foot across the floor, like she once did when she was small. "I mean, I—I can't stay here just for you. Right?"

Now, Maggie pulls up her skirt and stands. Barefoot, she pushes past her mother and moves onto the concrete. "So, what?" With a hand on her hip, her whole posture communicates nothing but sass. She's an adult, and yet currently looks to Ellie almost exactly the way she did as a preschooler, back when she was first beginning to unlock her own personality. "Are you going to *date* or something?"

"Date?" Ellie shudders—literally shudders—at the thought. She has absolutely no interest in this sort of thing. "No! Do you think that's what this is about? Dad and I are splitting up so we can go *date* other people again?"

In all the arguments and conversations Jonah and Ellie have had about their split—talks that stretched through entire nights and still weren't done by daybreak, the two of them reviewing every imaginable bit and piece of this new life they were claiming—she had not yet put serious thought into this concept. But now—Maggie in front of her, jutting out her hip and flailing her arms as she works to make some point, like she has any idea whatsoever what it takes to make a marriage work—Ellie thinks briefly of the idea. *Will* she date? What will she wear? Where will she go? And with whom? What on earth will she say? Will she need to invest in different—*better*—underwear?

But it isn't only the thought of dating that leaves Ellie with a slightly queasy feeling; it's the consideration of what could come *after* several successful dates. A relationship. *Oh God.* The thought of having to learn the ways someone lives his life all over again—how a person takes his coffee, or how many bed pillows he requires to comfortably sleep—feels like enough to make her break out in a flush of hives. No. Ellie will be fine alone. Dating is definitely out of the picture.

"So, what am I supposed to do?" Maggie plops herself down onto one of the slatted pool chairs, her arms two lean sticks set in her lap. "Where am I supposed to go?"

Maggie doesn't need to say it—this one unspeakable thing. The fact that, because of the circumstances through which they acquired their home, it's only right for Jonah to be the one to move out and sign a lease on some sad little apartment elsewhere in town.

Unlike dating, Ellie *has* thought about this part a lot. Their home— that midsize white Craftsman with black shutters and a covered porch, the one her parents had "sold" (at her mother's insistence) to her and Jonah for $11.11 (*for good luck!*); the home where Ellie grew up, and where Maggie grew up, and where now no one else will ever grow up, it seems—will not feel the same. Half of Jonah's belongings are already gone, packed up in a storage unit, where they will remain while he stays at an extended-stay hotel and looks for an apartment. A chunk of Maggie's possessions, which she's taken up to school, are also gone, her bedroom pared down and always looking too sparse and clean and empty, boxes of her childhood memories tucked away in the basement, the one part of the house no one ever has a real need to frequent.

"You'll come home," Ellie finally responds to Maggie's question. "Back to the house and your old bed," she adds, even though she knows she doesn't have a real say. Maggie is an adult, and so custody will not be a legal part of the split. Instead, she will get to decide who she wants to visit (or not visit) when she returns home on summer breaks and at the holidays. Their recent interactions having been so strained, Ellie has started to believe her daughter will elect to sleep on a pullout sofa over at her dad's. "But we have plenty of time to think about all this, Mags," Ellie concludes. "You'll only be home for a week after exams before you're away all summer, and then back at school again in the fall."

Much to Ellie's chagrin, Maggie and three of her college friends have decided to do that thing—that ridiculous *thing*—some undergrads choose to do: to pack up enormous hiking packs with months' worth of (vegan!) granola bars and specialty socks and head overseas to sleep in hostels. Like so many things with her daughter, there's not much Ellie can say. Maggie took a part-time job off campus and saved up for the trip herself. She's over eighteen. She doesn't need her mother's permission (or credit card) to book a flight. It doesn't help that Jonah, who took a similar trip the summer after his sophomore year, keeps telling Maggie it's a great idea.

"Yeah," Maggie says and rolls her yellow-flecked eyes at her mother's comment. "Sure."

"Isn't that the plan?" Ellie asks. "Aren't you still going on your trip? I mean, don't get me wrong. I'd be fine if you didn't go. I don't understand why on earth you'd *want* to—"

"You wouldn't, Mom," Maggie interjects, her tone suddenly condescending. "Understand, I mean. You just—you just wouldn't get it."

After college, Ellie moved her belongings back into her childhood bedroom (the one that would later belong to Maggie) like she'd never left. Unlike her friends, she didn't have a strong desire to go after a certain career. She needed a job—she knew that—and so she'd applied at a few small publishers in the city, not because she longed to work for them, but because she had a degree in English, and she didn't know what else to do. For two years, she climbed aboard that terrible commuter train every weekday morning before sunrise (the parking fees were outrageous, and so Frank dropped her off on his way to the deli, even though it made her feel childish) and then, too afraid to ride the subway, she walked all the way to her small, loft-style office on West Eighteenth Street.

The company published calendars (still relevant at the time) and fine art books, neither of which Ellie had a passion for or knew a thing about. But she had a desk, and that was something, and a cutout photo of Joan Didion taped to her space-age-looking computer, which felt possibly important, too. During her company's weekly Wednesday meetings, while every other employee her age took copious notes about who knew what, Ellie drew lines of scribbly illustrations over and over in her notepad and tried to understand why they were planning another photography book dedicated to horses. She hated her boss, a woman named Andrea (who insisted everyone pronounce it "On-drea-ah," like that was a real thing), and her yappy dog she always brought to the office, the one who often peed on the floor right next to Ellie's desk.

Ellie was not cut out for a big city or an office-based career, even though she felt as if that was what women like her—members of a generation who'd been brought up to believe they could have or be anything, girls who'd been granted the great privilege of attending good colleges and earning reputable degrees—were supposed to do. But the longer she stayed there, scraping by on her sad little salary, half of which went toward her silly commute, the more Ellie knew she didn't really want any part of it.

Shortly after she left that position, Ellie took a job at the bookstore in town and then signed a lease on a small, two-bedroom apartment a few blocks away from her parents. Her postgraduate life was simple, more a cozy romance than a splashy bestseller. And what was so wrong with that?

Apparently, everything.

It didn't take long into her adulthood for Ellie to learn that being a woman is inherently problematic. If you want something too much and then work and sacrifice too hard for it, you're selfish. If you don't want anything exclusively for yourself, you lack aspiration. As Ellie came to grasp a few years later—after she'd met Jonah and had Maggie, whom she'd left her bookstore job (too many nights and weekends) to raise—if you are content to be a mother and a wife, you are old fashioned, and that, she quickly came to understand, meant "bad."

Much like strong fictional characters, people expected you to have an interesting backstory, a healthy motivation for, well, something. According to the world—and, more recently, her own daughter—raising a family didn't quite count. It wasn't enough. The impact of your output was too weak. Other than the people inside your household, your efforts didn't have real reach.

That winter, after Maggie headed north for her second semester, Ellie sat in the kitchen and browsed job listings on her laptop, wondering if she'd feel better about her life if she launched herself into a fast-paced career. It was overwhelming. Not only the job descriptions (so much jargon—so many adjectives) but how much the world had changed. Who was she kidding? She didn't even understand how to download the software needed to upload her sad, fluffed-up résumé. She still had an AOL email address, for Christ's sake.

"Why are you doing this, Ellie?" Jonah had asked her in bed that night. "You don't need to get a job. I support you if you want one, but we've learned how to live comfortably on our current budget over the years. We're fine."

"You don't understand," Ellie said, holding a book she'd been pretending to read. "I've spent the last nearly twenty years focused on the two of you." She set it on her nightstand. "I need to finally find a way to focus just on me. To finally do something that matters."

"Come on. You don't really feel that way." He paused, waiting. "Do you?"

But Ellie didn't quite know how she felt. She clicked off the lamp and went to bed.

The next day, at her monthly book club meeting, the other women—their children finally receiving their own college acceptance letters—shifted away from the novel yet again. They were nervous, naturally, about their kids traveling so far from the nest, but also excited. One woman described how she and her husband browsed travel websites every night. Another said she and her spouse had started to frequent the animal shelter as they prepared to fill the new quiet in their home with a barking puppy. Someone else explained that she and her husband planned to list the house and downsize to a condo, the idea that they'd grow even closer with less space.

"Are we still happy?" Ellie asked Jonah that night.

Jonah sighed and clicked off the TV. "Is that question meant for you, or for me?"

A thought kept flashing through Ellie's mind. She could see it, like bulbs on a sign, but couldn't articulate it. Still, she felt it. Every time Maggie rushed her off the phone. Every time she and Jonah bickered about anything and everything. Maggie had finally moved on. Jonah, in his own way, had, too, every morning when he walked out the door to continue to pursue parts of his life that did not involve his wife. And what of Ellie? She'd given up so much of herself over the years that she wasn't even sure which parts of her were left.

That's when it hit her. Maybe, like her family, Ellie needed to move on, too.

Back in the pool area, Maggie—apparently having said what she needed to say—begins to walk back toward the fence. Ellie follows her. All around the complex, the vintage-looking lampposts that line the walkways turn on as quickly as if someone has snapped.

"Maggie, stop," Ellie demands. Maggie pauses and slowly turns around. "We're still a family," Ellie adds. "We're still us."

Maggie shakes her mane of long hair and briefly closes her eyes. When she opens them again, she releases an exasperated sigh. "I'm not a little kid, Mom," she points out, like Ellie needs the reminder. For a split second, Ellie allows herself to envision her daughter as exactly this—a little girl—anyway. Braided pigtails. A constellation of freckles along her nose and cheeks. Some plush toy forever in her tiny hands. "I'm nineteen. I know what's happening."

Ellie shakes away her vision, seeing the girl—the *woman*—again in the present day. Ellie wishes she could go back in time to talk in greater depth with Maggie about how this transition—moving away, acclimating to a roster of demanding classes, forming a new community—has been for her. She's asked, of course, during their phone calls. But if Ellie is honest with herself, she was often distracted. Behind the scenes, her marriage was falling apart. "Maggie, are you—"

"Am I what, Mom?" her daughter challenges.

Ellie pauses, considering the right way to ask. "Are you . . . I don't know, Mags . . . are you okay?"

"Okay?" Maggie's eyes widen, suddenly as round as the moon, which has faintly begun to appear in the sky. "Yeah, Mom," she says, though it's not sincere. "I'm just dandy."

Without another word, Maggie pivots and forcefully pushes her way beyond the pool gate. She hurries past a coral-hued hibiscus bush, then a fragrant magnolia, and disappears.

"Beauuutiful night!" Shelia announces as she and her gentleman friend round a corner, her wave as eager and energetic as a schoolgirl's. "Crystal clear!"

But for Ellie, nothing about this too-warm night is clear or beautiful. She nods her agreement anyway and waves back. Right as she does, a bulb on the lamppost beside her flickers—so desperate to hold on—and then dies.

It just dies.

"I think you're making a mistake."

Ellie is seated on a rattan chair in the sunroom, watching the final shards of sun leave the sky. She has a plate of pound cake—only a single bite taken from it—balanced on her lap.

"You and Jonah," Bunny clarifies and closes the glass slider behind her. She's changed into her cotton pajamas and lightweight robe, the whole matching set printed with a punchy floral and flamingo motif (*Florida!*). "This is not the right choice, Ellie." She takes a seat beside her daughter and breathes deeply, mustering up the courage for whatever she's about to say next. "This is a bad choice, in fact," she bravely admits, then leans back, satisfied that she's said it.

Above them, the palm-leaf ceiling fan whirs, moving the warm air around and around. Outside the room's screened walls, there is the sound of insects.

"Mom." Ellie briefly looks inside the house. Maggie, Jonah, and Frank are all on the couch, watching a game show, and looking like someone has died. Ellie swivels back to face the yard, the one her parents daydreamed about for decades. It occurs to Ellie that, in all their years together, she and Jonah have never seriously talked about their retirement. They've saved for it, sure. But they've never fantasized about it together—where they'd move or who they'd become during that stage in their lives. The absence of this conversation, Ellie now realizes, should have been a red flag. "Can we not do this, please? Not yet. I'm just . . ."

But Ellie fails to finish her statement because, honestly, she doesn't really know. What *is* she? Sad? Overwhelmed? Relieved? Worried? Anxious? It's like she sneezed—*Achoo!*—and every emotion she's ever felt has come to life inside her all at once.

Ellie was the one to say the word "divorce" first. She wasn't even fully sure that divorce was what she'd meant.

She was crouched on their bedroom floor, sorting laundry and feeling fed up and full of resentment and sadness and regret, when she said it. All those years of dedicating herself to her marriage and her home and her family, and for what? Look at the reward: a husband with whom she argued about nothing and a daughter who could hardly stand the sound of her mother's voice, let alone her opinion.

Ellie didn't know how divorce might solve her problems. She only knew she couldn't escape the idea that, for once, she needed to see who she was apart from her family—the one she'd given all of herself to—and to discover who she might be when given the chance to stand on—to focus exclusively on—her own two feet.

"You know, Jo," she'd said that evening, the d-word having just escaped her lips. "I keep wondering about who I might have become if I'd made other choices for myself. If anything I've actually done for this family, or this house, has really mattered." She shrugged, feeling defeated. "It's not like my commitment to this marriage—to our life—has changed the world, you know?" A pair of pilled athletic socks dangled from her fingers as she cried. "It's just—sometimes I think about what life might have looked like if I'd never agreed to have coffee with you that first day." She could have stopped, tossed the socks in the hamper, and left the room. But she didn't. "Lately, I think about the lives we might have lived—the people we might have become—if we'd never met. If the world would be different. Or if we would be different. If anything would have actually changed at all." She looked down at the drips of her tears on the wood floor. "Sometimes I think about what might have happened if we'd never actually been married at all."

Jonah stood at the bedroom door, his arms crossed over his chest. He bit his bottom lip hard. "So, you've finally figured out what you want then, huh?" His complexion grew splotchy with emotion. "This is it?"

"I—I don't know!" Ellie, frustrated and confused and full of envy and sadness and still crying, threw the sock. "I just don't want to live like this anymore. Us, always fighting. Me, always doing the laundry, and pretending the world is going to change as a result!"

But it was too late for her to backpedal. She'd been the one to click on the ignition, and now the car was in motion, heading right toward a crash. Once a word like that was out there, you couldn't just reach a hand into the air and take it back.

Jonah opened his mouth to speak again. Ellie thought he'd say this was foolish. Of course they weren't getting divorced. But he didn't. Which made her think that maybe it was what he wanted, too.

"Well then," he said, his voice flat. "I guess that's that."

And then he stepped out into the hallway and slammed the door.

In the sunroom, Bunny's gaze is cast on some indeterminate something out in the yard. "I'm sorry about what I said," Bunny admits. "I shouldn't have said it."

"Thank you, Mom." Ellie, grateful for this small serving of relief, lifts a bite of cake to her mouth. "I know it may *seem* like a bad choice right now, but it's not a—"

"No, no," Bunny immediately interjects. "Not about it being a bad choice. This is a terrible choice, Ellie. A horrible one." The bite of cake untouched, Ellie drops her fork back onto her plate. "I meant about calling Father Joe."

"You can call Father Joe, Mom." Ellie—tired in a way she's never been tired before—sets the plate on an end table. For as far back as she can remember, her mother has been religious. Church every Sunday (and, since she's been retired, most weekday mornings, too). A crucifix hanging above the front door. Her small gold cross around her neck, even when she sleeps. Bunny believes in angels, protective spirits that watch over and help guide her. Every time the clock strikes 11:11, Bunny insists that everyone stop and say a prayer or make a wish. Ellie has never much bought into these things. She's more like Frank in this way, going along with it all for Bunny's sake. Ellie and Jonah were married in a church (mostly due to Bunny's insistence). They had Maggie baptized and always took her to Mass on holidays. But that was it. They were lite-Catholics, like their faith was on a diet and therefore could only consume so much holiness in a given time frame. Maybe, Ellie considers now, this is another piece of their problems. "It's fine, Mom,"

Ellie continues. "Really. I'm not offended if you want to tell him that we're—"

"What?" Bunny practically explodes. "I'm not telling my priest you're getting divorced! He'll never look at me in church again!"

With this comment, Ellie decides it's time to go back inside. "I think I need to go to bed." She wants to take a shower, finally change out of her travel clothes. She lifts her plate, tugs the slider back open, and then winces, knowing instantly that she's jerked the door handle too hard.

"What *now*?" Bunny asks, noting her daughter's pained expression.

"It's my back," Ellie answers. "I tweaked something in it earlier at the airport."

"Oh Lord. I'll get the heating pad." Bunny stands. "I'll leave it in the front room—" She stops, a realization rushing over her like a forceful wind. "W-will you . . . ," she stammers. "Will he—"

"He's going to sleep on the couch with Maggie," Ellie explains. "We already talked about it."

"Great. Just great." Bunny locks the screen door and pulls her robe tighter. She makes the sign of the cross over her body, like she does every night before she closes up the house—a prayer, or a wish, maybe, that everyone inside stays safe. "I guess you don't need me, then." Bunny clicks off the ceiling fan light. The room goes dark. "It sounds like you two have everything planned."

FOUR

Saturday

The next day, the sun blazes, its rays like invisible flames that shoot down from the sky. After Bunny returns from morning Mass, the whole family piles into her and Frank's car. It's a midrange sedan—nothing glamorous, enough to get the job done. Frank's eyes are on the way out, and so Bunny—wearing a coral-colored cotton top—slides into the driver's seat (which is not to say her eyes are much better). The two of them work in tandem—a real grade A comedy act—to fold up the windshield's reflective shade. Behind them, Ellie, Maggie, and Jonah are crammed into the back seat, as tight as canned sardines, their knees practically in their throats.

"Everyone comfortable?" Bunny asks before she backs the car out of its spot and carefully turns onto their town's main drag. Above her, a palm tree–shaped air freshener hangs from the rearview mirror—the one Frank keeps peering in to cast a questioning glance at Jonah, as if his son-in-law of more than two decades has transformed into a serial killer overnight.

No, Ellie thinks as Maggie—who dons a pair of ripped denim shorts and a tie-dyed tank top printed with the logo of a jam band—works hard to keep her thigh from touching her mother's skin, exposed from her predictable chino shorts. *Not even a little bit.* Jonah sits on the far end of the back seat, still close and yet so far. They haven't exchanged more than a quick hello all morning. *No one here is comfortable at all.*

"We're great, Bunny," Jonah answers for the family. He wears his black sunglasses, a crisp navy-blue T-shirt, and tan shorts—vacation gear, even though this isn't a vacation. Sweat drips in petite beads from his hairline. He's trying to keep things amicable, to reduce the awkwardness and burden of their broken threesome being trapped here—smack-dab in the middle of the country's tourism capital and in the center of Bunny and Frank's retired life—for another full day.

The car moves forward. Through the window, the world is block after block of recently constructed condo developments and precisely manicured artificial lakes.

While Bunny drives, Ellie wonders if she and Jonah have made a mistake by telling everyone when they did. Maybe they should have waited until the end of the trip. But there's no one to blame. Making the announcement on the first night was Ellie's idea (Jonah couldn't decide on the right time). It would be like ripping off a Band-Aid, or so she'd thought. She'd figured everyone would sense something amiss between her and Jonah anyway—that they'd feel that their chemistry was off or that something between them had changed. But no one had.

Her gaze still out the window, Ellie thinks back to one of their last fights. It was only weeks ago, she and Jonah still sorting out what they'd say when they arrived here, how they'd explain this mess to the family. They'd been talking about the divorce for what had felt like ages by then. But that night, as they sat at their kitchen table, a half-empty bottle of red wine sitting between them, Jonah finally uttered the thing that so far neither of them had said.

"You know, *you're* the one who wanted this, Ellie!" he'd shouted, their black metal pendant light hanging above them in a way that suddenly made her feel like they were both under investigation for some unspoken crime. "*You're* the one who first brought all this up! This whole disaster—it was your choice, not mine!"

"That's not fair!" Ellie had shouted back, the swing of her hand nearly knocking over her wineglass. "Don't pin this all on me just because neither of us knows what we're supposed to say to everyone." She dropped her face into her hands, feeling like she'd aged about a hundred years in just a few weeks. They'd talked through their relationship so many times—their mutual unhappiness, their frustrations with all the disagreements and ridiculous tit for tats. But right then, Ellie thought back on that first night with the laundry basket. "We *both* wanted this," she added. Sure, she was the one brave enough to have suggested a divorce first. But he'd agreed, right from the get-go. He'd agreed. Hadn't he? "We've *both* been unhappy."

"Huh," Jonah said, the word not really meaning much of anything. It was just a sound, a filler.

"What?" Ellie asked, pushing away her glass. Who could drink right then? Who could even want that? "What do you want to say?"

Jonah stood, pressed his hands against the island's countertop, the muscles in his arms inadvertently flexing. "It's nothing, Ellie," he said, his tone evening out with each new breath. "We're both grieving right now." He tossed up his hands as if to say *Who even knows* and then dragged his fingertips across his scalp. They turned away from each other, neither of them sure where to look. Their focus simultaneously fell upon the stainless steel refrigerator, where one of Maggie's childhood marker drawings—a smiling illustrated sun wearing sunglasses—still hung, the paper yellowed with age. As delicately as if he were handling a newborn baby, Jonah pulled away the tape and held the paper in his hands. He looked at the drawing, then gently folded it and slid it into his pants pocket. "It feels like we're grieving so many things," he said.

Back in sunny Florida, Bunny pulls the car into a parking lot that looks out onto one of the artificial bodies of water. "We're here!" She shifts the gear into park, gathers her things.

The memory vanishes from Ellie's mind for the time being. "We're here already?" she asks, confused. They've been in the car for all of two minutes. She turns around, looks through the rear windshield, noting that her parents' condo development is still in plain sight. "We could have walked," she points out, not that she would have wanted to with her back and the heat.

Of course, no one is in the spirit for this lunch, the one Bunny had planned for them the instant Ellie told her they were all flying down for a few spontaneous days (or at least as spontaneous as the airlines would let you be anymore). But then again, what else are they all supposed to do? Sit around the condo and cry? No one is dead—it feels like it, but no one is. They're all here and healthy and, frankly, hungry. None of them thought a meal out was a good idea, though they all seemed to agree this is at least a *better* idea than sitting around the living room picking from yesterday's lunch meat tray and staring at each other.

Bunny opens the door, trying to seem unfazed. Nearby, an elderly couple briskly walks on a smooth pathway. "Come on, everyone," she says, like it's just another day in paradise, as if this casual Saturday meal is not a sort of Last Supper—a gastronomical tombstone here to mark the end of something. "You'll all love this place."

~

The restaurant is terrible. It's an old Olive Garden that has inexplicably been renovated into a different Italian restaurant that still looks exactly like an Olive Garden inside. Apparently, according to Bunny, the place is known for their delicious, fresh-baked breadsticks and bottomless salads. Again, not an Olive Garden.

"I've prepared a list," Bunny announces as the family's entrées arrive. Giant platters of chicken parmesan, dripping with melted cheese. Enormous bowls of pasta, ladled with steaming red sauce. It's all stuff one is dying to eat when it's nearly ninety degrees outside. Bunny digs through her handbag, pulls out her reading glasses and a notepad. "Is everyone ready?"

"Ready for what, Mom?" Ellie asks, picking at a bit of macaroni. She's hungry, and yet, in the past twenty-four hours, her appetite has pulled a Houdini and all but disappeared. "Why did you make a list?" Across the table, Jonah is piling the mozzarella-drenched chicken onto his plate (even though it will absolutely bother his stomach later) and nodding at his mother-in-law to show her how much he's enjoying the dish, the one he ordered upon her insistence. Beside him, Maggie nibbles her lettuce, as if anyone in the nonchain (but still basically a chain) establishment is concerned about her political stance. "A list for what?"

Bunny looks across the table. Her favorite creamy coral blush, another retirement favorite, is smoothed over her creased cheeks, a highlight to her perennial tan. She slides her readers down to the tip of her nose and looks at her granddaughter. "Why is she only eating vegetables again?" she asks the group, like Maggie is not sitting right here at the table with them. "Have you talked to her doctor? Maybe she has an—"

"She's doing it for the climate," Jonah says, but in a friendly, agreeable way. Maggie offers him a half smile, some camaraderie existing between them that's no longer present between her and Ellie. "Isn't that right, kiddo?"

Maggie looks at the food options on the table—many of which are her old favorites—and then back at her salad bowl. "The glaciers are melting," she tells her chopped romaine.

"The glaciers?" Bunny scrunches up her entire face. "What do glaciers have to do with chicken parm?"

Despite Bunny and whatever she's up to with her notepad, and Jonah and their impending divorce, Ellie's focus remains on Maggie. She's not the same as she was the day they packed the family car with plastic milk crates and twin XL bedsheets and then dropped her off at Middlebury's picturesque campus. The school had been Maggie's top choice. Unlike Ellie, who'd stayed close for college and then ricocheted right back like a boomerang after graduation, Maggie longed to go away *for real*. She wanted to find herself, she'd told Ellie so many—too many—times. To do things Ellie herself had never done. To explore and to see what existed outside the bubble that was her hometown community (too young to realize that schools like Middlebury are their own type of bubble). She loved to ski and be outside, and so Vermont felt perfect. Jonah agreed.

The weekend they visited Middlebury for an open house, Ellie and Maggie had a terrible fight.

"I love it!" Maggie had proclaimed on Sunday before they made the seven-hour drive back home. She was already wearing the *Vermont* sweatshirt Jonah had picked up for her in the campus store. "This is exactly what I want! This is exactly where I want to be!"

They were seated at a local restaurant, picking their way through an appetizer-size order of poutine. Ellie was happy for Maggie. But deep down, her maternal intuition kept insisting that her daughter's choice was not the right one for her.

"What?" Maggie looked at her mother and sipped her iced tea. "You don't like it?"

Jonah sighed, already knowing an argument was coming.

"I didn't say that," Ellie pointed out. "It's undeniably beautiful. The town is obviously very charming."

"Then what?" Maggie posed, her voice as sharp as a knife.

Ellie took a small sip of wine. "It's just—I just don't see you here at all."

Maggie's face appeared as hot as the fireplace that warmed the cozy room. "Why? Because it's not, like, a mile from our house?"

Ellie looked to Jonah, raised her brows. "A little help here, maybe?"

Jonah drank from his amber beer. "Look, this is between the two of you. Maggie, you need to speak more respectfully to your mother. And Ellie, if Maggie says she likes it here, then maybe it's not for either of us to question her choice to apply."

Maggie's yellowish eyes narrowed. "Why can't you just be happy for me?"

"I *am* happy," Ellie insisted and pushed away her plate. Obviously, she was done eating. "I just don't see why you need—"

"Because that's what kids like me do," Maggie interrupted and aggressively flicked her hand, splattering cheese on her new crewneck.

"I don't want to stay close to home forever and never actually do anything." She said the next part so fast that Ellie wasn't sure her daughter even knew she was saying it. "I don't want to do nothing with my life and just end up like—like—"

Maggie quickly cut herself off. But it was too late. Ellie had already heard the unspoken word in her head.

You.

I don't want to end up like you.

Here in Florida, Ellie traces her hand across the restaurant's tabletop.

"Anyway," Bunny says, tugging Ellie's focus away from her daughter. "Enough about the environment." She readjusts her glasses. "Let's talk through my list."

"Get ready for this one," Frank murmurs through a mouthful of baked macaroni. He's wearing another tourist T-shirt, today's selection printed with an illustration of a Floridian license plate.

"Oh, phooey." Bunny shoos him off. She clears her throat, a signal that she means business, and lifts her spiral notepad. "I'm taking back Christmas."

Ellie and Jonah—for the first time all day—exchange a look, both their eyebrows raised.

"Um, what does that mean exactly?" Ellie asks.

"Look, I know your father and I have celebrated down here for years now," Bunny continues. "That cold—it's too much for us at our age." She sets the notepad on the table. "That's why we're going to host it here—at our condo—this year." She turns to Jonah and suddenly chokes up. "Regardless of this *ridiculous* divorce stunt you two are pulling," she says before dramatically dropping the volume of her voice—"which will never last, by the way," she mumbles—"the five of us are still spending the holiday together." She gives one firm nod, as if her word is gospel. "It's one of the holiest days of the year for us!" She flips a page. "Speaking of which, let's talk about Easter. It's never too early to start to plan and to—"

"Bunny, I really appreciate this," Jonah acknowledges, his tone sincere. When he does, Ellie notices a glint of wetness in his eyes. "But Ellie and I should probably talk through some of the finer points of the holidays." His chest heaves with a substantial breath. "See what makes each of us comfortable."

"So, what?" Maggie flings—actually flings!—her fork across the table. A rogue slice of cherry tomato lands on the white tablecloth. "We just, like, never get to spend the holidays together—all five of us—again?"

Across the dining room, another family is staring.

"Mags," Jonah explains. "It won't be that bad." He pinches the bridge of his nose—a good one, angular, distinguished, but not so much that it's all you see—and blinks the emerging tears away. "You'll get to choose, you know. Spend one holiday with Mom, one holiday with me, so that—"

"You," Maggie spits and glares at her mother. "I choose you, Dad."

"Come on, kiddo," Jonah says. He's always been so soft on her. Dads often get to be this way with daughters; it's the mothers who have to be so hard.

"It's fine, Jo," Ellie tells him, even though it's not. She's had enough, reached her limit. She pushes her chair out from the table right as their waiter appears behind her.

"Can I interest anyone in dessert?" he asks, already prepared to pass out the slender, laminated menus.

"No!" Ellie, Jonah, and Maggie shout, one of the few things they currently agree on.

"I'll—I'll take a look." Frank reluctantly accepts a menu. "Do you still have that tiramisu?"

Ellie pushes her way through the dining room.

"Good Lord, where are you going, Ellie?" Bunny asks. "Come sit. I haven't even gone through my full list! That's only the first point. We haven't even discussed the matter of birthdays yet!"

"Not now, Mom," she says over her shoulder and navigates back toward the exit. "I—I need some air."

~

Ellie sits on a bench just beyond the parking lot and stares out at the artificial lake. It's pretty—Ellie can't deny this—even though it's not actually real. In the center of it, a series of three fountains artfully shoots sprays of water up toward the blue sky, like a mini Bellagio.

"Hey."

Ellie turns and finds Jonah behind her. He appears so familiar and yet so foreign, like some object from her childhood she's only now remembering ever existed. Jonah looks at his wife. She is, in this moment, still his wife. Nothing legal has been finalized or even officially started yet, both of them confident that telling the family was the appropriate first step. His expression, the distinct curves of it, suggests he wants to say something but doesn't have the right words.

"Want a breadstick?" he asks, like this is the whole reason he's come out here, and hands her a greasy golden carbohydrate tube.

Ellie pushes away her oval sunglasses, takes it, and begins to tear away little pieces, which she tosses into the grass where a family of ducks sits. They all quack in jubilation, pecking at the garlic-flecked bites with their orange beaks.

"What are we doing, Jo?" she asks, her gaze still cast on the water. She sets the breadstick beside her on the bench. "Are we really going through with this?" She looks up at Jonah, who's still standing, unsure what to do. "Are we really getting divorced?" For the first time since this word has become a part of their marital vernacular, Ellie wishes she hadn't been the first one to say it.

Jonah sighs heavily, finally takes a seat next to her. He pushes his sunglasses away from his face and onto his head. "I don't know, Ellie. I'm not sure what we're doing anymore." He picks apart the breadstick, throws another handful of pieces to their new feathered friends. "This is what we both said we wanted, right?" He turns, locks eyes with her. "To start over. To hit the reset button. To try to become better versions of ourselves and take a shot at a different life."

These are all things they've said before, lines they've crafted together, along with some they've adopted from the many self-help books about divorce they've both read in recent months, the ones they've told themselves make so much sense. But right now, the two of them side by side on this bench, the words don't hit right.

They did all the things they were supposed to do in the weeks that followed that night in their bedroom. They talked. They went to therapy (only a few times). They briefly separated, but not for long, the uncertainty of it (What *were* they?) riper with inconveniences than anything. In short, they tried. This much, Ellie can say with certainty, is true. They tried. Hadn't they?

"I'm worried about Maggie," Ellie admits. "I don't think she should take this trip overseas. I think she needs to come home after finals while we figure this all out."

"Home?" Jonah tilts his face, and in a rush, Ellie can sense it—the tenderness she felt toward him and their situation only one second earlier dissipating. His tone suggests that an argument is coming on, not because something Ellie has said is wrong, but because they're both just so broken and mad at themselves and each other for letting this happen. "And where would home be for her right now, Ellie? In our house, which will soon be half-empty? In the bachelor pad I still haven't found for myself yet?"

"I don't want to do this," Ellie admits and, frustrated, tosses the rest of the breadstick at the birds. They go berserk, their wings wildly flapping. "I don't want to fight with you anymore."

There are so many emotions that come with a marriage ending. More and more, Ellie is coming to realize that a divorce is very much a specific brand of grief. In the span of a day—sometimes in the span of a single minute—she experiences a whole spectrum of feelings. Denial.

Anger. Shock. Panic. Bargaining. Pain. Guilt. Sadness. And then, worst of all, acceptance that this decision they're making is in fact right.

"Mom!" Ellie turns and finds Maggie rushing toward them, a furious look painted across her youthful face. Behind her, Bunny and Frank exit the restaurant carrying multiple to-go containers. "You can't feed a breadstick to wild animals!" Maggie shouts. "That's *so* bad for them! For their whole ecosystem!"

"What?" Ellie looks around, a feeling of uncertainty settling on her, as if she suddenly cannot remember where she is or how she got there. Her heart palpitates in her chest. "What are you talking about?"

"The breadstick, Mom!" Maggie snaps. "I saw you throw it!" She tosses up her hands to show her annoyance, huffs as loudly as a hurricane, and then joins her grandparents at the car.

Ellie watches them all settle inside the vehicle and thinks back to that night in their bedroom, the one when her whole understanding of the world shifted with as much force as the planet's tectonic plates. Theirs is not a story of fate like she once believed. That day when they first met was only an accident, the result of a detour that Jonah, who'd been rerouted through Ellie's town, had been forced to follow on his way to someplace else.

Life, Ellie now recognizes, is not a study in destiny but an experiment in choice, less a quirky romance novel about serendipity and more akin to those Choose Your Own Adventure books she loved to read as a kid. You make one decision and flip ahead twenty pages. You make a different one and watch your marriage end.

Back at the waterfront, the breadstick is gone. The ducks all waddle into the lake.

"Are we making a mistake, Jo?" Ellie asks when they're alone at the bench once again. "Are we making a terrible choice by doing this?"

Jonah's chest rises and falls as he inhales and exhales a round of deep breaths. He opens his mouth to say something. But before he does, Bunny begins to beep the car horn. They both turn. She's waving from her spot in the driver's seat, like they all have some very important event to attend.

Ellie doesn't know what Jonah will say. Worse, she doesn't know what she even wants him to say anymore. That, yes, they're making a mistake. Or that, no, this is precisely the right choice. Which option is better? Which is more terrible?

The ducks swim away, leaving a gentle ripple in their wake.

"I mean, we already told the family," Jonah says.

FIVE

The rest of the day moves slowly, like a bad film that will not end. Everyone is in the condo, and yet it's as if they all exist on their own individual planes. Bunny spends the day heating and then reheating the lunch leftovers, which she schleps back and forth to the coffee table even though no one wants to eat. Jonah sits on the couch, vacillating between checking sports updates on his phone and periodically excusing himself to the bathroom, thanks to all that melted cheese. Frank sets himself up at the dining table with his multiple pairs of reading glasses, shaking out the flimsy pages of a newspaper and then slowly flipping through them to pass the time. Maggie hangs out alone in the sunroom, reading (or pretending to read and study) some book about ethical farming.

Ellie paces back and forth across the shiny white tiles, thinking about the ripple effect of her and Jonah's choice. One decision—out of the millions of decisions they've likely made together over the years—and look at the impact.

She pauses at her parents' entryway table and looks at the many framed photographs on it. Most of them are snapshots of Ellie, Jonah, and Maggie during better times. Nestled among them is one of Maggie's childhood drawings, her signature little-kid illustration, preserved in a frame: a cartoon sun wearing sunglasses and a wide smile, like the one back home once taped to their fridge.

Ellie looks away from the console and over at the back of Jonah's head of thick hair. They've mostly gotten along on this trip—a few blips here and there—though Ellie knows this is a type of performance they're both putting on, a small gift to each other to make up for all the fighting before they say goodbye, which is what they plan to do once their plane lands.

The doorbell rings, a shock wave to their quiet environment. They all turn to see. Bunny rushes to the door, drying her hands on a dish towel.

"Shelia?" Bunny questions, surprised, and maybe a touch annoyed. She tosses the rag over her shoulder. "What are you doing here?"

Shelia has been Bunny's neighbor for a few months now. Other than their brief interaction at the pool, Ellie is only aware of her from phone conversations with her mother. Since Shelia has moved into the unit several doors down, she and Bunny have said hello to each other—physically crossed paths—practically daily and made a habit of exchanging vague pleasantries. Still, Bunny hardly knows her. It doesn't matter. Ellie can tell that Bunny's already decided she cannot stand her.

"Hiya, Bunny." Shelia wears a pair of bermuda shorts and a windbreaker, even though the faint hint of a breeze does not warrant it. She cranes her neck to get a peek inside the condo. "I brought this for your visitors." She's holding a tray of something. "Cream puffs," she announces. "Who doesn't love cream puffs?"

"Thank you, Shelia," Bunny says, though Ellie can tell her mother's remark is not sincere. "They're leaving in the morning," she explains and accepts Shelia's offering. "Otherwise, I'd invite you in."

Shelia nods, still peering past Bunny's shoulder. "I understand." She touches her short, ashy hair and pauses long enough to suck in an audible breath. "I'd take every minute with my Johnnie if he were here visiting me, too."

They exchange a cordial farewell before Bunny closes the door. Ellie follows her mother into the kitchen to take a peek at the dessert Shelia has prepared—not that she has an appetite for it. Cream puffs are one of Ellie's least favorite desserts. It's the texture, plus the fact that they remind her of an old boyfriend who was obsessed with them.

"That's what you're going to end up like," Bunny admonishes her the instant Ellie steps into the room.

"Like a cream puff?" Ellie asks, confused.

"Like *Shelia*," Bunny whispers. "Look at her! Divorced. No husband. Just out galivanting around. No one knows her backstory. She doesn't talk about it." Bunny crosses her arms over the chest of her brightly colored top. "The other women in the neighborhood don't care for her," she announces. "Not even her own son—that *Johnnie*—comes to see her." She starts to wash some dishes. "Lord forgive me," she adds.

Ellie settles into a kitchen chair. Through the bay window, she sees Shelia outside talking to another neighbor. "Maybe divorce was the right choice for her, Mom. Maybe she wasn't happy being married."

Bunny turns and gives her daughter a look. "Please."

Ellie's whole life, her parents' marriage has been like something from a black-and-white rerun. Quiet mornings together with their newspapers and their coffees. Dinner on the table every night at 5:30 p.m. sharp. Everything about their relationship, as far as Ellie has always seen, has been framed by comfort. Ease. Contentment. A sense of infatuation and commitment that seems like an artifact from another time. Still, Ellie wonders.

"I'm serious," Ellie explains. "I'm sure at some point in the more than fifty years that you've been married to Dad, you've at least *thought* about what your life would have looked like if you hadn't married him."

"What?" Bunny asks, clearly offended.

"Come on, Mom," Ellie continues. "You mean to tell me you've never—not once—thought about what your life might have been like—who you might have become—if you hadn't ended up with him?"

"No," she says quickly. "Literally never." She turns off the faucet. "I made a commitment—a *vow*—to your father the day I married him."

Ellie thinks back to the night of her wedding. After the ceremony and the party and the dancing and the champagne, she and Jonah finally found themselves alone—still wearing their wedding clothes—on their hotel balcony. Jonah stood behind Ellie, wrapped his arms around her waist, the two of them looking toward the future that still waited for them.

"Out of all the people in the world," Jonah said, "what made you choose me?"

Ellie laughed, her bare arms prickled with goose bumps thanks to the mid-October air. "Your terrible driving," she joked, referencing the mishap that had first brought them together.

It was funny—in a charming way—that they'd picked each other. Jonah, with his love of numbers and sports, a bit of a jock. Ellie, with her passion for books and stories, someone who would have sat at a different lunch table than him in high school, that was for sure. Jonah, who'd traveled away from home for college to find himself. And Ellie, who'd more or less stayed put. He liked the lights in their apartment turned up bright, whereas she preferred them to stay dimmed. They were like two opposites who inexplicably matched—complementary hues on a color wheel.

"What made you choose me?" Ellie asked, her face tilted onto the shoulder of his suit jacket.

"Choose?" Jonah laughed quietly. "I didn't," he said. "It was fate." He kissed her head. "It did the choosing for me."

Back in the kitchen, Bunny folds a dish towel, sets it on the counter. She swats Ellie's hand away from the foil wrapping on Shelia's platter. "Don't eat those," she scolds her, quickly changing the topic, as if the homemade cream puffs are poison. "God only knows what she does over there."

~

"How's your back?"

Jonah appears in the doorframe of the front bedroom, where Ellie has begun to pack. He wears a long-sleeved shirt and a pair of cotton shorts, sleeping gear. It's getting late, the world outside the window fading to a deep blue, though not yet black.

"Not great," Ellie admits as she folds up the few articles of clothing she's actually removed from her suitcase in these last two awful days. "I should probably call the doctor on Monday."

Beyond the bedroom, the condo is mostly quiet. Bunny and Frank have both already fallen asleep in their respective reading chairs. Maggie, who's under a blanket on the couch, is starting to nod off as she half watches an old rerun of *Family Feud* (the irony of the show's title not lost on Ellie).

Jonah sits on the edge of the bed, runs his hands across his face. Speckles of dark stubble—a sign that the day is ending—have begun to appear along his cheeks. "The truth is that I don't know what we're doing," he admits, finally circling back to their conversation from earlier on the bench. "I have no idea if this is all a mistake or not."

Ellie sets her folded shirts down on the dresser, takes a seat next to him on the mattress. "I thought we'd feel better after we told everyone," she admits. "That we'd be relieved to not be holding on to this secret anymore." Jonah nods his agreement. They're both looking straight ahead at the bad beach art Bunny has hung on the wall. "But, in truth," Ellie continues, "I think I feel worse."

Neither of them says anything for a long beat. From the living room, they hear a familiar commercial jingle for a cleaning product.

"If you could go back," Ellie finally asks, breaking their silence, "would you do it all differently?"

Jonah turns to her, leans his head to one side. "What do you mean?"

"Our marriage," Ellie states. "Would you still do it again, even if you knew it would ultimately end?" She lets her question sit for a minute. "Not counting Maggie, of course," she adds with a wave of her hand. "Maggie would still exist in this scenario." She lets herself laugh quietly. Jonah does, too. "Just imagine that we had a one-night stand or something."

Jonah's nostrils widen as he inhales a deep, level breath. He exhales, bites his pink lip. "I think so," he admits. "I mean, despite where we're at right now, and not counting all the fighting and messy stuff from the last few months, I like to think we had a pretty good run." His mouth levels into a subtle smile. "I still think that, for the most part, we were a success." He watches Ellie, trying to interpret her expression. "What?" he asks. "You look like you want to say something."

She sighs. "It's nothing," she lies. "It's . . . silly."

Jonah raises a brow, a silent form of encouragement for her to continue.

"It's just . . . sometimes I wonder what it would be like if we met for the first time today. If, maybe through the wisdom of age or something, we'd approach our relationship differently." Ellie pauses, picking at her pale-pink fingernail. "Or if we'd choose each other out of a crowd if we didn't already share so much history." She stops again, a new strain of sadness infecting her. "Or if maybe we wouldn't, you know? If we'd just walk right past each other, not even notice one another at all."

Jonah rubs his hands across his thighs. "Who knows, Ellie." He stands. Outside the window, the neighborhood's lampposts have all turned on. "Unfortunately, in life, we don't tend to get those sorts of second chances." He stops, some thought crossing his mind. "But I'd like to think that we'd at least notice each other." He smiles softly. "Maybe say hello or something like that." He steps toward the doorframe. Before he leaves the room, he turns back to her. "You should get some sleep, Ellie," he says. "The car will be here early to take us to the airport."

Ellie nods, knowing he's right. This is what she really needs more than anything right now, this impossible thing she hasn't been able to get. Sleep. Rest. A chance to shut off her brain. To somehow not exist for a little while. Maybe then she could magically think.

With one blink of her eyes, their whole life and past together appear to Ellie in a flash. The fender bender. Their first months spent dating. The sunset engagement at the beach. Their wedding. Their first shared duplex apartment. The starter home. Maggie's birth. Watching together as she took her first steps. Listening, side by side, when she said her first real word. Infinite holidays and birthdays. So many choices that had led them through the maze of life and into endless happy moments. How had those same choices managed to lead them here, too?

"Good night, Jo," she says, knowing it's the last evening they'll do this—stand only a few feet from each other before they both retire to sleep. That the next night when she goes to bed—and all the nights that will follow it—she'll be alone.

"Good night, Ellie," he says and briefly closes his eyes, as if he's thinking the same thing or trying to capture the moment. He opens them again, slowly, a delayed camera shutter. "I hope you have good dreams."

He shuts the door.

Ellie bites her lip, but the tears come anyway.

SIX

Sunday

Ellie's phone vibrates across the nightstand, pulling her away from sleep. Confused and still half dreaming, she briefly believes she's at home, the whole weekend just a terrible dream. The phone continues to gyrate. Ellie blinks her eyes open. Several familiar objects take shape: the ceiling fan droning above her, the beach art, her suitcase, her mother's heating pad still warm beneath her back. She reaches for her device and notes the time: 4:16 a.m. *Great.* She'll never fall back asleep. Maybe not ever again.

Ellie presses her body against the headboard and swipes through the pesky notifications that have woken her, nearly all of them from her weather app. Apparently, a bad storm is brewing back at home. There are flood warnings, thunderstorm warnings, high-wind warnings. Ellie instantly panics as she imagines the turbulence they'll no doubt experience on their return flight—the overhead compartments flying open, the emergency oxygen masks dropping from the ceiling. *Super.* The way things have been going, she won't be surprised if their plane just falls like a dead bird from the sky. Before she paints the catastrophic scene any further, she notices one more alert from the airline. Their flight—thankfully? regrettably?—has already been delayed. Twice.

Her mind too busy for her to lie back down, Ellie slides on her sweatshirt and breezes through the condo. In the living room, Maggie and Jonah are asleep—feet to feet—on the sectional, the muted television still aglow. Ellie clicks it off and then adjusts Maggie's blanket, pausing long enough to softly trace the curves of her brilliant, freckle-marked face. Next to her, Jonah releases a throaty snore, half his thick body sliding off the couch cushions. Ellie sighs, wanting to walk away. But she can't help herself. Before she moves on, she adjusts his blanket for him, too. Some habits—despite the situation—feel impossible to break.

The condo quiet, Ellie navigates back toward the kitchen, figuring she'll brew herself some coffee, maybe watch the sun as it rises from behind the palm trees through the window. She steps into the darkness of the room, opens the fridge to pull out the bag of ground beans.

"It's already prepped," a voice announces from behind her.

"What the—" Ellie jumps, instigating a fresh wave of pain in her back. "Mom?" She blinks. Bunny is seated at the table, wearing her tropical-motif robe, her gold cross, like always, dangling at her neck. "What are you doing?" she asks. "Why are you awake?"

Bunny doesn't answer. Instead, she stands and clicks on the coffee-pot. "Your flight's delayed." She pulls two mugs down from the cabinet. "There's a bad storm. You'll probably spend half the day stuck in the airport," she reports, the bearer of excellent news. "For whatever reason, Maggie's flight is still on time."

Ellie sits. The coffee machine hisses and sputters, like a caffeinated dragon.

"What are you going to do when you go home, Ellie?" Bunny joins her daughter at the table. Her thinning, dyed-blond hair is brushed back away from her face, her skin a map of wrinkles and time.

"Well, to start, I plan to spend a few days wrapping my head around everything," Ellie explains. "On Monday, Jonah and I agreed that I'll call the attorney first thing, and then I plan to give myself a little personal day, maybe read, or take a walk, or do something for myself to help decompress and—"

"You're missing my point," Bunny interrupts. "What will you *do*? Things won't be the same when you go back. Your life. The house.

Everything will be different." The room begins to fill with the scent of her mother's favorite breakfast blend, a comforting contrast to the current conversation. "I don't think you realize how much of an impact your marriage has had on your life." She exhales long and slow, like an accordion that sighs with an extended note. "You won't be you without it."

Ellie lowers her eyelids, wishing she could fall back asleep—a hopeful fantasy. "That's a slightly outdated view of things, Mom," she points out and flutters her eyes open again.

"Oh, don't give me that," Bunny snaps. "I don't want to hear all that modern-day, patriarchal nonsense." She clears her throat, settling herself. "You know what I mean. And you know it's true."

In recent weeks, Ellie has spent more time than she'd care to admit visualizing what life without Jonah might be like. She envisions quiet evenings enjoying some television without the two of them fruitlessly bickering over what to watch. Simple dinners for one (certainly less cleanup) that will not involve them arguing about Maggie and the ways she's changed or this foolish trip she continues to plan. No time wasted tidying up the mess of personal items—keys, used dishes, dirty socks—Jonah has left all over the place, like a breadcrumb trail he creates in case he ever gets lost and needs to find his way back.

Yes, Ellie thinks. Her world *will* be different. Finally, she will have time to herself to sit and to think and to breathe. Maybe she'll have the space to do something for herself, to make something of her life, to carve out a more significant and noteworthy—a more appreciated— second act.

The coffee machine beeps, pulling Ellie back into the moment. "Look, Mom." In need of a task, she stands to pour them each their hot morning brew. "I know this seems unfathomable to you." She sets the mugs down on the table. Curls of steam rise from them. "But that's not because Jonah and I are monsters. It's because you and Dad have never gone through something like this, all right?" Ellie looks to her mother, in search of a sign on her face that maybe, even in the faintest way, some shred of her understands.

Bunny shakes her head. "Your marriage is important. Not just for you and Jonah. Not just for Maggie." She sucks in her cheeks, like she knows something that Ellie has not quite figured out yet. "It's important for all of us." She exhales through her nostrils. "I'm not sure you realize this."

Ellie's chest feels like it's been cast in concrete. "Things between us have just been so hard since Maggie left, Mom," she tries to explain. "We're not the same. Our marriage—I don't know . . ." Ellie trails off to collect her thoughts, though they're scattered. There are too many of them. It'd be like scooping her hand across the beach with the goal of picking up only a single grain of sand.

"You two made a vow to each other, Ellie," Bunny recounts, her mug still untouched. "Until death do you part." She allows her words to float, like buoys for them to cling to for safety. "You don't turn your back on something like that."

Ellie sips her coffee now and thinks back to their wedding. They were so young, practically children, though they'd felt so grown up—so very adult—that day. The ceremony was held in their town at the Adams's church, with Bunny's preferred priest back home, Father Donovan, officiating. Ellie held a bouquet of magnolias—her favorite flower, which would later come to serve as her future daughter's namesake—and wore a simple tea-length dress. Jonah was dressed in a navy-blue suit and a matching dapper bow tie. They were purely infatuated with each other that day, their love like helium. It lifted Ellie up, sent her floating in the clouds. She never wanted to come back down.

Father Donovan started the ceremony. Soon, the time arrived when he asked them both to repeat the vows back to him, like a pair of stylishly outfitted parakeets. All was fine until he arrived at the end of his script. That was when Ellie froze.

The priest sighed in a knowing fashion. He'd seen this sort of thing before. "There's no reason for nerves." He spoke slowly. "The line reads, 'Un-til death . . . do . . . us . . . part.'"

Ellie had understood him perfectly. She'd heard the line a million times in movies and at other people's weddings. She knew it word for word. Still, when it applied to her own relationship, she couldn't fully comprehend the somber sentiment contained within it. The idea of the end, the thought of them ever not being together and married, it was too much.

"Ellie?" Jonah had shifted on his feet. He suddenly looked a little pale beneath the church lights. "Are you okay?"

Ellie snapped to, shook her head—dismissing her feelings—and then quickly rattled off the line, desperate for them to hurry up and kiss.

I do, I do, I do, she thought as his mouth pressed into hers. *Forever and forever and forever.*

Back in Florida, Jonah exhales a loud, snorty breath in the next room. Across the table, Bunny finally pours a spiral of creamer into her coffee. "From what I can tell," she continues while tapping a spoon against the rim of her mug, "thankfully, neither of you are dead yet."

∼

Their bags packed, the family steps outside into the swampy morning. The Bakers' car has arrived. Ellie instantly notices that it's the same driver (What are the chances?) and then does her best to mentally prepare herself for another video game–inspired joyride across the highway and back down a bustling International Drive.

"Thank you for everything," Jonah says after he's piled everyone's respective baggage—some larger than others—into the trunk, as if he's casually acknowledging a weekend's worth of hospitality and not offering up one final bit of gratitude for the decades of kindness and love and memories that have come before it. He extends his arm and shakes Frank's hand. The two men somberly lock eyes. "Really," Jonah insists, not knowing when he'll actually see these people—his family—again. "I mean it." He steps away from Frank and pulls Bunny in for a long embrace. "I can't tell you how much I appreciate it," he whispers into her neck.

Following a few more hugs, the three of them gather into the car, like members of an impossibly sad parade. The doors hardly closed, their driver—who has zero time for pleasantries—zips backward out of his parking spot before any of them have even clicked their seat belts on.

Jonah wears his sunglasses, though it's unclear if their purpose is to block out the sun or to conceal his watery eyes. "Everyone okay back there?" he asks from the front seat, not because it's the appropriate question but because it's habit, and some habits are not easy to break.

Maggie doesn't say anything in response, only stares down at her lap. Ellie's back throbs, but she turns to look through the rear window anyway. Bunny has her head dropped down on Frank's shoulder, a soiled tissue in her aged hand. Ellie offers her parents one last pathetic wave—*I'm sorry*—before their driver, who fails to come to a full stop or to click on his blinker—erratically pulls the car out onto the main drag.

"We're fine," Ellie lies in response to Jonah's question. She turns back around to face forward, pulls her seat belt strap over her body. "Everyone is fine."

SEVEN

The inside of the airport is a disaster.

Apparently, every airline with routes up and down the Eastern Seaboard has been changing, canceling, and rerouting flights all day. Despite the bold tropical sun that beams down in golden tubes from the main terminal's glass ceiling, based on the electronic departures board, which Ellie has hardly taken her eyes off for the last hour, everywhere else on the planet is a mess of black storm clouds and gale-force winds.

"This doesn't make sense," Ellie announces as she and Jonah inch forward in the security line. She wears the same jeans and a similar white T-shirt to the one she had on when they flew down, her trusty cardigan in her book bag in case she gets cool on the plane. But she can't imagine feeling a chill right now. They're crowded in on all sides by a sea of frazzled, frantic, and furious travelers. Children are crying. Parents—officially *over* it—are cursing under their breath. Unlike when they first landed at the start of the weekend, there's not a *Happiest Vacation on Earth!* T-shirt—the ones Jonah thought were corny, unlike Ellie, who believed they were cute—or a pair of whimsical mouse ears in sight. Everyone around them, it seems, is tired. Overheated. Pissed.

"What doesn't make sense, Ellie?" Jonah asks and waves to Maggie, who awkwardly squeezes her way back toward them through the infinite mass of frustrated people after sneaking out to find an earth-friendly snack. Something has changed in him since they arrived inside the airport and checked Ellie's suitcase, the emotional, sentimental nature he wore this morning now gone and replaced with a hard-to-place edge. "What's the problem?"

Ellie—taken aback by Jonah's confrontational tone—twists her hair off her neck and into a bun, securing it with the tie she always wears on her wrist. She fans her skin with her boarding pass, which Frank—a product of his generation—insisted on printing for all three of them, perhaps in case the airport's Wi-Fi went out, like some sort of aviation-exclusive Y2K. She considers calling Jonah out on his attitude—reminding him that *this* is part of the issue. The way they snap at each other. The way they've learned to argue over nothing. She takes a breath, decides not to bring it up. It doesn't matter now.

"The problem," Ellie explains, "is that I don't understand how Maggie's flight is the only one still taking off on time." She points up at the departures board, which refreshes every few minutes and reveals more altered itineraries. Their flight back to New Jersey has been bumped back by three hours, but so far no cancellation. "It makes no sense," she continues, the familiar feeling of anxiety washing over her: the one that almost always accompanies her—an unwanted travel companion—anytime she or her family must venture away from home and the safety of their familiar surroundings. This time, though, it's hard to say if her nerves are caused by the thought of Maggie flying through storm clouds or the thought of Maggie flying anywhere—and in any condition—away from her. "She's heading north, too. How can it be safe for her flight to take off but not for ours?"

"I—I don't know," Jonah stammers, and when he does, Ellie notices that he's sweating at his hairline, his face simultaneously pale and flushed. "I'm not a pilot." His soft blue T-shirt—preppy, clean, tasteful—is rimmed with a faint line of perspiration. "I don't know the flight routes, Ellie."

"Yes," Ellie acknowledges, becoming progressively more annoyed with him. Whatever civilities they extended to each other all weekend, whatever brief glimmers of doubt they may have expressed, Ellie now realizes are gone. She slides her foot into and out of her leather sandal, something to try to distract herself from her rising nerves. "I'm aware of this." She tilts her head at him. He's being short with her, yes. But there's something else. "Are you all right?"

Above them, the departures board refreshes yet again. Several new cancellations blink in ominous red digital letters. "Come on!" someone yells out from behind them in the line seconds before an announcement about the cancellation booms through the airport's overhead speakers. "You've got to be kidding me!"

"I'm—I'm fine," Jonah stutters, even though the quickened quality of his chest—*inhale, exhale, inhale, exhale*—suggests otherwise. He turns from Ellie as Maggie rejoins them. "D-did you find anything?" he asks. His tone, Ellie can't help but notice, is softer with her, the difference akin to wearing sandpaper all day and then slipping into cashmere. Still, something about the way he speaks is off, stammered, the sound of his voice not quite right.

"Just this." Maggie, who wears a hunter-green sweatshirt with the word *Vermont* stamped across the chest and a pair of frayed denim shorts, holds up an overripe banana. "All the nuts and dehydrated fruit were manufactured in the same facility as dairy and eggs, so . . ." She trails off, looks down at her sad, brown-spotted snack.

"Maggie, don't be ridiculous," Ellie snaps, her eyes still half on Jonah as the three of them step forward in the snaking security line. She pulls off her travel book bag, sifts through it, and produces a granola bar. "You can't just eat a banana." She offers it to her daughter, but Maggie—likely suspecting some form of antivegan contamination—declines. "It'll be hours before you're back in your dorm room." Ellie stops and looks back up at the board in time to catch another round of cancellations. "That is, if you—or any of us—get out of here today."

And maybe, Ellie thinks, this is what she really wants, the reason she's kept focused on the board ever since their erratic driver dumped them off on the curb—her hope not so much that they'll all depart on time and jet off into their new, broken lives, but rather, that they'll all stay. Deep down, perhaps some part of her hopes their flights to New

Jersey and Vermont will be scrapped, that the three of them will get stuck here in this crowded airport and forced to talk and to comfort each other and to try, in some small way, to make a form of amends.

"I'm going back to school," Maggie announces more forcefully than Ellie expects, her voice a decibel below a shout. She takes a bite of her mushy snack, which may as well be a puree, and tries not to wince. "Come hell or high water, I'm getting back there tonight."

"Mags," Jonah offers, a weak response to his daughter's unruly tone.

"Seriously?" Ellie shoots him a glare, though honestly, she's not surprised. In every household, one parent gets to play good cop, which means the other parent must be cast as bad. For Maggie's whole life, Jonah has been the one to bring home surprise toys and bags of candy. Ellie has been the one to remind Maggie about upcoming tests and dental appointments, the parent to stand her ground on discipline. "That's all you're going to say to her? We're going to let our grown daughter speak to me like this?"

"What do you want from me?" Jonah questions, a subtle quiver in his voice.

It was not so long ago that Maggie and Ellie spoke to each other in a different, kinder way. But by the time they arrived at that final summer, all their interactions had become so strained.

"Can I come in?"

Ellie stood in the doorway of Maggie's bedroom, watching as she packed one more duffel bag.

"Um, yeah." Maggie shoved another shirt inside it. "What's up?"

Ever since the electronic acceptance letter had arrived that winter, Ellie had done her best to swallow her emotions and express nothing but her pride in and excitement for Maggie, even as she felt her daughter drifting further from her, and on a course she wasn't sure was right.

"I guess it'll be pretty quiet around here in a few weeks." Ellie sat on the edge of the bed.

Maggie sighed and set down her things. "That's the way it's supposed to be, Mom."

Ellie nodded her understanding. "Can I ask you something?" She knew this was likely one of their final private moments together before her daughter left.

Maggie huffed. The same human who'd once run full speed into Ellie's arms, now annoyed by her mother's voice. "What is it?"

Ellie rubbed the comforter. "Why, exactly, did you have a change of heart? Was it pressure from your friends? Or your guidance counselor? Dad, maybe? I know he can be pretty excitable when it comes to talking about his college days." She didn't mention the last thing she'd been thinking, the chorus that had sung the same sad song over and over in her head for weeks. *Or is it because you just want to get away from me?*

"We've been over this a hundred times." Maggie zipped her duffel. "Practically every girl in my graduation class is heading off to someplace new for school," she explained. "My generation, we're going to do big things. Really find ourselves and our identities, figure stuff out, leave our mark on this world." It sounded like she was reading from a page someone else had written. "I'm not like you, okay?" Maggie looked down, absently tugged the hem of her well-worn preppy shirt. "I don't want the same life as you."

Ellie blinked hard, like she was both seeing and hearing imaginary things. "Has my life really been so bad?" she asked, feeling hurt and taken aback. "I mean, I raised you, and—"

"I didn't mean it like that." Maggie rubbed a hand across the rug. "Can we not make this about you, please?" She stood, pulled more clothes from her closet. "This is part of the problem."

"What's that?" Ellie couldn't keep her emotions down anymore. "The fact that I've been trying for months to help you make the most informed possible decision?"

"No!" Maggie replied. "The fact that, for months, you've been trying to make this decision for me!"

"That is not true, Maggie! You made the decision! You made the choice! You're leaving, whether I think it's best for you or not! Which I don't!"

Maggie tossed a pile of sweaters onto the floor. "You're right, Mom." She balanced a hand on her hip. For a long beat, they just looked at each other, like strangers, and breathed. "I made the choice. And right now, I'm really glad that I did."

Now, in the airport, Maggie dramatically adjusts her silly patchwork bag on her shoulder. "Look, I just need to get back, all right?" She rolls her eyes—a stark reminder that, although she's an adult according to her age, she's not really. Not fully. Not yet. "This wasn't exactly the best time in the world for you to drop this bomb on me," she points out, and looks exclusively at Ellie, as if she's the only one responsible for everything that's unfolded, as if her father is an innocent bystander—just as blindsided as her—and not half-responsible for this decision. "In case everyone forgot, I start finals soon."

"Can we—can we just not do this right now, gang?" Jonah asks as he tugs on the neckline of his shirt. "Can the three of us just—"

"Why are you guys doing this?" Maggie shouts, startling the many travelers who surround them, as well as a pair of officers who instantly move closer to their family's place in the line. "This is so dumb!" she exclaims and throws up her hands. A squishy-looking piece of banana falls onto the airport's teal-patterned carpeting. "None of this even makes sense!"

"Is everything okay over here?" one of the officers asks, wearing a stern look.

"Not really!" Maggie goes on, oblivious to the new threat of authority. "Apparently my parents are getting divorced! So, I guess—*poof!*— we're just, like, not a family anymore! I don't have a home anymore . . . or whatever!"

"Mags," Jonah repeats again as everyone around them looks on. He continues to pull at his shirt, as if the fabric has shrunk, everything suddenly too tight for his muscular body. "Christ. Is it really hot in here?"

"Mags." Ellie bends down to pick up the banana piece, ignoring both Jonah and the officers. She stands and then, with her free hand, reaches out to touch her daughter's arm, hoping to soothe her, the way she used to be able to do when Maggie was small. Maggie pulls away, fast and hard, nearly hitting another traveler who stands behind her. "Maybe the three of us should step out of line and talk."

"What is there to talk about, Mom?" Maggie's eyes are glassy with tears. "You and Dad already made this choice without me. What am I supposed to talk about? What is there for me to say?" She launches her hands back up toward the glass ceiling. "Oh, right. That's just it! I don't get a say!"

"Ma'am?" one of the officers asks, his question directed at Ellie.

"We're fine, sir," Ellie asserts, still holding the mushy fruit, hoping this man—and everyone else around them—will magically disappear into vapor and go away. She shoots her daughter a look, sees she's slowly calming back down. "Really."

The officers exchange a glance and then nod—their silent agreement that bigger problems likely require their attention—before they move on.

"Have you lost your mind?" Ellie shout-whispers at Maggie once the police are gone. She tosses the banana piece in a nearby garbage can, where other travelers begrudgingly empty their water bottles before they arrive at the head of the security line. "Are you trying to have us all arrested?" she asks and wipes her soiled fingers on the thigh of her classic light-wash jeans.

"Hey, gang," Jonah says, but Ellie is too fired up with Maggie to let him speak.

"I get it," Ellie continues, a burning ball of anger rising quickly inside her. "This isn't ideal for anyone. Trust me, this isn't a position your father and I ever thought we'd be in, either. But this is what's happening, and this is what's—"

"Dad?" Maggie quickly turns away from her mother, her expression softened, like melted butter. "What's wrong? You're breathing sort of funny."

"I—I don't know." Jonah gasps, waving a hand at his face. "There are too many people. There's too much happening."

"Jesus, Jo," Ellie blurts out, suddenly realizing what's going on. "Are you—are you having a panic attack?"

In all the years they've been a couple, Jonah has never been the one to panic. Yes, he shows emotion. And, yes, he worries like everyone else. But panic is just not a part of his personality, as if this piece of him was simply cut out of the fabric of his being at birth. For the duration of their marriage, Jonah has always been the one in the proverbial driver's seat (well, often the literal one, too), the person who knows what to do, where to go, and how to get there. But this—this is new.

A TSA employee waves their family onward—panic attack or not, there's no time to delay here. Not wanting to cause another scene, they abide and move up to the security machines, where they're all forced to quickly slip off their shoes, empty their pockets, and dump their bags like criminals—the days of luxurious Pan Am–style travel long gone. Jonah's breathing sounds labored—his hands shaking—as he walks through the x-ray machine and collects his things.

"Jo." Ellie stops him on the other side of the security area as he lifts his wallet and slides it back into his pocket, looking like a shell of himself. She stands a foot in front of him, watching and waiting as he slowly catches his breath. Behind them, Maggie gathers her belongings. "What's going on?"

"I just—" He sucks in one more deep inhalation. The color slowly returns to his face. "I guess I just didn't realize this would be quite so hard." He forces a small smile as Maggie steps up beside him. He playfully tousles her long, straight hair, like she's still a kid. "You ready to go ace those exams, kiddo?" he says then, as if the whole thing—this visible display of his emotions—has not happened.

Another TSA employee signals for them to keep moving before Ellie can say anything further. They can't stand here in the security area forever, though now Ellie wishes they could—that these giant x-ray machines saw one level deeper, not just to determine if anything they carry is dangerous, but rather to see what pieces inside each of them are broken.

Together—but not really—they step in the direction of the airport's monorail system, the one that will bring them to their respective gates and force them to separate from each other.

"Why don't Dad and I come with you, Mags?" Ellie suggests as the train pulls into the modern, neon-embellished tube. As it does, she thinks about those silly vacation shirts, the ones they never bothered to wear as a family. Ellie wishes they could go back in time so she could insist—not merely suggest—that they wear them, something to prove their bond, as if doing so might have helped. "Our flight's delayed anyway. We can help you get settled at your gate," Ellie continues as the train's electronic doors slide open. A crowd of happy travelers, all ready for a memorable few days (*Best Vacation Ever! Happiest Family Trip on Earth!*), pours out of them. "We have time."

Maggie shakes her head, her drapery of shiny hair shaking along with it. "I'll text you guys when I land."

Nearby, one of the other families strolls past. The mother is playing a game with her young child, a sort of impromptu charades. "Are you a *zebra*?" the mother asks. "Are you a *hamburger*?"

Ellie recalls playing games like this with Maggie. Children love when you pretend you don't know them, or don't know what they are, like they're strangers from a different universe. When Maggie was small, Ellie engaged in a similar game with her daughter. *And who are you? Do I know you? I don't remember you being like this.* Once Maggie hit a certain age, though (*Ugh . . . Mom . . . seriously?*), she stopped finding it funny. A few years later (*But really, Maggie . . . who are you now? I hardly know or recognize you . . .*), the game stopped being fun or funny to Ellie, too.

Back near the monorail, Maggie hugs Jonah first, long and hard, before she breaks away and offers Ellie a much shorter embrace. "I guess I'll see you guys later," she says, and Ellie knows it's because she doesn't want to have to say goodbye.

Maggie joins the crowd of other travelers, her bohemian bag swinging at her side, and steps inside the train.

"Please stand clear of doors and hold on to handrails," an automated voice announces overhead. "The doors are now closing."

Through the glass, Maggie gives her parents one last wave.

"The doors are now closed," the voice says as the monorail begins to move backward.

Ellie stares ahead, not taking her eyes off Maggie until the train is gone.

EIGHT

The plane lands at night.

It was, simply put, the worst flight of Ellie's life. The aircraft bounced and shook and at one point dropped so hard and so fast, like a trackless free-fall ride, that all the seat-back television screens went black and never turned on again. Not once did the pilot click off the seat belt signs. The flight crew stayed strapped into their fold-down seats, unable to safely push the beverage cart down the too-narrow aisle. From the minute they took off until the wheels touched the runway, a woman behind Ellie screamed out "Oh, Jesus! Oh, Jesus!" every ten seconds while her toddler furiously and forcefully kicked the back of her seat like a frightened donkey.

Other than their fellow passengers, the airport is practically empty when they deboard. The other gates are mostly quiet, save for a few stranded strays who use their travel gear as pillows. The snack stand's lights are clicked off. A cleaning crew vacuums the carpeting. In silence, Ellie and Jonah pass through a hallway of windows. Outside, the world is all wind and sideways rain. Their transparent reflections blend with it.

Ellie can hardly walk, her back a mess of knots and spasms thanks to their awful flight. Her fingers ache from gripping the armrests. She feels the way she imagines one must feel after participating in one of those intense boot camp–style exercise classes—the sort that she, an almost newly single woman, ought to consider taking but won't. She already feels beat up. Fatigued. Sore.

Ellie and Jonah—still travel partners, if only for a few more minutes—pause outside the restroom near the departure gates. Jonah—who, despite the panic-inducing environment, managed to calm himself down midflight—steps into the bathroom first. While she waits, Ellie slides her phone from her pocket and sends her two obligatory texts, one to her mother and another to her daughter, whose plane somehow arrived back in Vermont hours earlier, to let them know they've landed. Bunny sends a return message almost immediately.

Think about what I said, Ellie, Bunny types back without posing a single question about the treacherous weather and flight. Ellie imagines her mother seated in her reading chair, unable to sleep, wearing her tropical robe while she watches old game show reruns and thinks and thinks and thinks. The vow, Bunny writes, as if her point is not already clear. A new bubble appears. Also, I meant what I said about Christmas.

Ellie shakes her head at her mother (How can she even *begin* to think so far ahead?) and swipes back to her message chain with Maggie. She sees from the time stamp that her daughter has read her note, though she's chosen not to write back. Frustrated, Ellie is about to close the screen but then sees three dots appear, an indication that Maggie is right here with her and typing back. Her heart racing in her throat, Ellie waits. But her efforts are a waste. A few seconds later, the bubbles disappear, Maggie disappearing along with them.

"Here," Ellie says when Jonah walks out and rejoins her. She clicks her screen closed, then hands him her book bag, like always, so she doesn't need to carry it into the bathroom stall. "Just give me a minute."

Maybe it's the harsh fluorescent lights or the fact that it's late or that she's been awake and moving since roughly 4:00 a.m. Whatever the reason, as Ellie sets her phone down on the counter, washes her hands at the filthy sink, and then splashes cool water on her face (probably filthy, too, though she needs it—she feels like she's dead), she can't help but notice that she looks terrible. Her skin appears a touch gray. Two puffy bags hang like unwanted accessories beneath her eyes. Back outside the bathroom, Jonah looks washed out and terrible, too. Is this what they wanted? Are these the people—these new, fabulous versions of themselves—they felt so desperate to become without each other? Or is this only the start—the chrysalis before the final, sought-after metamorphosis?

"Are you going to be okay?" Jonah asks Ellie when she exits the bathroom. He hands her back her book bag. His T-shirt is wrinkled from a long day of travel. His hair, typically styled, is rumpled. Although impossible, it appears to contain more silver strands than it did when they departed forty-eight hours ago. "Your back," he clarifies, scratching at the new stubble that's grown in on his face since the morning. "You're practically limping."

"I'll be fine," she insists while maneuvering her arms through the bag's nylon straps. "Really. I have some of those pills at home." They're nothing too strong or too dangerous—she's not a dummy—just something she needs sometimes to subdue the muscle spasms so she can rest. "I just need to get home and sleep in my own bed," she adds, and the words hit them both like bullets, even though she hadn't meant for them to sound this way. *Home. My own bed.* The suggestion that these two things are now hers—no longer his.

A short while later and they are at the baggage claim, Ellie's suitcase collected, everything they set out to do on this weekend trip officially done. They stand a few feet away from each other near the airport's wall of glass doors. Outside, several cars are parked at the curb, trunks wide open, hazard lights flashing. Other travelers, also anxious to get back home, hustle out into the miserable weather.

Jonah runs a hand through his gray-flecked hair, sucks in a deep barrel of a breath. He offers Ellie a timid half smile, like a kid with something embarrassing to say. "Maybe we should turn back around," he announces, and for a second Ellie can't tell if he is joking. "Maybe we should go back through security, get on a different flight, go someplace else, and run away from all this."

Ellie gives herself permission to release a quiet puff of a laugh. "Oh yeah?" Her body—her bones and her brain, just everything—is so tired. This small dose of entertainment—she needs it. "And where would we go?"

His eyes—which often shine gold but now look so dimmed—are locked on hers in a way they haven't been in a very long time. "I don't know," he says, his voice a hint above a whisper, like it's just the two of them who stand in this public space. "Somewhere far away," Jonah continues. "Someplace where we can start over. Have a second chance, maybe." He smiles, but it's quiet. Sentimental. Sad. "Or maybe just a good beach."

"Yeah." Ellie nods and imagines the two of them at some poolside bar, sipping fruity drinks, this whole weekend and the many months that have led them to it merely a bad figment of their imaginations. "That'd be nice, wouldn't it?"

Jonah tosses his hands up at his sides, shrugs his wide shoulders. "Well," he says, "I guess this is it, then." He leans in and hugs her, not too long, and not too brief, just enough for a proper goodbye. When he pulls back, he looks at her—his wife of over twenty years—for one more extended beat. "We'll talk in a few days, Ellie. Okay?"

A lump of emotion clogs Ellie's throat, heavy and cumbersome like a brick. She nods again, reminding herself that this is what they wanted. That no one has made this choice but the two of them. That the decision Jonah references—for Ellie to be the one to call the attorney first thing tomorrow morning to get the legal process started, and in the interim for the two of them to not communicate for the rest of the week so they can both take a cool-off period before litigation begins—is all part of the agreement they made together, too. "Okay," she echoes as she twists her simple wedding band on her finger, just so she'll have something to do with her hands.

Jonah steps forward first. The electronic doors open in front of him. "You know . . . ," he begins before briefly turning back. "I meant what I said last night, Ellie. Despite where we're at, I still think our marriage was a success." Behind him, a family from their flight—two exhausted, sun-burned children passed out like rag dolls over their parents' shoulders—exits the building, tired but satisfied to have collected several days of new happy memories together. "And even though I know how our story ends," Jonah continues, "if I got to go back to the first chapter, I'd still do it all again."

Ellie sighs heavily. It feels like whatever she releases has been held inside her for ages. "That's quite the literary metaphor for a guy who thrives on numbers," she says with a smile. It's the only thing she can do so that she doesn't cry.

Jonah chuckles. Lines crease around his mouth and eyes. "I wanted to make sure I phrased things in a way you'd understand."

Outside, the world is dark, flooded, the whole state wet thanks to this absurd, theatrical storm. Ellie briefly thinks of her books, wondering if maybe the weather is symbolic, like a form of baptism, a ceremonial cleansing before she and Jonah go their separate ways. Ellie shakes the thought away, knowing, of course, that life is most certainly not a book. Not a series of happy endings. This moment—the last real one in her marriage—is not a proverbial purification rite. Not an emblem. Not an example of fate or free will. It is not anything, really. It just . . . is.

"I'll see you soon," Jonah says as he steps outside and into the rain. "We'll talk next weekend."

Ellie lowers her eyelids like window blinds so she won't have to watch him walk away. When she reopens them, he's gone, and she's left here alone. She tugs the handle of her scuffed suitcase and moves forward, too. Before she exits, she peers back over her shoulder, as if she's outside herself, like she might see herself and Jonah still standing there behind her. When she does this, she notices the time on a digital clock above the baggage claim.

11:11 p.m.

She doesn't even know what she's wishing for. Not really. Even so, certain habits, as she's come to learn, are hard to break.

Ellie closes her eyes and wishes for it anyway.

PART TWO

The Arrival

NINE

Ellie wakes up in bed alone. Her eyes still closed, she feels drowsy, her body heavy but in that good, satisfying way, a signal from her limbs that she's actually—miraculously—slept. But not just slept. Rested. Based on her current groggy state, the control center that is her brain finally agreed to shut down for eight solid hours, allowing her muscles and her cells and every one of her organs to slip into a regenerative dream state.

Thank God, Ellie thinks, rubbing her feet across the sheets and noticing for the first time in ages that her back does not ache. After a night of repose and one of those magical little pills, she can actually move somewhat fluidly.

With the bed linens embracing her like soft, generous clouds, Ellie releases a long, deep yawn and stretches with all the intensity of a newborn learning to use her body for the first time. It's been forever since she's slept this way. Fairy-tale sleep, as she's sometimes called it—when you wake up feeling like Aurora or Rip Van Winkle, as if you've been lost in slumber for one hundred years and slipped off into another dimension.

Ellie bats her eyes open and finds that the room is awash with morning light—a stark contrast to the drenching storm that greeted her and Jonah when they arrived in Newark late last night. The blankets still pulled up to her chin, Ellie briefly thinks back on the scene: the two of them in that near-empty baggage claim, that aggressive rain practically assaulting the wall of automated glass doors as they said goodbye.

Ellie kept her torso pressed against the steering wheel the whole ride home, her eyes strained in a tight squint so she could make out the lines in the roadway, wishing they hadn't taken separate cars to the airport and that he'd driven her home one last time. Ellie never drove on highways anymore, let alone at night. For years, she'd gladly let Jonah take the wheel and click a sports broadcast on the satellite radio while she sat in the passenger seat drinking a to-go coffee and reading some novel with the help of the book light she kept in the glove compartment.

As if the drive wasn't bad enough, Ellie (wet and cold and still foolishly wearing her leather sandals) had arrived home to find that the oak tree in their front yard, the one where Ellie had carved her initials as a girl, and where Maggie had done the same, and where Jonah had etched their family name—*Baker*—when they first moved in, had toppled over, tangling its branches in the electrical wires like a clumsy dancer and tugging them down on its way. In the meantime, the home's small generator had clicked on, providing all the electricity Ellie needed. Maybe it was a sign: like those downed lines, by the time she finally made it to her bed, Ellie was ready to power off, too.

Now, Ellie inhales and exhales one long, slow breath. It's time. Once she gets out of this bed, maybe has some coffee and something small to eat, she will make the call—the one that will set the rest of this awful process in motion—to tell their attorney that, after more than twenty years, the Bakers—no longer the unit they once were—have decided to go their separate ways.

With this thought, Ellie is now fully awake and coherent. She looks around, acknowledges that the space is marked by a certain emptiness—an invisible void—that wasn't here a few weeks ago. Jonah's clothes are not haphazardly tossed across the bench at the foot of their bed. His small possessions, a mishmash of assorted knickknacks, are gone from the top of the dresser. The book he'd been reading—some athlete's memoir—no longer sits on the nightstand. Ellie knows if she peeked inside his closet or drawers, she'd find that the rest of his belongings are also gone, either packed up in the duffel bags he brought to his hotel or arranged in plastic containers in his new storage unit across town.

Ellie feels both sadness and relief at this realization. The worst part—telling the family, having Jonah leave, waking up for the first time alone in their bed, now *her* bed—is over. The bandage has been ripped off, the wound they've created now exposed to the air, where it can begin to heal and to mend and to breathe and to—

Pound. Pound. Pound.

Before Ellie can further process these thoughts, she hears a series of loud knocks at the front door. She drops her feet to the floor, slides on her slippers and a sweatshirt, and quickly peers through the bedroom window. Outside, the world is an ode to spring. Yellow sunshine. A canopy of green leaves. A sweep of blue sky. It is a contrast to the sound of machines and the sight of the power company's work truck parked near the end of their driveway. Ellie stretches her neck and sees that a pair of uniformed men have begun to saw through the trunk of her family's fallen tree—a necessity thanks to the storm, but a regrettable one.

Pound. Pound. Pound.

"Hang on!" Ellie shouts as she turns away from the window and begins to traverse the upstairs hallway. She moves past Maggie's closed bedroom door—the one she shut before she and Jonah left for the weekend. She couldn't bring herself to look inside and to think about—

Pound. Pound. Pound.

"I'm coming!" Ellie takes the steps two at a time, prepared to launch into a tirade about the value of patience to whoever stands opposite her door. *Pound. Pound.* "One minute!"

Once downstairs, Ellie flings open the door, expecting to discover a power company employee prepared to deliver information about when her home's full service might be restored. But the work crew is off in the background, wearing their hard hats and reflective vests.

Here, on Ellie's porch—the one with the charming bench swing, the blooming spring flower planters, and the WELCOME HOME doormat—is someone else, a familiar face belonging to someone she was most certainly not expecting to see this morning. Ellie opens her mouth, but no words arrive. She stands, blinking unnaturally, her mouth as agape as a dying fish.

"I'm leaving your father," Bunny announces as she pushes a pair of black sunglasses away from her face and onto her neatly combed blond bob. "He's driving me absolutely mad." She purses her pale, thin lips to prove she's serious. When she does, Ellie—more or less paralyzed at the moment—notices the black leather weekender bag at her mother's feet. "I can't stay with him for another minute. Not a single second!"

Ellie's throat has gone dry, as if someone has stuffed her full of cotton like one of Maggie's childhood toys. She expels an awkward, nervous gasp of a laugh. "Umm . . . Mom?"

"What's the matter with you?" Bunny swivels her head up and down, taking in the sight of her daughter. "And why are you still in your pajamas?" Her face tilts, like a broken figurine. "Are you ill?" She slaps a hand across Ellie's forehead, then shakes it away, satisfied by the temperature of her skin. "Because, honestly, the *last* thing I need right now, Ellie, is to get sick."

Across the yard, Ellie observes the crew from the power company slicing the enormous tree trunk in half. It divides into two giant rounds, revealing decades' worth of faint age rings inside it. "What do you mean you're leaving Dad?" Ellie peers up and down the block, as though a commercial jet might be parked among the damaged electrical lines. "For a day? Or for a week?" She thinks about the storm, the many flight delays and cancellations, the sheer factor of time. "Wait." She stops, rubs her eyes like a tired child. "How are you *here*?"

"Are you using something different on your face?" Bunny disregards Ellie's stammered questions. "A new moisturizer or serum or something?" She lifts a hand, pokes Ellie's cheek with her fingertip. "I'd go back to the old one. I don't like the way your skin looks right now."

"I—I—"

"I know. It's a shock, Ellie." Bunny lowers her arm. "We'll talk more inside." She grips the handle of her bag. "In the meantime, I understand you're taking a little personal day, but you need to pull yourself together. It's time to get out! See the world! Go on dates!"

Ellie stands in the doorframe in her pajamas and her slippers, the patterned cotton shorts loose on her narrow hips, wondering if her brain is bleeding, if perhaps she is hallucinating, or maybe still dreaming. She pinches her arm to double-check but instantly feels the pain of her own fingers. "I—I don't understand."

"I already told you." Bunny steps forward, past Ellie and into the home's foyer, where she dumps her weekender bag at the foot of the family's staircase. "I can't live with him anymore." She quickly makes the sign of the cross over her body. "Lord forgive me."

"I—I don't follow." Ellie takes a last look over her shoulder, as if she'll discover that her sidewalk has been transformed into an airport tarmac. "What *exactly* is happening here?"

Bunny slips off her dark, quilted spring jacket and tosses it over the wooden banister. "Isn't it obvious?" She removes her sunglasses, neatly folds them, and then sets them on her bag. "I'm moving back in."

～

"How many scoops do you use?" Bunny stands beside the kitchen counter, a metal coffee scooper hovering from her hand. "Six, right?" She answers her own question, then instantly shakes her head. "That's way too many." She dips it into the bag of artisanal beans she's pulled out from the fridge. "I'm using four."

"I—I'm sorry." Ellie glances at the stove clock to quickly calculate numbers and time, to see if this can all possibly add up. Her efforts are a waste. The digital clock, disrupted by the storm, stubbornly blinks the incorrect numbers: 11:11. "How—how are you here right now?" Ellie can't see her own face, though she imagines it looks as if she's having an aneurysm, or at the very least some type of minor, not-fatal stroke. "Physically, I mean."

Ellie's instinct is to contact Jonah. Yes, they've agreed not to talk all week so they can both step away (her words) and process things (their three-time therapist's words) and just think (everyone's agreed-upon phrasing). Still, there must be a stipulation, some fine print they didn't consider when hashing out their plan, to factor in for emergencies. And this—whatever it is that will explain how Bunny, who hours earlier had bid their family a heartfelt goodbye from her Orlando curb, waving her sad little tissue while they drove away, is now inside Ellie's New Jersey kitchen, opening and closing all the drawers and cabinets as she prepares a pot of coffee, as if her presence here is a completely normal thing—is certainly some sort of calamity.

An only child, Ellie didn't grow up knowing what it felt like to run to a sibling's bedroom and exchange cringeworthy stories about her parents. She'd never been the type to claim another woman as her best friend. There are no extended family members with whom she feels particularly close. For her entire adult life, Jonah has been Ellie's in-case-of-emergency contact, the initials "ICE" listed next to his name in her phone.

"You need to work on your greetings." Bunny opens the refrigerator. She bends down, her gold cross necklace dangling from her neckline, and sets the beans back inside. "Really."

Ellie needs her phone. In addition to her desire to call Jonah, the whole point of this morning—the only significant item on her to-do list—is to call the attorney and tell him that the Bakers plan to file for divorce. After Bunny dropped her bag at the staircase, Ellie launched into a CIA-level search but couldn't find it. She shook out her bedding, checked her en suite bathroom, inventoried her nightstand, retraced the few steps she'd actually taken since arriving home late last night. Now, she's watching her mother sweep a little pile of coffee bean dust up from the counter and brainstorming what she'll say to the attorney (*I have some bad news . . .* or *I have some good news . . .* or just *I have news?*)

or to Jonah when she finally finds her device and calls him (screw the agreement, she has to, no question; she absolutely *must*).

"I—I . . ." Ellie can hardly speak. It's like she's trapped in a fairy tale in which some crazed villain has stolen her voice. Her use of language temporarily gone, she stares at her mother's dark blouse, which she's accented with a colorful jeweled brooch, the shiny stones on it forming the shape of a palm tree. The whole time, Ellie wonders if her mother's visor and punchy tops are packed in her weekender bag. "Also, what—what are you wearing?"

Bunny reaches into the cabinet, clearly familiar with her way around this space, even though she hasn't visited (*The snow! That cold air!*) in years. "Boy, you're really something this morning, huh?"

Ellie dismisses this comment, choosing to continue her mental backtracking to the last time she used her phone. Not at the house. Not on that treacherous drive. Not at the baggage claim.

"Do you like these beans?" Bunny asks. "I didn't care for them the last time. I should have sent you a message last night, asked you to pick up that breakfast blend I like."

Bingo! The message. Of course! Bunny. Maggie. The last two texts Ellie sent before she stepped into the airport bathroom. *No!* She must have left it on that filthy counter.

"Can—can I use your phone, Mom?" Ellie asks, realizing her error and still trying to understand how her mother has arrived here from Florida so fast. "I was distracted because of Jo last night, and I think I left it—"

"Jo?" A sly expression crosses Bunny's face. "Well, that explains the pajamas." She smirks, reaches into her trouser pocket, produces her own device. "Good luck. It's hardly working from all those downed lines." She raises a defensive hand. "I *only* called your father while you were upstairs to let him know I got here safely. *Not* that it means anything."

Ellie thinks for a second. "Actually, never mind." Now that she considers it, maybe her call to Jonah can wait. She knows her mother. She'll find a way to overhear Ellie's conversation or to read any message she sends. On the counter, the coffee machine beeps. Ellie, in dire need of caffeine, pours herself a steaming mug and takes a long, scalding sip, not even pausing long enough to add her creamer. "Where *is* Dad, by the way?"

"What do you mean?" Bunny asks as Ellie pours her a mug. "He's home. At the condo."

Ellie's face scrunches into a question. "And he knows you're . . . here?" she asks, handing over her mother's beverage and then consuming another piping-hot sip.

"Of course he knows!" Bunny exclaims. "I told you I just called him." She purses her lips into a capricious beak. "Where else, exactly, would I *be*?"

Ellie's insides start to settle. At least *this* part makes some sense.

"I told him he's lucky, though," Bunny continues. As she does, something in her tone makes Ellie's nervous system swing back into high alert, her internal alarms all going off. "If I had my way," Bunny explains, "I would have booked myself a ticket and gotten on a plane."

Time slows down. "What do you mean you *would* have gotten on a plane?" She takes one step closer to Bunny, suddenly wondering if she's having some type of medical episode, or perhaps if Ellie is having one herself. "How *else* would you have gotten to my house?"

"Ellie, what nonsense are you talking about?" Bunny winces at the terrible coffee. "What a completely ridiculous question." She pauses, smacks her tongue. "The same way I get here every day." She looks down to adjust her pin. The multicolored jewels on the palm tree catch the bright May light that leaks in from the kitchen window. "I walked."

TEN

The waiting room at the local hospital's ER is a scene from a posta-pocalyptic book. Or, at the very least, a leftover set from a B-list zombie flick. Every chair is occupied by some injured or ill person. Glimpses of infected cuts, oozing gashes, and limbs twisted at unnatural angles are on display, like a free art exhibit themed around pain. Bunny, who slipped back on her sunglasses and quilted jacket before Ellie all but wrestled her into the car (*I haven't even finished my coffee!*), has her arms tight against her sides. Since they've arrived, she's reminded Ellie at least a dozen times not to touch anything.

"I don't understand why we're here," Bunny whispers as she awk-wardly stands near—though not against—a wall. There isn't a single vacant seat. In the last two minutes, Bunny has slid her hands beneath an automated sanitizer station three times. "The germs here, Ellie. We're both going to leave with a disease." She rubs her palms together, the overpowering alcohol scent enough to make a person sick. "I'm in my eighties. Are you trying to kill me?"

Ever since Bunny appeared on the porch, Ellie's heart has been engaged in a full-on gymnastics routine. Her mother, a senior citizen who hasn't traveled alone in decades, is now here, despite storms and nightfall and the unbendable rules of time. Ellie's opening reaction—aside from shock—was that Bunny's outrageous announcement and unplanned visit were meant to be a lesson about the sanctity of mar-riage. Of course, she quickly erased this thought from the whiteboard of ideas in her mind. Bunny had said she'd *walked* over one thousand miles through the night. And though her knees aren't so bad for a woman her age—all those humid morning jaunts around the condo community have helped to prevent full-blown arthritis from eating away at her joints—the situation does not make sense. Which is how Ellie arrived at conclusion number two: her mother is in the midst of an extreme form of fast-moving dementia. But she half wrote off this narrative, as well. If her mother's neurology is indeed short-circuiting, she would not have been capable of navigating the world of airplanes and taxis.

Honestly, Ellie does not have a clue.

As Bunny sat sipping her allegedly terrible coffee, the only thing Ellie could think to do was to call Frank from Bunny's phone. Her call went straight to his voicemail box, which—no real surprise (he still hardly understood how to use his device)—was full. Left with limited options, Ellie threw her travel clothes back on—previously worn white T-shirt, wrinkled jeans, still-damp leather sandals, not a stitch of makeup—tossed on her book bag, and instructed her mother to put down the mug (*You don't even like that roast!*) and get in the car.

Now, Ellie stands inches from Bunny, who inexplicably looks perfectly fine. Around them, humanity, on the other hand, appears to be falling apart at the seams, the air inside the ER just one stale, probably contagious cough.

"We need to have you checked out, Mom." Ellie strains an ear toward the check-in desk, gathering information about wait times, half wondering if she is the one experiencing a health crisis, maybe a full-blown mental health break, a consequence of the trauma set off by the impending divorce. "Something's not . . . right."

Bunny tugs up the neckline of her inky-colored blouse, pulling the fabric over her nose and mouth, like a makeshift face mask. "I'd certainly agree with that," she declares, her movements shimmying her palm tree accessory like an exotic dancer.

"When did you get that pin, Mom?" Ellie's eyes are focused on its jewels, a more preferable sight than their surroundings. "I've never seen you wear it."

"What are you talking about!" Bunny practically shouts, the volume of one's voice mattering less as one ages. "I wear this every day! It's my Florida pin! You know that!" Her brows furrow like two disgruntled caterpillars. "The one that makes me think about my perfect retirement." She pulls her face away from her shirt, a tortoise coming out of its shell. "Not that I'll ever get it," she mumbles.

"What does *that* mean?" Ellie feels her eyes taper at their corners. "Not get *what*?"

"Oh, don't worry about it." Bunny reaches for more hand sanitizer. "Anyway, I've had this pin for years. Your father bought it for me on that trip."

Ellie glances down at her twice-worn T-shirt, which she acknowledges smells less than fresh. She thinks about Jonah, about *their* trip, wondering about his morning. If he took a hot shower in his hotel, if he hopped on a train and headed into his office, if he's spoken with Maggie. Or if, like Ellie, he is also up against some type of bespoke marital-inspired mental malfunction. She exhales long and slow, adding to the room's decaying air, and wishes he were here, but she quickly brushes the thought aside. Handling situations like this is her job now. Bunny is her mother, after all, not his. She'll call Jonah shortly, she decides, once she's pieced together more concrete information about the puzzle that has been her morning.

"I'd really like to leave." Bunny shakes her hands to dry the remaining alcohol foam. "I know my news is very surprising, though it does not, based on my current understanding, constitute a medical emergency." She drops her voice. "Though I could probably benefit from some antacids. I have terrible heartburn and agita from that coffee you insist on buying." She turns, but before she reaches the exit, a female nurse steps into the room.

"Adams?" the young woman asks, her eyes glued to her clipboard.

Bunny's shoulders instantly perk up, pleased by the sound of her own last name, even though she gained it through the marriage she's about to leave. She pivots, as if being summoned for a desirable dinner reservation (a knockoff Olive Garden, say) and not a seat on a springy hospital bed. "That's us!" she declares with an amicable wave of her hand.

"Yup," Ellie says, already dreading what the rest of the day may bring. "That's us."

~

The actual ER is a symphony of beeps. Bunny lies on a cot, which she's made a point to let every nurse know is *very* uncomfortable. A blood pressure cuff and assorted wires dangle from her arms like tentacles. The only thing that separates them from the rest of the crowded room is a not nearly thick enough fabric curtain.

"Mom, *what* is going on?" Aside from some of Bunny's planned surgeries, for which Ellie always flew to Florida, she has never sat with her mother like this. For a woman her age, Bunny is in good health. She remembers to take her medications. Ever since their big move, she's enjoyed her daily walks, paired with late-afternoon swims. She likes her sweets (Who doesn't?), though mostly she eats okay. "Give me something to work with here."

Bunny tugs at one of her cords. "Your father and I are not happy anymore," she explains, failing to mention her travel itinerary, as though her announcement is the most confounding part of this day.

While they talk, Ellie uses Bunny's phone to contact Frank again. The calls go straight to voicemail. Her messages are trapped by a green line, like a type of electronic purgatory.

"I know it's difficult for you to understand," Bunny continues. Beneath the harsh hospital lighting, her skin appears pale, any hint of the sun-kissed color or creamy coral blush that brightened her face over the weekend now washed out from the fluorescents. "Marriage, Ellie—it's—it's harder than you can even imagine."

Ellie feels her eyes widen, like a cartoon character faced with a stack of TNT. She looks at Bunny with a new sense of curiosity and confusion and tries to determine if her brain is powering down or if, in some very cruel and dramatic way, her mother is out to prove something.

"How are we doing in here?" The doctor pulls back the curtain and walks straight to Bunny's bed. He has his back to Ellie as he notes the numbers on Bunny's machines. "What brings you in?"

"Before we go any further, are you Catholic?" Bunny taps her cross necklace, not yet far enough inside the hospital's innards for her jewelry to be removed. "Because if I die here today, I'd like to make sure someone knows to call in a priest to read off the last rites."

Ellie feels her chest heave at this comment. "Mom!" Before she can apologize for her mother, the phone pings, an alert that her messages to Frank have finally gone through.

"I am Catholic, though I assure you it won't matter." The doctor chuckles. "You're not dying today." He pats Bunny's IV-strung hand, then finally turns around to face Ellie. "And don't worry," he adds. "My mother would have asked the same thing."

Ellie looks up, prepared to thank the doctor for his understanding, and hopefully to share a short-lived laugh in this awful place. But when she sees his face, the blood from her head rushes down to her feet—a vascular waterfall—as she takes him in: peridot-green eyes, cheekbones like arrows, square jaw, flaxen hair. Their gazes connect, and when they do, Ellie sees a flash of recognition steal across his expression, too.

"Jack?" Ellie asks.

And then she promptly blacks out.

~

When Ellie finally comes to, she's on the bed. Jack—whom she has learned is known around the hospital as Dr. Collins—hovers over her, peering into her pupils with a pen-size medical flashlight.

"Welcome back," Jack says, his smile a banner of perfect teeth. "It's certainly nice to see you." He tucks his light into the pocket of his medical coat and then leans back, giving Ellie some personal space. "Glad to see you're okay."

Ellie blinks—one, two, three times—before she sees Bunny, who stands at the foot of the bed, gripping her gold cross.

"Jesus, Mary, and Joseph!" Bunny proclaims the second she sees that Ellie's eyes have opened. "What's the matter with you?" She poses this question as if Ellie has self-elected to collapse. "You're not pregnant, are you?"

"Mom!" Ellie hasn't even sat up yet. "Are you serious? I'm forty-nine. And I'm—"

"Single," Bunny quickly chimes in, a newly minted matchmaker. She gives Dr. Collins a look. "And Catholic!" She contorts her aging face. "Not fully practicing, but . . ."

Ellie suddenly feels like she's sixteen, like her mother has just embarrassed her in front of the cute high school quarterback.

"Well, it looks like I've kept my word." Jack smiles and looks back and forth between mother and daughter, his cheekbones somehow lifted even higher than normal. "Everyone here is leaving perfectly alive and intact."

"Thank God." Bunny reaches for her jacket, still draped across the foot of the bed. "In that case, I need to excuse myself." Behind Jack's back, Bunny makes a dramatic nudging motion, as if Ellie should launch herself at him. "I'll meet you near the main exit," she says with a wink as she leaves through the fabric curtain.

"What's going on with my mother?" Ellie asks the second she's gone. Not *Hello*. Not *How have you been the last two decades?* She pulls herself up, remembering her appearance, and does her best to smooth her knotty, sleep-matted hair into a low bun. "What did her labs show?"

Jack's face glows with the confidence of a man who's about to deliver positive news. "Everything looks good. The nursing staff filled me in about what you told them happened earlier today." He tilts his head at Ellie now, the attractive curves in his facial expression newly shaped like a question mark. "To be honest, what she told them seemed to check out."

"No, no, no." Ellie swings her legs off the uncomfortable bed. "That's not right."

"All the information is detailed in her medical history in the hospital's computer system," Jack explains, and as he does, Ellie is overwhelmed by a familiar prickly sensation, the feeling that he's trying to convince her of something she already knows is not true. "The nurses triple-checked."

Ellie thinks back to the last time she saw him. She was twenty-six and seated on that scratchy yellow couch, listening as he broke her heart into a hundred pieces, his announcement like a verbal hammer straight to her chest.

They'd dated for just shy of one year—which in the span of a whole life, isn't very long, but when you're in your twenties, it can feel meaningful. He'd attended Princeton and then stayed in New Jersey to attend medical school, which he was halfway through when he met Ellie. She sold him a copy of Fitzgerald's *Tender Is the Night*, a fact that in retrospect probably should have been her first sign. They'd had a good run—reading books and drinking beer and going out for Indian food and sometimes saying "I love you," and honestly for a while Ellie really believed she might marry him.

That morning, as she'd sat on his awful couch and listened to him talk about how he hadn't cheated on her—though, he guessed he hadn't *not* cheated on her, either, since he'd been driving back home to Westchester every Thursday for over a month to hang out with his high school flame—some part of her felt broken.

Back in the ER, a commotion erupts outside the fabric curtain. From what Ellie can hear, another patient—obviously in much worse shape—is screaming show tunes.

"I'd better go." Already sensing that her choice to bring her mother here has been a waste, Ellie reaches for her book bag and slides the straps back on, right as a new question pops into her mind. "Have you lived around here this whole time?" she asks before she leaves, thinking back to the last time she saw him and that whole wild, transitional time in her life. Ellie is not the sort of woman to waste hours stalking people from her past on social media. She's never crossed paths with him in their not-so-big town. Still, she feels like she should have known he was living here—not back in New York, near his own parents—all this time. "I thought you moved home all those years ago."

He half smiles, revealing a sliver of his perfect, white teeth. "Change of plans." He shrugs and stuffs a hand into his lab coat pocket. "I decided to stay."

Ellie nods at Jack, a sort of thank-you for his time. "I'll, um—I'll see you around, I guess."

Jack's thin, pink lips remain in a subdued U shape as he steps aside so Ellie has the space to walk freely past.

She pulls open the curtain and takes a step.

"Hey, Ellie," Jack says before she leaves, his green eyes narrowing with a thought.

She glances back at him over her bag's shoulder strap, not sure she even wants to hear what he has to say.

"Despite the circumstances . . . ," he tells her, his face quickly flushing, as if he's downed a pint of beer. "Well, it's just—" He bites his bottom lip. "You look good."

ELEVEN

Bunny is seated at the kitchen table when Ellie walks downstairs. She's writing a list on a small pad from the junk drawer and sipping a fresh mug of terrible coffee. They've been home from the hospital for over an hour, and still Ellie doesn't quite know what is happening. She keeps wondering if she's dead or dreaming or on one of those prank TV shows, like she's about to get stormed by a laughing crowd here to explain the day's many chaotic turns.

"The clock on your stove is still blinking," Bunny points out, her face cast down on her notepad. "Did you notice the time?" She looks up, directs her eyes to the flashing numbers: 11:11. "Hmm," says Bunny, leaving her observation at that.

Ellie, disregarding this, notices the dark-gray cardigan Bunny has thrown over her shoulders. "Is that a sweater?" Beyond the window, the sun paints the scene with its buttery warmth. The edge of the yard is lined with a carpet of pale spring flowers. "It's in the sixties," she points out, even though Ellie is frequently guilty of committing the same sartorial crime.

Ellie steps farther into the room, feeling slightly human for the first time since this morning. When they arrived home, she'd gone straight upstairs, past Maggie's still-closed bedroom door, and into her primary suite, where she stripped off her filthy travel clothes and showered, hoping the water might wash away the more bizarre instances of the day. She'd stayed in there until her skin turned lobster red, though she could not relax. Even with the water turned up and the bathroom fan running, she could hear Bunny—who was *supposed* to be far away in Florida, soaking up her retirement—through the floorboards as she banged around in the kitchen.

"I'm freezing, Ellie," Bunny announces and then sets down her pen. The overhead black pendant light is off—the generator is still running, the power not yet fully restored—the room illuminated by what Bunny believes is frigid sunlight. "I despise this weather. I hate the cold." She looks at the notepad before she says the next part, as if she's unsure she wants her daughter to hear. "I shouldn't be here in it."

"Well, Mom," Ellie replies, noticing her mother has started to unpack, her plastic pillbox now set on the counter, alongside the zip-lock bag full of hard butterscotch candies she always carries with her just in case (in case of what, no one is sure). Ellie opens the fridge, thankfully still running from the generator, and pulls out one of her atmosphere-destroying seltzers and a piece of cheese. "At least right now we can agree on that."

Finally, Ellie wears fresh clothes—a pair of clean jeans, her old low-top tennis sneakers, and a washed T-shirt. Her face looks a touch more alive thanks to some simple makeup, while her hair—wet and smelling like ultraclean floral-based chemicals—is neatly combed from her center part. She embraces this feeling of freshness and enjoys a cold sip of her fizzy water, not quite knowing what to do next.

"By the way . . . ," Ellie starts. Opposite the window, she sees that the caravan of power company trucks has returned, a pair of men already ascending upward toward the damaged lines in a sturdy crane. "What are you writing?"

Despite her multiple layers, Bunny shivers like it's the middle of winter. She gives a little shake, her poof of blond hair making her look like a human Q-tip. "What, this?" She looks down at the notebook. "It's a list of things I need to tell your father," she explains. "He never remembers what time to take his medications or how to use the laundry machine."

Divorce, Ellie recognizes, is strange. For years, you are intimately connected to a person—sharing everything from your medical history to your toilet to your groceries—and then one day you just drive away, even though in all reality only one of you likely knows how to get to the next place you're going, and the other person is the only one who remembered to fill the car with gas. Ellie watches her mother with her list. It isn't easy to unlearn the many ways you've come to rely upon your spouse. It's like trying to unbake a cake. How do you fully separate all the ingredients and return them to their original state once they've already been mixed?

"Maybe," Ellie points out to Bunny and sets down her already half-empty seltzer can, "that's why separating from your husband in your eighties is a bad—"

Pound. Pound. Pound.

Someone knocks at the front door—again. Ellie takes a fast look at her mother. After this morning, she isn't so sure she wants to know who waits for her on the other side. She inhales deeply, like a free diver preparing to submerge beneath the water for a too-long time, and then takes a step forward. But before she reaches the entryway, the door swings open.

"Your power lines are down!" Frank announces as he boisterously steps inside. "Your generator is running!" He looks like himself—like regular old Frank—except that he's wearing a casual button-down shirt and closed-toe shoes. In his arms, he gingerly balances a reusable grocery bag. "That was some storm last night, huh?"

Ellie has stopped in the middle of the hallway, as if someone has bordered off the space with an electric fence.

Well then, that's that, she thinks and concurs with herself that she must be dead. Although she does not remember it, her plane must have been struck by lightning and crashed into the Atlantic in a glorious blaze. Whatever she's witnessed today is just a distorted first step of the afterlife.

"What are you doing home, by the way, sweetheart?" Frank asks, like the surprise of the morning is that Ellie is the one who is here. He hands his only daughter the bag. She quickly peers inside it, thinking she'll find a dozen tiny angels flapping their wings. This is heaven, after all—a very dysfunctional version—right? "Don't you have things to do?" He's practically shouting, even though he stands a few feet away. "It's Monday!" he yells while smoothing out the sides of his short white hair.

"I told you she gave herself a little personal day, Frank!" Bunny shouts from the kitchen. "The breakup!" she continues, like Ellie isn't standing here, more or less between them, as if caught in a game of verbal keep-away. "She's a real mess this morning!"

"I'm sorry about everything," Frank says and then kisses Ellie's cheek. She resists the urge to poke his face to determine if he's real or maybe animatronic. "Take it from me." He gestures toward the kitchen. "Heartache is never easy, Ellie. No matter your age." He drops his voice. "Not that she'll ever go through with this," he mumbles to himself, then pulls back. "Bunny!" he exclaims as he takes the reusable bag and marches into the kitchen. "I brought your coffee!"

"Oh, thank God!" Bunny cries out. "The heartburn from this other one! It's terrible!"

Any amount of freshness Ellie felt is gone, the concaves beneath her underarms dripping with sweat, like her body is a hot spring. She follows her father into the kitchen. He pulls Bunny's favorite breakfast blend from the bag, as well as three parchment-wrapped submarine-length sandwiches.

"I stopped by the deli and picked up lunch," Frank adds, laying out his provisions. His drugstore readers sway from the neckline of his shirt with his every move. "Your mother said neither of you ate."

"Don't even look in the fridge, Frank," Bunny announces. She tears her list from the notepad and hands it to him. He nods his understanding. "There's hardly anything in it."

"What do you mean 'the deli'?" Ellie asks.

Frank sneaks a quick bite of his sandwich before he responds. "What are you saying, Ellie?" he asks through a full mouth. "*My* deli. The one I've owned your whole life!"

Ellie watches her parents unpack the rest of the food, feeling overcome by both shock and extreme calm. *Of course* her father is here and talking nonsense. *Of course* her mother is here and doing the same. Because Ellie has somehow turned into Alice and become lost in Wonderland. Because at some point in the last twenty-four hours, her brain has turned into mashed potatoes.

"You sold the deli years ago, Dad," Ellie recounts in an even tone, now wondering if all three of them are dead, or all battling some highly transmissible, lightning-fast amnesia.

Bunny sucks her teeth, gives Frank a look as she picks apart her sandwich.

Ellie knew when she woke up today—the first real day without Jonah in it—that things would feel different. That life would take on a new, unfamiliar shape. But this feels extreme. She watches her parents. It appears to Ellie that they (or she?) are losing their minds. Other than their separation announcement, however, the two of them don't seem to notice anything amiss.

"Hey, Dad." Ellie drags her damp hair off her neck, secures it with her rubber band. "Hypothetically speaking, how would you say you got yourself from *your* house and over to *my* house just now?" She pauses like a well-seasoned game show contestant. "In a train. On a bicycle. In a trolley. In an airplane or—"

"An airplane?" Frank nearly chokes on a bite of ham. He coughs, covering his mouth with his age-spotted hand, and offers Bunny an inquisitive glance. "What's the matter with her?"

Bunny pulls a single fold of turkey from her sandwich. "I *told* you."

Ellie closes her eyes, already knowing the answer, the one her father will inexplicably—but inevitably—give her. She doesn't know *why* or *how* it is the answer, but she does know it. "So, I'm guessing that means you . . . walked?"

Her mind flashes to *Family Feud*, the show's vintage reruns often turned on in the background of her parents' Floridian home. *Survey says: Walked!*

"Walked?" Frank's weathered face lifts into an amused smile. "No, no, I parked my cruise ship out front." He laughs, playfully swats Bunny's arm. "Did I walk?"

Ellie gives one firm nod, already reaching for her book bag. "Well, it seems I'm currently spiraling my way through some sort of mental breakdown, so I'm going to scoot out for a bit." She grabs her car keys. "Oh, one more thing." She begins to walk backward toward the entryway. "In case I don't have a chance to say this later, you two really are not very good at splitting up." Ellie pauses long enough to take one last glance at things, then swiftly turns around to see herself out.

"Oh, Ellie!" Bunny calls before her daughter leaves. "Hang on! There's one more item to discuss!"

Ellie sucks in a deep breath. She turns her head back over her shoulder, half expecting her mother and father to burst out laughing, or at the very least to explain the inner workings of this very peculiar day. "Yes, Mom?"

"I don't trust that fridge right now," Bunny states, her biggest concern. "Wherever it is that you're going, make a point to stop and pick up some fresh creamer on your way back."

TWELVE

Ellie is driving.

Racing, actually. Or, at the very least, barreling her white, midsize Volvo SUV (practical, classic, safe) erratically enough through her town's quiet streets to no doubt make her Floridian driver, the one who deposited her family at the airport just one day ago, impeccably proud.

Everywhere she looks are fallen trees, downed wires, and broken-off branches—a hundred small obstacles. She doesn't care. Ever since she left her house several minutes ago, said goodbye to her parents, and engaged in a brief chat with a man from the power company ("At least a few more days, ma'am"), she's been speeding down the twenty-five-mph roadway like a stunt driver. There is no possible way she can slow down.

Beep! Beep!

Another driver pounds his car horn like a punching bag as Ellie passes. He's right. Of course he's right. Ellie should *not* be behind the wheel. And certainly not in this reckless way. She knows this. She can hardly think, let alone see straight or operate heavy machinery. Her palms? A sweaty mess. Her "fresh" shirt? Same issue. It doesn't matter. She knows what she needs to do: retrieve her phone, call Jonah (likely already at work for the morning)—even though she's not supposed to—and see if he can help her make sense of this lucid dream.

Ellie continues to career the car along her town's otherwise peaceful streets. Talk radio buzzes in her immediate background, the host of whatever program she left clicked on last night reminding listeners that the world is more or less on fire. Ellie stabs her finger against the stereo panel so the woman will vanish. *Go away, go away, go away.* She has no mental space available for the host's harangue of bad news. Ellie has more immediate issues to solve. The climate, the dolphins, the ice caps, whatever political drama currently unfolds across the globe like a badly wrinkled-up map, all of it—much to Maggie's likely disappointment—must wait.

Oh no, Ellie thinks as she barrels over another haphazard pile of fallen twigs. *Maggie.* She should check in with her, too. And say what? That another branch of her small family tree is about to break? That her grandmother (and possibly her grandfather) is in the midst of an overlooked neurological episode? Or, worse, that Ellie is herself? *No,* she decides. It's best to leave Maggie alone so she can focus on exams, let the announcement about her own parents' divorce sink in before Ellie adds any more uncertainty to her daughter's plate.

Up ahead, a stop sign. Ellie skids the car to a dramatic stop. Her heart races a thousand miles per minute. She peers in the rearview, panting. Thankfully, no one is behind her. She jabs her fingers at the stereo one last time and finally hits the correct button, a minor win. The woman's voice disappears. In its place, the soft, soothing (and maybe a little bit sad) sounds of an alternative rock station hum through the vehicle, a melodic sort of white noise. *Perfect.*

Another driver slows behind Ellie. She consumes a deep breath, neatly realigns her hands on the wheel, and mentally rattles off her plan. She'll go to the airport, find her phone (or at least file the appropriate lost and found paperwork to retrieve it), call Jonah to discuss Bunny and Frank, and then, item by item, begin to make sense of this day. *Easy.*

But first—*deep breath*—before she begins her forty-minute high-way drive back to the airport, she absolutely must stop and get a coffee. A very strong one. A very large one. Something to help her better focus and to see straight. Stat.

Ellie turns the car onto Main Street. Outside her windows, save for the power company trucks and damaged trees, the world mostly appears normal, an ordinary Monday. Locals are outside walking dogs. A few runners sprint past. The town's elegant homes appear as always, a muted rainbow of desirable whites: dove, chantilly, lace. Another few blocks and the residential section fades out, giving way to a bustling downtown, a collection of shops and boutiques and tasteful window displays, cafés with wrought iron tables that spill out onto the sidewalks, and floral window boxes flecked with spring shades of pinks and whites and greens.

Ellie turns the car right, then left, then right again, weaving her way beyond the more crowded streets. Up ahead, she spots additional sights that soothe her—the bookstore where she once worked and still sometimes visits, and her favorite coffee shop across the street.

The quiet music still thrumming, she flicks on the car's blinker, ready to pull into a vacant spot. But before she can, another driver—some obviously terrible human—cuts her off and steals her space. Ellie blares on her horn like it's a bagpipe, but the awful person couldn't care less. He offers a wave, slides out of his car, and then—*chirp! chirp!*—locks the doors and walks off on his merry little way.

Her brief interlude with calm quickly deteriorating, like a beautiful cake left out in the rain, Ellie is forced to circle the block, not once, not twice, but three times in search of a new place to park. Before she turns back onto the street a fourth time, the light ahead of her changes to red. Ellie taps the brake pedal and stops at the busy four-way intersection. Beneath her, the car idles and vibrates, gently shaking her like a bad masseuse. With her eyes trained on a newly vacant space up ahead, a song Ellie remembers but has not heard in a very long time pipes through the stereo. The lyrics come back to her in a rush. She tries to recall the last time she listened to this band. It was ages ago. Another lifetime, practically. Ellie wasn't even the same person then.

Up ahead, the crosswalk signal changes, a blinking warning. Finally, the traffic light that hangs overhead turns green. Ellie lifts her foot from the brake and eases it onto the gas pedal. She spins the steering wheel and sees that her parking space remains available. She smiles at this small victory—*Yes, yes, yes*—and completes her turn. The car moves forward. And then—SMASH!

She punches her closed fists against the steering wheel. Of all the days in her life, why must this have happened today? One brilliant person's choice—to steal her original parking spot—and look at the consequences.

Ellie opens her glove compartment and digs out her insurance booklet and a peppermint before she slides on her oval sunglasses. She inhales a minty breath, tells herself she will *not* dig into this person who has caused this entirely avoidable accident on this already terrible day.

Knock, knock, knock.

She turns back toward her driver's side window. When she does, Ellie squints, like her glasses are smudged. She removes them—a double take—then buzzes down the window. She huffs loudly, emitting a puff of hot, angry air. Probably terrible for the environment.

"You've got to be kidding me," she says.

~

"I'm so—I'm so sorry!"

Jonah stands at Ellie's driver's side window, looking like a severely disheveled version of himself. His typically styled hair is rumpled, several unkempt strands dangling like too-short curtains above his eyebrows. His usual weekday office wear—a baby-blue button-down, maybe one of those silly bubble vests if it's chilly—has been swapped with a wrinkled white T-shirt, which Ellie notes may actually be an undershirt. Apparently, based on the timing of things, as well as appearances, he's decided on a personal day, too.

"I'm glad you found me." Ellie clicks off her seat belt. In the rearview mirror, she sees flashing red lights a few blocks behind them. "Well," she says, editing herself, "I'm not glad you *smashed* into me."

She tries for a smile, but he only half returns it. His mind, she can tell, is someplace else. "But I'm happy you're here." She twists to open her door, and when she does, she feels it—the familiar ripple of pain. That one stubborn muscle that hugs her spine, which has been in hibernation since she woke up, has been triggered from the impact of the crash. She doesn't have time to think about it. She stretches her torso, hoping to subdue the sensation, and steps out of the car. On the sidewalk, onlookers have gathered, perhaps to serve as witnesses to this completely unnecessary event. "Anyway, I've had a horrible morning," Ellie tells him, shaking her head just thinking about it.

"I'm very sorry." Jonah looks at her with a somewhat blank—maybe a touch cold?—stare. Ellie can tell he's trying to work some problem out in his head. "I didn't mean to add to it. This is obviously my fault." He squeezes the back of his neck, fuzzy with fresh hair growth. "I—I didn't mean to cause this."

"Honestly, in the grand scheme of today, this is the least of my problems." Ellie massages the bones above her eyes. "I don't even know where to begin." As Ellie says this, she pauses, really looks around. Suddenly, the inherent strangeness of this accident hits her: the fact that it happened here, on the exact corner where they first met. Ellie's brain does not process numbers in the same lightning-fast way Jonah's can, though she imagines this is why he seems off. He's preoccupied as he wonders about the likelihood of this repeat meeting.

"Huh." Ellie puffs out her lips. "This is . . . strange, isn't it?" She lets herself smile. "Not exactly how I thought this week might kick off."

"Yeah." Jonah still has a glazed look in his attractive hazel eyes. "Tell me about it."

Frazzled and confused, they're both silent as they stand a few feet from each other, their cars pressed together like a mechanical kiss. Ellie thinks back to their initial crash here. They were both twenty-six, old enough to be considered real, functioning adults, yet still young enough that they were in the process of becoming other versions of themselves.

Jonah had felt so badly about that first accident (the one he'd caused after he briefly tilted his head toward the radio to search for a specific sports broadcast). Ellie had been so flabbergasted by her breakup that she couldn't help but laugh. After they exchanged insurance information and spoke to the officer on the scene, Jonah asked if he could take her out for coffee. They drove their damaged cars two blocks, then shared a table in the window, a cascade of plants trailing over their heads.

Ellie had been so taken aback by Jonah. He was handsome and kind and gentle and warm and humble and apologetic and polite. He was every good adjective. From the second they sat, he made Ellie laugh over practically nothing. When Ellie asked him about where he'd been heading at the time he crashed into her car, he vaguely said he'd been on his way to meet a friend, but there'd been a detour. And wasn't that true for her, too? When Jack had called her the night before and said he had something important for them to discuss, she foolishly thought he might propose. She had pictured a meal and a bottle of wine, maybe a picnic blanket laid out on the living room floor of his apartment. Instead, they'd argued straight through the night, until finally, the next morning on that terrible couch, she got dumped.

A detour. It didn't take long for Ellie to forget about Jack. She fell for Jonah the way one might fall off a cliff—it was fast and hard and unexpected. In the weeks that immediately followed, she soon felt not like she was falling, but rather like she was arriving. She'd finally found her way to the right destination.

Now, back at the scene of the current accident, Ellie feels a tugging in her heart as she recalls those early days.

"So, I took a quick glance on my walk over, and it looks like the damage to both cars is minor." Whatever thought had occupied Jonah's mind a minute ago is gone. His tone is now flat, this event suddenly nothing more than a business transaction. "I have a good mechanic. I'm happy to pay for the damage out of pocket," he offers, like they don't still share all the same accounts. "I have a hell of a week. This will probably be easier than dealing with a dozen phone calls to insurance companies."

Her wistfulness instantly gone, Ellie feels her eyes tighten. "Yup." She makes a loud popping sound with her mouth when she arrives at the final *p*. "Would *hate* to inconvenience you."

Jonah runs his sturdy hands through his thick mess of hair. "Great." He pats his pockets, produces his phone, swipes the screen open, then meets Ellie's gaze. "Do you—I'm sorry, maybe this is awkward." He hands it to her. "Do you mind punching in your number?"

Ellie does not need a mirror to know her neck is all red, angry splotches. Her insides are fire—a heaping pile of burning orange embers—and yet simultaneously empty—cold, dead, black, as gutted as a fish. He's already forgotten her number and deleted it from his phone? Already removed her from his favorite phone contacts, neutering her of the letters "ICE" beside her name?

"Sure." Ellie takes his device, punches in her information, and hands it back. She's fuming, nothing but flames, a fireworks display ready to burst. She's going to get her phone. And she's going to call that attorney the second she taps open the electronic screen.

"Again, I'm really sorry," Jonah stammers, pulling Ellie away from her thoughts. His lips have parted, as though he is amused by some detail of the scene Ellie does not see. "Well, it's that—" The bold May sun catches in Jonah's eyes, the ones that, over the course of her life, Ellie has stared into a million times. "I—I just—" He pauses again—he's like a bad TV signal today, constantly glitching. He tries to shake his thought away, but she can see in his expression that it is obstinate and comes right back.

Before he speaks anything further, Ellie can feel a change, the way you sense a storm coming just by the way the air shifts. "What?" she asks, already knowing he's about to drop a soon-to-detonate bomb at her feet. She considers the bizarre ways her day thus far has trended. Every cell in her body begins to intuit something bad. He's looking at her funny now, part of his lip curled, one eye in a squint, like a student who can't quite see the blackboard. "Just say it." *Tick. Tick. Tick.* "Really." She prepares for the explosion. "My day has been pretty terrible so far. I can't imagine that whatever you're about to tell me can possibly top it."

Jonah nods, considering Ellie's statement. "Well, this may sound strange." He pauses, bites his generous pink lower lip, the one she's pressed her own mouth upon innumerable times. "I—I don't know. It's hard to explain." He scratches his presently unruly hair. "I just—I feel like I know you from somewhere." *Tick, tick.* "Have we—have we met?"

Ka-boom.

THIRTEEN

I don't have it."

Ellie stands at the lost and found window at Newark Liberty International Airport, where she's been positioned for the last hour. A man in a blue TSA uniform, whom Ellie has begun to feel confident is at least part sloth, has sifted through every relevant bin, or so he says. Who could know? The room behind him looks like it's sponsored by Rubbermaid. There are plastic boxes in every size and variety full of items—maybe meaningful, maybe not—that other travelers have left behind. There are forgotten toys, abandoned bags, tangles of misplaced cords and chargers, metal rings full of keys, an entire rolling rack of jackets. Humanity is careless, Ellie acknowledges as she takes it all in. People neglect so many things.

"Are you sure?" Ellie asks, even though she's personally witnessed him sort through his box of lost cell phones multiple times. "*Really* sure?"

The man turns away from Ellie. He's had enough of her, she can tell. "You said you lost it here last night, right?" He sets his bin back on a shelf. "Maybe no one's turned it in yet," he suggests as he takes a seat at his cluttered desk. "Could still be where you left it."

"I'm pretty sure I left it in a bathroom near my gate," Ellie explains.

"Near your gate?" The man blows out his lips. "That means it's on the other side of security. The only way you'll get through there, ma'am, is with a ticket."

Ellie—angry and frustrated and confused and still without her phone, adjusts her backpack straps and walks away from the window. It's midday on a Monday and so the crowd inside the airport isn't bad. Here are the business travelers with their laptop bags and stoic expressions—wherever they're heading, they just want to go and get back. Here are the families with their overpacked luggage and their strollers and their fussy children and their many snacks—the parents likely having snagged affordable tickets to get ahead of the summer travel months. All around, there are scattered singletons like Ellie, too—people who do not fit into either of the aforementioned categories.

Ellie moves across the shiny floors, past the snack stands and the escalators and the officers with their drug-sniffing dogs. Airports, she notes, are strange places. Dependent upon which traveler you ask, they are both beginnings and endings, starting points for celebrations, final moments before gut-wrenching goodbyes, their corridors home to heartache and happiness, pain and joy, memories some people hope will live in their hearts and minds forever, and other memories different people will wish they could immediately wipe away. They are not, she recognizes, so different from divorce.

Ellie stops in front of the main terminal entrance that will lead her back to long-term parking. The automated doors open, and another round of travelers rushes inside. *Think, think, think.* If she gets back in her car and drives home, she doesn't know what will happen, what new catastrophe or surprise guest or weird unforeseen world awaits. Maybe, Ellie thinks, she should just fly away.

On a typical day, Ellie hates airports. The anxiety of flying, the stress of whether or not she'll have time to make one last bathroom stop, the ruminating about whether she's remembered to pack all the correct things. But today? Today is different. Ellie is not herself. While the rest of the world carries on normally, her pocket of the universe is no longer right. Now, the thought of getting on a plane, strapping herself in, and arriving someplace else sounds sort of nice.

"I need a ticket," Ellie says when she approaches the airline's desk.

A woman in a navy-blue skirt-suit looks at Ellie like one of them is malfunctioning. Her name is Brenda, according to her wing-shaped nameplate. "You want to buy a ticket . . . here?"

"Yes." Ellie looks up at the departures board. "Whatever the next available flight is to Orlando, I guess," she decides, knowing someplace vaguely familiar might be a good thing.

Brenda's eyes widen, like she's not sure if this interaction is a nothing or one that requires a fast call-in to security. "You . . . guess?"

Ellie pushes away a strand of frizzed-out hair that has come loose from her black tie. Maybe going away is what she should have done for herself from the start. Over the years, Ellie has dedicated her entire life to her family, Jonah and Maggie specifically. And for what? Did Ellie think there'd be some reward waiting for her at the end? No one needs her in the same way anymore. What would it matter if she and Jonah split up, get divorced, and go their separate ways, if he knows her anymore or not? What would it matter if she flew away?

"You know you can do this from your phone, right?" Brenda punches her fingers across her computer keyboard, peers up at Ellie through a wisp of dark hair. "That's how most people do it nowadays."

Ellie nods. "I've heard this."

Brenda looks down at her computer. "There's a seat available on a flight to Orlando that begins boarding in about an hour."

"I'll take it." Ellie digs through her backpack, thinking about what she'll do when she arrives. Find a taxi. Pop off somewhere to buy a few simple outfits and hygiene products. Book a hotel, call her parents and Maggie from her room phone to explain her whereabouts (or maybe place the call from her cell phone, if she can find it near her gate before she leaves). She pulls out her credit card and ID, hands both items over.

"Return flight?" Brenda lifts Ellie's license and types in her information.

Ellie chews her lip. "No thank you," she decides. "I don't know when I'm coming back."

Brenda's expression does nothing to disguise her judgment. She drums her fingers across her keyboard, pulls Ellie's boarding pass from the mouth of her countertop printer, and hands it to her.

Ellie slips her credit card back into her wallet, then shoves her ID and boarding pass into her pocket so they'll be easily accessible for security.

"Have a safe flight, Ms. Adams," Brenda says.

Ellie's head snaps up. "What did you say?"

"Ms. Adams? That's what's written on your ID." She lifts a thin brow toward the ceiling. "Did I get it right? Because if not, I'll need to type your information in again. You'll never get through TSA otherwise."

Ellie pulls out her license, the day's events quickly transforming from something illogical to something almost clear, like swirling a finger through muddy water and then watching as the sediment settles.

"Is there a problem?" Brenda asks.

She feels it again. That out-of-body sensation she's had too many times already today. Out of all the unexplainable situations she's faced since waking up this morning, this is the one that rattles her the most and makes her think she is not just dreaming or dealing with the trauma of a divorce or going through the motions of a brain that no longer quite works. It is something else. Something much worse.

"Ms. Adams?"

"I—I'm sorry." Ellie's mouth has gone dry, as if she's swallowed a bucket of sand. "I just—I haven't heard someone call me by my maiden name in a while."

She steps out of line, looks down at her ID.

And here it is:

Eleanor Grace Adams
116 Cherry Lane
Great.

～

Ellie Adams—not Ellie Baker—is seated at her gate, turning her ID in her hand like a bouncer on the hunt for fakes. On her way here, she discovered that the bathroom she used last night is closed for renovation, any hope of finding her phone now gone. She sets her license on her lap, not knowing what to make of it. She only knows that, somehow, in a dozen different ways, she's no longer the same person living the same life as she was yesterday. She is herself, reset. Or herself, after everything. She doesn't know which yet.

"Good afternoon, travelers on flight 2017, with direct service from Newark to Orlando," a voice pipes through the overhead speakers. Around Ellie, other travelers start to gather their belongings and stand. "We're ready to begin our boarding process and now welcome group one passengers as well as active military and families traveling with small children."

Through the window, Ellie sees the planes on the tarmac. Since marrying Jonah, she has not traveled any place more than an hour or two away from home by herself. Vacations? Jonah was always at her side. Trips to see Bunny and Frank? He was always the person seated next to her on the plane.

"We now welcome groups two and three to begin the boarding process," a member of the flight crew announces a few minutes later. "Please remember to place your smaller personal items under the seat in front of you to help us speed up the boarding process."

Ellie pushes herself up from her chair and makes her way toward the line. She thinks about the flight, about navigating the turbulence without Jonah at her side, as well as the turbulence they've already survived. She thumbs her ring finger, noticing for the first time all day that her slim gold wedding band—the one she's hardly removed in years—is gone.

"All remaining passengers are now welcome to begin the boarding process," a staticky voice announces. Nearby, the last groups of travelers wheel their carry-ons to the gate.

Ellie's pack is back on her shoulders. Her paper boarding pass and ID are in her hand. This is her moment. The one perhaps she didn't know she was waiting for until right now, when she actually arrived at it. She can leave behind this whole confused, out-of-order day and all her choices that have led her to it. She can fly away, start over, make new decisions, try again.

~

"Any luck finding it?"

A few minutes later, Ellie sees the man from lost and found on the escalator. The boarding pass is shoved in her bag, her car keys now dangling from her fingers. She steps off and heads into the baggage claim area. "I think I left it at home, actually," she lies.

The man shakes his head at her and then goes off on his separate way.

For the second time in twenty-four hours, Ellie finds herself standing alone in this public space. From the corner of her eye, she catches a glimpse of a digital clock overhead, the same one she saw last night. She rubs her bare finger, a highlight reel of the day playing in her mind.

In front of Ellie, the airport's automatic doors open, then close, then open again.

She doesn't know what will happen when she arrives home, who or what will be waiting. From a place deep within her, she only knows she needs to get back. That, while here in this baggage claim last night, she broke something. Or that, months ago, that night on their bedroom floor with the laundry when she'd said that word—"divorce"—she'd broken something, too.

Now, for better or worse, she needs to figure out what exactly.

And then she has to try to fix it.

FOURTEEN

W e need to talk."

Ellie drops her book bag on the kitchen table across from where her mother sits and stares out the window at the spring sun that has slowly started to set.

"Did you remember the creamer?" Bunny asks.

"No, Mom. I've been pretty . . . preoccupied today." Ellie looks around for Frank. "Where's Dad?"

Bunny sighs, her breath as heavy as the dark cardigan she still wears. "I don't know." Her gaze is set someplace outside. "It's not my job to keep tabs on him anymore. He's on his own now." She waves a dismissive hand at the air, lowers her voice. "Not that he'll have a clue how."

"I need to ask you an important question." Ellie sits across from her mother, produces her ID from her jeans pocket, and slaps it down. "What is this?"

Bunny leans forward, her entire face scrunched up, as if even her cheeks need to strain in order for her to see anything clearly. She pulls her readers from the neckline of her blouse, shaking them away from her cross necklace. After she slides them on, she takes a peek, then raises her chin and looks up at Ellie. "What are you talking about?" She looks like she's just eaten something incredibly sour. "It's your driver's license."

"Right," Ellie agrees, the laminated rectangle set between them. The whole drive home, Ellie thought more about last night. In her life, she's wished for so many things. For her and Jonah to stay happy forever.

And later, for the fighting to stop. For Maggie to remain young and innocent and in need of her for eternity. "And you don't notice anything unusual about it?"

Bunny fiddles with her palm tree pin, her eyes narrowing as she takes in the too-tiny text. "Nothing," she says, which is what Ellie expects. "Except that you've self-elected to be an organ donor." She shudders. "Do you really want someone to cut up your body like that?"

"Did she buy the creamer?" Behind Ellie, Frank steps into the room, his reading glasses hugging the tip of his nose. He wears more comfortable clothing now—cotton pants, a pair of well-worn slippers. His hair, she can see, is freshly washed, the thinning strands neatly combed. Beneath his arm, he carries a set of Ellie's bedsheets.

"Why are you carrying around my bedsheets, Dad?" Ellie squeezes her temples as the kitchen fills with shadows. This day—this illogical, enigmatic day—is beginning to taper.

"I'm putting them on the couch for when I go to sleep." He looks to his wife, but her gaze is lost out the window again. "I'm not letting your mother stay here without me." He cuts across the kitchen, pulls the undesirable creamer from the fridge, and takes a quick sniff.

Ellie drops her face into her palms. "Let me get this straight." She looks back up. "The two of you are getting divorced . . . but for some incomprehensible reason, you're both here . . . and staying . . . together . . . in my house?"

"Your mother is in her eighties," Frank adds, as if he himself is not a member of this same age bracket. He squints through his glasses, peers at the container's small font, then catches Ellie's attention. *Don't worry,* Frank silently mouths to his daughter while Bunny stares off in the other direction. "She'll never go through with this," he adds quietly so that Bunny can't hear him. He pours the perfectly fine creamer down the drain.

Ellie sighs, unclear if her father is simply humoring Bunny or what. "You two really are not very good at splitting up." She tugs away her hair tie—her honey mane still partially damp—and looks at her parents, trying to figure out how one of her own choices has so deeply altered life for them. "I need to ask you both something. And I need you to answer me very clearly." Bunny turns and folds her hands in a neat pile, like an obedient schoolgirl. Frank tosses the empty container and sits at the table next to his soon-to-be-not-wife. "When was the last time either of you set foot on a plane?"

"Oh, good Lord," Bunny starts and then unfolds her hands. "What kind of ridiculous—"

"No, no," Ellie interrupts. "Just answer the question, Mom."

Bunny's nostrils flare as she exhales her annoyance. "I don't know, Ellie. Four, maybe five years ago." She looks to Frank, as if to compare notes. "It was that long weekend your father and I took when he bought me my pin." She points at her colorful accessory. "Why are you asking us this?"

A recollection: the night, roughly seventeen years earlier, right here in this house. Maggie in her high chair with her teensy, cut-up pieces of meatballs. The four adults gathered around the table as Frank told Ellie and Jonah the news about the house. For years, whenever Ellie has thought back on the event, this is the part of the story her brain has always zoomed in on: the fact that her parents were bequeathing her this home she loved so much. It's only now that Ellie recalls another part of the conversation.

After dinner, the buzz of the announcement beginning to die down, Jonah took Maggie upstairs for a diaper change while Bunny began to clear the plates and bring out fresh ones for dessert. Ellie and Frank were alone at the table, stacking up dishes and serving platters.

"You know, sweetheart," Frank said as he shook out a cloth napkin, "this is all your doing."

A young, thirtysomething Ellie looked up, her mother's favorite salad bowl in her hands. "What do you mean?"

Frank, who seemed old to Ellie back then, even though he'd only recently stepped into his sixties, set down the table linen. "This," he said as he looked fondly around the room. "This whole night. Everything with Mom and me. Our retirement. Me finally selling the deli. The move. Just . . . all of it."

Ellie's brows revealed her confusion. Frank gestured at their dining chairs, an invitation for them to both sit.

"Your mother and I have wanted to do this forever, Ellie," Frank explained. Tufts of soft coffee-colored hair, which would fade to silver in several years, framed his newly aged face. "But we knew we never would unless you were happy and settled into your own life." Frank's eyes, concealed behind the reading glasses he'd recently started to wear with greater frequency, began to mist over with emotion.

"Dad, you still would have—"

"This life you've built for yourself, Ellie," he continued, "it's a good one. I know it seems simple sometimes, choosing to stay at home for your family. But your choices have made a world of difference, not only in Jonah's and Maggie's lives, but in ours." From beneath his crisp shirt, Frank's chest rippled with emotion. "We'll miss seeing the three of you every day." He inhaled deeply in an effort to hide the shaky quality that had started to weave its way into his voice. "But we know you'll be okay, that you won't be alone, that you'll be here and happy with your own family. Your own purpose." He smiled, deepening the lines that hugged his mouth. "We know you don't need us the way you once did anymore."

Now, Ellie picks up her photo ID and takes another look at her name. "The two of you never retired to Florida, did you?" She taps her license on the tabletop and meets her parents' confused stares. "You always talked about it—I remember from when I was younger—but you never actually did it." She sets the ID down. "Why?"

"Oh, stop." Bunny looks away. "You know I'd never leave you to live up here by yourself."

Frank huffs at this comment. "Yes, Bunny," he says, a new, atypical gruffness in his voice. The skin around his eyes wrinkles. "But we all already knew that."

Bunny waves a hand at the air, exhales an annoyed breath.

Ellie glances back and forth between them and begins to assemble all the pieces in her mind. It's like a jigsaw puzzle that once seemed impossible but now, with the edges finally in place, has begun to take shape. She's starting to understand. In no small way, her parents have stayed put here, steeped in their own unhappiness, because of their only daughter, the one whom they believed would eventually grow up, move on, and form a family of her own, but did not.

"And, Dad, you never sold the deli, right? Because you didn't need to." She pauses, allowing her words to sink in like a heavy cream. "You knew your employees could run it most days, so you could finally slow down," she goes on, "but you didn't need to get rid of it, since you'd be here—not moving away—and available to keep a regular eye on things." Frank is looking down at his clean fingernails. "Am I—"

Frank nods at his hands—all marked with brown spots—his signal that her story adds up. "Yes," he sighs.

Ellie peers through the window, the sun almost fully gone. Out there, the world, the one she never played a huge part in—never discovered another planet, never founded a movement, never rose in the ranks at some important company—is mostly the same. Though inside this simple house, everything is different.

Ellie thinks about the book she once skimmed, and the idea of choices, as well as the ripples that result from each of them. She wonders about her life, this strange, edited version of it, and the decisions she has or has not made, as well as their consequences.

"Neither of you traveled very far to get here this morning, did you?" Ellie asks. "Your condo, it's right here in town, isn't it?"

"Ellie, cut it out." Bunny wraps her cardigan tighter around her shoulders. "I know this is a surprise, this news about Dad and me. But I assure you—"

"Why did you both give me the house if you never moved away?" Ellie asks, and suddenly, like her mother did earlier, she feels a chill run through her. "Why didn't you stay?" Already, her heart hurts, like some invisible force has kicked her square in her chest and bruised this most vital muscle.

Frank hasn't looked up. Whatever is happening—or is about to happen between them—Ellie can see Bunny is the one in the driver's seat, that Frank is unwillingly along for this ride.

"The house got to be too big for us, Ellie." Bunny redirects her gaze to the kitchen's black-and-white floor, the words she's preparing to deliver about to unravel the delicate tapestry of everything. "And that's the truth."

"But not all of it," Frank admits, so low Ellie isn't sure he even meant for anyone else in the room to hear him.

Bunny peers at Frank, unpleased by this verbal betrayal. He absently touches his thinning hair with a frail hand, one that just days earlier—and in another place—looked younger and healthier, a touch sun kissed.

For perhaps the first time in her adult life—the one she's recently felt has not mattered much—Ellie finally begins to see she was wrong. Her choices have mattered. They have had an impact. And here—wherever and whenever she is—her choice *not* to make this her life has mattered, too.

"Mom?" Ellie presses.

"We—" Bunny fills her lungs with air. She releases it long and slow. "We just thought by now you'd, well—" She stops, pushes away her readers, and closes her eyes. "We had assumed—hoped—you'd—"

"Be married," Ellie interjects to spare her mother from having to say it herself.

Bunny opens her eyes again, looks at her daughter. "Yes," she sighs.

FIFTEEN

Tuesday

Ellie opens her eyes the next morning and sees drips of sunlight through her bedroom window. She barely moves at first, too unsure of what to expect from this new day. For a few minutes, she lies as still as a corpse and listens. So far, she hears no movement from elsewhere in the house. No sound of Bunny banging the kitchen cabinets. No noise from Frank shuffling around in the downstairs hallway.

Slowly, Ellie slides away the blankets and pulls herself upright. She presses her back (*Does it still hurt?*) against the upholstered headboard and sees that the room looks as it should. She exhales deeply, a soft smile settling on her face. She'd read in several books that the trauma from divorce can instigate all kinds of unpleasant things in one's body. Upset stomach. Irritability. Change in appetite. Elevated blood pressure. Loss of sleep.

She quietly laughs at herself. Finally, in the light of a new day, she recognizes that the whole thing—her parents, the accident, the airport, her ID—only exists in that wild, incomprehensible part of her brain, the place that manufactures her fears and her dreams and—

Pound. Pound. Pound.

Or not.

"Oh, come on!" Ellie exclaims and instantly sinks back into her bed.

"Ellie!" Bunny shouts from downstairs, like she did when her daughter was in high school and running late. "Your friend is here!"

Ellie grabs the pillow and shoves it over her face in case she needs to scream, but then quickly removes it.

Wait.

"My . . . friend?" Ellie repeats back to herself.

The truth is Ellie doesn't have many close friends. Acquaintances, sure. Her fellow book club members. Mothers of Maggie's friends whom she still sometimes meets for coffee. Familiar faces from her childhood whom she socializes with from time to time. But *real* friends? The type who show up unannounced on her doorstep? Ellie was a girl—just a few years shy of Maggie's current age—the last time she shared that sort of intimacy with other women.

Ellie has two friends from childhood who also settled back in town. They've known each other for years. Middle school slumber parties. Friday-night football games under the lights. As adults, they live a few miles from each other, though to Ellie it sometimes feels like they live a universe apart. At their monthly dinners (or at least the months when they can make their schedules miraculously align), the evening always starts with lots of laughs. Comical motherhood anecdotes. A few funny childhood memories sprinkled in for good measure. But by the time they finish their entrées, the conversation almost always pivots to the other women's careers (important meetings, business travel, the night-mare of childcare, even when your children are grown), leaving Ellie feeling like the third wheel.

Back in her bed, Ellie still holds the pillow.

"Ellie!" Bunny calls out once more.

Great, she thinks. *Here we go again.*

Ellie shoves away the comforter—though not without a generous, annoyed huff—and drops her feet to the floor. She slides on her slippers, twists her bed hair back into a low bun, and marches into the hallway, past Maggie's still-closed bedroom door, and down the stairs, all as if through one giant, sweeping, overly annoyed step.

"What *now*?" Ellie moans when she arrives in the entryway. Her parents—both dressed in heavy-looking flannel pajama sets, as if it's the middle of December—are positioned in the front doorway, blocking any view of the porch. Ellie adjusts her floral-patterned pajama shorts set, as if to compose herself, but there's no point. She feels like a contestant on a game show, waiting to see what terrible thing awaits her behind door number two.

"I told you your friend is here," Bunny says as she and Frank slowly part like curtains on a stage. "What did you say your name is again, sweetheart?"

"Gabby," a vaguely familiar female voice announces.

"Nope!" Ellie exclaims before she's even seen her, instantly swiveling back in the direction of the stairs. "No frickin' way! Not in this life or in any other one!"

"Eleanor Adams, get back over here!" Bunny demands, making Ellie feel like a teenager all over again, and then lets out a hard, dry cough. She lifts her fist to her mouth and coughs a second time. "See?" Bunny adds and places a hand on her wheezy chest, her light hair still sleep matted. "I told you that ER would make me sick!"

Even with her back turned, Ellie hears through the open front door the muted hum of the generator still running, a sign that nothing inside this house has yet been fixed.

If yesterday was any indicator, she knows even if she walks back upstairs—tries to hide, tries to sleep, tries to run away—this day and all its absurdities will still find her. Understanding she does not have much of a choice, especially not with her parents staying in her house, Ellie slowly pivots back around. When she does, the movement triggers her stubborn back muscle yet again.

Frank shakes his head as Bunny continues to cough. "See what I mean, Ellie?" Her father arches his thick, gray brows in a knowing way, like they're trying to make contact with the ceiling. "It's good I was here," he reminds her, and he pats the neckline of his pajamas for his reading glasses—not that he needs them, but more for the security of knowing they are there. "Your mother was up sick half the night."

It's not that Ellie doesn't care about this detail. Of course she does. Her mother is getting older, and so sickness—even a simple cold—doesn't hit her body the same way. Still, she can't focus on it right now. Her gaze has panned over to the porch like a film camera. There's a person here, yes, but Ellie can only focus on singular details, as if she's looking at a work of abstract art but doesn't yet see how all the disjointed shapes add up. Those giant blue eyes, the ones that look like a child's drawing brought to life. The wild strands of kinked golden hair, which always made her seem part mermaid. That messy heap of wooden necklaces, the sheer quantity of them making her look like a preschool teacher or camp counselor gone mad.

"Dare I ask why *you're* here this morning?" Ellie asks, feeling like her life (Ha! *Is* this her life?) these last twenty-four hours is the world's worst dating show. "Or what ridiculous world I've woken up in that would warrant you being on my porch?"

"Well, good morning to you, too, Ellie." An entertained look lights up Gabby's heart-shaped face like light bulbs on a marquee. "Sounds like your mother is right." She offers Bunny a playful wink. "You really are a mess from this breakup, huh?" She readjusts the macramé bag that hangs from her shoulder, a tangle of knotted rope. "Now go get dressed." She waves a hand—her fingernails painted with bright-purple polish—toward the staircase. "We can talk about the whole thing on our way to work."

It's as if someone has plunged Ellie into a hot bath. Drips of sweat run down her back beneath her cotton pajamas. "Work?" Ellie gasps, realizing Gabby may still be just as much of a loose cannon as she remembers.

"Correct." Gabby exchanges an inquisitive glance with Ellie's parents. "You know, the bookstore you own." She puckers her lips, which are painted with a dramatic iridescent-pink gloss. "Remember it?"

Ellie feels like someone has put glue in her eyes. They're stuck wide open.

"The bookstore?" Ellie repeats back. On second thought, she has no clue who the unbalanced person is in this current scene. "The one I . . . own?"

"Are you *sure* you want to drive us this morning?" Gabby wears what appears to be a thrift-store T-shirt, a pale-yellow ringer with the words *Ray of Sunshine* stamped (perhaps ironically, perhaps not) across the chest, paired with baggy ripped jeans. She looks like a late-forties woman dressed in costume as an art student, except it's not a costume. It's just her. "Because I can walk back up the block to my apartment and get my car if—"

"I—I'm fine," Ellie stammers, which, of course, is a lie.

In the kitchen, the coffee machine beeps. Frank shuffles down the hallway.

"Frank!" Bunny coughs and starts to follow him. "I forgot to ask. When you walk back to the condo this morning to get more of our things, make sure you pack up my VapoRub!" She coughs again. "I want to put some on my chest before I go to church this afternoon to talk to Father Donovan about this situation! I won't move forward with another step in this process until my priest knows!" She dabs her nose with a crumpled tissue. Behind her, Frank stops moving. "Come to think of it, maybe you ought to talk to those younger boys who work at the deli, see if one of them will carry my reading chair over here for me." Bunny looks back at Ellie and Gabby over her shoulder. "I can't be expected to live here forever without my reading chair."

Frank turns, moves back toward them from the hallway. "Where did you say you're going this afternoon?" he asks, his words slowly pouring out of him.

"To church! To tell Father Donovan!" Bunny restates. "Open your ears, Frank!"

Frank pushes away his readers, as if for once he hopes not to see what's in front of him. "You wouldn't do that." He shakes his head.

"You wouldn't tell Father Donovan something like that unless you really meant it."

Gabby glances around at the three of them, takes a backward step. "Maybe I should—"

"You think I'm kidding, Frank," Bunny states, a straightened finger pointed toward the ceiling. "But I'm not! I can't live this way anymore! We both want different things!"

Ellie massages her eyebrows and tries to wrap her head around whatever is unfolding before her. She turns to Gabby while her parents begin to bicker uncharacteristically. "Give me ten minutes to get dressed," she tells her. "I'll meet you outside."

"Sure." Gabby's shimmering pink mouth settles into a straight line. "Sounds like we have a lot to catch up on at the moment."

"Gabby." Ellie puffs out her cheeks. "You have no idea."

~

"Here." Ellie tosses Gabby her car keys. "I—um—I have a terrible headache." What else is she supposed to say? *I don't know what life I'm living and so I'm not sure of the directions to get us to where we're going*? "I changed my mind. I think I do need you to drive, after all."

"Huh." Gabby ponders this news for a second. "Oh, and for the record, you know that in the years I've worked at the shop, I've met your mother, like, probably two dozen times, right?"

"Yes?" Ellie queries, her response framed out as a question. "That— um, that seems right." She gives Gabby a shrug. "Her, uh—her memory is a bit distorted this week. As is mine, I think," she mumbles.

"Sweet," Gabby says, like some kind of grown-up teenager. "So what's the deal with your parents?"

Ellie rubs her eyes. "I think they're getting divorced, but also both inexplicably living with me."

"This breakup really got to you, huh?" Gabby playfully rolls her eyes, then gives Ellie a fast once-over. "Also, yeah, no chance you're driving," she confirms. "You look like you woke up on another planet."

Ellie gives one firm nod. "That is the most accurate thing I've heard all morning."

Back in her twenties, after her short stint working at the art book publisher in the city, Ellie moved into her own apartment in town. She worked at the bookstore full-time, which it turned out she enjoyed. She liked to be surrounded by stories, to make recommendations, to unpack new books and neatly arrange all their spines in clean lines on the shelves. Even so, she couldn't deny it was not the most lucrative gig.

Jack had been the one to suggest that Ellie put an ad for a sublet on Craigslist, which came as a disappointment. Deep down, she'd hoped Jack, who lived alone in an apartment funded by his parents while he worked to complete his medical residency, might ask her to move in with him. It was an unrealistic fantasy. They'd been dating only a few months. Plus, her parents—especially her mother—would have killed her if she moved in with a boyfriend out of wedlock. Bunny and Frank didn't even know Jack. They'd met him once, maybe? They weren't at that level in their relationship yet. It turned out, they never would be.

The day Gabby came to view the apartment, Ellie had put out a platter of store-bought cookies, which she could hardly afford, on her IKEA coffee table. She'd hated having roommates in college and did not look forward to living with a stranger again. She wanted this Gabby person to know Ellie's apartment was a cozy, undebauched, grown-up space.

Gabby, who grew up several towns away, had initially seemed normal—a touch artsy, though that wasn't bad—as they nibbled cookies and viewed the closet-size second bedroom Ellie had advertised. Gabby had been a library science major, she explained, and currently worked at the town library, a fact that pleased Ellie. After all, how bad could a librarian be?

It turned out terrible, actually.

The first week Gabby lived there, Ellie came home to find her and three strangers taking bong hits in the living room, their ridiculous weed apparatus, which apparently had a name (*Thor!*), leaving a giant water ring on Ellie's Allen wrench–assembled table. Things went downhill—fast—from there.

Now, back in Ellie's driveway, Gabby walks around the back of the vehicle, making her way to the driver's side door. "Also, what happened to your car?" Gabby asks right as the power company truck pulls up and parks alongside the curbside. "Your bumper is all banged up and scratched."

Ellie—outfitted in her comfortable jeans, a clean T-shirt, and her old tennis shoes (regardless of which lifetime she is in, at least some things, it seems, don't change)—opens the passenger-side door. She slides off her book bag, the one she's carried around with her for days, and gets into the car.

"It's a long story." Ellie pulls her seat belt across her body, as if this thin fabric strap can protect her from whatever this new day will bring. In front of them, Bunny, still dressed in her winter pajamas, steps onto the porch and waves her crumpled tissue. Behind her, Frank—wearing his street clothes and a livid expression—opens the door, suddenly looking like he has some other place to be. Ellie pulls her tortoiseshell sunglasses from her bag, slips them on. "Now let's get out of here before my mother—or either of my parents, for that matter—sees it."

~

"Everyone on their best behavior!" Gabby shouts not ten minutes later when they step into the bookshop, a delicate set of bells jingling on the glass door. Two twentysomething girls—both dressed casually in jeans and cute, comfortable shirts—are seated on the floor, unpacking boxes of books. They glance up and wave. "Boss lady is back from her one-day detour on the heartbreak highway!" Gabby's bag—which looks like something college-Maggie might wear—slaps against her side as she comfortably breezes through the space. "No one give her a hard time!"

Ellie pauses and looks around, her mouth agape, like she's on a mission to catch flies. She has stood right here in this exact spot numerous times in her life—as a young girl out shopping with Bunny, as an employee here in her twenties, as a mother on the hunt for good picture books with her own daughter at her side. But right now, her feet planted on the charming white penny tile that makes up the small shop's entryway, it all feels different. This store and everything in it is no longer someone else's story. Today, for the first time ever, it is hers.

Magnolia Books.

At least, this is what's painted on the front window, the one Ellie walked past on her way inside. Magnolia. Ellie's favorite flower. The one that, in a different life, serves as the namesake for something—someone—else.

Maggie.

"So, are you going to tell me what happened?" Gabby asks. Her vintage T-shirt rides up a touch as she speaks, revealing an inch-wide sliver of her flat stomach.

Ellie watches her old roommate (Dear God, is she *really* friends with Gabby—the one who twice nearly burned down their apartment—in this bizarre, altered version of her life?) as she steps behind the store's front counter—pretty, rounded, white, and accented with a few small potted plants. It is exactly the sort of thing Ellie herself would have picked (and apparently has), something to replace the store's old dark wood that was inside this space when Ellie was last here several weeks ago to buy another round of sad self-help titles (*Flying Solo: A Guide for a Happy Empty Nest*; *Uncoupling Your Heart: A Road Map to Healing*).

But this is not the only change. Outside, the shop's redbrick exterior has also been painted in a fresh coat of white, two classic potted topiaries on either side of the door, like Ellie always felt the longtime owners—a couple who had earned their AARP cards years earlier—ought to do.

How, she privately wonders, did she not register these changes when she drove down this block yesterday?

Gabby opens and shuts some counter drawers, then drums a computer keyboard, its screen illuminating with life. She looks up at Ellie. Her clunky, presumably handcrafted necklaces, which look just a step above the macaroni jewelry Maggie once made, bang into each other when she moves.

"So?" Gabby asks.

But Ellie hardly hears her. She slides off her book bag, drops it in a heap beside her, and glides toward the walls of bookshelves, where the titles are arranged not by genre but by the mood the texts evoke (Dreamy, Hopeful, Sentimental, Uneasy, Safe), just as young Ellie, unpacking boxes of new shipments much like her two employees are doing (Does Ellie actually have employees?), used to imagine would be a fun way to organize things.

"Yoo-hoo?" Gabby arranges some papers on the counter into neat piles. "Earth to Ellie!"

"Huh?" Ellie turns, a subtle smile creeping across her face as she takes it all in.

Gabby tugs a strand of her long, crimped-looking hair. "Based on the dumbfounded face you're currently wearing," she says with a laugh, "it seems like I'm going to need to guess."

Ellie blinks, not sure what to say. How could she ever possibly explain the unexplainable turn her week has taken?

"Anyway, honestly, you're better off without him," Gabby narrates, thankfully starting to fill in some gaps. She picks up a spray bottle and spritzes water on the neatly potted plants, just one of the many small gestures of care she's exhibited for this space since they've arrived.

Nearby, the two young girls (Ellie probably should find a clever way to learn their names) are still busy unpacking new titles on the shop's wood floor—stylishly outfitted with pale-blue-and-white area rugs. They perk up, ready for a taste of gossip.

"I mean, didn't you tell me he's a professional scuba diver?" Gabby uses her arms to mock-swim. "What were you going to do? Live with him on a boat?" she questions as she repositions the plants in a new, neat arrangement. "Granted, I never met him. You only dated for what, like, a month?" She turns back to the computer, types something. "Based on everything you told me, the only things he seemed capable of talking about were oyster shells and neoprene." She smiles through her pearlescent lips. "Trust me, Ellie. I know you're sad, but in the long run," she adds and then briefly offers her best backstroke, "this is a very good thing."

"I dated a scuba diver?" Ellie asks. She thinks of Maggie and their conversation this past weekend at Bunny and Frank's pool. *I'm . . . dating?* "Really?" The corners of her eyes crinkle right before she laughs. "We live an hour from an ocean. That's . . . weird. I think."

"Tell me about it." Gabby breezily walks away from the counter. She stops beside a display marked "Farcical." With a light tap, she pushes aside one of the white library ladders that accent the floor-to-ceiling shelves. "Whoever thought you'd top the unintelligible chef who *swore* he'd worked at a five-star restaurant, yet always managed to burn your toast, right?"

Nearby, the store's glass door opens. The bundle of bells gently rings, the sound as delicate as angels' wings. A middle-aged woman with a canvas tote bag thrown over her shoulder takes one step inside and then stops.

"Oh—oh, I'm sorry." She quickly looks from left to right, then glances at her wristwatch. "Are you—am I too early? Are you open yet?"

Gabby smiles, and when she does, a shallow dimple (Ellie had forgotten this small detail about her) forms in one of her cheeks. "What do you say, boss lady?" she asks, and she glances at a simple black clock that hangs on the wall. "It's ten minutes before ten." She playfully tilts her head, her cascade of hair swaying from one side to the other. "Are we open yet?"

Ellie takes another quick look around her current setting. Through the window, she sees the shop's hand-painted sign—MAGNOLIA BOOKS—staring back at her in reverse.

"Um—yes." Ellie exhales. For an instant, all the messes of these last few days—everything that unraveled in Florida, and everything that has continued to disentangle since she's been home—temporarily melt away. "Yes." She takes a step forward. "We're open."

SIXTEEN

Book people are nice.

Ellie had forgotten this fact. All morning, she's allowed herself to temporarily brush aside the absurdities of the last day and a half and just be swept along with the motions of this new space. Every few minutes, another customer wanders through the glass door wearing an obvious look of contentment on their face. They're happy to be here. Unlike most other areas of retail, people don't tend to find themselves at a bookshop because it's a chore, just another item to cross off a never-ending to-do list. Rather, stepping inside here is a reprieve. Customers want to stay, slow down, take a break. No one is in a rush to leave.

Back in her real life, Ellie sometimes thought about returning to work here. Every few years, she'd tell herself this next chapter in motherhood would be easier, but it was never true. It's a big misconception, the idea that as your child gets older, she'll need you less. When Maggie entered her elementary years and Ellie believed she might have a few free mornings to take on part-time bookseller shifts, she learned that her daughter's school relied on mothers like her to cover the front desk and to sign up as room parents and to organize fundraisers and to chaperone field trips. By middle school, Maggie's cocurriculars and budding social life more or less required Ellie to become a chauffeur, and never at convenient hours. By high school—well, just forget it. Those four years were such a blur of prep courses and guidance meetings that Ellie often wondered if the other mothers had hired personal assistants to keep track of everything.

It was true Ellie's own mother had worked part-time, though things were so different then. Life—parenthood, in particular—was not nearly as demanding. As a child, Ellie was a Girl Scout—a commitment that required her and Bunny to attend one event every month at a town park. By the time Maggie was in sixth grade, she was on three travel sports teams, which meant she (and, in turn, Ellie) had lengthy commitments to keep literally seven days per week all year long. It wasn't that Maggie particularly loved any of the sports or thought she might become a professional athlete. It was just how things worked—it was just what you *did*.

"Why are you walking funny?" Gabby asks, her mermaid-esque hair wildly framing her face. She balances a stack of new fiction titles—a happy, literary rainbow—in her hands. She slides them, one by one, onto a shelf, an orderly arrangement of well-executed plotlines.

Ellie takes a seat on a comfortable chair—one of the few set up throughout the store. They're like upholstered invitations for shoppers to sit and read. She tucks a piece of her straight, honey hair behind her ear, noticing her bare ring finger. "That little fender bender," Ellie explains. Her back has been acting up ever since the crash. But today, thanks to all the new sights and sounds around her—this most unexpected setting—she's almost briefly forgotten about it, or at least been able to ignore it for the time being. "I think I tweaked my back again," she adds now, newly reminded of the pain.

"Again?" Gabby asks, her pink mouth twisted, as she turns away from the shelf. "What do you mean? What'd you do to it the first time?"

Right, Ellie thinks. Because here, in this cozy bookshop and in this current life, as far as Ellie understands, it is not a pain she ever would have mentioned, one that would not even exist.

Ellie waves an unbothered hand. "It's—it's nothing," she explains, a lie.

The night Maggie was born—well, the whole twenty-four uncomfortable hours Ellie spent in the Labor and Delivery wing at the local hospital, all of which had ultimately led up to that most climactic of events—was the most emotional of Ellie's entire life. She'd never been admitted to a hospital before—not for surgeries or to have her tonsils removed or for a broken bone. For thirty-odd years, she'd managed to bypass that whole side plot of one's upbringing. She was terrified from the minute she entered the vast building. Although it sounded juvenile, she hadn't even really known (other than the fictionalized knowledge she'd gained from movies) what the inside of a hospital actually looked like.

Jonah sat in a chair in the corner of Ellie's delivery room, putting on his best calm face, although she knew he was all jumping beans inside. For the first few hours of labor, the pain had been uncomfortable but manageable enough for the two of them to laugh a few times about the terrible reruns they were forced to watch on the hospital TV. Ellie wasn't allowed to eat anything, which felt like a form of torture right then, even though she knew she was fine and hooked up to an IV. Even so, every half hour, Jonah walked down to the nurses' station and got her a lemon Italian ice, the only thing she *was* permitted to consume—a small, sugary, paper-wrapped luxury that, for a few minutes once per hour, made her feel a little bit like herself again.

For as slow as her labor was, the actual birth came shockingly fast. The nurses—who'd been so sweet a little while earlier, fluffing Ellie's pillows and making jokes when they came to check her vitals, anything to make her forget the contractions—instantly turned into aggressive sports coaches who shouted a barrage of demands. *Push! Harder! Now! Breathe!* Ellie's lower body was paralyzed by drugs—if she couldn't physically see them, she might honestly have thought she'd lost her legs. Terrified of screwing up and damaging this perfect human she and Jonah had created, she did as they said, every single muscle in her body tense and in full use and shaking.

Less than forty-eight hours later, the three of them were discharged, which in and of itself felt insane—the fact that Ellie and Jonah, who had absolutely zero real training, were just sent home with the task of caring for another human for the rest of their living days. But it was fine, just as it often is for people—not always, but usually—the two of them quickly figuring out a new rhythm for their shared life, like learning the steps of a dance and then working to perfect it a little more each day. It wasn't until a week later, once the drugs and the adrenaline and a little thing called sleep had fully worn off, that Ellie first noticed the pain. In the months that followed, she visited multiple doctors, though none of them could find anything definably wrong.

"This is just motherhood," one of the physicians had said, gaslighting her. "Sometimes, it's simply the price we pay," he explained, even though he had never given birth, and thus had paid nothing.

As time passed, Ellie often thought of that terrible doctor, not wanting to admit it, though privately acknowledging that part of what he'd said had been right. That *is* motherhood in some ways, isn't it? The invisible pain mothers carry. The aches inside their bodies and their hearts that can never be explained or pinpointed or healed.

"So, where'd you get into an accident?" Gabby moves back behind the shop's pretty white counter. She taps her fingers across the computer keyboard like a pianist. "I thought you planned to stay home watching bad rom-coms and eating pints of ice cream."

"The corner of Elm and South," Ellie explains and then watches as a young mother and her toddler daughter push open the glass door. The bells jingle. The little girl, dressed in Velcro sneakers and a polka-dot dress, runs across the store—clearly familiar with the space—and heads right over to the children's section—all pint-size shelves and pastel-colored beanbag chairs—in the back.

"Elm and South?" Gabby lifts a purple fingernail to her mouth, nibbles her cuticle. "Didn't you get into an accident at that intersection years ago?" She lowers her hand and tilts her head at Ellie, who looks at her blankly, hoping this topic will—*Abracadabra!*—magically go away.

"Remember?" Gabby nudges. "With that cute guy. It was the day you and Jack broke up."

Her jaw clenching, Ellie breathes through her teeth. "Jack?" she repeats, playing dumb, as if she did not just run into him in the emergency room yesterday. Or as if she has not been replaying that original accident over and over in her head on a perpetual loop for the last day. "Remind me what happened with him?"

Gabby is smiling, but in a scandalous way. "You can't possibly still be burned by that one," she says as a customer approaches the counter. She exchanges pleasantries, then continues the conversation with Ellie. "I mean, yes, he was a total fool for what he did," she explains as she drops the customer's purchase—some recent popular beach read—into a small brown shopping bag. "And, yes, it was probably a mistake that, after our conversation in our apartment, you totally went against my advice, talked to him again the next day, and then proceeded to date him for another six months. But, I mean—"

"Another six months?" Ellie questions and notes the way Gabby looks at her, as if she's suddenly begun to speak in a different, never-before-heard-of language. "I . . . did?"

Gabby laughs out loud. "Guess you decided to mentally block that one out?" She sends the customer on her way. "I don't blame you." She smiles. As she talks, Ellie feels herself taking copious mental notes, like a stenographer has moved into her brain. "Anyway, when you came back to our apartment after your little car crash that day and sobbed to me for hours—" She stops herself. "Wait a minute." Some light bulb clicks on inside her head. "Come to think of it, that whole breakup—well, the first time around, at least—is sort of the reason you and I finally became friends, isn't it?"

"Right," Ellie agrees, even though she hasn't the slightest clue if this is true. Her gaze begins to shift away from Gabby—too much eye contact makes it feel impossible to lie—and lands on the little girl. She is now sprawled out on an area rug as she flips through a book Ellie recognizes—one she once read to Maggie—about a magical kingdom.

"That's how we finally became friends," she adds, her voice somber. "Because I just came home."

One choice, Ellie thinks to herself. *One small choice and you changed everything.*

"You feeling all right, Ellie?" Gabby grabs a stack of books from near the register and carries them to a shelf. "You're sort of, like, staring off into space."

"Um, yeah," Ellie acknowledges. "I'm fine. I was just thinking about how weird it is."

"What's that?" Gabby asks as she begins to display the new titles.

"Just—I mean—I don't know," Ellie says. "Imagine if I'd gone someplace else that day. Like if I'd stopped off somewhere with the guy who crashed into me or something."

Gabby's big blue eyes widen. "Oh, that would have made for a fun twist!" She sets down the rest of her books, then places a hand on her slender hip. "What was his name? Do you remember?" Behind them, the bells on the door chime again. "I feel like you talked about him for a few days after that."

"Who can remember?" Ellie fibs, her eyes still set toward the picture-book section. "It was so long ago." She shakes her head, as if nonchalantly dismissing an unimportant set of memories. Finally, she turns back to Gabby. "It feels like something from another life, right?"

~

"I'm going to get a coffee," Ellie announces a little while later. This whole afternoon has been lovely, like watching an enjoyable theatrical production, but she knows it's not real. She needs to refocus and remember the task at hand.

What *exactly*, she thinks, is that again?

Gabby—who's trying to talk a customer out of purchasing a terrible, though somehow bestselling, novel written (probably ghostwritten) by an "it" celebrity—gives Ellie a wave as she slides on her book bag straps and walks to the glass door. The bells jingle as she steps back outside and into the warm spring sunlight.

Rather than go immediately across the street, Ellie spends the next few minutes walking. She needs time to think. Her hands shoved in her pockets, Ellie moves up the block, all lined with pink and white dogwood trees. Out here, the world looks exactly the same. Here is the café where she's dined dozens of times and its blooming window boxes. Here is the sweet little flower shop where she's sometimes popped in for fresh bouquets. Here is the artisanal olive oil store that is pretty but never seems to sell a thing (Ellie hasn't a clue how it survives). In the near distance, she hears the distinct whistle of the commuter train pulling into the local station, some people coming home, and others traveling away.

Ellie has lived here in this town for nearly her entire life. She's never jetted across oceans, the way Maggie soon plans to do. She's never headed out west the way Jonah did for college, just to see for a few years what a life of constant sunshine and citrus is all about. Other than those trips back and forth between Newark and Orlando, she's never really gone anywhere too distant. And yet, while she walks alone today as Ellie Adams—not Ellie Baker or anyone else—on this stretch of pavement that in all reality she's likely traversed more than a thousand times in her life, she's never felt someplace more foreign or far away.

What is she supposed to do? What is the solution? Does she try to fix this life—the goal she set for herself only yesterday—even though she has no idea how? Does she try to sleep it off, like a bad hangover? Or does she just go with it, like picking up a book you're not sure you'll like, but seeing it through to the end just to find out where it leads?

Ellie has no real logical clue how she's ended up here, inside this strange, not entirely terrible, though most definitely bizarre, alternate version of her life. Perhaps worse, she doesn't know how long she'll be stuck in it. Is this whole thing akin to a short-lived weekend trip away? A long, extended vacation? A permanent move?

Ellie turns at the corner to loop back around the block. How is it possible that the rest of the town seems normal—not a pothole, not a crooked street sign, not a single thing out of place—except for her small pocket of it? Up ahead, Ellie sees the bookstore (*her* bookstore, apparently—*pffft*) and her favorite coffee shop across the street, outside of which is a chalkboard sidewalk sign. *Come try our new signature breakfast blend!*

Her mind immediately flips back to Sunday morning in Florida, Ellie and her mother at the kitchen table, talking over their steaming mugs. *Things won't be the same when you go back. Your life. The house. Everything will be different.* Ellie cannot imagine a world in which her mother would ever mean for those words to be taken quite so literally. And yet . . .

Now, Ellie pushes open the glass door. The inside of the coffee shop is thankfully the same as always. Wooden beams crisscross the ceiling. A wall of shiny espresso machines behind the counter hiss with steam. A dozen or so wood-top tables are scattered, in no particular pattern, throughout the space.

At the counter, Ellie orders a large hot coffee with a splash of cream and a sprinkle of cinnamon. It's her usual order—nothing fancy that requires too many descriptions or steps. The twentysomething barista, a young man who wears an unseasonable beanie hat, shreds of lettuce hair poking out its bottom, works to prepare it. While she waits, Ellie looks through the glass display at all those sweets—croissants and brownies and those silly little cake pops that never actually taste very good.

"Want anything?" the barista asks, noticing her eyeing the case. He hands over her coffee, then taps the glass. "The cream puffs." He points to a pyramid of golden rounds. "They're my favorite."

Ellie's nose wrinkles at the suggestion. "No thanks."

After she pays, Ellie briefly closes her eyes and takes a hot sip of her fresh breakfast blend. It's good. Light. A little nutty. Comfortably predictable. Easy to drink. She opens her eyes and takes a step, scanning the place for a vacant table, then immediately swallows another sip of her coffee as she takes a shaky breath.

There, at the window seat—*their* seat, the one beneath that trailing cascade of green leaves—she sees him, like a ghost from a past life. He wears that undershirt again, the one that in his (in *their*) real life, he'd never be caught dead sporting out in public. Although she can only see his back—his strong shoulders visible beneath the cotton—it is obvious that, once again, his thick chestnut-and-gray hair is a freestyle mess and in need of a trim (something Ellie is always the one to schedule for him).

She opens her mouth to speak but doesn't know what to say. Does she call him by name? Does she reference yesterday's accident as a segue? Does she—

"Ahh!" Someone bumps into Ellie from behind. Her perfect, hot, freshly brewed coffee somersaults out of her hand. It explodes on the floor, brown splatters splashing up onto her jeans.

"I'm so sorry!" a random man behind her gasps, already reaching for a stack of paper napkins. "This is completely my fault."

"It's—it's fine," Ellie decides as she bends down to help the stranger clean the mess he's made. She picks up the empty cup and spreads the napkins over the puddle.

"Here," a familiar voice announces above her. "Let me help with this."

Ellie looks up, and there he is. Jonah. He smiles at her. When he does, for the first time in years, the sight of it triggers something deep inside her, some feeling that may be nerves or anxiety or excitement. It's hard to tell. Sometimes, they all feel the same, like cousins—distinctive in their own ways and yet all stemming from the same family tree. It doesn't matter. Whatever the feeling, Ellie forgets how to breathe.

Jonah, who moved away from his window seat while Ellie's head was down, assists now with the spill. As he does, she smells the piney scent of his deodorant, the earthy aroma of his skin. He gathers a sopping pile of coffee-soaked napkins in his hand and then turns to meet Ellie's face. Time stops. He parts his lips to say something. It could be anything. It could be nothing.

"I remember you," he says.

It is everything.

SEVENTEEN

"I got you a fresh coffee."

Ellie looks up from her place at the window seat and sees a smiling Jonah, his white shirt now stained with several noticeable brown drips, just like her jeans. The table is empty, other than a silver caddy full of expected coffee shop provisions—sugar packets, a glass jar of honey, some scraps of paper and golf-size pencils meant for the creatives who camp out in places like this all day. Above her, a cascade of viridescent stems and leaves hangs. Her lips settle into a straight line. She accepts the cup and double-checks that the lid is secured tightly this time.

"Thanks," she tells him and then waits. She has no idea what will happen—what either of them might say—next. She decides to let him lead.

Seated this close to Jonah, Ellie notes the uncharacteristic rash of brown stubble across his typically smooth chin and cheeks. In their real life, the only days he fails to shave are on Sundays or when he is sick. When they were younger, back in their early thirties, he'd sometimes let it go now and again. A little bit of laziness does, in fact, look handsome on certain men. But that habit quickly came to a halt when Maggie was a child. She always told him it felt too scratchy, and he obediently listened, never wanting to sacrifice a single second of snuggling with her cheek to cheek.

Now, Jonah slides into a black metal chair, places his own coffee on the table. "I realized after you left yesterday where I recognized you from," he recalls, and Ellie sees a glimmer of something in his eyes.

From our home? From our wedding day? From our daughter? From this past weekend? From the more than two decades of life we've shared together?

"Hmm . . . ?" she poses, an open-ended sound for him to complete.

Jonah points with his bear-claw-size hand at the window. "There." He extends a finger, pointing directly at it. "The bookstore." His pink mouth curves into an understated smile. "You work there, right? I've seen you through the window sometimes, coming and going."

Ellie joins his gaze and stares through the glass at that pretty, white-painted brick facade. "I do." She inhales, her breath reaching way down to her toes before she slowly releases it again. "Work there, I mean." She laughs to herself. "At least, that's what they tell me." She smirks.

Jonah nods, not sensing anything off about Ellie's comment. It's just a joke, a charming throwaway. "How's the coffee?" he asks while gesturing at her cup. "It's the new breakfast blend," he says and redirects his finger to the sidewalk sign. "They're really pushing it. It's good, right?"

Ellie lifts her cup to her mouth, enjoys another small sip of what tastes just a teensy bit like normalcy. "It is," she agrees.

Jonah enjoys another mouthful of his own beverage. "You know, I tried to call you a few times last night," he admits, and when he does she sees that his stubbled cheeks turn a pale shade of red. "About your car," he quickly adds, so as not to suggest anything otherwise. "And the mechanic. I—I need to make sure to give you the right amount of money for that."

Ellie bites her lip. "We'll figure it out," she says, unfazed by this nothing of a problem, not in light of everything else. "Anyway, I don't have my phone right now." She briefly closes her eyes, huffs. "I lost it." She opens them again. "I'm currently completely off the grid."

"Off the grid, huh?" Jonah nods his head to show his understanding. "That's not always a bad thing." He smirks. "I've been feeling a bit off the grid myself recently," he adds, though she doesn't quite understand what he means.

In the last few months of their marriage, Ellie and Jonah completely stopped sharing moments like this. A simple cup of coffee. A casual conversation to break up the day. But why?

"Have we really never met before?" Ellie asks Jonah now, and when she does he turns. Their eyes catch, a hook to a fish. For a split second, Ellie observes the way he peers at her, as if the inner workings of his mind are piecing together an important equation. "Never anytime before that car crash yesterday?"

She wants to ask him if he feels it. This sense of déjà vu. Her heart beats in her chest like a caged bird, her palms simultaneously hot and cool from sweat. She feels like she's been here before with him in this exact same moment and this exact same place, because in another life—one that exists here and yet does not—she *has* been with him at this same table, back before they were a couple, long before they described themselves as an "us" or a "we." They were just two individuals, not yet a unit, not yet anything, really. They were only at the beginning then and taking their first steps toward getting to know each other, no clue what joys and sadness their future together might bring.

"Not before yesterday's crash." He reaches into the metal caddy and pulls out a scrap of paper and a miniature pencil, on which he absently scribbles a series of lines that don't look like they'll add up to much of anything. He tilts his chin at her ever so slightly, like he's afraid to look her in the eyes again. "I feel pretty certain that if we had met some other time before that accident, I would have remembered."

Her cheeks flush from both his words and the many mixed emotions she's felt on this very unusual day. She doesn't know what to do. She doesn't want to get up and leave, for this unexpected coffee date between husband and wife—between strangers—to end. She wants to tell him she's stuck here—somehow living in the wrong timeline—and that he is, too. But there's no right way to say something like this.

Instead, she follows in Jonah's footsteps, picks up a sheet of paper, and begins to doodle on it, just to extend the moment.

Ellie is not—nor has she ever been—a good artist. She's a mom artist, all her drawings dating back to the ones she'd draw over and over and over with Maggie during her preschool years. A silly jack-o'-lantern. A happy butterfly. A smiling flower. She's not even thinking about what she's creating, these witless illustrations she makes arriving to her in such an instinctual fashion. She feels her fingers sketching out the circle of the sun—the classic picture she and Maggie drew together so many times—and the triangle rays that extend off it.

From inside Jonah's pocket, his phone rings. He looks annoyed by the sound—the interruption—of it, but he slides it out regardless so he can take a peek at the screen.

"I'm really sorry," he says, and he looks like he sincerely means it. He briefly silences the device. "I think maybe I should take this call."

Ellie sets down her pencil on top of her unfinished drawing. Through the picture window, she sees another pair of customers walk into the shop—*her* shop—across the street. "It's okay," she tells him. "I should probably get going, anyway."

Jonah stands and then starts to walk away. Before he makes much progress, he quickly turns back. "Hey," he says. "About that whole accident. If you don't have your phone, what's the best way for me to get in touch with you?"

She's the one who points her finger at the glass this time. "You'll know where to find me." Her tone is brushed by flirtation. "I won't be far."

Before they part, Ellie takes one last long look at his face. She recalls their conversation from the other night in her parents' spare Floridian bedroom when she asked him what he thought it might be like if they had the chance to meet again for the first time. She'd meant the question purely rhetorically, not ever imagining a world in which they'd have the chance.

I'd like to think that we'd at least notice each other, he'd said. *Maybe say hello or something like that.*

Jonah's phone vibrates in his palm. He presses a button on the side of it and slides the device away, deciding that whoever is on the other end of the call can wait one more minute.

"It was nice talking with you," he says as a quick flash of realization spreads across his face. "Ellie, right?" he poses. "That's what you put in my phone when you typed it in, I think."

She nods.

He extends a sturdy hand. She lifts her own to meet it, the two of them briefly joined, if only for this quick second.

"Jonah," he says, by way of an introduction. "Jonah Baker."

Ellie smiles, unsure which emotion waits right behind it. Laughter? Tears?

"It's nice to meet you, Jonah Baker," she says.

EIGHTEEN

After coffee, Ellie stops back into the bookstore to tell Gabby she isn't feeling well. She needs to head home, lie down, work out a few thoughts, but will return after she gets some rest. A headache, she says, and blames it on the breakup, which isn't untrue. It's just not because of the specific breakup (A scuba diver? Really?) Gabby thinks.

Ellie is back in her car now and driving through town. The alternative rock station she'd clicked on yesterday, right before her accident with Jonah, is still turned on. Some sad, acoustic love song—a perfect soundtrack—plays as she navigates the vehicle along the bustling suburban streets, past the window displays and picturesque cafés, and tries to figure out what she's meant to do next.

Unlike yesterday, Ellie no longer needs to call the attorney (*Hello, I would like to divorce my husband, who isn't actually my husband, because we've never been married, and because we technically just met for the first time this afternoon*). She has a deep desire to contact Maggie. (Where is her daughter right now? When she stepped onto her respective plane, did she somehow escape all this?) But she's afraid to hear what strange something might greet Ellie on the opposite end of this communication. She no longer needs to call Frank to tell him Bunny is inexplicably at her house in New Jersey and saying unhinged things, because Frank is here.

Click, click, click.

Ellie flicks on her blinker and turns the car down a quiet side street, a little ways off the beaten path. For her whole life, her family has been the epicenter of her universe. Bunny and Frank. Jonah, more or less from the first day they met. Maggie from the second the doctor set her in Ellie's arms. Whenever she's had a problem, these are the people she's turned to for help. Whenever she's felt lost, their small circle has served as Ellie's true north. But not today. This time, Ellie needs to solve this issue alone.

Ellie shifts the car into park. She walks up the marble steps of Saint Mary's Church. It's the middle of the day, no masses anytime soon, but the door, as always, is open. Ellie pulls it wide. She dips her fingers into the holy water, like she was taught to do when she was small, and makes the sign of the cross over her body. A faint scent of incense lingers in the air. Up high, the stained glass windows are illuminated by the late-spring sun, though not enough to actually provide light to the darkened church nave. Ellie takes a step forward, her tennis shoes creating a dramatic echo each time they hit the shiny floor. She moves past several empty pews, all of them cast in shadows, before she settles on one closer to the altar and slides in.

"We almost retired to Florida once," Bunny explains without turning around. She coughs. "You were in your twenties. You'd just broken up with that boy."

"How did you know it was me?" Ellie asks from a few pews behind her mother. "It could have been anyone who walked in."

Bunny twists the upper half of her body. "A mother just knows, Ellie. I can sense when you're near me even when you're still miles away."

Ellie scoots out of her pew, joins Bunny. "So, why didn't you?" She looks down, noticing that both she and her mother are rubbing their ring fingers—Bunny's, for the time being, still outfitted with a metal band.

"It wasn't the right time, Ellie," Bunny explains, turning her decades-old wedding band on her aging skin. "We flew down for a week, just like for any other trip. Before we went, your father made some appointments with a Realtor in the area, lined up a few properties for us to see. She showed us one we liked."

Before Bunny speaks another word, Ellie already knows how she will describe it.

"Let me guess," Ellie says. "A little sunroom. A community pool. Shuffleboard courts."

Bunny looks at Ellie, her forehead creasing.

"Those types of places are always the same," Ellie notes and bites her lip.

Bunny clears her throat and then laughs softly at the memory of the place. "There was this big palm tree out back," she continues. "I joked with your father that if we bought that place, I'd wrap the trunk of it up in multicolored lights every Christmas." She smiles at this thought. "A little tropical holiday."

It's hard to fully see inside of a marriage, especially one that is not your own. What unfulfilled wishes exist inside it. What broken promises or abandoned dreams haunt it. What disagreements or fights have remained hidden from public view. An only child, Ellie had always felt especially close to her parents growing up, as if they also functioned as her stand-in siblings. As narcissistic as it sounded, she'd often believed she knew everything about her mother and father's relationship, as if there wasn't a single secret in their home she hadn't been briefed on. Now, while seated in this church pew, Ellie wonders what other secrets her parents have kept from her—in this life and in any other. She thinks about the secrets she's kept from them, too.

"Did you tell me you were doing that?" Ellie asks, unsure where her actual memory stops and where new memories—ones she isn't familiar with—set in. "That you two had planned to look at condos on that trip and that you wanted to move?"

Bunny unlaces her hands, waves one, slapping away Ellie's question. "For what? To give you stress that we were going to leave?" She looks at her daughter over the shoulder of her unseasonable sweater. "We were only daydreaming." Bunny shakes her head at some private thought.

"We knew we wouldn't do it until you were settled into your own life first."

"But I am settled, Mom," Ellie states. "Right? I have a job and the house. And I think I have a few friends," she tries, still in disbelief that Gabby now falls into this category. "Maybe I was never meant to be married," she suggests. The church is so empty that every sound is amplified. Her words all echo back at her. "Maybe that's just not my destiny for this life."

Looking up at the altar, Ellie can almost see her and Jonah—two children in their twenties—dressed in their fancy clothes, minutes before they said "I do." Neither of them realized how much they were agreeing to with that vow. They had so much life ahead of them. Good and bad, a whole spectrum of experiences and emotions. How could they ever have known as they slipped the rings on each other's fingers what their future might have in store for them, how they might change or stay the same, or how they'd react to it all?

Ellie inhales deeply, the residual incense fragrance tickling her throat. She coughs, causing her eyes to become wet with tears. They fall down her cheeks. She wipes them away, looks back at the altar, and wonders what she and Jonah might say to each other—what new vows or promises they'd make—if they had the chance to stand up there again.

Unlike some of their friends, who'd taken extravagant honeymoons to Hawaii and to Europe, when Jonah asked Ellie where she wanted to go after their wedding, she said home. She'd meant it partially as a joke, though not entirely. Ellie had no desire to jet off to Paris or to Bora Bora or wherever it is that some people they knew had gone. That all felt to her like pretend. She wanted their life together—the *real* one they'd live every day—to begin right away.

Jonah did ultimately convince her to go someplace, though they'd settled on a pretty resort nearby. For a week, they drank wine on their hotel balcony—only an hour from home—and looked out at the changing autumn leaves, both of them enjoying the subtle change in scenery and the chance to step away and be alone.

"What do you think we'll be doing twenty years from now?" Ellie had asked Jonah on one of those nights. She was buzzed from the wine and also drunk on the idea of those vows.

Ellie had half expected Jonah to make a joke about some fabulous, over-the-top life they might be living together. He didn't. "I don't know," he said as he looked out at the rust-colored landscape. "I hope it's something simple and easy like this, though."

Here in the present, Ellie's eyes remain on the altar, that sturdy slab of stone.

"I told Father Donovan the news," Bunny admits, shifting the topic. "So I suppose it's official now." She clears her throat and then lowers her voice. "At least in the eyes of God."

"What?" Ellie's heart begins to race. She knows her mother, and what her faith means to her. To tell her priest this information is more significant than if she'd told an attorney. The many legal steps involved in making a divorce official are merely bureaucratic details. To Bunny, this announcement to her church is what makes the situation real. "You can't leave Dad. You two made a vow. An important one."

Behind them, a noise.

"But apparently not important enough," a voice announces. Ellie and Bunny both turn. Frank stands at the far end of the aisle. "How could you, Bunny?"

Ellie bolts up, energized by panic. "Whatever it is you two are going through, it's—it's not real, Mom." As Ellie speaks, the sun catches the stained glass windows. "Dad, tell her it isn't real!"

"I can't tell her that, Ellie," Frank says, his expression nothing but hurt. "It's real now, whether it's what I wanted—what I thought would happen—or not."

Bunny looks back at the altar. Her tone remains calm, a suggestion that she's thought through this topic again and again. "Marriage is hard, Ellie," she explains. "Even at our age." She sighs, which makes her cough again. "It never gets easier. People think it does, the longer a couple has been together, but that's not true." She turns to face Frank. "It's just not true."

Never in all their years has Bunny spoken about marriage—her marriage, in particular—like this. Her face looks old. Tired. Sad. And yet, beyond all this, Ellie can still see it: right here, past the pale, wrinkled skin, the sagging neckline, and the thinning hair, the young woman who still lives inside it. The one who took a vow all those years ago. It's like seeing superimposed images, these two women who sit next to Ellie in this church pew.

"You guys can't do this," Ellie pleads, her words catching with tears in her throat. "You can't just leave each other."

"It's too late, Ellie," Frank states. "Your mother already made the choice." He pivots toward the door, his brows tightly knit. "Now it seems it's time for me to make mine."

And then he walks out.

NINETEEN

Ellie needs to find Jonah. Again.

This is all she thinks about as she buckles her seat belt and shifts her car into gear, leaving her mother—who decided to stay in her pew and pray a little while longer—so she can drive back across town to find him.

The truth is she has no clue if he'll still be where she left him, hanging out in the coffee shop, maybe still taking that call on his phone, drinking a fresh cup of breakfast blend. They parted ways there well over an hour ago. Plus, it's late afternoon. She has to guess the shop closes up soon.

Why did she leave him earlier in such a loose fashion? Why hadn't she made a plan, insisted on some formal time and place for them to meet again? *Would you like to meet here again tomorrow morning for coffee?* Why, for the second time in her life (lives?), had she allowed her husband to more or less just walk away?

The church in her rearview, Ellie throws on her blinker and pulls back out onto their town's main drag. Teenagers from the local high school, their sports practices and various cocurriculars complete for the day, walk around carrying smoothie cups from one of the local shops. Some café employees have begun to set the metal tables that line the sidewalks with votive candles in preparation for the evening. While Ellie drives, she peers through her windows, half expecting to see him casually walking up the street. Part of her hopes that maybe, for reasons he doesn't quite understand, he's out here, scoping out their town and looking for her, too.

A few minutes later and Ellie turns onto the correct block. She slows the vehicle, cruises past the bookshop. Through the window she sees Gabby behind the counter, in full charge of the place. Across the street, Ellie notes that the coffee shop is still open. She strains her neck to look through the glass. But this is fool's work. Of course he's not there, sitting in the window seat, doing nothing. He probably left the shop ages ago. Another car beeps behind Ellie, nudging her to speed it up. She taps the gas pedal, then brakes at the stop sign up ahead. Still, she thinks to herself. Maybe he didn't. Maybe he relocated to a different table in the back.

She turns, ready to loop the car back around the block so she can park, run inside, and double-check. Her entire body tingles. Her hair, her skin, everything is suddenly electric. It's been so long since she's experienced this feeling, this flutter in her chest, these pins and needles in her hands, as her anticipation and hope to see him continue to build. She's reminded of back when they first met, when every time they parted felt like heartache, and every time she saw him felt like coming alive again.

Ellie turns left now, then left again as she makes her way back around the block. She inhales but her breath is jagged, her insides all nerves and suspense and expectation. She wants to see her husband. For the first time in forever, Ellie is overwhelmed by the knowledge that they're making a mistake. Of course they can't get divorced. What are they doing? They love each other; they're just going through a terrible rough patch, like Bunny and Frank. They made a vow, a commitment, an entire life. They can't throw their world away.

Up ahead, the traffic light turns red. Ellie brings the vehicle to a stop. With the car idling beneath her, Ellie experiences a sense of calm she hasn't felt in ages. No, they're not getting divorced. Ellie just needed a minute, a chance to step away and see her world without him, the whole "absence makes the heart grow fonder" bit. And it has. She misses him. She misses them. She misses everything—their family, their simple life, their home.

Jonah is still in that coffee shop. Her cells thrum with this knowledge. For reasons she cannot explain, she knows he's there and waiting for her. Maybe it's intuition. Maybe it's just love—this most powerful energy that can transcend time and logic. Or maybe, Ellie considers, this is fate: that idea she gave up on now coming back to find her and reminding her that if she and Jonah are meant to meet again—and they are, of course they are; she knows this now—then they will. That they'll cross paths as easily and naturally as water flowing down a river. Without much effort, things that are meant to be will just be. They'll find each other.

Opposite the intersection where she's currently stopped, Ellie sees a parking space open in front of the coffee shop's chalkboard sidewalk sign. *Perfect,* she thinks, as if this whole world—this whole quiet town—is falling into place just for her. Up ahead, the crosswalk signal changes, a blinking warning. The traffic light that hangs overhead turns green. Ellie lifts her foot off the brake pedal, and when she does, she almost stops breathing as she falls so quickly into this all-encompassing feeling of déjà vu.

It's like she's looking into a crystal ball. Of course this is how it will happen. Of course! Ellie actually laughs—laughs!—at the situation she knows is about to unfold. It's so perfect, so brilliant, she honestly might have thought to orchestrate it herself if she'd only known how.

Her knuckles turn white as she grips the steering wheel at ten and two and then waits for it: the feeling of impact, the sound of metal grating, the two of them coming back together like she knew they would.

Behind her, a car horn. A warning. But Ellie ignores it. She smiles and begins a countdown in her head. *Three. Two.* Any second now. *One.*

And then—SMASH!

Ellie doesn't move. Instead, she leans back and closes her eyes, knowing when she opens them, he'll be there, just like always. That they'll laugh, both of them caught in the knowledge that yes—*yes!*—they've already been here before.

She hears it now, the sound of his fingers drumming the glass. Ellie lets her eyelids rise—*showtime!*—ready to see him and finally, after all these months of turmoil they've lived through together, prepared with what to say.

The afternoon sun beams through the window, creating an impossible-to-see-through orange glare. She squints, presses a button, buzzes down the glass. But even without this transparent, breakable divider between them, nothing about Ellie's current view, or who stands in front of her, has changed. The peridot eyes. The flaxen hair.

"Jack?"

"Hi, Ellie," he announces. "Funny running into you here."

She drops her free hand from the wheel.

No, she thinks. *It's not.*

TWENTY

"Here," Jack says a short while later as he approaches the table—the one right beside the window. He hands Ellie a disposable coffee cup. "I wasn't sure how you take things nowadays." He smiles. It's warm, kind, the man who wears it clearly more mature than the boy who once broke Ellie's heart. "I went classic. One cream. A teensy sprinkle of sugar."

Ellie accepts it and takes a sip, but it's too sweet. "Thank you," she says as he sits next to her, the two of them side by side beneath the trailing greenery.

Jack sips his coffee. He looks at Ellie over the rim of his cup. Other than in the hospital yesterday, she hasn't seen him since the day they broke up on his couch, the image of him in his tattered twentysomething jeans and loose-fitting concert T-shirt branded into her memory. It feels like a surprise to see him now in a crisp white button-down tucked into a pair of nicely cut khaki pants, looking like the type of man who might appear in a Ralph Lauren ad. His face appears older now than it did all those years ago when they were a couple. Of course it does. Not even physicians can defy the laws of gravity or time. Still, sitting this close to him now, she sees he also looks somehow almost exactly the same. People change, and they don't.

"I'm really sorry about earlier." Jack sets down his beverage. "I don't know what happened, honestly." He lifts a hand, squeezes the back of his neck, his hair neatly trimmed. "I'm not sure if it was the glare or if my foot slipped or what." His complexion flushes pink, giving away his embarrassment. "I just—" He cuts himself off, shakes his head, and ever so briefly closes his eyes. A fan of blond lashes brushes the tops of his cheeks. "Anyway," he says, opening them again. "I'll take care of it. Whatever it is that needs to be fixed."

The accident is the least of her current concerns. Ellie can't stop worrying about her parents, her own marriage, and all that she's damaged. She's nodding at Jack, but really, she's looking around the coffee shop's interior, which has begun to empty out. It's coming up on dinnertime, not the most popular part of the day for a leisurely caffeine break. A few tables over, a group of high school girls sit together and work through some group project for a class. Beside them, a woman Ellie's age sits alone and stares out at nothing, like her brain is both entirely empty and completely full. Much to Ellie's disappointment, Jonah is not at any of the tables. Ellie knows this as fact. While Jack stood in line for their coffees—the one he'd insisted on treating her to as a form of apology for their crash—she scoped the whole place out, as if Jonah might have left a clue for Ellie to find. So far, she hasn't seen or found a trace of him.

"So." Jack crosses one of his slim legs over the other. He has a runner's body, all lean and compact. Ellie recalls this detail about him now, his love for a certain class of sports: cycling, tennis, rowing, his specific brand of athleticism stamped with a mark of pedigree. "How are you feeling since I saw you last?"

"Oh. I—I'm fine," she says, recalling her reaction when she first bumped into him again in the ER. "I was—um—just having a strange day."

He nods. "And your mother? She's okay, too, I assume?"

No, Ellie thinks. *She's not okay. Her entire life is broken because I broke it.*

"She's all right," Ellie lies, wondering if Frank has wandered back to her house, or if he and Bunny have found a way to make amends.

Jack smiles. "Tell me about your life, Ellie. I'd love to hear about it."

Ellie stretches her neck, retrains her eyes like a telescope lens, like maybe if she repositions her gaze or refocuses, the image she hopes to see will appear to her clearly. She sighs. "Which version of it?" she asks. With her eyes cast down on the table in defeat, she reaches for the metal caddy, pulls out a scrap of paper and a pen, and begins to absently doodle on it.

Jack lifts a brow, a corner of his mouth rising at the same time. "I guess whichever version you'd be willing to tell me."

"Right." Before she explains anything further, Ellie notes her book bag, plopped down on an empty chair beside her. Inside it, her ID—that simple, laminated rectangle that provides proof of her current identity—still sits inside her wallet. Where does she even begin? "Apparently, I own that place." She points to the bookshop across the street.

"You do?" Jack questions. A pair of classic mirrored aviators hang from the neckline of his shirt. Ellie's reflection looks back at her from the lenses. "How did I not know this?"

Ellie's lips tug themselves into a straight line. "Sometimes, Jack," she says, "it's still a surprise to me."

"I'll have to stop in sometime now that I know," he says. "To be honest, I don't have the time to read as much as I used to, unfortunately. And, I'm sure you'll hate me for this, but usually when I do, I order my books while half-asleep in my bed."

"No offense taken," Ellie informs him. In her real life, she's often guilty of the same bibliophilic crime.

Jack nods. "Well, it's nice to hear. I remember how much you loved to read." He smiles at this casual memory. "Books are important. Stories are important." He breathes in through his nose. "I see plenty of them unfold daily at the hospital." He shrugs. "Some happy. Some sad." Nearby, the same young male barista who helped Ellie earlier in the day waves a hand in their direction. "I'll be right back," Jack says and stands.

Through the glass, Ellie sees the lights inside the bookstore click off. Her two young employees, whose names she hasn't yet had a chance to learn, exit and walk down the block. A beat later, Gabby steps out, her macramé bag slung over her shoulder, and locks the shop's door.

"I figured after that little fender bender, we owed it to ourselves to enjoy something sweet." Jack reapproaches the table, a small plate balanced in his hand. He sets it down in the space between them and reaches for a butter knife in the metal caddy. The yellow custard pours from the center of the pastry like a puddle when Jack slices through it. "Cream puff?" he offers.

Ellie can't help but laugh as she thinks of her mother over the weekend, acting as if her divorced neighbor's baked goods were poison. "No thanks," she says.

Deep down, Jack is not, in fact, terrible. Ellie knew this back then and she senses it now, too. What he did to her all those years ago, well, it had more to do with the fact that he was young than anything else. People make all kinds of mistakes in their twenties. Bad wardrobe choices. Bad jobs. Bad drunken nights. Everyone is entitled to be youthful and foolish for a stretch of time, Ellie supposes now. It's part of growing up, she guesses.

"How did I not know you live around here still?" she asks as he takes a bite of his favorite pastry. She tries not to gag at the sight of all that custard, remembering when he often kept a store-bought tray of similar desserts on his messy apartment countertop. "Have you been here, living in town, this whole time?"

Jack takes another bite. A drip of custard falls on his lip. He reaches for a napkin, dabs it away. "For the most part," he explains. "I've bounced around a bit here and there, though mostly I've been a ghost in those hospital corridors all these years." He smiles. "I like my work, though. It suits me, being there."

Small towns can be strange places. Some days, it can feel like you've memorized every inch of a place, the name of every person on every street, and then on other days you realize those same streets are as big as a metropolis, full of a million secrets you never knew.

Ellie sips her too-sweet coffee. As she does, she can't help it. She wants to know. Her eyes fall down toward his hand. His ring finger is bare, no trace of a circular tan line from years of repeated wear. "You've never been married," she tries and thinks back to that day on his apartment couch. That whole morning and the night that had bled into it had been so terrible, but not only for the most obvious reasons: the fact that their relationship was over and that he'd been talking to someone new. It was the specific look in Jack's eyes when he'd told Ellie about the other girl—what was her name?—and the way they'd sparkled with some hidden power source that never flickered to life when he looked at her.

"I thought you and, you know . . ." Ellie waves a hand, an invitation for Jack to complete her thought, and then trails off.

"Kristin?" He smiles at the sound of her name. "Nah." Lines as fine as hairs appear around Jack's eyes, a curtain of sadness dropping down within them. "It wasn't meant to be."

"What happened?"

He pushes aside his dessert plate and leans back in his chair, his expression suggesting he isn't sure if he should speak the thought that occupies his mind.

"It was a long time ago," Ellie says with a laugh, knowing at least part of what he's thinking. "I promise, I've healed from—well, whatever it was we went through."

Jack chuckles at himself. "Right." He licks his bottom lip, allowing a certain set of memories to pour back through him, like water into a pitcher. "It was nothing particularly unique, you know?" he explains. "After you and I rekindled things and got back together for those few months, she met someone, moved on." He recrosses his legs. "Hard to blame her." He grins. "Hard to blame you, either, for dumping me a few months later the second time around. I was kind of a—hmm—a not-so-grown-up-yet person back then." He smiles. "I promise I'm not quite so terrible now, though."

"So she got married?" Ellie asks. "Kristin? She found another life for herself?"

Jack nods. "She did," he agrees, then lifts his brows, a hint that some other story lives beyond the surface of what he's told her so far. "They divorced a few years ago, though." He laughs, though it's not one built around humor, but rather one that sounds more like an echo of regret. "I reached out to her a little while after, invited her to dinner. She was still living in Westchester at that point, up near where we both grew up."

Ellie tilts her head as she listens to this more tender side of Jack. "How'd that go?"

"Nice, I thought," he admits. "But apparently I was the only one who felt that way. Based on the story I've heard, she had such a horrible time with me that she took herself out for a drink here in town after dinner before she drove home." He shakes his head. "She met someone else that evening. They've been together ever since." He shrugs, as if to show he's over this—whatever has happened through the years between him and Kristin. "It was always an issue of bad timing between us," he concludes, a wistful look in his eyes. "Our lives—I don't know. They never seemed to align, no matter how hard we tried."

At the counter, the barista begins to wipe down the metal espresso machines. Another employee moves across the shop and flips a sign that hangs on the door so it reads CLOSED.

"What about you, Ellie?" Jack asks. "Have you ever been married?"

Ellie exhales a shuddery breath. She thumbs her bare finger, her pale-pink polish looking somehow sad beside it. "I, um—I don't know how to answer that question, actually." She lifts her hand, brushes a strand of hair away from her face. "It's, well, it's complicated."

"I understand." Jack sets his hands on the thighs of his khaki pants. "Based on my experiences, love often is."

Through the window, Ellie sees the light in the spring sky starting to shift. The bright blue of the afternoon is becoming brushed with yellow and orange streaks. Another day in Ellie's present life is preparing itself to end. She looks away, not wanting to think about this fact, and resumes doodling on her scrap sheet.

"Ellie, if I can be forward," Jack says, "if your situation isn't *too* complicated, well, it's just that . . . I'd very much like to take you out on a date sometime." He smiles, the flushed color in his cheeks revealing his embarrassment. "A proper one," he explains and then looks over both his shoulders at their current setting. "Dinner, maybe. That is, if you're not—"

"Wait!" a familiar voice shouts out, interrupting Jack's thought. The shop door swings wide open, despite the flipped-over sign on the glass. "I only want a tea! You don't even have to brew it for me! My ride ditched me! I need it for my walk!"

"Gabby?" Ellie looks up.

"Oh, there you are," Gabby casually states. She adjusts her bag strap before the full details of the current scene she's stepped into occur to her. "Wait." She pivots her head from left to right, like an anxious child who's nervous to cross the street. Her many necklaces swing along with her body. "Are you—is this?" she stammers right before she starts to laugh. "I—I definitely need a second." She blinks once, twice, shakes her head in disbelief. "What have I missed in the last few hours?"

Jack and Gabby briefly reintroduce themselves to one another. Before they get too deep into anything, his phone rings inside his pocket.

"Excuse me." He glances at the screen. "It's my mother," he explains, already pressing the device against his ear. He holds up one finger—*I'll be right back*—and moves to the far end of the shop, his back turned to them as he takes the call.

"Man, talk about a weird week, huh?" Gabby whistles loudly to showcase her amusement with things. "The scuba diver. A car crash." She points to the opposite end of the shop. "Running into that old flame, who for the record is *quite* handsome!" She's shaking her head, her wild hair dancing around her face. "Wouldn't blame you if you decided to drink something a bit stronger than coffee." She lowers her voice by a notch. "Especially with him."

Ellie doesn't offer up a response. Her focus is back on the window and a new sight that has presented itself beyond the glass. Jonah and another woman. They walk together up the sidewalk, their bodies close. Before Ellie can even process what's happening, she watches as the woman—pretty in a predictable way—blond hair, petite frame—turns and places a soft kiss on Jonah's cheek. A moment later, the coffee shop door opens again. She steps inside.

"Pardon me," she says, already walking up to the counter, even though it's clear things inside here are winding down for the day. "Any chance I can get two quick regular old coffees to go?" Her voice sounds as sweet as Ellie's too-sugary beverage. "We have a long night ahead of us with about a million things to do." The woman points to Jonah, who waits for her beyond the glass. The barista, ready to get out of this place for the day, looks at her through his most bored expression. He couldn't care less about whatever it is she's going to say. "It's—well—" She stops herself, too bubbled over with excitement, like a bottle of good champagne. The woman glances over each shoulder, as if to see if anyone around her is listening. She bites her strawberry-pink lips. "It's just—we're getting married this weekend!"

All of Ellie's blood rushes from her head down into her feet. Suddenly, she's glad Jack is still standing in the back of the coffee shop, that he's nearby, as she feels rather certain she will pass out or that her heart will simply stop beating inside her chest.

"Ellie? Yoo-hoo! Earth to Ellie! Did you hear me?" Gabby asks, though Ellie hardly registers her question. "I said I'm going to walk. I don't want to third-wheel whatever it is that you've got going on here," she adds and, like a misplaced hitchhiker, points her thumb toward the back, where Jack is still on the phone. "I'll see you tomorrow?"

Tomorrow. The word vibrates through Ellie like a song she cannot shake. Who even knows what that day will bring?

"Ohhh-kay, then," Gabby says. "So . . . byyye!"

Ellie doesn't turn around to watch Gabby as she exits. Her focus is still on this stranger who's about to ruin everything. The woman thanks the barista, walks away from the counter, and then, like Gabby, steps back outside. She hands Jonah a coffee and kisses his cheek.

Before they disappear, Jonah strains his neck in the direction of the bookshop, as if trying to steal a glance through the windows. He speaks to the woman—*Wait here*—and moves to the store entrance. His hand touches the door, but the rest of his body stops. He dramatically shakes his head, second-guessing something, then turns back. In the process, their eyes meet through the glass: Jonah, out there, and Ellie, in here.

The world stops spinning for a breath.

Jonah, his expression newly conflicted, looks back and forth between them—his current fiancée, and the woman he doesn't realize once was in some other life. For the briefest of seconds, he closes his eyes—a broken compass stuck between two directions—before he ultimately pivots, takes the woman's hand, and leaves.

"I'm sorry about that," Jack says a minute later, rejoining Ellie at the table. Her focus is still outside the window, even though Jonah is gone. "What did I miss?"

Everything, Ellie thinks. "Nothing," she actually says.

Jack nods and takes his seat as he slides his phone back into his pocket. He follows Ellie's gaze and looks out the window, even though no one is there.

"Why did you say what you said before about love?" Ellie asks Jack. The barista, officially done with his shift for the evening, clicks off the lights. "About your experiences? And about it being complicated?"

Jack exhales heavily. "Love can be funny, you know? It's like a book about a happy couple, the whole focus exclusively set on them. You rarely get to hear about all the other characters involved—not their full backstories, anyway."

"What do you mean?"

"Love stories are never about only two people," he explains. "There's always some hopeful fool off on the sidelines—just waiting and watching—who ends up getting burned in the end." Jack looks down at the table, this topic suddenly feeling too personal perhaps. "At least, based on my encounters."

"Unfortunately," Ellie says, her thoughts turning back to the church altar and their vow. The one she and Jonah once made together. The one, she now understands, he is days away from making with some-one else. "I can relate to that." Finally, she looks away from the empty sidewalk—Jonah's choice hurting her in new ways with each passing second. But this hurt, it does more than wound her. It fuels her. "So, when were you thinking?"

Jack brushes some crumbs up into a napkin. "About what?"

"About our dinner," she states and offers her best smile.

"Oh." Jack's back straightens. "Oh, um, great." His cheeks flush again, though for a different reason this time. "I—uh—anytime that's good for you, Ellie. I'm not on shift at the hospital tomorrow." His eyes sparkle with something. "Any chance you're free?"

Ellie looks back through the window again, just to see. But no one is there. "Tomorrow?"

"Sure. Unless that doesn't work for you, in which case we can—"

"No, no. Tomorrow's great," she says. "I'll be at my shop, so you can meet me there early, take a look around beforehand."

"I'd love that."

"Perfect." She turns away from the glass, meets Jack's attractive face. "Consider it a date."

TWENTY-ONE

Ellie is upstairs in bed alone and staring at the ceiling. It's late, too late for her to still be awake, but she can't sleep. How can she? The life she knows, the one she took for granted—her marriage, the day-to-day workings of her home, her parents' life and happiness—it's all broken because Ellie decided to break it.

I want a divorce, Ellie had said to herself so many times in recent months.

I wish we'd never been married. She'd had that thought more than once, too.

In her head, she hears Maggie's question.

Are you going to date or something?

Apparently, yes.

Ellie was the one who'd said it, who'd wished for all of it. Jonah had agreed, yes. But her mouth, not his, was the one the word—"divorce"—had fallen out of first.

And why? Were things between them really so bad? Bad enough for Ellie to believe that throwing it all away would somehow be better? Or was it just that Ellie was sad. Sad that the best chapter of her life was ending. The three of them living together in the house. Ellie always so busy, and yet always having some defined purpose. Even if it was for a million small somethings—tasks other people might have overlooked—for many years, Ellie had felt so needed. All the invisible work she filled her days with—all the invisible work every mother fills her days with—it was important. It kept the ship running. It kept everyone safe. Healthy. Happy. Forward moving. It made Ellie feel like what she was doing mattered. That her choices mattered. That her life mattered and made a difference.

But then, as abruptly as a car crash, it all stopped.

Ellie's job—the one she'd chosen all those years earlier—was over. Maggie was gone. The house felt empty. Her days lacked the same impetus. Every part of her life began to fall flat.

Ellie pulls the comforter farther up her chest and continues to gaze at the ceiling, as if it is a movie screen. A thousand memories replay in her head. Her and Jonah on the living room floor in their starter home, encouraging a months-old Maggie to roll over, her little body propped up on one of those silly U-shaped pillows. Watching toddler Maggie blow away the cottony wisps of the wish flowers in their back-yard. The two of them pretending not to cry (allergies—always such terrible allergies) as they watched Maggie up onstage for her first theater performance, or sprinting across the turf on those two long, gorgeous, healthy legs at her first soccer tournament. The three of them playing board games in the living room. Ellie creaking open Maggie's bedroom door every night and stealing a few quiet, private minutes to watch her daughter—her most precious blessing—peacefully sleep.

Watching Maggie grow up was a privilege. Ellie knows this. Still, it hurt. Over the years, Ellie was constantly forced to watch pieces of her only child's younger self die, like being a guest at a thousand funerals. The first time Maggie left the house without a kiss. The moment she released Ellie's hand, desperate to walk ahead of her. The afternoon Maggie decided she no longer needed a push on the swing. The last time she played with her favorite tea set. Her first doll. The bicycle with the rainbow streamers. Not once in those useless parenting books Ellie had bought when Maggie was a baby had any "expert" brought this part of child-rearing to her attention: the fact that "motherhood" is a synonym for "grief."

Knock, knock, knock.

At first, the sound is so low Ellie believes she's imagining it. It's like someone tapping on cotton. A noise, sure, but soft. Beside her, the window is open a crack. The quiet song of insects seeps through the screen. The generator, that temporary source that still powers this house, hums.

Knock, knock, knock.

Ellie looks away from the ceiling, pushes down the bed linens. Someone is here, on her porch, yet again. She's not sure she has the mental capacity after these last two days to discover who it is that waits.

She swings her feet off the mattress, slides on her slippers, and pulls a sweatshirt over her head. The hallway is dark when Ellie opens her bedroom door and slowly tiptoes down the staircase. Before she steps into the entryway, she peers into the living room, hoping maybe her father, whom neither she nor Bunny have seen since their encounter this afternoon, has come back. The sofa is vacant, Ellie's sheets still lining the cushions from the night before. Beside it, Bunny softly snores in her reading chair, which Frank had someone cart over prior to their church episode earlier in the day.

Knock, knock, knock.

Another few steps and Ellie is at the door, her hand wrapped around the metal knob. She takes a breath and then another, preparing herself for whatever unplanned destiny waits for her on the other side.

"Here," he says as soon as she opens it.

Jonah.

Her husband. Who is no longer her husband. Because they've split up. Or because they've never been together. Or because he is days away from marrying someone else.

"You forgot this earlier," he announces as he extends his hand.

It all happens so fast. The words exist in her head—*How are you here? How did you know where to find me? What has happened to our life?*—though it takes too long for them to arrive at her lips. She never asks. Instead, with her eyes locked on his, Ellie extends her hand and accepts the folded sheet of paper he passes to her.

"I have to go," Jonah announces, already turning to walk away. "I can't stay."

"Wait," she says, and nervously crinkles the paper in her hand. She's furious, and yet longs for him. "W-will you come back? Will I see you again?"

"I—I don't know, Ellie." Jonah steps down the porch stairs, two at a time. "I'm not sure what I know anymore," he tells her and then quickly disappears down the block.

Ellie moves back inside, shuts the door, feeling like she's seen a ghost.

"Who on earth was at the door at this hour?" Bunny whispers from her reading chair, a thick blanket pulled up to her chin. She glances at the empty sofa beside her, then pats her head in search of her reading glasses, perhaps to confirm that she's seeing the empty cushions clearly.

"It was just a friend," Ellie explains, her breath feeling short. "He—he had to drop something off to me."

Bunny coughs, makes a disapproving grunting sound. It's unclear which situation the noise is directed at. "Well, make sure you remembered to lock the door."

Back upstairs, Ellie peers through the window to see if maybe he's still there, or what other surprises might wait for her outside. Her street looks normal. Patches of manicured grass. Sleepy houses. The only things that look even remotely out of place are the damaged power lines at the end of her driveway and the sawed-through pieces of her family's favorite tree set in a neat pile on the lawn.

The room is illuminated by silver moonlight as Ellie gets back into bed. Slowly, as if it is glass and may somehow shatter in her hands, she unfolds the paper, one crease at a time. She flattens it against the comforter, smoothing out the wrinkles, just to be sure she hasn't missed anything.

Here, on the page, a most familiar drawing. The bold circle. The triangle rays. And there, in a different-colored ink, the silly cartoonish sunglasses, the ones Ellie herself did not have time this afternoon to finish drawing in, the ones her daughter always liked to sketch out, once upon a time. Ellie looks at the finished picture, the one Jonah—despite time and timelines—knew how to complete.

"Maggie," Ellie whispers to herself into the night.

He knows.

PART THREE

Standby

TWENTY-TWO

Wednesday

E llie doesn't wait for someone to knock. She's been awake for hours. She's already seen the sun rise, already showered, dressed, and run a fast errand. She's ready. This morning, unlike the ones that came before it, she's prepared for whatever waits for her in this new, not entirely real, day.

"You're leaving," Ellie announces when Bunny, just having risen from her reading chair, shuffles into the kitchen. Behind them, the coffee machine beeps predictably on the counter. "And I made you your breakfast blend." She pulls two mugs down from the cabinet. "Now sit."

After Jonah appeared on the porch—Jonah, *her* Jonah, not a stranger, not some person who accidentally crashed into her and whom she was meeting for the first time—and handed Ellie the completed drawing, she stayed awake nearly all night looking at that creased sheet of paper and mapping out a plan.

The drawing itself was silly, literally a child's drawing that, over the years, Ellie had produced and reproduced alongside her daughter, and yet it told the story of their family's whole life. The dozens of birthdays and holidays when Maggie was too small to find real value in stores and so instead gifted assorted versions of her signature illustration to her parents and grandparents as gifts. The trail of marker caps and broken crayons she left all over their house and their cars and even the yard for years and years and years. Her hand-drawn pictures, the ones Ellie often taped to the fridge, a happy greeting there for her and Jonah anytime they needed to pull open the door for milk or eggs.

Jonah knew how to finish that silly drawing because, like Ellie, he'd watched Maggie draw it dozens of times. And although Ellie hasn't solved all the *how*s and *why*s yet, she comprehends enough to recognize that he understands what's happening. That something about their life has been flipped.

"What do you mean I'm leaving?" Bunny asks as she pulls her robe tighter around her body. Her short bob of hair is frazzled from sleep. "To go where? And when?" She coughs, a slight rattle of mucus in her throat. "I'm not going anywhere until I've had my coffee first."

Ellie is already wearing her jeans and a clean white T-shirt. Her favorite taupe cardigan is folded up in her book bag nearby. Her car keys are out and waiting right beside it. "Here." She sets a steaming mug down in front of her mother and then reaches into the refrigerator for the new carton of creamer she picked up earlier from the store. She places this down on the table, too. "It's fresh," Ellie confirms, already anticipating Bunny's line of questioning. "Now drink."

"Are you kicking me out?" Bunny asks before pouring way too much creamer into her mug. Her coffee is basically a milkshake. She takes a sip, adds another splash. "I don't know where I'll go now," she mumbles, partially to Ellie and partially to herself. "I suppose I'll live on the street," she rambles while nervously fidgeting with her cross pendant. A sudden thought transforms her face. Bunny throws up her hands. "I knew it! You're sending me to a home, aren't you?"

"A home?" Ellie squeezes her eyes shut, shakes her head. "No! What are you saying?"

"Well, I can't think of any other place I'd go," Bunny continues. "I certainly won't move back into the condo, not with everything going on between—"

"Wrong," Ellie states, newly pleased with herself. After months and days of turmoil and uncertainty, for this brief snippet of time she feels, thankfully, in control of things again. "That's exactly where you're heading, Mom." She begins to gather her mother's belongings—her blue tub of VapoRub, her plastic pill case—from the counter and sets them on the table in an orderly pile. "We're going to find Dad."

~

Knock, knock, knock.

Ellie swings the door wide open a little while later, already knowing what to expect. Inside the house, Bunny continues to take her time as she organizes and gathers her things.

"I can't," she tells Gabby, who stands opposite her on the porch. Her macramé bag is slung over her shoulder like a fashionable knot, while her long, crimped hair forms an unruly crown that drips from her head. "I know what I'm about to say won't make much sense—or maybe it will—but ever since I woke up on Monday morning, my entire life has been completely out of order."

Gabby, who wears a different vintage T-shirt today (some relic from an old camp resort upstate), tugs a piece of her hair, pulling her head toward one side. "Is this because of the scuba diver?" Her face illuminates, her tone lifting. She releases the long strand. "Or because of yesterday in the coffee shop with Jack?" Her pink-painted lips mold themselves into a smile. "Because, honestly, I *definitely* did not see that one coming!" She lifts her hands, offers a dramatic slow clap. "By the way, A-plus for whatever *that* was all about."

"Um." Ellie bites her lip, slicked with a hint of bare shimmer. So much has transpired—so many loose threads have unraveled in her head since yesterday—it's hard to believe it was only a few hours ago that she sat in the coffee shop window with Jack. "It's partially about that run-in," she explains. Around them, the world is heavy with springtime perfume—all blooming flowers and clean air. "Though, if I'm being honest, that's not quite the full story."

From behind Ellie, a forlorn Bunny appears in the hallway, carting her things.

"Should I ask?" Gabby poses.

Ellie shakes her head. "Just take care of the shop," she says. "That seems a lot more like your world right now than it does mine."

~

"This is silly," Bunny keeps saying, over and over like a broken record, as she hands Ellie her overnight bag in the driveway. "We'll never find him."

"Of course we will, Mom," Ellie insists as she hoists her mother's bag into the back seat, even though the movement makes it feel as if her back will rip right in half. "There are only two places in the whole world where Dad would be right now."

Before she gets in the car, Bunny cranes her neck toward the back of the vehicle. "What happened to your bumper, Ellie?" She slides her readers from her head and onto her nose. "It looks like you got into an accident!"

"I did." Ellie slams the door shut. "But I'm fine."

"Oh, Jesus, Mary, and Joseph!" Bunny exclaims, as if an accident might be happening right now. "When did that happen?"

"Yesterday," Ellie announces and then shoos her mother into the vehicle. "And another the day before that."

Ellie opens the driver's side door, clicks her seat belt into place. In the rearview, she sees the power company's truck parking against the curb. Two employees lumber out. Like her, they're intent on fixing everything that's been damaged these last few days.

"You got in *two* accidents this week?" Bunny asks from the passenger seat as she thumbs her gold cross. "How can you expect me to drive with you after this news?"

Ellie takes one last glance at the porch, praying Jonah will miraculously appear on it again. "Right now, Mom," she says as she shifts the gear into reverse, "I don't think you have much of a choice."

~

Frank is nowhere. Not at the deli (the only place other than his home where Ellie thought he might be). Not out walking through town. Not at church. Not at Ellie's house (which they circled back to twice). And not here, in his and Bunny's New Jersey condo, which Ellie now sees exists just a few blocks over from where she lives.

"I told you we wouldn't find him," Bunny says as she moves around her tight, windowless kitchen. "I'm sure that, by now, he's long gone."

Feeling claustrophobic, Ellie steps out and paces through the living room. This doesn't look like the place where her parents live at all. Yes, she sees familiar objects—her father's reading chair, some framed childhood photographs of Ellie. But the room is missing something. A lot of somethings.

"Wait." Ellie turns back to face the kitchen entryway. "What do you mean . . . 'gone'?"

Bunny joins her daughter in the living room. "This is the problem, Ellie. Your father wants his life, and I want mine."

While Bunny talks, Ellie rummages through the room, as if a clue about her father's whereabouts might exist beneath a couch cushion. "What does that mean, Mom?"

A creature of habit, Bunny walks to the empty space where her reading chair was previously positioned and nearly tries to sit. She stops, lowers herself into Frank's chair instead. "Your father told me weeks ago that if I ever did go through with this, the first thing he'd do is put himself on a plane and go someplace sunny, finally follow our original plan."

This is when it clicks for Ellie. Without another word, she races down the condo's short hallway and into her parents' bedroom. She pulls open the closet and sees that her father's old blue suitcase is missing. "Mom!" Ellie calls out and then zips through the room, hunting for the specific items her father has packed. She flicks on the light in their small, en suite bathroom, sees his toothbrush is missing. "Is this a joke?" she shouts. "Dad's in his eighties! He doesn't travel by himself anymore! He hardly knows how to use his phone! What if something happens?" She swings open the medicine cabinet, revealing a half dozen orange prescription bottles. "And he didn't pack his heart medication!"

Bunny appears in the bedroom. "See? I told you he never remembers a thing about his pills." She purses her lips. "I suppose he didn't pack the list I wrote out for him, either."

Ellie slams the cabinet closed and rushes back into the bedroom, searching. "There!" Beneath the printer that sits on her parents' shared desk is a mess of loose papers on the carpeting. Ellie gathers them, notices the duplicate printouts of the same thing—testaments to her father's inability to understand electronics. "Jesus Christ, Mom. You're not kidding." She shoves the papers at Bunny. "This is a flight confirmation. His plane leaves in an hour!"

Bunny hands the papers back, then nonchalantly straightens up the bed linens—Frank's side of the mattress the only one that's been slept in. "Well, he finally got what he wanted. A tropical retirement. With or without me."

Ellie is sweating through her shirt. "But it should be with you. That's what you've always wanted, too."

Bunny closes her eyes, breathes deeply. She opens them, tugs the comforter tight. "Not now," she states. "Right now, you need me here."

"No! I don't!" Ellie exclaims, realizing she sounds like an angry teen. "You can't put your whole life on hold—you can't throw your whole marriage away—because of me!"

Bunny shakes her little blond bob. "I'm not."

"You are," Ellie insists and then moves back toward the closet. She drags out Bunny's suitcase. "But I'm not letting you anymore."

"Don't be absurd, Ellie." Bunny straightens her back—or as much as her spine will let her these days—to assert her maternal dominance. "You're my child. You don't get to make these choices for me!"

"Well, today, I do." Ellie heaves the suitcase onto the bed, triggering her back once more. "Now get moving." She wipes some perspiration from her forehead. "You have exactly ten minutes to pack."

TWENTY-THREE

"This is absurd," Bunny says as Ellie races the car down the high-way. They've hit nothing but obstacles—traffic, closed lanes, construction—on this drive. "I can't just get on a plane and go to Florida! I need to go shopping! I don't have the right blouses! I need to pick up sunscreen! Plus, your father and I aren't even speaking!"

Ellie has zero plan. By now, Frank is likely already at his gate and preparing to board. She's called and messaged him a dozen times from Bunny's phone. (*What are you doing, Dad? You can't get on a plane and fly to Florida with no place to stay by yourself!*) But in all his heartache, he has yet to respond. Though she won't say it to Bunny, Ellie hasn't a clue what she'll do once they arrive. Buy her mother a last-minute ticket on the same flight? Beg a TSA agent to let her unticketed elderly parent through to the gate to find her spouse?

Finally, the airport exit appears on the right. Ellie clicks on her blinker, veers the car toward the off-ramp, and then drives into the airport complex. Every few feet, enormous signs are staked alongside the roadway to remind travelers of all the places in the world available for them to see, and all the ways for them to arrive there.

"I don't care for this car," Bunny states. The minute the words escape her mouth, so does a hacking cough. "I don't—*cough, cough*—I don't like the way it—*cough*—drives."

"Really?" Ellie attempts to swerve into the short-term parking area, though naturally there's a detour. Based on the completely roundabout manner in which the alternate route loops them, an alien from outer space who shot down to visit might believe airports are places that operate purely by the laws of leisure, and not by very strict timelines. "That's your big concern at the moment?"

Bunny coughs again. "One of them."

Ellie peers at her mother over her shoulder. "Are you all right, Mom? I don't like the sound of that."

"I'm fine, I'm fine," Bunny says, even though she's still coughing. "It's only a tickle." She pulls a hard candy out from her handbag and pops it into her mouth. "See?" she poses through half of a gasp.

~

Ellie is sweating. With her book bag accosting her back (*thump, thump, thump*), she wheels Bunny's suitcase behind her, doing her best to get her to hustle to the terminal entrance.

Finally, they step past the electronic glass doors, both of them briefly pausing to catch their breath. Bunny looks around, fluffs her short hair with a hand, then points upward at the digital departures board, looking through her reading glasses to better view it.

"It's too late," she announces. "The door on his flight is already closed." She removes her glasses. "He's probably already met someone else by now," she suggests, as if domestic flights are the go-to dating destination for the soon-to-be-divorced, eightysomething set.

Ellie rubs her hands over her face. *Think, think, think.* She begins to pace.

"You're limping," Bunny points out, matter of fact. She wears her dark, quilted spring jacket—the same one she wore on Ellie's porch when she arrived Monday morning. Her palm tree brooch peeks out from it and sparkles beneath the airport's artificial light.

"Yes, I know," Ellie says, cautious not to say too much. "I hurt my back. But I'm fine."

Bunny's eyes thin themselves into slivers. She reaches into the pocket of her coat and digs out another hard candy. "What is all this about? Why are we really here? What are we actually doing?"

A memory: a cold winter morning. Ellie was twenty-two or maybe twenty-three. She'd been out of college for well over a year and living at home in her childhood bedroom while commuting back and forth like a pinball into and out of the city. It was early in the morning, the sky still so black it looked like night, and Ellie was seated on her pale-pink comforter, already dressed in a black sweater and shift dress and impossibly uncomfortable black tights.

"Why are you doing this, Ellie?" Bunny asked as she creaked open the bedroom door and watched her daughter struggle to pull on her knee-high boots, which looked exactly like the ones all the other girls in Ellie's office had been wearing that winter, which was the point. "There's a blizzard outside," Bunny said. "There's a foot of snow on the ground. Are you really going to get on the train right now?"

"The weather's different in the city, Mom," Ellie said, a ball of emotion lodged in the base of her throat. She hated that job and the commute and those silly boots she'd spent half a paycheck to buy. "It'll be fine."

"This isn't the right track for you, Ellie," Bunny, still dressed in her heavy winter pajamas and bathrobe, boldly said.

Ellie finally tugged her boot onto her calf. She looked up at her mother, biting her lip. She was dreading getting on that freezing train and then trudging through the humid corridors of Penn Station and then sloshing along the slush-filled streets along with every other pissed-off commuter in the tristate area. But she couldn't admit all that to her mother. She had to at least pretend to put up a good fight.

"This is what girls like me do nowadays, Mom," she said as she yanked on her other overpriced boot. "We graduate college. We get jobs. We change the world, you know?"

Bunny lifted her eyebrows on her pale, makeup-free face. "You're going to change the world in this snowstorm? Doing what? Slipping on a patch of black ice?"

Ellie threw up her hands. Outside her bedroom window, she saw the headlights on Frank's car click on. "You know what I mean."

Mother-daughter relationships are so complicated. It feels like Ellie has known that forever, and yet it seems like it's something new she's learning more about every day. She and Bunny have always been close, a fact she loves and usually feels grateful for. But it's moments like that one—when Bunny seemed to have a superhuman ability to look inside her daughter, as if with some invisible microscope or magical x-ray machine, and see the parts of herself she tried to keep hidden from the world—that their closeness and their relationship in general drive Ellie completely mad.

"I know you don't want to hear it, Ellie," Bunny had said. Outside the window, Frank beeped the horn. "But this isn't the right path for you."

Ellie stood from the bed, collected her things. "And what makes you think that?"

Bunny sighed, pulled her bathrobe tighter. "Sometimes, a mother just knows these things."

Now, back in the airport, Bunny sucks on her candy, suppressing another cough. "Well?" she asks. "What is it that you're doing, dragging us here? What do you think you're going to change?"

Before Ellie can answer, she sees him: Frank, yelling at an airport employee and haphazardly stabbing his finger against the screen of an electronic kiosk.

"You just need to trust me, Mom," she says and then grabs Bunny's hand. She tugs her forward as other travelers zip past. "Whatever has happened recently between you and Dad, well, you have to believe me when I say it's not the right path."

~

"The three of us need to talk."

Frank looks up from his kiosk, blinks his confusion. "Ellie?" He furrows his brows. "Bunny?" he states in a sharper tone. Behind him, the airport employee, relieved this transaction has been interrupted, slips away. "Wh-what are you both doing here?"

"You're not running away to Florida by yourself, Dad," Ellie tells him.

"I sure am!" he insists and then pats his head in search of his glasses, which are not there. "I just need to figure out how to use this machine so I can book myself a new ticket. I misread the time on my last one and missed my flight."

Bunny remains silent and just shakes her head. She reaches into her jacket pocket, produces a spare pair of drugstore readers, and hands them to him.

He hesitates, but ultimately takes them and slides them on his face. "Anyway," he says as he turns back to the machine. "If you two are here to try to stop me, you're wasting your time." He jabs a finger at the screen again. "I'm leaving today. It's time for me to start this next chapter of my life!"

Bunny rolls her eyes and huffs loudly. "For God's sake, Frank, you're not going any place without these!" She reaches back into her coat pocket and pulls out a plastic bag full of his prescription bottles. "You'll be dead in a day if you don't take them!"

"What does it matter to you?" Frank asks, finally giving up on the kiosk. "According to our church, I'm not your husband anymore." He tosses up his hands. "I'm no one!"

Bunny huffs out an annoyed breath at Frank's drama. She begins to say something, then stops, then starts again. "I"—*cough, cough*—"I—I didn't actually tell Father Donovan."

"What?" Ellie and Frank say in unison.

"I—I wanted to," Bunny admits and, not willing to make eye contact with either of them, studies her hand. "But it turns out he was away on retreat this week."

All around them, the airport terminal buzzes with activity. But right here, for these three people, the world has stopped.

"I don't understand," Frank says. "Then why did you say you did?"

Bunny rubs one of her fingernails. "I'm not sure. Perhaps it was a sort of test run. A chance for me to hear how it would sound to finally say it out loud."

"So Father Donovan was never there?" Ellie asks.

Bunny shakes her head.

Overhead, an announcement chimes through the terminal's vast speaker system.

"Maybe you weren't meant to tell him, then," Ellie suggests.

Bunny pauses, then finally looks up. "I'd thought of that."

Another traveler steps up beside them, gestures to the machine. Frank moves away from it. "Do you mean it, Bunny?" he asks. "You never told him?"

"No," Bunny says. "I mean it. I never did."

Frank nods his understanding.

Bunny tucks the bag of medications back into her pocket. "You know you'd never survive without me, Frank."

"You think I don't know that?" he responds.

Bunny tugs at her gold cross. "But if I'm honest," she says, finally meeting his gaze, "thinking about you leaving—well—I'm not so sure I'd survive without you, either."

Behind them, the other traveler grabs his printed boarding pass and hurries on his way.

"So, what do we do now?" Bunny asks, though it's unclear who she's asking. Ellie? Frank? Herself?

Ellie looks up and notes that Brenda is still working at the airline's main counter, as if she's never left. "Give me twenty minutes, and one of your phones," she says. "I have a plan."

~

Together, the three of them move across the slippery white floors, then down the narrow escalators, and finally to the end of the security line.

"I'm not so sure about this," Bunny admits as she and Frank step forward. "I—I'm not even sure if I packed the correct toiletries!"

"You're not going to the moon, Mom," Ellie points out. "You're going to Florida. The entire state is designed for people who travel there from elsewhere. I assure you that ninety percent of visitors there forget something."

A few minutes earlier, Ellie used Frank's phone to book her parents airline tickets and all the other reservations needed to safely get them to where they're going, to where they need—where they're *supposed*—to be. At least until Sunday, which is the date marked on their return tickets—enough time, Ellie hopes, for them to see this fact for themselves.

"I don't like the way you're walking," Bunny points out. "You're going to be alone in the house with your back like this?"

"What's the matter with her back?" Frank chimes in. "What did I miss?"

"Nothing, Dad." Ellie walks beside them as the line moves forward. "I'm okay," she says, right as what feels like an electrical shock sparks the lower half of her body. "Really."

"Tell me again, Ellie," Frank says. "What do we do when we get there?""

"I promise," Ellie insists, believing herself. "Everything will run smoothly. All the reservations I made for you—hotel, car service—are in your email, as well as a list of step-by-step instructions for everything you'll need to do to get safely to your hotel and then back here again in a few days. Okay?" She leans forward, embraces both her parents, and then kisses each of them on their respective cheeks. "No one here is getting divorced, all right?"

"Well, what are we supposed to do if we need to get in touch with you?" Bunny asks. "You don't have your phone."

"I plan to check the lost and found again before I leave," Ellie declares without thinking.

"The lost and found?" Bunny proclaims. "Here? Oh, good Lord. For what?"

Ellie briefly covers her face with her palm. "Just . . . never mind, Mom."

Ahead of them, the other travelers inch closer to the security checkpoint.

"Listen." Ellie begins to wrap things up. "I'll be okay while you're gone. I promise." She hesitates before she speaks the next part. "I won't be alone." Her parents look at her inquisitively. "I—I think I met some-one," she admits, not knowing how else to put it. "I'll tell you more when you get back. But in the meantime, I promise you don't need to sit around and worry about me, okay? I'll see you both in a few days," Ellie reassures them. "Now go. It's time to get your life together back on track," she says as she starts to walk away.

Before she makes it far, she feels a hand on her shoulder. She turns back.

"Sweetheart," Frank whispers after Bunny has nudged herself a few paces ahead. He lowers his arm, squeezes his daughter's hand. "Thank you for this."

TWENTY-FOUR

Home.

Ellie pulls into the driveway and finds Jonah waiting for her on the porch. He sits on the bench swing, gently rocking back and forth, like he and Maggie used to do together on warm days when she was small. He's cleaned himself up since their last meeting—his hair is neatly trimmed, the edges clean around his face, and he's put on a fresh button-down shirt and nicely cut jeans. It occurs to Ellie that he looks like he's going on a date, only she doesn't know if it's the one he's about to share with her, or a different one in this uncanny life with his fiancée.

Ellie shifts the car into park and steps out, her eyes focused only on him. She walks, one step and then another, closer to the house, not sure what either of them will say or do when she arrives. Hug? Kiss? Cry? Fight? Her hands tremble, like she's a schoolgirl about to come face-to-face with her crush. She tugs at a loose piece of her hair, like she used to do when she felt nervous as a child.

"Hi." One side of Jonah's mouth lifts into an uncertain smile, like he's unsure if this is the correct thing to say.

"Hi," Ellie says and stuffs both her hands into her pockets. The late-spring air is warm, comfortable, that ideal temperature when you're not hot or cold, but just perfect. Even so, a chill runs through her body. She contemplates walking back to the car for her book bag so she can grab her cardigan and slip it on like a security blanket.

Nearby, the men from the power company are two stories above them in their giant crane. The tools they use—whatever it is they're actually doing up there—send a shower of electrical sparks down toward the ground. Above them, the May sky is a brilliant blue. *Cornflower,* Ellie thinks, the name of Maggie's favorite crayon color.

One of them needs to say something now. Who could ever know where to start? How will they even begin?

"Hey, Ellie." Jonah's voice—him saying her name—sounds so comfortably familiar.

She lifts her face and meets his eyes.

"Would you like to go for a walk?" he asks.

Another shiver runs through Ellie's body, though this one feels different.

"Yes," she says.

~

They walk. All through their neighborhood, along the ribbons of alabaster sidewalks. Beneath the blooming dogwoods and Japanese cherry trees, the delicate petals falling all around them like a soft snow. They walk past their first apartment—that sweet little duplex with the pleasant back porch and the yellow bathroom tile—and past their starter home—that charming money pit they brought Maggie back to after they were discharged from the hospital, and where they'd paced the hallways night after night trying to get her to sleep, and where Ellie and Jonah had nearly lost their minds with happiness the first time they heard her laugh.

They keep going.

Together, they walk past the old playground, with that terribly steep plastic slide, and Maggie's elementary school (which, at one point in time, was Ellie's elementary school, too), where dozens of small children are outside running for playtime. The whole time they walk, Ellie and Jonah are quiet, both of them listening to the breeze and the birds and whatever thoughts are bubbling up in their respective minds.

"Would you like to sit?" Jonah finally asks when they arrive at the small park across the street from the schoolyard, and gestures to a wooden bench.

The park itself is not big, only a few blooming trees, a small fountain, and a half dozen benches for people to take a pause and think or read or talk or cry or whatever it is people need to do in places like this.

They both take a seat, though not too close to each other, neither of them quite sure of how distance should or should not function between them right now.

"I contemplated if I should come see you again," Jonah admits, his face directed straight ahead at the schoolyard, where all those happy children still play. The breeze blows and sends a thick strand of his dark, silver-accented hair waving across his forehead. "I'm still not sure what's right."

In the near distance, a teacher blows a whistle.

"Why didn't you tell me you knew what was happening from the minute you saw me?" Ellie asks, her hands set on her thighs, her gaze cast forward. "On Monday," she continues, "when you crashed into me. Why didn't you say something right away?"

Jonah takes a long time to answer. He just breathes and breathes and breathes. "This is what you said you wanted, Ellie. To see what life would have been like if we'd never existed together, you know?" He shrugs his wide shoulders. "For all I knew when I first saw you Monday, maybe you wouldn't have remembered me." He sighs sadly. "Or maybe you wouldn't have wanted to."

She shakes her head, suddenly annoyed. "I mean, yes and no. I sort of think waking up and finding ourselves in an alternate version of the present might have warranted a conversation or something, though, right?"

"Look." Jonah turns away from the schoolyard. "I don't know how we ended up here." He offers her an exasperated face. "I woke up in this place just like you." He opens his mouth to continue, but pauses, and instead pulls in a long breath.

"What?" she asks, sensing something. "What is it?"

"It's—it's nothing."

"I know that tone," she points out. "It's not nothing."

He sighs, something about the sound revealing to Ellie that he's stuck at the intersection of sadness and embarrassment. "All those months, Ellie, you spent time wondering about what life might be like without me. Without us. You said those words—or some version of them—to me so many times." He bites his bottom lip. "Maybe I just finally needed to do the thing I never seriously did back then." He pauses, then presses on. "To see and consider for myself what my life might be like without you."

The words hit her right in the chest, as heavy and hurtful as bricks.

They both cling to silence again. Off in the distance, the children enjoy their final few minutes of unstructured freedom before the remainder of the school day and its schedule takes control of everything again. Ellie watches them all, a feeling pulsating in her belly, one that simultaneously feels like love and like pain. She's flooded by a million remembrances. Walking Maggie to school every weekday morning, her small, doll-size hand tucked safely in her own. Ellie and Jonah laughing and crying happy tears as they sat side by side in the school's multipurpose room every year at the holidays to watch Maggie and her peers parade around onstage, all of them dressed up like cardboard snowflakes and merrily singing off-key.

Back then, as they were living through all those moments they both knew would ultimately come to serve as some of their life's happiest memories, Ellie felt like what she and Jonah were really doing was creating a sort of glue, one that would hold them together tightly. But that was before Maggie grew up and left. Before all the fighting got underway like a theatrical production she and Jonah had been forced to attend but that neither of them had ever wanted to see. Before Ellie knew firsthand all the different ways a woman's heart can break.

In the distance, the teacher blows the whistle again. The children hustle into a chaotic line and march their tiny bodies back inside the building.

"I followed you that morning," Jonah finally admits. "I parked down the street a little ways before the house a few hours after I woke up and pieced together what was happening. I was right behind you the whole time, but you never even noticed me." He's quiet, thinking, then continues. "When I woke up in my hotel room Monday, before anything had even really happened, I felt like the whole earth had shifted." He rubs his hands across his thick thighs. "I figured it was anxiety. I knew you had planned to call the attorney and that we'd finally arrived at the day when things—" He sighs, waves a hand in front of him. "When all this—us, no longer being together—became real." Nearby, a pair of runners, dressed in all sorts of spandex, sprint past and through the park. "I called you a dozen times to ask you not to make the call, and to tell you we needed to talk things through again, that we were wrong, that it was all a misunderstanding, that we were making a giant mistake." He drops his head into his sizable hands. "I don't know why I waited, Ellie." He rubs his fingers through his hair, turning it back into a mess. "I called and I called, but you never picked up."

She turns her whole body now to look at him. "I lost my phone at the airport the night we flew back," she explains. "I've been completely untethered all week. I *told* you that."

He pulls his posture up, straightening himself. "I tried to call Maggie after I called you." He closes his mouth and inhales a long, deep breath through his nose. "It didn't go through." He shrugs. "It was one of those weird error messages." Jonah shakes his head. "I don't have a clue what that means."

Ellie has so many questions, though none of them seem quite right. Her eyes burn with the threat of tears. She blinks, releasing one of them, and inhales a long, slow breath, too. For now, she decides to just listen.

"At first, I thought I was hallucinating or dreaming or, I don't know, that maybe I was dead or something," he explains. "It was around then that my phone rang. I assumed—hoped—it was you calling, but when I answered, another woman's voice was there, telling me I was running late, that I needed to come meet her right away." His chest shakes with a soft laugh. "I have no idea why I went," he explains. "Curiosity, I guess. Or a search for answers. When I met her down at the coffee shop, she started to talk so fast, it was like she was throwing a hundred different clues at me." His lips—his soft, generous mouth—lift into something that almost resembles a smile. "None of it made any sense, of course. It still doesn't." Finally, he turns to look at Ellie again. "Some things don't."

They're so close Ellie can make out every small detail of his face. The smattering of sunspots on his cheeks. The 11 lines that have formed between his brows over the years. His pores and the exact shade of his complexion, which is somehow always both pale and a tiny bit tan, enough for him to look healthy.

"I'm supposed to be getting married this weekend, Ellie," he says.

It feels like someone stabs her in the heart—over and over—with a million tiny pins. "I know."

"So, what should I do?" he asks. "Which life am I meant to pick?" He tilts his chin to look at her. "I don't know how to get back to the way things were." He inhales deeply, his shoulders rising right before he exhales. "And what's worse is that I don't even know if you'd want me to."

Close by, the park fountain bubbles a gentle background melody.

"I miss you," Ellie says, plain and simple. "We made a mistake. A terrible one."

"I know," he agrees. "But now that we're here—" He stops himself, sighs out so many feelings. "I—I worry that it's too late."

She wants to reach out her hand and touch him, to cup the curve of his jaw in her palm, or to feel the coarseness of his hair between her fingers, to let her face fall onto his chest and to listen to his heart as it beats and beats and beats. Instead, she poses a question.

"Did you mean to crash into me?" she asks. "Or was it really just an accident?"

"Which time?" On the sidewalk in front of them, a young couple walks by pushing a baby carriage. "This week? Or all those years ago?"

Ellie watches them walk away. "Both."

"It's hard to say," Jonah admits. "I don't think I'd ever *choose* to crash a vehicle into you."

Although neither of them has moved, something about the space between them suddenly feels both smaller and infinite.

"Maybe something or someone else chose for you," she suggests, remembering her old belief, the one she abandoned long ago.

"And what's that, Ellie?" he asks, waiting for her to say it.

Ellie takes a deep breath and then another. "Fate," she says.

"No," he instantly counters, surprising her. "That's where you're wrong. It wasn't fate," he explains. "It was me." His voice is both stern and tender. "I'd find you in any lifetime, Ellie Adams," he says.

TWENTY-FIVE

Ellie wants to show him. Everything that she's built. Everything that she's become.

The bells ring as she swings open the glass door. Jonah follows her. Inside, the atmosphere is just as Ellie left it yesterday. Warm. Inviting. Calm. She waves to Gabby, who's perched on a stool behind the long, rounded white counter, her neck predictably weighed down by wooden beads as she sifts through a stack of papers. The two young, college-aged women who were here yesterday are back again and tastefully arranging a summer reading display in the window. Around the shop, a handful of customers browse the neatly arranged shelves in search of the feeling that best suits them today, what mood they're willing to buy into for a several-hour span.

Jonah pauses on the penny tile entryway and takes it all in. He breathes deeply, the fabric of his clean button-down shirt rising and falling in an even rhythm. "You made this," he says. His words are a statement, not a question.

Ellie steps deeper into the space. "I did."

He nods. "I see you everywhere in here."

Why hasn't she done this for herself in her real life? Created a place like this—something away from her home and her family, something that exists only for her, something to fall back on later when she isn't needed in the same ways anymore. Then again, motherhood sometimes feels like a study in guilt. If you leave your child when she's young to pursue something for yourself, you feel the guilt of it early. If you don't and then realize later that your purpose has grown up and moved away, you'll feel it at the end. It's really just a matter of whether you want to front-load or back-load the emotions.

"I didn't think I'd see you again today," Gabby playfully notes without lifting her face from her work. A customer approaches the counter and sets down two novels to purchase. Near the window, the other employees twist their heads in preparation for some idle chatter. "Planning to introduce me to your new friend?"

How can Ellie say it? How can she possibly explain? But then again, how can you ever really explain marriage or love or divorce to someone who isn't steeped inside it?

"This is Jonah," Ellie offers and looks over at him. When she does, she sees all the versions of him she's ever known. The unsure twenty-something. The nervous boy who offered her a ring. The young man in that dapper suit who stood across from her at the church altar. The doting new father. The thoughtful son-in-law. Over the years, he's been so many different people to her. So many versions of himself. Right then, Ellie becomes overwhelmed by an emotion. It feels like drowning, and yet like floating, as if she's just now coming to the surface of something. She misses him. All of him. All of them. All the lives they've ever lived together. All the versions of himself he's ever been to her.

Gabby's eyelashes flap like butterfly wings while she waits in anticipation. She sets down her papers, looks up at Ellie, and then back at the customer, whom she begins to ring up. "And did you just pick Jonah here up off the street, or . . . ?"

Nearby, the girls pretend to do everything except eavesdrop on this exchange.

"We lost touch for a little while," Ellie explains, knowing it's the truest thing she's spoken in days. "But I guess you could say he's an old friend."

Back in their twenties, Ellie and Gabby had practically nothing in common other than their communal living room and their shared admiration for literature. Ellie liked things quiet, while Gabby preferred life to be loud. Ellie chose to present herself in a simple fashion—straight hair, a pale-neutral nail, classic jeans—whereas Gabby outfitted herself like a toddler given too much freedom—everything clashing and wild and full of color—and yet, for her, it worked. Why hadn't they been friends then? Why had Ellie completely shut her out?

It's been so many years since Ellie has had a real friend, one outside her family and her home, one she's not connected to because of Jonah or Maggie, but someone who is just hers. There was a woman in college, a fellow English major, whom she was close with for several years, but it didn't last. There was a friend in high school, though that fizzled out shortly after graduation. Yes, Ellie could have—*should* have—put in more effort with the women from town—her fellow book club members, the other moms from Maggie's school—though she never did, through no one's fault but her own. Some part of her always felt their relationships were not entirely organic but were rooted in their children's friendships instead.

Standing near Gabby now—Gabby, who's been nothing but nice and knowledgeable and reliable and kind in her own quirky way—Ellie regrets not putting in any real effort with her back when they were roommates. She wonders about what other opportunities she might have missed.

A look of amusement lifting her glossy opalescent lips, Gabby steps away from the counter. "Well, it's very nice to meet you, Jonah, the old, long-lost friend." She turns in such a way so only Ellie can see her face. *What is happening?* she mouths and then drifts off toward a shelf.

Jonah stands beside Ellie and squeezes the back of his neck. She hovers beside him, unsure if they should stay or leave. Before either of them has a chance to decide, a pair of tiny hands pushes the shop door back open, the bells tinkling like glitter for one's ears. The little girl in the Velcro sneakers rushes past, just like yesterday, and straight toward the children's section in the back. A second later, the girl's mother—looking happy and tired and content and drained—steps inside, a beige book bag strapped over her shoulders, which Ellie guesses is filled with her child's many things.

"I'm sorry," the woman says and fruitlessly waves a hand in her daughter's direction, as if this motion will quell her excitement and make her slow down.

Mothers always apologize for their children. Anytime they say the wrong thing. Anytime they act even an iota out of line. Really, though, they're apologizing to and for themselves. *I'm sorry. Am I doing this right? Is this the way she's supposed to behave? Is this the way I'm meant to feel? This is all so much harder than I ever imagined.*

"She's fine," Ellie reassures this stranger. *You're doing fine. More than fine.* "Really."

"Friend of yours?" Jonah gestures at the child as her mother joins her on the area rug.

They don't need to say a word to know what they're both thinking. The girl looks just like her. The big, wide, jack-o'-lantern-tooth smile. The woven pigtails. The sweet cotton dress and stretchy, patterned leggings. The way she sits on her hands and bounces, and then quickly plops herself down onto her belly, and then pops straight up and sits on her hands again, like her body is made of springs.

Back when Maggie was about this age, on the morning Ellie and Jonah dropped her off at preschool for the first time, they were both such messes. They'd walked together—the three of them hand in hand like an inseparable chain—to their church, the same place where Ellie and Jonah were married, and to the secured preschool entrance, which was accessible in the back. After they helped her hang up her precious pink book bag and find her pint-size seat, they waved goodbye to her from the carpeted hallway. They both knew Maggie would be safe and happy there. But they were also smart enough to know they stood at the start of it. The letting go. It hurt so bad. Jonah had held it together for Ellie's sake on the walk home, though a short while later, she heard him sobbing through the bathroom door. Years later, when things between them had begun to crash, she would look back on this day all the time—during those long stretches of night following a particularly noxious fight, when they went to bed without a kiss or an apology and she couldn't even think of sleep—and recognize that, in more ways than one, it had been the beginning of the end of everything.

"Excuse me?" a tiny voice interrupts, pulling Ellie away from this memory.

Ellie blinks several times in fast succession, briefly forgetting where—or when—she is, everything she's nearly thrown away.

"Is there a Cinderella part two?" the girl asks now. "I want to know if she stays married."

"Oh, um." Ellie hasn't read children's books in years, though she wishes this were not the case. She loves these books, all of them fairy tales in their own ways. Inside these brightly illustrated covers, anything can happen. Animals can talk. Any old fool can become a superhero. Everyone always finds her happily ever after. Characters can fall asleep in one place and magically wake up somewhere else, without any real purpose or explanation. No one is ever left feeling hurt in the end. "Hmm." The child's question is both heartbreakingly innocent and deeply profound. "I'm not sure, actually. But maybe I can recommend something else?"

Close by, Gabby—taking a brief pause from her tasks—plops herself down into one of the shop's comfortable, upholstered chairs. Jonah steps backward and watches Ellie—his wife, or his old friend, or both— as she navigates this new circumstance. She moves with the child across the store and back toward the children's section, where she crouches down and browses through the kid-size shelves.

"How about this one?" Ellie squats and pulls down a book with a cartoon castle on the cover. "It's an old one, but a classic." She smiles at the girl's mother. And then, without thinking, she utters the next part. "It used to be my daughter's favorite."

Her words are like a record scratch.

"What did you say?" Gabby instantly asks, her voice akin to tires screeching. At the window, the twentysomething employees' eyes double in size, suddenly looking as wide and round as dinner plates. "Your *what*?" Gabby scoffs.

Ellie quickly pops back up, the fast movement triggering the pain inside her body all over again. "I—uh—I meant—" She feels herself fumbling, like a clumsy child who's trying to catch a ball. "I meant my daughter—no, no, my friend's daughter, it was her favorite when—" She can't get the words out. They're caught in her throat like a too-big bite of something difficult to swallow. It doesn't matter. She already knows it's too late to save face. Children are fiercely curious creatures. The questions immediately pour in, like spilled paint.

"Are you married?" the child asks, her mother behind her already becoming red faced. "How many kids do you have? Are they boys or girls? Is there a baby in your belly right now? Do you have a dog?"

"Ellie?" Gabby asks as she rises from her seat. "Are you okay? You look, um, kind of flushed. And are talking like maybe your mind is going a bit cuckoo or—"

"Ellie?" Jonah interrupts her.

"I just—I—"

But Ellie can't speak. Not really. Deep inside her, she feels something about to detonate. This setting—this barrage of unsolicited questions, none of which she has the capacity to answer, but which she wishes she could—it's breaking her.

There is no logical way to explain it. That, yes, she has a daughter, but she's far away from this disaster her mother has intentionally (she did, in fact, utter the word "divorce" first) or unintentionally (she did not, however, intend to make a wish and screw up the entire concept of time) created. Or that, yes, technically she is still married to the man who stands right here, because she lost her phone and never called the attorney. That her life—her *real* one, which she only now realizes was so wonderful—exists someplace else, somewhere that is not here, in a space she cannot wish herself back into right now, let alone try to articulate.

"I—I—I don't know. I don't know what's happening." She looks at Jonah, his nostrils slightly flared, his breath quickening like hers, both of them becoming enveloped in panic. "*Am* I married, Jo?" she asks him. "*Do* I have a kid?"

"Ellie?" Gabby's face is awash with new worry. She moves toward the counter, shoos another customer closer to the glass door so she'll quickly leave. "Maybe I should call someone. Are your parents still—"

"Sweetheart," the child's mother says, hurriedly and sloppily reshelving the titles her daughter pulled down. "I think it's time for us to go." She looks at Ellie, briefly makes eye contact with her. *I'm sorry. Please don't judge me. Please don't judge her. She never acts like this. She always acts like this. I don't know why she behaves this way. I don't know why I do, either. I'm trying. She's trying. I'm trying. I'm trying. I'm trying.*

"I think we're going to head out now," Jonah decides. "I should get you home so you can rest." He places a gentle hand on Ellie's back.

She winces beneath his light touch. The pain. That muscle. Every emotion and memory stored inside that set of cells, it aches and aches and aches. She doesn't want to be here. In this store. In this life. She thinks of Bunny's comment the other morning as the two of them sat at her table in sunny Florida.

You think marriage is about love?

Um, yes, Ellie had foolishly said then.

It's only now that she fully realizes it's about more than that. Marriage, love, relationships—they're also about history. And about memory. Right now, all of hers feel convoluted. Mixed up. Like she can't recall what's fiction and what's not.

The mother—her face burning with embarrassment—and her sweet, adorable, not-meaning-to-cause-any-trouble daughter, quickly exit the store.

"I'm—I'm sorry, Gabby," Ellie stammers as Jonah begins to guide her out the door. "It's been a really strange week. I think I need to go—"

"I've got this," Gabby insists, her nostalgic T-shirt tugging at her chest. "Really. I promise I'll take care of everything."

"Thank you." Ellie nearly stumbles over her own feet. The pain ripples through her. Jonah stays beside her, his hand still tenderly set on that part of her that aches. "You seem like a good friend, Gabby."

Gabby quizzically tilts her head. "I *seem* like—"

"I'll see you soon," Ellie says, and she hopes her words ring true. "I'll find you. I promise I'll reach out, okay?"

"Come on," Jonah whispers, and together they take a step toward the door.

"Wait a second," Gabby interrupts, her pupils glazed over with questions. "How did you two say you know each other again?"

Jonah turns to Ellie, a look in his eyes silently asking her for permission. Ellie nods. "I'm her husband," he states.

The bells tinkle. Someone is pushing the door open. No one inside bothers to look in the direction of it.

"What the—" Gabby gasps. Her brightly made-up lips pull back on her face, like she's caught in a wind tunnel. "This has seriously been a week for the books! You can't make stories like this up!"

"Ellie?"

A voice. One Ellie has not heard in years, though in recent days it's become familiar to her once again.

She looks over at the door.

"Jack?" Ellie asks, as if she's not seeing things quite right, like she's wearing smudged-up glasses or has a piece of fuzz in her eye. "What are you—" Ellie feels breathless for a myriad of reasons, one of them being that she feels Jonah, clearly taken aback by whatever is happening, pull away from her. "What are you doing here?" And then, she remembers. "Oh God. Our date," she says, not meaning to actually say this aloud, her interior thoughts just slipping out. "I—I forgot."

"Your *what*?" Jonah moves away from her, as if she is made of poison.

Jack takes another step inside the shop. He's wearing khaki bermuda shorts and a crisp, white button-down, a pair of preppy loafers. His aviators are pushed up onto his head of golden hair. In his left hand, he holds a colorful floral bouquet. His green eyes dart from Jonah to Ellie and then back to Jonah again, like he's watching a tennis match.

"I'm—I'm sorry." Jack offers up a confused look, one that is also ripe with disappointment. His high cheeks blush, like they've been pinched. He quickly averts his gaze to the ground, and—clearly embarrassed—positions the bouquet behind his back, as if no one in the shop has noticed him holding it. "I—I think I misunderstood something." Jack takes a backward step. "I'll come back some other time," he stammers and quickly walks out.

The next part happens so fast that Ellie hardly even processes it. As Jack backtracks onto the sidewalk, looking defeated and delirious, he stumbles right into a passerby: an attractive blond woman in a pale-pink sweater, her eyes hidden behind a pair of black sunglasses, though not enough to conceal the rest of her face, which quickly reveals she's been crying.

"Oh no," Jonah blurts. "It's her."

"It's who?" Ellie asks and swivels her head to look at him.

"My fiancée," he sternly notes. "The one I called things off with this morning." His face grows red with anger. "Because I foolishly thought I could patch things up with you."

"What?" Ellie is breathless. "Wh-why didn't you tell me that?"

"Man," Gabby proclaims. She's on her tippy-toes, staring through the window behind the counter. "The plot twists today!" She kisses the tips of her fingers, offers up a chef's kiss.

Jonah doesn't immediately respond. Instead, they all watch together as the woman slowly lifts her sunglasses away from her face. She laughs at something. Jack—his face scrunched up in question—laughs, too. He pulls the bouquet out from behind his back and offers it to her, his face aglow with disbelief.

"I need to get out of here," Jonah states, a new sense of urgency cropping up in his voice. He takes a step forward, then stops, realizing he can't go out through the front entrance just yet. He spins in a circle, as if looking for an emergency exit. "This was a mistake, Ellie. This whole day. I don't know what I've been thinking."

Ellie knows she needs to respond. But at the moment, she feels too emotionally paralyzed to move. She watches Jack through the glass—the boy who, once upon a time, broke her heart because his heart was beating for someone else. She sees the whole narrative unfolding, page by page. Line by line. Choice by singular choice.

"Jonah, wait." Ellie's focus remains set on the windowpane. "I need to ask you something." She feels like her body has been cast in stone. There's no way she can move. "I—I need to know. What was your fiancée's name?"

Jonah throws up his arms. "Does it matter?"

"Yes," she says, suddenly desperate to hear him say it, even though, deep in the pit of her, she knows it. It already sits on the tip of her tongue.

He huffs. "Kristin," he says, like she knew he would.

And isn't this just life, Ellie thinks.

In any given moment, for some people, the timing is off. And for others, finally, it's exactly right.

TWENTY-SIX

"You met someone? You were planning to go on a date?"

These are the first things Jonah asks when they step inside the house, which Ellie pleaded with him to come back to with her. Bunny and Frank are gone, likely hours into their sunny trip. Maggie is—well, not here? The home is so quiet that their footsteps echo as they stomp through it. The only sound other than their angry voices comes from outside—the gentle, incessant hum of the generator, still running, and the men from the power company who chatter and pack up their tools, ready to wrap up another long day.

"No!" Ellie kicks off her tennis shoes in the entryway and then moves into the kitchen. "Or, yes!" She reaches into the cabinet for some ibuprofen to help dull the pain. "I don't know, Jo!" She fills a glass from the faucet, swallows two brown tablets. "I'm not sure what's happening—what's real, what's not—anymore."

Ellie takes a seat at the kitchen table and looks around the room. She's spent hours of her life right here in this exact space. It is so full of history. Today, the walls are white—Swiss Coffee, the paint can had read when Ellie picked it—but before, when Maggie was little, there was a time when they were canary yellow and, for a brief window, a pale, icy blue. When Ellie was young, Bunny went through a bad wallpaper phase, dressing the walls in Laura Ashley–style floral prints and regrettable rooster motifs.

Now, as Jonah takes a seat across from her, squeezing his temples as if for dear life, Ellie longs to peel away all the layers on these walls and go back and back and back through the decades her family has lived inside them. The pain. The joy. The good times. The hard ones. She wishes she could see them spread out wide before her so she could pinpoint for herself the exact minute when things began to go wrong.

"What would have happened if I wasn't there?" Jonah asks. His face looks like a distress signal. "Would he have walked away?" His forehead creases. "Would he have stayed?" He repositions his weight on the chair. The wood emits a low creak. "Would you have let him?"

Ellie thinks of that old book. The one she read all those years ago, back when she was a single, twentysomething woman who felt so desperate to find her way. Thirty-five thousand choices, all in a single day. It feels to her right now—the chalky, medicinal taste of those brown pills still lingering on her tongue—like too much to bear. For every small choice we make, we walk both toward and away from a prescribed version of our existence. Life is like skipping stones. The instant you make the choice to release that warm, smooth rock from your hand, a series of chain reactions is set into motion. The ripples you've created spread and spread and spread.

Ellie doesn't answer. Instead, she volleys a question back to him. "Would you have gotten married if you hadn't run into me earlier in the week?"

Neither of them responds. Because the painful truth is that they don't know. Who or what might they choose if they each lived a life away from one another? What lives might they have chosen for themselves if they hadn't—back in their real one—crashed right into each other that very first day? What if she turned left instead of right? What if he did? What other versions of themselves are out there, just out of frame and waiting for them? For every new door we open in our lives, another one must remain closed. With each new choice we make, no matter how small it may seem at the time—to grab a coffee, to stay put a minute longer, to go home and sulk or not—we commit ourselves to a particular path. A certain destiny. And, often without ever realizing it, we commit all the people we love to this path, too.

"Why didn't I do something more for myself in our real life?" Ellie poses, pivoting the conversation by a few degrees. It's a rhetorical question, one really meant for herself, but still she asks. She can't stop thinking about the specific life they chose—that she chose—and all the lives they might have lived with or without each other. "The bookshop," she continues. "Or a friend." The pills are kicking in now, the pain in her back starting to subside, though a new one—a burning, searing emotion—ignites inside her chest. "I gave the two of you all I had," she admits. "And in the end, it wasn't enough."

Jonah looks at her inquisitively. "Ellie, I—I never asked you to give up those things. Those were choices you made, not me."

In the months that led up to Maggie's departure, Ellie wanted someone to blame, and she often chose Jonah. It was easier than blaming herself, even though that was where the blame belonged. The choices were always hers. Jonah simply did his best to support them.

Through the window, Ellie sees that the late-day sun is setting. The sky is touched by clouds, their edges appearing as puffy as a child's drawing. In the distance she notes the sweep of cornflower-blue sky becoming a different shade. Midnight blue, another of Maggie's old favorites. For a split second, her heartbeat drumming the inside of her throat, Ellie wonders if her daughter—wherever she is, or whoever she is right now—can see this same sky, too.

"Why didn't you fight harder?" she asks him. "When I first said it. Why didn't you fight harder to make me change my mind and to keep me around?"

Jonah closes his eyes, remembering. "I did, Ellie. You just didn't hear me." He opens them. "You never heard me."

Ellie looks all around the room again. The memories are everywhere. They're as omnipresent as the air. "I want to go back," she whispers. "I want to go back to the start. When she was small. When she still needed me." She sighs with everything in her. "I miss that part of my life so much."

"But you can't, Ellie. And neither can I," he states.

"Why?" she asks, not actually expecting him to have an answer. No one does. It's so unfair, these unbendable rules of time.

"Because she doesn't need you in the past," he explains. "She needs you now, back home, back in the present. The real one." He exhales a sad, heavy breath. "And so do I. But . . ." He trails off.

"But what?"

"But I don't know if we can get back there," he says. "I worry that we're too far past it now."

Neither of them speaks. Their words, their memories, they're all just floating here.

"What was that?" Jonah asks, concern cropping up in his voice. "Did you hear something?"

"Hear what?" Ellie asks. "I don't hear anything."

Jonah moves closer to the window and peers outside. "I thought the generator made a funny noise." He brushes the idea off. "Never mind," he decides. "It was probably just in my head."

For an extended beat, they stand a few feet from each other, watching and waiting.

"I think I'm going to go," Jonah finally says, his tone ringing with sadness. "I don't think I should be here right now."

"Go?" Ellie asks. "You're leaving? To go where?"

"I don't know," he admits. "To get air. To take a long walk. To think."

A feeling of panic begins to rise in her, bubbling and bubbling like boiling water. "Are you coming back?"

Jonah shakes his head. It's clear from his expression that he feels every feeling, and yet is all out of them, too. "I don't know, Ellie. I don't think it's up to me."

Her eyebrows lift in two uncertain arches. "What do you mean?"

"You're the one who got us here." He takes a step into the entryway. "I can't fix this. It's up to you." He takes another step away from her and then opens the door. Before he leaves, he meets her eyes. When he does, it feels to Ellie like it's both for the first and the last time. "You're the one who needs to make a choice and decide how this story ends."

~

Ellie is alone, still seated at the kitchen table. Jonah was right earlier. Something is wrong with the generator. It's clicked off, and she hasn't a clue how or why. The whole house is dark except for the faint glow from the glass-enclosed candle she's lit on the counter and the pale hints of blue moonlight that stretch through the windows.

Knock, knock, knock.

Someone is here to see her. Again. She doesn't know who. She hopes it's him, that he's come back, but she can sense already that it is not.

Only a few hours earlier, Ellie felt like she was on the right path to fixing this mess. That she was putting the pieces of her life back together one by one, like building something with a set of wooden blocks. But that was before. Now?

Knock, knock, knock.

Ellie stands and walks across the kitchen's black-and-white floor, like she's done a thousand other times. What if she ignores it? What if she goes back to the table and pretends she didn't hear? What then? Can she hide from whatever it is that waits for her right now on the other side of the door? Can she choose to turn around, to pick a different destiny for herself and for this whole life she's living in instead?

Knock, knock, knock.

But this isn't the answer. Ellie knows this. You can't turn your back on your choices or the path you've picked. All you can do is face them.

She opens the door. The porch light is out, like all the other lights inside. Even so, she doesn't need it to see him, to recognize the lines and curves of his face, to immediately know something is wrong.

"Dad?" Ellie poses. "What are you—why—how are you here?" she stammers.

"Christ! Don't you check your phone?" Frank stands on the porch, a look of worry painted across his aging face. "You're always yelling at me about that, and yet—"

"What?" Over her father's shoulder, she sees a yellow taxi—its headlights still beaming—parked in the driveway. "I told you. I lost it. The other day. I haven't—"

"They bumped our flight back four times," he explains. "They finally let us board, and we sat on the tarmac for three hours. But by the time we deboarded—"

"I—I don't understand," she interjects, confused. "So you never went? You've been up here the whole time?" She's spinning, her thoughts circling around and around like a broken toy. "Maybe there's another flight. Maybe we can still get you both there tonight."

"Tonight?" Frank scoffs. "Ellie, there's only one place we're going right now."

Ellie widens her eyes in question.

"The hospital," he explains. "I've been calling and messaging you for hours. It's your mother," he states. Ellie feels her heart drop into a free fall. "She's sick."

TWENTY-SEVEN

Thursday, 12:01 a.m.

But it could have been any time or any day. It is so hard to tell in places like this. Yes, it is dark beyond the window in Bunny's fourth-floor hospital room, a clear indicator that it is night. In all the rooms stacked against Bunny's, other patients like her are asleep. But any sign of night ends there. Everyone else—the nurses who keep checking in, the anxious family members who pace and pace and pace—is wide awake.

Frank was right. Bunny is indeed sick. This is all Ellie can think about as she sits in an uncomfortable hospital chair—everything about it cold and slick to make it easier for the custodial staff to wipe the germs away—next to her mother's bed. It's a virus, the doctor—some physician who is not Jack—explained shortly after she was admitted. It's nothing serious in theory, but then again at her age, anything that triggers a high fever or affects her breathing can turn very serious very fast. They need to get the fever down, though so far they can't get it to break. Whatever it is, the doctor said, she likely picked it up while here in the ER on Monday.

Now, while Frank speaks to someone at the nurses' station, Ellie sits and watches her mother sleep. Tangles of cords are attached to her body like unwanted leashes meant to keep her here. She looks so pale, her skin practically translucent when set against her blue hospital gown.

Ellie decides she hates this gown. It doesn't suit her mother at all. She should be dressed in something punchy and bright, her skin smoothed with coral blush and a tan, as she walks around and around her condo development, her body basking in the hot sun and the damp humidity.

But there is no sun here. In this sad hospital room, there are no tropical insects singing their lullabies into the night. It's just machines beeping. It's so cold, Ellie thinks as she wraps her cocoon cardigan—the one she finally pulled out from her book bag and slipped her lean body back into—tighter around her frame. Ellie briefly closes her eyes and pretends to feel that warm, southern sun on her skin. She can't. When she opens them again, her vision is blurred by tears. The only heat in this room radiates from inside Bunny's body. None of this is right.

"Hi, sweetheart." Frank appears in the doorway, his demeanor and tone more subdued than it was back on the porch. "Tough night, huh?"

Ellie can see in her father's face and the specific expression he wears that he's had such a long day. Such a long week. Like her, he's been placed in so many unexpected settings—and so many unanticipated circumstances. He's tired. Ellie is, too.

Ellie stands so her father can sit. A true gentleman, in most cases, he'd decline such an offer. Tonight, he accepts it.

"How's she doing?" he asks, like Ellie knows. Like either of them do. People give up so much control in places like this. You put all your trust in a stranger and hope they'll do the right things—make the correct choices—to get you or your loved one back on track. But no one ever knows if the choices they're making are right. Doctors, after all, are just people. "Has her fever come down?"

Ellie shrugs and stands at the foot of her mother's bed. The only light source in here comes from the hallway and the small in-room television that's mounted near the ceiling. The ibuprofen she took earlier is wearing off, a subtle quiver of pain suddenly reintroducing itself to her body, like an unwelcome party guest.

"This is all my fault, Dad," she says, which takes every imaginable effort not to cry. She does not want to break down in front of him. He doesn't need to worry about her right now, too. "If I hadn't brought her here on Monday or if I hadn't tried to ship the two of you off today or—"

"Stop," Frank insists, which surprises her. Through the window behind him, a pale trace of white moonlight illuminates part of his face. "This isn't your fault, Ellie. You didn't cause any of this."

"But I did, Dad," she pleads, a part of her wanting him to believe this, even though she doesn't want it to be true. "I'm the one who chose to—"

"You didn't, Ellie." In the hallway, a pair of nurses push a wheeled stretcher. "Who's to say where one choice ends and another one starts? You can just as easily make the argument that this is all my fault for not absolutely insisting that she stay put at home on Monday, instead of turning up on your porch and bogging you down with all this."

Knock, knock, knock.

Ellie and Frank both turn. A female nurse, a woman with beautiful mahogany skin and a smile as warm and inviting as a freshly made bed, stands at the door.

"I'm really sorry," she says, her tone apologetic. "But visiting hours ended a long time ago. There's only supposed to be one guest per room overnight in this wing."

Ellie gives a firm nod, a signal to this nurse that she understands and has no intention of giving her a hard time. The woman turns at this gesture and disappears down the hallway.

"You should get some sleep, Ellie." Frank stands. He takes a step closer to his wife's bed and presses the back side of his hand against her forehead, the way Bunny has always done for them when they've been sick. He pulls his hand away and adjusts her thin, hospital-grade blanket. "You need to rest." He turns back to face his daughter. "You've had a long week, too."

Ellie buttons her cardigan, this single layer meant to keep her protected and warm. "I'll be back in a few hours," she tells him.

Frank nods and then drags the hospital chair closer to Bunny's bed. He sits and takes her hand in his. "I'll be right here."

~

The town is empty. Ellie knows this because she's driven all around it—past the bookstore and the coffee shop and around those familiar streets—at least a dozen times.

She keeps looking, but he's nowhere. He's everywhere, too. Still, she can't find him.

Click, click, click.

Ellie flicks on her blinker so she can turn and drive home. All the traffic lights blink red at this hour. It's up to each driver—not that there are many of them out right now—to stop or to yield or to say screw it and just keep on going.

The car rolls into the driveway. From the outside, Ellie sees the whole house is black. The power is still out. The generator has exhaled its last, tired sigh. She slides on her book bag straps, her keys dangling from her fingers as she steps onto the porch, hoping perhaps she hasn't seen things clearly because of the darkness. Maybe he's hiding somewhere in the shadows, waiting for her. She opens the door and knows instantly he's not here.

Upstairs, Ellie sits alone in the dark on the edge of her bed. Is she really going to get changed and go to sleep? She can't. It'll never happen. She already knows this as fact.

A memory: the night of Maggie's birth. By the time the nurses, each of them angels in their own right, had gotten her settled in her room (Had minutes or hours or entire days passed?), she had absolutely zero concept of time. She kept blinking, half in shock and half in relief that it was over, that she'd made it, that she and the baby had both survived. Maggie, all swaddled up in one of the good hospital cloths (so much better than the silly muslin ones the stores convince new mothers to buy), was on her chest and asleep. A nurse—a woman who looked to be only a few years older than Ellie, and whose eyelids were painted with the boldest shade of blue—appeared at her bedside.

"Why don't you let me take her to the nursery for a few hours for you, Mama," the nurse said, already lifting the baby off Ellie's chest. "You need rest."

Maggie didn't so much as stir from the movement, just slept peacefully as the nurse set her down in the wheeled bassinet. Ellie didn't know if she was supposed to act like she didn't want this time away from her new daughter—the guilt of motherhood already setting in. She didn't know what she was supposed to do or say or want right then.

"Enjoy it," the nurse said, reading her mind. "You won't get much alone time from here on out."

Back in her dark bedroom, Ellie realizes how right that nurse was. For years, it's felt as if Ellie hasn't had a single moment to herself. But right now, while seated on the edge of her bed, she sees that life has come full circle on her. Finally—unwillingly—Ellie is alone again.

Through the blackness, she reaches for the drawing from the coffee shop—the one Jonah had completed and dropped off the other night—and thumbs the paper, knowing what she finally needs to do, the one thing that's been hurting and worrying her the most this week, which she finally must force herself to see.

Even without light, Ellie knows the way. She can walk this path without issue, regardless of time or space or which life she's trapped living in.

There's no need to knock. She knows, regardless of what magic has unfolded around her in recent days, that the person she's looking for is not on the other side of this door. Still, she wants to see what is.

Moonlight filters through the linen curtains, lighting the room as though from within. It's all still here. Her bed, with its fuzzy throw pillows. The pale-pink walls, which she adored when she was a child but learned to roll her eyes at the more she aged. The beanbag chair where she loved to sit alone and read. Her favorite photos of her friends and some inspiring quotes, as well as a printout of the electronic acceptance letter she'd received from Middlebury, pinned to a corkboard.

Ellie steps deeper inside, the scrap of paper with her and Jonah's drawing on it still in her hand. The whole room smells like Maggie. Not like perfume or cosmetics but like her. The same distinct scent she carried that first night the nurses laid her curled-up body on Ellie's chest. This space should not exist here. And yet, it does. But then again, perhaps its presence makes perfect sense. Mothers are the gatekeepers of their children's memories, the only people who know all of them—even the early ones their children themselves will never recall.

Yes, Ellie thinks. *Of course this room is still right here, despite logic.*

Because a mother's love is not made from logic. It knows no boundaries. No limits.

Not even time.

The bed is soft. Ellie allows herself to sit on the edge of it, running her free hand across the cozy comforter, the one with the pretty watercolor design. For a long time, Ellie has only allowed herself to miss a certain part of her daughter. The younger one. The little girl with pigtails and Velcro sneakers, the one who left a trail of crushed-up cereal pieces and stray toys all over the back seat of Ellie's car. The one who danced in front of the television every time her favorite cartoon's theme song came on. The girl who said, "One more, one more, one more," every night—no amount of stories her mother could read to her ever seeming to be enough—before she finally tired herself out and fell asleep in Ellie's arms.

But that was then. Right now, Ellie misses a different part of her daughter. The bouncy teenager running out the front door to meet her friends. The one who did her homework every evening at the kitchen table, the black pendant light glowing above her as she worked so hard. The one who insisted on a daily basis that she no longer needed her mother, even though it was so clear she still did. That she still does. That they all do.

Ellie takes a big breath and moves across the bedroom. She pauses in front of the corkboard, her head tilting to one side as she takes in the sight of Maggie, her wide smile staring back at her from all those pinned-up photographs.

"I'm going to fix this, Mags," Ellie whispers to the air, some part of her hoping the words will carry through the window and over mountains and right to her daughter's ears. "Not just for you." She pins up the scrap of paper. "Not just for Dad. But for me. For all of me. And for all of us, too."

This time, Ellie leaves the door wide open when she exits the room.

TWENTY-EIGHT

Ellie is driving, even though it is the middle of the night. No one is anywhere. The streets, the sidewalks, the whole town is empty, as if every single person who lives here has just up and left. The traffic lights keep blinking red, but Ellie doesn't halt or yield.

No.

This time, she refuses to stop until she finds him.

Click, click, click.

She turns the car, keeps going. He's somewhere out here. She knows this as much as she knows anything. She feels it deep down inside her, like some telepathic message he's sent. Where else would he be? He's not at their home. As far as she knows, he doesn't have another home here. Is it possible he's back at his hotel, the one he brought his baggage back to on Sunday night, shortly after their plane landed? But he's not. Ellie is certain of it. Jonah wouldn't be sitting and staring at a wall right now, not with everything that's happening. Everything that has already happened.

Click, click.

She flips on her blinker, even though it isn't necessary because no one else is on the road. Even so, it's a hard habit to break—this practiced instinct to let people know where you're heading, which direction you hope to end up traveling. The car moves past the cafés and tiny shops and charming window displays, the store interiors beyond them black and closed up until morning, the whole world dark and empty and quiet. Her hands set on ten and two like always, Ellie peers through the windows anyway. *Please, please, please.* She knows any second she will look up and see him, that he'll be right here in front of her, that together they'll finally be ready to both apologize and make amends.

Up ahead, a familiar intersection appears. Elm and South. *Of course,* Ellie thinks. Why hadn't she thought of it before? This place, this four-way stop that points in every direction and yet more than once has managed to point them right to one another. It makes perfect sense. This is where she will find him. This is where they will meet again.

The car idles beneath her. She peers in her rearview as she approaches the blinking light. No one is behind her. Not yet.

Click, click.

She turns left, arrives at a stop sign, and then turns left again so she can circle the block. She arrives back at the intersection—their intersection—the light ahead still flashing red. Red. Red. A heartbeat. Ellie looks around. No one. She circles again. And then again.

A few minutes later and she finds herself back at the start, the traffic light dangling above her. She only tilts her head down for a second. Just long enough to click on the heat and shake this chill that hasn't left her alone ever since she was in Bunny's hospital room. It makes no difference. She doesn't need her eyes on the road to know that, finally, he's here. Ellie feels him—his energy, his presence—before she sees him. Even if all her senses simultaneously shut down and stopped working right now, she'd still know that Jonah was close by.

It only takes one second—one small choice—to know she's made a terrible mistake.

Their eyes catch for half an instant. But she can't stop. The vehicle moves forward. It all happens too fast.

The car makes contact. Her head slams against the steering wheel. Even so, Ellie sees what has happened. Jonah, in the crosswalk. Jonah, out for a walk, just like he'd said. Jonah, lost and alone in the middle of this tragic night and searching for her, too. The sound of it—both silence and noise—bleeds in her ears.

She bolts from the car and screams out into the night, but no one else can hear.

~

Jonah, his face young and lineless, his dark, thick hair free from any grays, standing in the middle of the intersection, apologizing again and again and again, and then asking if he could buy her a cup of coffee.

~

Jonah, lying next to her on her springy apartment bed, both their teeth stained red from wine, and just talking.

~

Jonah, the orange sun dipping itself into the calm sheet of ocean behind him, the delicate ring placed between his fingers, and the question she always knew he'd ask.

~

Jonah, wearing his new navy-blue suit and dapper matching bow tie as he stood at the altar, the autumn sunlight smiling down on them through the panels of stained glass, and the way he whispered in her ear before he kissed her. *Forever and forever and forever.*

~

Jonah, flipping pancakes in their first apartment—the one with the pleasant back porch and the yellow bathroom tile—and both of them laughing.

~

Jonah, standing in the unfinished cement basement of their starter home, holding a metal tool he had no clue how to use, water spewing from a pipe overhead, as if they stood together in the rain.

~

Jonah, trying to look brave even though he was afraid, as he walked back into the hospital room and unpeeled the lid from another lemon Italian ice.

~

Jonah, his face a bit older, a little patch of grays forming alongside his forehead, as he moved back and forth and back and forth across the porch, carting her parents' boxes out of the family's house and moving their boxes inside.

~

Jonah, chasing Maggie through the living room and pretending to be a monster, one who always hugged and tickled her in the end.

~

Jonah, seated on the edge of Maggie's bed, her head down on his chest as she cried and cried and cried about some boy, with Ellie looking on from the hallway.

~

Jonah, his arms crossed as he stood in their bedroom doorway, watching Ellie toss the laundry all around and then listening—like a verbal gunshot—the first time she said it.

~

Jonah, beside her on the plane, and watching his seat-back television, pretending.

~

Jonah, slicing yellow pound cake at Bunny and Frank's table, and trying. And failing.

~

Jonah, in the baggage claim, his black wheeled carry-on at his side, not knowing where he was going, or where he'd ultimately end up, or how to say goodbye. *I'd still do it all again.*

~

Jonah, in the window seat and handing her a cup of breakfast blend, that small, seemingly insignificant gesture that he knew, even in this strange place, would offer her a small sense of home.

~

Jonah, the red traffic light blinking. Her foot pressing the gas. And then . . .

And then.

~

And now.

Jonah, in the back of an ambulance. Strangers poking and prodding him and pushing her off to the side. Her own head bleeding, a gash above her brows—but nothing compared to him.

Him.

Eyes closed. No sound. Nothing looking quite right.

"Is he—will he be—"

"Ma'am, please," the EMT repeats over and over and over as the crew presses and presses and presses their hands against Jonah's chest—the one where she has rested her head, and where Maggie has rested her head, that hulking, tender cavity.

"I didn't mean it!" Ellie is screaming. It's like she's outside of herself and looking down, as if she's witnessing someone's else's life and tragedy unfold. "I didn't mean for any of this to happen! It was an accident! It was all an accident!"

"Please, ma'am," the EMT insists again.

"He wasn't supposed to be there!" she screams out. "We aren't supposed to be here!"

The EMT doesn't say anything this time. He's too preoccupied.

"This isn't supposed to be our life," Ellie sobs, but no one is listening. Not really. "This isn't our real life," she cries to herself.

Beneath her, the vehicle begins to slow down. It feels like a plane pulling back as it begins its final descent.

"This isn't real," she whispers, like a prayer. Or like a wish. "None of this is real."

The man removes a walkie-talkie from his belt, holds it close to his mouth.

"Dispatch," he says into his device. "Please prepare for trauma arrival." He turns, looks at his team. "Everyone ready?" he poses. *Please secure your seat-back trays and personal belongings.* "We're almost there."

TWENTY-NINE

Ellie is back in a cold, slippery chair. Only this time, she's in a different room in another part of the hospital, away from where her mother sleeps. Jonah's body looks like it's sprouted new limbs. There are cords and tubes connected to every part of him—his mouth, his arms, his chest, just everything. Nearby, a half dozen ominous-looking machines hum and beep. Ever since the accident, his eyes have remained closed. She doesn't know what this means.

A swath of white gauze taped to her own forehead, she's watched for the last twenty minutes as nurse after nurse has hurried into the room doing things to Jonah's body that she fails to understand. She doesn't need to question them to know that everything they do is urgent. Ellie can feel it in the way they move (fast) and the way they speak (direct). She doesn't even know if she's supposed to be in here, if visitors are allowed in this hall. She hasn't asked. So far, no one has told her to leave.

For now, Ellie sits and watches and waits.

There's nothing else she can do right now except wait.

∼

A dream. The two of them at home in their bed. The sunlight through the window. The feeling of soft cotton. Morning. Both of them are smiling.

~

Her chin hits her chest, waking her from her unintentional sleep. Another team of nurses, another new doctor at their helm. Ellie quickly wipes the dribble from her chin, rubs her eyes.

"What?" Ellie asks, her voice panicked. Frantic. It doesn't matter. She knows they're used to reactions like this. "What is it?" She can tell by the looks on their faces that either something has changed or nothing. It's impossible to say which scenario is worse.

No one answers. They don't have an answer to give.

There is not a clock in the room. Not in the hallway. Not anywhere.

Time—precious time—keeps moving forward while also standing still.

~

Ellie needs to leave. That's what one of the nurses said a few minutes ago. They need the space. They have work to do. Also, what is your relationship to the patient? Are you his . . .

Ellie is lost. Why are hospitals always so confusing? They're like white, sterile mazes made of infinite wings, all of them looking almost exactly the same. But they're not. Each wing, really, is built around an emotion, a particular mood it evokes. Panic in the ER. Worry and despair in the ICU.

Ellie keeps walking, her back throbbing from the impact of the crash, from everything—she needs to ask one of the nurses for something she can take for the pain—hoping to find her way. Outside the windows in the corridors that connect each different section of this place, she sees the night sky is black. Inside here, though, everything is illuminated by bright-white light. Artificial. Fake. And yet as real as it comes.

She stops. Her breath catches in her throat, like it's trapped there by a powerful net. Up ahead, a familiar wing—the only one she really knows. Beyond the automated glass doors that lead into it is a security desk. An officer with a gun on his belt sits and drinks a to-go cup of coffee and listens to the quiet hum of music.

She doesn't move at first, just stands absently in the middle of the hallway and watches through the glass doors, waiting. For what, she doesn't know. Maybe to see if a younger version of herself in her slippers and pink hospital gown, her lower back and abdomen trembling from the contractions, walks past.

"Are you looking for something?" the officer asks, this man with a gun whose job it is to protect all the new mothers from having an intruder come and take their precious cargo away, all those women too early in the game to understand that one day those sweet babies will stand up and walk away all on their own.

"N-no," Ellie stammers. Through the glass doors, Ellie sees a woman slowly walk by, carting an IV pole at her side, as her partner walks next to her and rubs her back. Right now, Ellie's back aches, too. She breathes deeply, lets herself feel it. Really feel it. This pain that is also, strangely, a reminder of love. Of life. "I—I've already been here. A long time ago."

The officer nods—*Nothing to worry about here*—and looks down at his desk.

Her one unruly back muscle still contracting, Ellie turns to walk away.

One step. And then another.

She has to let go of this part. She has to keep going.

She knows it's time.

~

"Dad?"

Frank is asleep in his chair. He holds Bunny's hand, which is already bruised from the IVs. He startles at the sound of his name and quickly lifts his head, like a puppet on a string.

"I'm up! I'm up!" he proclaims. He lifts his reading glasses, which sit crooked on the tip of his nose, onto his thin bed of hair. "You're back. Is it visiting hours already? What happened to your head?"

Ellie lifts a hand and touches the gauze. She'd nearly forgotten it's there. "I got into an accident," she explains.

"An accident?" He attempts to bolt from the chair, but it takes more than one attempt. He's not so young anymore. "Nurse! Nurse! My daughter! She's been in an—"

Ellie holds out a hand, a signal for him to stop. "They already know, Dad. They're the ones who gave me the gauze. I'm fine." She motions for him to sit back down. "Really."

Frank heaves out a heavy breath and follows her orders. His body settles into the chair. Behind him, Ellie leans herself against a windowsill.

"How's she doing?" Ellie asks.

In the bed, Bunny is still asleep. The skin on her face appears as thin and crinkly as old paper. Her chest rises and falls, but the movements look shallow.

"Her fever's come down a little bit," Frank answers, and adjusts her blankets. "She'll be all right." He gently pats her black-and-blue hand. "She's a tough cookie."

In the hallway, a group of nurses walk past, talking. Ellie can over-hear from the pieces of their conversation that float into the room that their shift has ended.

"What happened, Dad?" she asks. "Why did Mom show up on my porch the way she did on Monday?"

Frank's lips settle into a subtle, downward slope, not quite a frown, but close. "I knew she wasn't going to leave, Ellie," he says. "Not really. Not for long." He adjusts his posture. "That's why I was so shocked—so hurt—that day in church." All around them, the machines spit out a symphony of white noise. "I didn't believe she'd ever really go through with it. I just went along with things because I knew—I thought—she just needed time to process some stuff."

"Like what, Dad?" Ellie asks, confused. "What did she need to process?"

"The truth, Ellie," Frank begins, "is that your mother has been in horrible grief for a while now."

"Grief?" Ellie poses.

He sighs. As he does, Ellie wonders if maybe this is why the air in these places feels so stale. It's all the heavy emotions people here are constantly expelling.

"Your mother just . . . saw a different life for you, I think," he states. "Before you even say it, I know what you're thinking," he continues, even though Ellie herself isn't quite sure of what's happening inside her head. "You girls these days, you can *do* anything. You can *be* anything. And you should," he insists and then points one long, crooked finger in the air to prove he means it. "You *should* have every choice available to you and have the whole world at your fingertips." He stops himself for a second, considering his ideas. "But sometimes, Ellie, I think your mother feels that people get all wrapped up in the notion that their life has to be so big, so earth shattering, that they forget how significant a simple and quiet life can be, too. How meaningful love and commitment are in such an unpredictable world." Frank exhales through his nose. "To your mother, marriage is the most important thing out there, which is more or less how I knew that, no matter what, she wouldn't go through with any split between us." His chest rises and falls. "Maybe her sentiments are old fashioned." He shrugs. "Maybe not."

Beneath Frank's soft touch, Ellie sees her mother's fingers start to move. She wonders if Bunny can hear him, which of the two women in this hospital room his message is truly intended for.

"Marriage isn't for everyone," Frank acknowledges. "It's hard. And it takes a lot of work. More work and fine-tuning than most people can imagine."

"Then why do it, Dad?" she asks, genuinely wanting to know. "Why get married? Why *stay* married? If a person can have or be anything, why choose that? Especially if it's so difficult?"

Frank softly squeezes Bunny's hand. As he does, one of her machines releases a different beep. Something inside her has shifted. Ellie considers if it's the pure and simple fact that she feels her husband here with her.

"Because in a world where everything is always changing, sweetheart," Frank says, "where nothing is certain, sometimes it's nice to have at least one thing that feels constant. To know that wherever you are in life, wherever your journey might take you, when you have this other person at your side, you'll always feel like you're at home."

~

On her walk back to Jonah's room, Ellie sees that one of the small hospital cafés is open. She has no idea of the time, only the fact that it is so late that it has become early again. She buys herself a coffee and takes a seat at a table.

"Mind if I join you?" a familiar voice asks from behind her.

She turns to peer over her shoulder and finds Jack in his white medical coat. Ellie gestures at the empty seat across from her. "I'd say I'm surprised to see you here, but . . ."

Jack sits. His peridot eyes land on his tan coffee. He takes a sip, looks up, and meets Ellie's gaze. "I saw your mother's name come up in the system when I checked in for my shift."

Ellie feels her body pull forward, inching across the table, desperate to know what secrets he's read. "And?"

"She'll be all right, Ellie," he assures her. "I popped into her room a little bit ago and checked on her. She'll likely need to stay for a few days so they can make sure her sodium levels remain balanced, that she doesn't get dehydrated or anything like that. But she'll be okay."

A rush of relief pulsates through her.

"It looks like you've had a tough night yourself," Jack points out, nodding at the gauze on her forehead. "I saw your name when I logged in, too."

Her hands are wrapped around the paper cup so she can feel a bit of warmth in this cold place. "I was in an accident earlier," she explains. Jack's blond eyebrows lift in question. "With—with my friend," she offers. "He's upstairs. He's—not doing so great."

"What's his name? I'll check on him for you."

"Baker," she says. The name she knows is meant to belong to her, too. "Jonah Baker."

Jack drops his head toward one shoulder. "Your friend?" he questions, clearly reading some message that's written all over her face. "From yesterday?"

Her eyes close, like curtains. "It's so . . ."

"Complicated," Jack adds, completing her thought.

Ellie's eyelids part back open. "Yes," she agrees.

Jack takes another sip of his coffee. He spots someone beyond Ellie's shoulder—a colleague?—and waves. "You'll never believe who I ran into after I saw you yesterday."

"Hmm?" she questions, as if she does not already know.

"Kristin," he says, his lips trapped somewhere between a smile and a frown.

"And?"

His shoulders rise as he inhales. A moment passes before he lets it all back out again. "We had a cup of coffee," he explains. "We talked a little." He sighs again. "We can just never get our timing right together, though." His face shifts, and he looks at some indefinable spot on the ceiling. "It turns out she just got out of a relationship this week."

"I'm sorry about that," she states.

He flips his hands upward. "What can you do?"

Outside the café's windows, the shades of darkness in the sky are starting to slowly change. Midnight. Navy. Denim. There's no light yet, but it's coming.

"Do you ever wonder, Jack, what might have happened if we never dated?" She lets herself laugh a little. "Or if we never dated again, I guess."

Nearby, a few more hospital employees stroll in, ready for this new day and whatever traumas await them to begin.

"I have sometimes," he admits. He delays the next part, his chest moving fluidly beneath his white coat. "I hope you won't take this personally," he says, and she nods to communicate to him that whatever he's about to tell her is okay. "It's just, sometimes I've wondered if I made the wrong choice. If I should have gone rushing to her back then, moved home instead of staying here. If maybe we would have gotten married, had kids, made a whole life for ourselves together, you know?"

"I do."

He shakes his head at himself. "I don't know. It's my own fault. My parents got divorced when I was a kid, and, well, I guess I've been a little funny about commitments and relationships ever since then," he admits. He smiles at a different colleague.

"I didn't know that about you," she admits. "You never once told me that in all the months we dated. Not that I can remember, at least."

Jack's cheekbones rise in a smile. "It's hard when you're young to talk about hard things," he explains. "It's hard to talk about hard things when you're old, too, but here we are," he says, and they both laugh. "Anyway, my dad was a great guy. He just—he made some mistakes along the way."

"Was?" Ellie echoes, pointing out Jack's use of the past tense.

Jack wraps his hands around his carry-out mug. Maybe he's looking for a source of warmth, too. "He died a few years ago," he explains.

"I'm sorry."

"It's okay," Jack says, even though, of course, it's not. He takes one final sip. "Anyway, whoever knows what's possible when it comes to love, right? Maybe it'll still happen one day. It'd certainly make my mother happy." He laughs again, thinking of this woman—his mother—who, in the time they spent together in their younger years, Ellie never once met. "No matter how successful I am in my career, all she ever asks is, 'Johnnie, have you met a nice girl yet?'"

Ellie's face scrunches into the shape of a question. "Johnnie?"

He chuckles. "Right. It's this silly Irish Catholic thing," he explains. "I have absolutely no clue why, but if you're an Irish American kid and your first name is John, at a certain point in your childhood, everyone just starts calling you Jack." A corner of his mouth lifts. "Well, everyone except for my mother." He waves a hand. "Shelia," he says. "She's a real hoot."

The pieces all fall in front of Ellie like dominoes. The cream puffs. The trace of a New York accent. "Shelia," Ellie echoes. "Your mom." In any given instant, the world can feel both infinitely vast and comfortably small. "And where is she now?"

"Probably at home, looking at some dating app for me," he jokes. "She still lives in Westchester," he explains. "She always said she'd eventually retire to someplace warm, but she never did." He shakes his head. "I guess she wanted to stay up north, so I wasn't alone, even though we live an hour from each other." He smiles. "Who knows? Moms, right?"

"Right." Ellie stuffs a paper napkin into her empty cup.

But she'll get there, Ellie thinks to herself. *Which means you must have gotten yourself somewhere good, too.*

"Speaking of which," Ellie says, "I'd better get back. Not that I know which room to check in on first."

Jack nods his empathy. "I promise I'll keep an eye on both of them for you, Ellie."

"Thank you." Out in the hallway, more people begin to appear, the quiet shuffle of feet on cold, hard flooring. "What time is it?" Ellie asks.

Jack flips his wrist to look at his watch. "A little after four," he says. "Still a bit of a stretch before the sun rises."

She pushes out her chair and stands. "It was nice running into you these last few days, Jack."

He smiles. "It was nice running into you, too, Ellie." He pauses, processing a thought. "Not literally, though," he says with a laugh. "We probably could have done without that little fender bender, huh?" He rubs his temple, a physical sign that he still feels terrible about this event. "I'll get on the phone with my insurance company on Monday," he assures her. "We'll get it all squared away. Okay?"

She nods. "Okay."

Outside the window, the sky remains mostly dark, though some new hues begin to yawn themselves to life.

"Take it easy, Jack," Ellie says and then takes a step.

"Thanks, Ellie," he says. "You too."

THIRTY

Jonah is alone in his hospital bed. His eyes are still closed, every imaginable cord and tube attached to him. The machines around him hum and beep, a whole electronic language that they speak to each other to communicate what's happening inside of him.

After she left Jack in the café, Ellie walked back to Bunny's room to check on her but saw that both her parents were fast asleep. Frank was still in his chair. Bunny was still in her hospital bed. They weren't in the place they should have been—not as far as Ellie could see it—but they were together, and to her, their only daughter, that felt like something, at least.

Beep. Beep. Beep.

How, she wonders, have they traveled this far? How did they go from that night in their bedroom with the laundry and that single word she'd said and ultimately found themselves here?

Her head and her back and her entire body aching, she lets herself sit beside him. His hand is like a pincushion to a dozen different needles. She weaves her fingers into his, the feel of his skin comforting and warm.

"I'm so sorry, Jo," she whispers. "I'm so sorry for everything."

Knock, knock.

A nurse in the doorway. "Hi," she says. "I'm sorry, but there aren't really supposed to be visitors overnight in this wing."

Ellie pulls in a significant breath. She waits a moment—a long one—before she asks: "He's not doing well, is he?"

The nurse pauses. "No," she finally admits. "He's not." Machines beep around them, a sad, terrible song. "Are you his . . ." The woman trails off, giving Ellie the space to answer.

But what should she say? Love is so hard to explain or define. The titles we give to it, what do they even really mean? If you add a certain one, does it really change the way you feel about a person? If you take it away, do your feelings really go away, too?

Love is not built on titles. Not on legal documents or diamond rings. It is built on the stories you create with a person. All those shared moments that ultimately turn into memories.

Do you remember when . . .

Remember that time we . . .

"Can I please have a few more minutes with him?" Ellie asks, the desperation in her voice not doing a thing to hide from itself. "And then I promise I'll leave."

The nurse takes a deep breath and looks over both her shoulders. An expression of empathy transforms her face. She's been in love before. Ellie can see it. "Five minutes," the woman agrees. "Okay?"

Ellie nods and watches her step into the hallway. She thinks back to a few nights ago, down in Florida, and the words her mother said.

You two made a vow to each other, Ellie. Until death do you part.

Now, Ellie wonders if maybe they have, in their own way, stayed true to that vow. The two of them here right until the bitter end.

For so long, Ellie has wondered if in order to find happiness again, she must choose between her family and herself. One or the other. Either or.

What do you want, Ellie? What do you want?

Although impossible, it's as if she can hear him ask.

"I'd still do it all again, too, Jo," she whispers, their hands laced together. "Even now. Even knowing how it all ends."

Outside the room's single window, faint streaks of yellow daylight off in the far distance begin to mix with ebony. It's not quite night anymore, and yet it isn't morning, either. It's some hard-to-define in-between time. Not yet tomorrow, and not quite yesterday.

"I'll see you soon, Jo," Ellie says as a form of goodbye. "I don't know where or when. But I know I will."

Ellie stands to leave, taking one more look through the window and not having a clue what this new day might bring. Before she exits his room, she peers back, as if when she turns around she might see something else other than the current scene.

For a moment so brief it's as though it doesn't even happen, she closes her eyes. Ellie doesn't know the specific minute or hour. These last few days, it's felt as if these concepts do not really exist. But it doesn't matter. Certain habits, she now understands, are impossible to break.

This time, she knows exactly what she's wishing for, even though it seems improbable.

She doesn't care.

Ellie allows herself to wish for it anyway.

PART FOUR

The Return Flight

THIRTY-ONE

Ellie wakes up in bed alone. Though "wake up" is a generous phrase. She's hardly slept, more just tossed and turned with anxiety before her body finally shut down and then forced—for a few uninterrupted minutes, tops—her mind into a kind of dream state.

She keeps her eyes closed for a long time, not ready to know what unwanted surprises this new day will bring to her. It's been one week since she and Jonah left this house together, put their travel gear in their respective car trunks, and drove to the airport to officially begin the process of disassembling their shared life. Right now, her body aching in every imaginable way, it feels like so much longer than only a few days. More like an entire lifetime.

The bed linens are soft, comfortable, familiar. In an alternate reality, she'd stay here and allow herself to rest for a few more hours. But not today. She needs to get herself up, get back to the hospital, check in, and see what's transpired since she left. She's not sure she's ready for all of it.

Finally, Ellie's eyes part themselves open. She pulls herself up, brushes a strand of hair away from her face, and adjusts her matching pajama set. The house is silent—no one, she knows, is here anymore—as Ellie stands and moves toward the bathroom. She turns on the shower, allowing the room to fill with steam, disrobes, and then steps in. The hot water hits every part of her. The top of her head. Her face. Her aching shoulders. The delicate skin of her chest. Her throbbing back. She lathers herself in scented bubbles, but they do nothing to help her feel better or fresh in any way. *I can't do this,* Ellie decides, a shampoo bottle dropping from her hand as she allows her body—fire-engine red from the heat—to slide down the tiles. *I can't face this day.*

She sits on the floor of her shower, the hot water still running over her, so determined to cleanse her of everything. The water swirls itself into the metal drain. If her life were a book, she knows this scene would serve as a symbolic form of rebirth. But her life is not a work of fiction. It is not a story someone else has penned. Right now, all the most important pieces of it shattered, she knows it is not anything. Not anymore. She closes her eyes again. A guttural sob escapes her. All by herself, she cries hard and loud, the burning water trying its best to wash these emotions away.

A few minutes later, the water starting to cool, she pulls herself up, twists the faucet handle, and steps out. She wraps herself in a thick white towel and pauses at the sink, trying to gain some strength. This is when it occurs to her, this most obvious detail that, in her current state, she hadn't even noticed or considered: her windowless bathroom is flooded with light.

Ellie blinks, like she's imagining it, and then flicks the light switch. The power—finally, miraculously—is back. A small victory in a week of losses.

In her bedroom, she clicks on the overhead lighting and gets herself dressed in her daily uniform. Jeans. A clean white shirt. Her favorite low-top tennis sneakers. A comfortable cardigan, which she folds into her book bag. All neutral, familiar choices, so that she's ready for wherever this dreaded day decides to take her.

Downstairs, Ellie brews herself a pot of coffee, knowing she needs the caffeine. While the machine bubbles itself into action, Ellie moves over to the stove, its digital clock still blinking 11:11, just like it has been all week. She presses a button so she can reset the time but realizes she doesn't know it. The coffee machine beeps. She leaves the clock alone and allows it to continue to blink and blink and blink.

Her steaming mug in her hand, she takes a seat at the table. The early-morning sun, as yellow as butter, has begun to pour into the room. She sips her coffee, her eyes glazing over all the seats around her. One for Maggie. One for Jonah. One for each of her parents. They're all empty. It's just Ellie.

Knock, knock, knock.

Until now. Now, someone is on the porch once again. Some unsolicited surprise waiting for her on the other side of her door. Ellie sets down her mug and closes her eyes. She allows herself to breathe—*in, out, in*—for a long minute, unsure if the best strategy is for her to hide or to stand up and face it.

She twists open the dead bolt and then slowly—so slowly it's as if she isn't even really moving—opens the door. At the edges of her vision, her porch looks the same as always. The charming bench swing. The blooming springtime floral planters. The WELCOME HOME doormat. There is only one thing that has changed.

"You locked me out," Jonah says. He wears a pair of medium-wash denim, a nice cut for his age and stature, and a fresh salmon-colored T-shirt. His chestnut-and-silver hair looks damp and is neatly combed away from his cleanly shaven face.

Ellie doesn't speak. She can't. Her bottom lip falls away from her top, like a leaf from a tree. No words come out. It doesn't matter, though. Even if they did, she knows none of them would be quite right. She doesn't want to talk. She wants to launch herself at him, to feel him and know he is real. But she restrains herself. After the last few days, she's not sure what she believes yet.

"You're—you're here," she finally—cautiously—manages to say. "Y-y-you're okay." Her tone hovers somewhere between a statement and a question. Slowly, Ellie raises one hand and cups it against Jonah's smooth cheek, his skin warm with life. "You came home."

A memory. The first night her parents officially lived in Florida, Ellie broke. She wanted to be happy for them—and she was, of course, deep down past the pain of it—but a piece of her, an important one, felt off, like she'd walked outside and forgotten to put on pants. Something was missing. She'd held it together all day—so grateful for the home her parents had bequeathed to her—calling them several times, laughing through the line to prove she was okay. But by the time evening rolled in and Maggie was asleep, she could no longer keep it all in.

She snapped at Jonah while she was washing the dishes, her despair over the feeling that her family was changing—that two people she loved so dearly were too far away for her to physically reach—ran so deeply through her that her hands were shaking. A dinner plate slipped from her soapy hands and smashed on the floor. Jonah didn't say a word as Ellie continued to shout at him for no real reason. He didn't say a word, either, when, a few seconds later, he reached for his keys and walked through the front door.

For the next twenty minutes, Ellie's whole world grew black with panic. She believed he was gone, that she'd sent him away. When he walked back through the door a short while later holding a small brown bag, her mind spun with confusion. "Where did you go?" she sniffled, her tears not yet fully dried up. She was seated on the checkered kitchen floor, her back pressed against the cabinets. "I—I thought you left."

Jonah's eyes widened. His brows lifted themselves up toward the ceiling. "Left?" He handed her the bag. From inside it, she pulled out a pint of her favorite ice cream. "Where would I go?" He opened the utensil drawer, which was only half-full. The house was still so new to them. They hadn't even fully unpacked. "This is my home, Ellie," he said as he handed her a spoon. She removed the lid and indulged in a rich, chocolatey bite, right as Jonah sat down beside her, the two of them shoulder to shoulder on the black-and-white tiles. "Where else would I go?" he asked, taking the spoon. "Where would I want to be if not right here with you?"

In the present, her hand still lingering on his cheek, Jonah stares at Ellie with a quizzical expression. "Of course I'm back. I only ran out to pick these up," he explains, producing a pack of batteries from his pocket. "I wanted to change them before we leave. Otherwise the beeping from the carbon monoxide detectors will drive you nuts next week."

Beyond Jonah's wide shoulder, Ellie observes the power lines, all properly strung back up to the wooden poles that connect them. Her favorite tree—the magnificent oak that for decades has grown on her family's front lawn—its branches dressed up in bright-green leaves—stands tall. Ellie lowers her hand and glides away from the porch like a ghost, her feet moving through the grass, still damp with morning dew. She touches her fingers to the bark and traces the letters carved in the wide trunk: *B-a-k-e-r*. When she does, the light from the sun—newly risen—catches on her wedding band, the one that inexplicably hugs her ring finger.

Back on the porch, Jonah—healthy, vibrant Jonah—stands and watches her. "It'll only take a minute to change the batteries," he notes, a curious look on his face. "When I'm done, we should probably get on the road," he adds, then turns toward the door.

Ellie looks over at the driveway, where their unscuffed cars are parked in a neat line, their luggage obediently standing upright, before she redirects her full attention back at him.

Does she try to explain what has happened, even though doing so would make her sound unhinged? Does she tell him she's realized this is all a big mistake? They made this choice together. But Ellie initiated it. It was her doing. And now, she recognizes, it's her job to fix it.

"Jonah, wait!" She swallows hard, chokes down a tear so nothing can block the words she wants to get out now. "Why haven't you told me you don't want this?" she asks, the question she's privately held inside for too long. "Why haven't you outright said you think this is all a mistake?"

He turns, then lifts a hand and squeezes the back of his neck. "I—I don't know." Jonah looks down at his feet, then lifts his gaze again. "At first, I thought you just needed space to process things." Nearby, a car backs out of a neighboring driveway. "To be honest," Jonah continues, "I never actually thought any of this would have gone on for so long."

Marriage is so hard. It's just a bet you make on your heart. When you recite those vows—regardless of the specific words a couple chooses to exchange—you create a promise so big you could never possibly try to carry the weight of it in your arms. Which is why, Ellie supposes now, you're meant to carry it with the help of someone else.

"What if we don't tell them?" Ellie proposes and takes one step forward. "What if we just say we were desperate for an impromptu visit, a chance for us all to be together for a few days?"

"Ellie—" He closes his eyes, sighs, and shakes his head before he reopens them. "Wh-where is all this coming from?"

"It's hard to explain," she says. "I've just had a lot of time to think the last few days."

He runs his hands through his hair. "Ellie, you've been saying—"

"I know," she interrupts. "And I was wrong." A new feeling of desperation comes over her, the situation suddenly so clear it's like she's opening her eyes and seeing the world for the first time. "But think of everything we've been through. The history we've built. Our home. Our whole life." She moves up the porch steps. "I'm sorry I put us through this," Ellie admits and then touches his face once more. "I'm sorry about all the choices I made that led us here."

Jonah's lips and eyes narrow. His face is both full of emotion and void of it. Ellie doesn't know what will come next. "I'm sorry, too," he finally tells her. "You aren't the only one whose choices got us here." He brushes a strand of hair from her face. "I made choices along the way, same as you."

Ellie allows her cheek to fall against his chest. Inside him, she hears the even drumming of his heart as it beats and beats. "So what do we do now?"

All around them, the world is scented with spring, the air a perfumed blend of freshness and flowers and life. Suddenly, everything familiar also feels new.

"It's up to you, Ellie," Jonah says, his chin propped on her head. "What do you want?"

There are so many ways for her to answer. Yet just one answer is true. "I want to go. With you," she clarifies. "I want us all to be together right now."

Jonah gently pulls away from her, checks the time. "Well, in that case, we'd better get moving," he notes and glances back at the house. "Is there anything else you need to do before we leave?" he asks, a direct question, but also an open-ended one.

Ellie's eyes settle on the curves of his face. "No." She inhales, taking it all in. This life. This setting. "There's nothing else I need to do." For the first time in a long time, she sees all of it. "I'm ready now."

THIRTY-TWO

"I already checked us both in."

Ellie, who returns from a newsstand with a bottle of water, finds Jonah standing beside one of the airline's many stand-alone kiosks, his sleek, hard-shell carry-on positioned at his side.

"Your boarding pass should have gotten sent to your phone," he continues.

Oh God.

"What?" Jonah notes the expression of worry—confusion?—on Ellie's face. "What is it?"

"My phone," Ellie says, not knowing how to explain things. "I—um—I think I forgot it."

Jonah blows a heavy breath through his lips. He quickly glances up at the departures board. "I—I don't think you have time to go home and get it."

"It's fine," Ellie decides, because what else is she supposed to do? She can't travel back through time—or forward, even—to find it. "I'll ask for a paper boarding pass. I'll make do."

Jonah nods firmly and offers Ellie a smile—*You okay?* She nods back—*I'm fine*—before they turn and glide past the other travelers—families with small children strapped into strollers, their tiny bodies still half-asleep, the business travelers, all sharply dressed, who've been forced to jet off to places they don't want to be—and then approach the airline counter. Brenda still stands behind it in her two-piece navy-blue skirt-suit, a pair of wings pinned to her chest.

"IDs?" she says, already hoisting Ellie's suitcase onto her giant scale.

Jonah slides his leather wallet from his pants pocket, hands Brenda his driver's license. Beside him, Ellie pulls her book bag from her back and digs out her own wallet, already knowing what she'll find inside it. She doesn't even look, just hands the ID over. It's too much to even try to comprehend.

Brenda stabs her fingers across her computer keyboard, hands them each a printed-out boarding pass. "Enjoy your flight, Mr. and Mrs. Baker," she says.

$\sim$

Ellie and Jonah sit side by side at their gate. Despite their early-morning departure time, their flight, she can already see, will be packed. Everyone wants to get away ahead of the weekend, to land at their chosen destination early enough for them to actually take full advantage of the day. Beside her, Jonah reads some news articles on his phone, checks a few sports scores, and skims his email. Ellie, on the other hand, doesn't know what to do. Should she ask him if he remembers? If he recalls what happened last night or in the nights that have led them here?

"Good morning, ladies and gentlemen on flight 1251, with direct service from Newark to Orlando," a voice announces overhead. Nearby, other travelers—all of them anxious to find their seats and get settled— start to stand and collect their things. "It is my pleasure, on behalf of our whole flight crew, to welcome you. In a moment, we'll begin our boarding process, starting with group one passengers, active military members, and any families traveling with small children."

Opposite the wall of glass that separates the gate area from the tarmac, Ellie sees their plane and the clear blue sky in the backdrop beyond it. She rubs her thumb over her ring—the metal cool and smooth and familiar. Airports, she privately acknowledges, are unique places. Here, every minute matters. If you make a choice and turn up one moment later than intended, the door closes, the path you believed you were about to travel nixed, just like that.

"I'm going to use the bathroom before we board," Ellie announces. Jonah, who's still seated, nods. She gestures to her chair with her chin. "Do you mind watching my bag?"

Ellie moves past the snack kiosks and joins the winding line of other women. They inch forward—why does this always take so long?—and eventually arrive at the crowded room of stalls. Behind Ellie, a young mother and her daughter wait, too. The little girl, whom Ellie suspects is of preschool age, bounces up and down like her feet are made of trampolines.

"I'm going to burst, Mama!" the child exclaims. She and her mother wear matching T-shirts. *Vacation Mode!*

Ellie, who is next in line, turns to face them. She sees the look of panic on the mother's face. *Oh God, please hold it in, baby. I don't remember if I packed your backup pants or if I left them home on the bed. I'm always forgetting something lately. Please hold it. Please, someone, help me. Please, please, please.*

"You two go first," Ellie tells them and points to the end of the line of identical stalls. "There. One just opened."

"Are you sure?" the mother asks, already pushing her daughter forward through the crowd. "I'm so sorry." *Potty training isn't working. I've given her a thousand M&M'S, and still, nothing. What am I doing wrong? Is she okay? Am I doing all this okay?*

"Absolutely," Ellie assures her, nudging them on their way.

A minute later, Ellie locks herself into the stall next to them. She uses the restroom and laughs to herself, watching the little girl's feet dancing and wiggling and spinning in circles on the floor next to her while her poor mother simply tries to pee. *You'll miss those little feet one day,* Ellie thinks to herself as she exits. *You'll hate all that privacy.*

Up ahead, a bank of communal sinks. Ellie washes her hands beneath the too-hot water and takes a peek at herself in the mirror. She looks the same, like regular old Ellie. A few simple sweeps of makeup. Her professionally dyed honey hair hanging in two straight curtains around her face. And yet, here in this reflection, there are so many versions of herself she sees. The recent college graduate, so unsure of everything and just hoping to eventually find her way. The blushing bride, her heart pumping to the rhythm of her own love song. The new mother, with the bags beneath her eyes and the smile as bright as neon.

"Thanks again," a voice says.

Ellie turns and sees the other mother beside her, her daughter humming the ABC's as she washes her hands. "No problem." Ellie's heart warms for this woman who reminds her so much of another version of herself, one who exists in a different time. "I remember those days." Ellie turns away from them, reaches for some paper towels, and dries her hands.

"Here," the woman says from behind her. "I think you forgot this. It was up on the ledge."

When she turns back around, the woman holds Ellie's phone in her hand, the one she herself was apparently too distracted to notice as she studied her reflection. Ellie takes it, noting that it's not only somehow still here, but still turned on. A photo—an old favorite—of her, Jonah, and Maggie stares back at her from the screen.

Once outside the bathroom, Ellie swipes the device open, unsure what else she'll find on it. The airport Wi-Fi is terrible—only a single bar—but it's enough. She taps open her message history with Maggie, and then her history with Bunny, curious to see if their last correspondences—the ones Ellie sent to them when she landed here on Sunday night—are somehow there. But they're not. Of course they're not. Those conversations, Ellie understands, have not happened yet.

"You found it?" Jonah asks when Ellie reappears beside him and gestures at her hand.

"Oh—oh yeah," she stammers, still fruitlessly trying to wrap her head around it. "I, uh—I forgot to tell you before that I found it earlier at the bottom of my bag."

Jonah nods. There's no reason for him to question this response.

All around them, the seats have emptied. The majority of other travelers heading to their destination have gone ahead.

"At this time, we invite all remaining passengers on flight 1251, with direct service from Newark to Orlando, to begin the boarding process," a member of the flight crew announces through the overhead speakers.

Jonah stands and hands Ellie her book bag, which he's kept guard over during her absence. He snaps up the handle of his wheeled carry-on as she slides it on. Together, they step into line and show their tickets—their proof that they belong here—to the female flight crew member. The woman briefly looks down at the items they've provided to her, then back up at their faces, double-checking that it's really them. She pauses for a second that feels too long. Ellie's heart thumps in her chest. *Oh please, God,* she thinks. *Not again.*

"Here you go." The woman hands everything back to them—her acknowledgment that they're who they say, and that they're in the right place and time.

"Looks like a nice morning for flying," Jonah—a lover of small talk—says before they disappear into the accordion passenger bridge. He points to the window and the canvas of clear, cornflower-blue sky.

"From what I can tell"—the woman nods and waves another passenger ahead—"it should be a smooth flight."

THIRTY-THREE

E llie?"

Her head snaps up with a jolt before her eyes have even opened. She gasps for breath—a fish on shore—temporarily forgetting her whereabouts and wondering if the whole morning has only existed in her mind. Her eyelids part. Slowly, the scene comes into focus. The shape of the seats in front of her. The flight attendant breezing through the narrow aisle. And beside her: Jonah.

"Are you all right?" he asks, a trace of concern evident in his voice. All around them, the world is white noise. The sound of air rushing past. The low murmur of voices. The gentle hum of electronic parts. Ellie rubs her eyes, taking it in. "You never sleep on flights," he points out.

Ellie straightens her posture, blinks herself awake. She has her cardigan on, a soft and familiar layer of comfort while she finally let herself rest. "I'm all right," she decides. Outside the porthole-like window beside Jonah, the clouds have disappeared, and the world has begun to present itself again. Everything appears in miniature. Tiny houses. A tapestry of land. Threads of black roadway. "What time is it?" Ellie asks, unsure if she's been asleep for minutes or hours, if they're in the midst of departing or landing. It's so hard sometimes to determine if what you're looking at is the beginning or the end of something.

Jonah offers a soft chuckle. "You've been asleep for a while," he tells her and gingerly taps the glass. "Look." Together, they both peer through the window at the hot, tropical landscape that waits for them. "See?" He smiles. "You slept through the worst part of things," he notes. "We're almost there."

~

The minute they step off the plane and into the passenger bridge that leads them inside, Ellie feels the heat. Even though it's early—still morning for all intents and purposes, though she's already been awake and moving for hours—the humidity is thick. She doesn't need a mirror to know her hair, which was smooth and neatly brushed when she boarded their flight, is a catastrophe of frizz. She doesn't care. Her focus right now is exclusively on Jonah, who walks several paces ahead, his head of thick hair bobbing through the crowd like a stylish buoy.

"Jonah, stop!" she shouts out, surprising herself as well as everyone else who navigates this corridor. All around her, a handful of passersby look on, not sure if this woman they see and hear is about to make a scene. "Please."

Up ahead, Jonah turns, his feet—just seconds ago moving swiftly—locked momentarily in place. Outside the glass, a plane pulls away from its gate, all those souls on board it ready and waiting to arrive someplace new.

She needs to ask him. To know that this day is real.

"Tell me everything you remember," she says.

Jonah squints, unsure of what she means. From outside, the bold sun and the relentless heat radiate through the glass.

"About the last few days." She shifts her weight from one foot to the other in her leather sandals, which she slid into before they left. "About everything that got us here."

Jonah tugs the sturdy handle of his carry-on, the luggage obediently spinning to a stop at his side. "What do you mean, Ellie?"

Nearby, dozens of other travelers—all of them happy to have their feet back on the ground after speeding through the clouds from whatever place they came—zip past. Time is important here. Every minute and small choice counts. They can't wait and watch.

"I—I don't know," Ellie admits, suddenly doubting herself. Close to them, two young children, dressed in the vacation gear typical to this place, run past—both of them screaming and laughing (much to their mother's audible annoyance) as they wrestle each other onto the public space's teal-patterned carpet. "You really don't remember?"

"Remember what?" Jonah asks.

Overhead, an announcement pipes through the airport's speaker system. A traveler on another flight is running late. The main cabin door on his aircraft is about to close, whatever destiny awaited him in his chosen destination now on a final countdown.

"This week," Ellie says. "And, you know, anything . . . funny?"

"Funny?" Jonah questions. "No, not that I can think of." He smiles. It's clear he's telling the truth. This chapter, she understands, is closed.

Jonah steps forward, wheeling his carry-on at his side. He lifts his arms and begins to wrap them around Ellie in an embrace, though his movements are far from smooth. He can't find a place to comfortably position himself because of her backpack. He pulls away and laughs.

"What?"

"Your bag," he says, already sliding it off her. "Give me that."

Ellie's shoulders instantly settle, relieved by this new absence of weight, this sudden feeling of lightness. She smiles and watches him slide the pack onto his own back.

"I should have offered to help you with it anyway."

"This is the final boarding call—I repeat, the final boarding call—for passengers on flight 1180 with direct service to Los Angeles," a voice announces through the speaker system. "Please procced to gate four immediately."

Jonah circles his arms around Ellie's body. "So, what made you ask me that?" He kisses her forehead. "What stories are you spinning in your head?"

"None," she says, holding him just a bit tighter. "None at all."

They stay like this for a minute, a sea of other travelers parting around them.

"Well, in that case, what do you say?" He pulls back to meet her face. "Coffee?"

Ellie smiles, though really it's more of a grin. "Absolutely."

~

"Maggie!"

Ellie and Jonah yell out her name in tandem. She stands near the baggage carousel, nibbling on some dehydrated something. She's so brilliant, like a perfect work of art. Her glossy, sandy-brown hair hangs loosely down her narrow back. This time, Ellie is not the only one who sprints across the airport's shiny terrazzo floor to get to her.

"Oh, Maggie." Ellie burrows her face in her daughter's hair as Jonah stands beside them. But already, Ellie feels her daughter pulling back. She mentally prepares herself, ready to be scolded for this public display of affection.

"Dad?" Maggie adjusts the patchwork bag that hangs limply from her shoulder. "Are you—are you crying?"

"Hmm?" Jonah dabs his eyes. "No, no. It's from my coffee." He nods at the cup in his hand. "I, uh—I just took a really hot sip."

"It's cold brew, Dad," Maggie points out. She turns to her mother, gives her a look, and then playfully rolls her eyes. Ellie smiles and laughs, grateful for this brief moment of solidarity between them. "You're in Florida," she points out. "You never drink hot coffee here."

"Right." Jonah indulges an icy mouthful. "Come here, kiddo." With one arm, he pulls Maggie in for a hug, wrapping his free arm around Ellie. "I missed you girls."

From the corner of Ellie's eye, she sees a man positioned near the baggage claim's wall of automated glass doors. She recognizes him immediately: the slightly wrinkled dress shirt, the loose slacks. And, of course, his sign. THE BAKER FAMILY, it reads.

Jonah sees it, too. "That's us!" he shouts at the man. "We just need a minute!"

Together, their bodies form a tight little triangle right in the middle of this public space. All around them, other travelers hustle to grab their luggage and hurry off on their way to wherever it is that they're heading. But not them. Not just yet.

Nearby, the doors open and then close and then open again.

Still, they stay put.

Right now, this moment feels like their real destination.

In so many ways, regardless of what is stamped on their respective tickets, it is the only place where they've hoped to arrive.

THIRTY-FOUR

"Frank! Get out here, Frank. They're here!"

Bunny stands at the edge of the terra-cotta-colored walkway that leads to the front door of the condo—the exact place where she and Frank are meant to be. She's waving a dish towel above her head, which she's accessorized with her favorite visor (*Florida!*) and her bright-as-the-tropical-sun shirt. These things suit her here. The dark clothes she once wore are gone now, just a relic from another time. She doesn't need them. In this life—the right one—Bunny isn't busy grieving anything anymore.

"Oh, Jesus, Mary, and Joseph!" Bunny—her face noticeably sun kissed and brightened by creamy coral streaks—proclaims as Frank saunters up beside her in his favorite tourist T-shirt. They both have their drugstore readers predictably perched on the tips of their noses. "You're taking forever!" She grabs his phone from his hands, which he's been fumbling around like a football. "Give me that." Bunny pushes her glasses closer to her eyes, even though they're not intended for tasks like this. "I don't want to miss a chance for a good picture!"

Nearby, Jonah pulls all the luggage from the trunk and settles up with the driver. Ellie and Maggie both take hold of their respective suitcase handles and drag them—*clunk, clunk, clunk*—against the steaming black pavement. The sweat drips down Ellie's back as if her spine is a waterslide. Already, her T-shirt is soaking wet.

"Everyone stop!" Bunny begs and holds up the camera. "I want to take this before you all come inside!"

"It's so hot," Maggie mumbles, droplets of perspiration collecting in the delicate concaves above her collarbones. "Do we really have to—"

"Just smile, Mags," Ellie suggests, though her tone is kind. She reaches down and takes her daughter's hand. Maggie lets her. "Who knows? Maybe it'll make you happy to look back on a picture like this one day."

"Perfect," Bunny announces as Jonah wheels his carry-on up beside Ellie and Maggie, striking a casual pose. Behind them, all along the perimeter of the parking lot, a dozen or so slender palm trees reach up toward the clear, blue sky. "That's just perfect."

~

"Into the living room!" Bunny, like always, herds everyone onto the couches. On the television, an old rerun airs on the Game Show Network, same as it did the last time (and the time before that . . . and that . . . and that) they were all here.

Ellie, still standing, leans against the sofa's armrest. On the screen, she notes the familiar stage set from *Let's Make a Deal*, which consists of three large doors, each contestant forced to choose to see what's behind just one of them.

She turns to walk away, leaving Jonah, Maggie, and Frank to watch which destiny the contestant has picked. In the kitchen, she joins Bunny, who's busy putting the final touches on her deli meat tray.

"What are you doing?" Bunny snaps when she notices Ellie peering inside the fridge. "I have everything right here."

Ellie closes the door, a bag of baby carrots and a head of celery in her hands. "It's for Maggie," she explains. In the other room, she hears that the contestant has selected door number three. "She's just . . . choosing to explore some new sides to herself."

Bunny peers at her daughter over the top of her reading glasses, which slide down her nose. "She's exploring herself by way of the crisper drawer?" But Bunny doesn't give Ellie a chance to respond. Already, she's waving a hand, asking for the items. "Lord, I don't need to know. Just give me those. Let's at least put them out on a plate."

~

Dinner comes and goes with the ease of any other meal. Bunny prepared spaghetti and shrimp, as well as a large salad, on top of which Ellie added a can of garbanzo beans she found in the cabinet for Maggie. When the family is done eating, Jonah begins the process of helping Bunny and Frank clear the table.

"It looks like Dad's got this all under control," Ellie tells Maggie, who sits across from her, taking a final bite of her oil-slicked salad. "Would you like to take a walk with me?"

A few minutes later, they sit side by side on the pool deck. Their feet drift through the water. Above them, the orange sun has begun its slow descent. Everyone else in this small community is back inside, preparing themselves for evening. Right now—right here—it's only the two of them.

"We haven't talked as much as we should since you've gone away," Ellie states. All around them, the palm leaves gently sway with the evening breeze. "I've had a really difficult time since you've left, Mags. It's been hard for me not having you around and trying to figure out for myself what it is that I'm supposed to do next."

Maggie doesn't say anything. She just sits, kicking her feet through the warm water, her long hair delicately draping itself over her slender arms.

"Can I ask you something?" Ellie poses, filling in their silence. Maggie tilts her head up at her mother. The sun's final rays create a glare. Ellie squints through it. When she does, she sees every version of her daughter sitting right here with her.

Maggie, with her pull-up diaper and whale-spout ponytail.

Maggie, up onstage for her first dance recital—and that adorable, stiff pink tutu—tapping her toes off beat.

Maggie, the first time she rode off by herself on that bicycle with the rainbow streamers (*Look, Mama, look!*).

Maggie, seated on her bed and studying for a test with her headphones on.

Maggie, sliding down the staircase banister—like someone from a movie—in her pale-blue prom dress.

Maggie, waving goodbye from her second-story dorm window the first time her parents pulled away.

Maggie, right here on the pool deck, her white maxi skirt bunched up in her hands so it doesn't get wet, some unspoken thought or question etched across her perfect face.

"Um, sure," Maggie finally responds. "What's—um—what's up?"

Ellie inhales and exhales slowly. "Mags," she begins. "Are you . . . I don't know. Are you okay?"

"Am I okay?" Maggie echoes and bites her lip.

Ellie's chest tightens. In her mind, she's wishing she could edit herself, certain she's said the wrong thing. "I just—"

"I'm—I'm miserable," Maggie interjects. A wash of emotion instantly falls from her hazel eyes and down the gentle curves of her smooth freckled cheeks.

"Wait." Ellie is taken aback. "What do you mean you're miserable?"

"I made a terrible choice, Mom," Maggie admits. "That school," she clarifies. "I hate it. I don't fit in there at all."

It takes everything in Ellie not to wrap her arms so tightly around her daughter and pull her face against her chest, like when she was small. "Okay" is all Ellie says, so Maggie has the space to keep speaking.

Maggie's tears drip from her chin and into the blue water, each of them creating a delicate pattern of ripples that spreads across the pool's surface. "I hate the cold," she tells her mother. "And the snow. I don't like the taste of all the hoppy local beers, which, *yes*, I know I'm too young to even technically drink. I don't even like to ski, really. I don't want to eat tempeh. I don't want to sleep in a hostel all summer."

Along the edge of the pool area, the community's old-fashioned lampposts all click on.

"What do you want, then, Maggie?" Ellie asks, unsure of what answer her daughter will provide.

"I—I—" She stops herself. "You were right, Mom. I know I'm supposed to want all this—to move mountains—to be *in* the mountains, or whatever. But I just . . . don't. I'm not ready. I don't like being so far away," she says through a sniffle. "I thought I would. That's what practically every person during junior and senior year kept telling me. That I needed to challenge myself and break out of my shell. To go somewhere new. To explore. That I'd love it once I was there. But they were wrong. I don't like it. It's not for me." Her chest shudders. "I just want to come back home."

All around them, a gentle, tropical breeze blows, rustling the flowers on the nearby hibiscus and magnolia trees. The air fills with their unique perfume.

"Can I do that, Mom?" Maggie wipes her face with the back of her hand. "I'll finish my finals first," she clarifies. "But once they're done, can I—"

"Of course," Ellie says and then takes her daughter's hand. She gives it a loving squeeze.

With this secret—which Ellie now suspects her daughter has held inside for months—finally out in the open air, Maggie's breathing starts to settle. For the first time in as long as Ellie can remember, her daughter—suddenly so in need of her—drops her head onto her mother's shoulder.

"Are you disappointed?" Maggie asks.

"What? No, not at all," Ellie reassures her. "Why would you ask me that?"

"I don't know." Maggie continues to sway her feet through the water. "I made such a big deal about going away." Her toes pop through the surface like fish. "I just feel like I'm supposed to go out and seek adventure and change the world—really leave my mark or something."

Ellie wraps her arm around Maggie's back. "You still can, Mags. But you get to choose how you want to do it." In the sky, a faint outline of the moon reveals itself, a nod to the world that this day and everything it's contained will soon end. "Sometimes," Ellie says, "you can make a big impact close to home."

"I'm sorry I said some of those things to you, Mom," Maggie says through her tears. "I didn't mean them. I like your life. I like where we live. I like being close to you and Dad." She nuzzles herself tighter against her mother. "I don't know. I think maybe I'm a lot like you."

Nearby, the pool gate opens.

"Girls?" Jonah asks, taking in the sight of them. "Everything all right?"

They both nod.

"I just needed Mom for a minute," Maggie explains.

Jonah smiles at them. His eyes catch the early, pale moonlight. "Okay," he says, not wanting to interfere with this moment. "I just wanted to tell you both that dessert is out. Grams picked up a pound cake."

"Come on." Ellie pats Maggie's thigh. "I promise not to tell any of your college friends that one of your favorite desserts is made with butter and eggs." She pulls herself back up to a standing position, then pivots in the direction of the gate.

"Hey, Mom," Maggie says from behind her. Ellie swivels herself around. "I know you've given up a lot over the years to always be there for me. And, I don't know. I guess I just want to say, well . . ." Her freckled cheeks subtly lift in a quiet smile. "Thanks."

THIRTY-FIVE

Saturday

The sun blazes as boldly as ever, so much so that the blacktop in the condo parking lot literally steams. If there's even a trace of a breeze, Ellie cannot feel it. The atmosphere is sticky and thick, the air like hot honey. Any suggestion of her morning shower is already gone, the scent of fragrant bubbles replaced by the slickness of sweat.

The whole family piles into Bunny and Frank's car. Bunny clicks on the air. After a minute of blowing out a stream of forced heat, it cools. Everyone buckles themselves in, prepared for this meal Bunny has planned for them, and for this whole new day.

"Everyone ready?" she asks as she and Frank fold up the windshield's reflective shade, her palm tree–shaped air freshener swinging from the rearview mirror.

In the back seat, Ellie, Jonah, and Maggie are pressed together in the too-small sedan. But this time, no one winces or complains about the need for private space.

On this trip, there has been no announcement. No news of a split. No fracture to their family, as jarring as a bone breaking. No reason for any of them to worry that their collective life—the one they're all living in together right now—is anything other than what it seems.

"We're ready, Mom," Ellie announces on her trio's behalf.

Beside her, Maggie is dressed in an old preppy nautical-striped T-shirt that Ellie remembers purchasing for her in high school—she must have packed it in her carry-on—which she's tucked into a pair of clean-cut denim shorts. The Jesus sandals, much to Ellie's chagrin, have stayed. But it's okay. Right now, for the first time in months, her daughter looks exactly like herself—a hybrid of who she used to be and who she's still busy becoming.

The car moves forward. Through the window, the world is both palm trees and concrete, blue sky and artificial lakes, block after block of neat tropical landscaping.

"It's nice here," Maggie decides, her gaze somewhere outside the glass.

Jonah wears his classic black sunglasses. Even with them on, it's clear that he smiles with his eyes.

Ellie smiles, too, as she gives her daughter's thigh a quick squeeze. "It really is."

~

When they return to the condo after lunch, the rest of the day carries on like a vacation. Together, the five of them enjoy an afternoon swim, the water practically as warm as a bath. They each take turns napping in the pool area's chaise lounges, all their cheeks becoming a subtle shade of pink. Later, after a family game of shuffleboard on the community's shared court, they all sit in Bunny and Frank's yard, sipping iced tea from perspiring acrylic tumblers.

In a blink, it's nearly evening again. They all head inside, taking turns to shower and change into fresh, comfortable clothes. After she's slipped into a clean T-shirt and a pair of cotton shorts, Ellie joins her mother in the kitchen, helping her pull out all the leftovers from lunch and slide them into casserole dishes to reheat.

The doorbell rings. Bunny looks up, confused by this unexpected interruption. A dish towel slung over her shoulder, she moves to the door.

"Shelia?" Bunny questions, her tone not doing much to hide her annoyance. "What are you doing here?"

"Hiya, Bunny," Shelia says, stretching her neck to gain a peek at who and what is beyond Bunny's shoulder. She wears her windbreaker and bermuda shorts—just like last time—a foil-wrapped tray in her aging hands. "I whipped up some cream puffs for your guests. I remembered you telling me you had company this weekend."

Ellie steps out of the kitchen and joins her mother in the condo's small entryway. "Hello." She accepts the tray from Shelia. "I'm Bunny's daughter, Ellie." She smiles as she says it, and she thinks of Jack, wondering if it's all actually possible, that maybe he and Kristin did end up together after all, thus allowing Shelia to relocate to here.

Shelia smiles, pleased by this warm greeting. "Pleasure to meet you." She lingers for a minute. "Well, I'm certainly not here to intrude on anyone's family time." She pats her short, ashy hair, and pauses to breathe. "Trust me," she says. "I'd take every minute with my Johnnie if he were here visiting me, too." She gives a friendly wave. "Byyye-ya, ladies," she says and then takes a step back. "Enjoy your night."

Bunny closes the door and steps back into the kitchen. Ellie follows her and sets the tray on the table. Not a minute passes before she excuses herself and steps outside.

"Shelia?" Ellie asks once her feet have touched the walkway.

Up ahead, Shelia—who's walking back to her own unit—pauses and turns around. "Oh Lord, you're not allergic to cream puffs, are you?" She gasps, her insecurities suddenly on full display. "I didn't mean to offend anyone. I was only trying to—"

"No," Ellie says with a laugh. "It's not that." An instant look of relief settles back on Shelia's aged face. "It's just, well, I have a bit of a strange question, actually."

Nearby, the leaves on the palm trees rustle from the gentle and warm evening air. Shelia looks at Ellie in question, her hair softly swaying, too.

"By chance," Ellie begins, "is your son—Johnnie, the one you mentioned—well, is he a physician?"

Shelia's expression simultaneously lights up and goes dark, like a neon sign someone has turned on right at the exact moment when all the bulbs have burned out. "Yes," she says. "Why, yes. A very good one, in fact." Her expression, already wrinkled from time, continues to wrinkle now with thought. "How did you know that?"

Ellie licks her lips, thinking.

"It's—well, your face," Ellie decides. "It reminds me of him." She smiles softly and thinks of the Jack she knew back in her twenties, wondering if Shelia might remember her old name—Ellie Adams—and the mystery girl her son once left behind. "He—um—he treated me a few times," Ellie offers as further explanation. "How is he?" she asks, wanting to know how it all ended up for him—how their single, shared choice to part ways, and to never rekindle things for those extra six months, has influenced his life—his real one. "I don't believe he practices in my area anymore. I haven't seen him in a very long time."

As soon as Ellie asks these questions, though, she knows it was the wrong thing to do.

Shelia sighs heavily through her nose and briefly closes her eyes. "We lost Johnnie last year," she tells Ellie. When she reopens her eyes, the tears fall. "The twins were on their way home from college for the summer that afternoon." She shakes her head at this thought. "He was so excited to see them. He was rushing home from his shift at the hospital near our homes to help get things ready." She stops, bites her quivering bottom lip, and rubs a nervous hand across the front of her knee-length shorts. "Anyway, another driver sped right through a red light." She inhales a shaky breath. "One person's foolish choice," she explains, "one completely avoidable accident, and it ruined everything."

Ellie feels like someone has sucked all the air right out of her. "I'm—I'm so sorry." Tears begin to form in her eyes, too. "I had no idea. I'm terribly sorry I asked."

Shelia waves a hand, as if this whole transaction has been no big deal, even though, of course, it has been. "It's fine," she assures her. "Since moving down here, I haven't talked about him much with the neighbors. I still feel so guilty about leaving my daughter-in-law behind. The memories," she explains; "they were too much for me." Her breath starts to even out, right as a touch of a breeze picks up. "I needed to turn the page and start over someplace new."

Ellie cannot help herself. She already knows the answer. Still, she needs to ask.

"Your daughter-in-law," Ellie says. "How is she? I—I can't imagine—"

"Kristin?" Shelia poses, speaking the name Ellie knew—or rather, *hoped*—she would say. "Terrible. But, you know, the twins, they keep her going."

Ellie nods. She does know, in her own way.

"The three of them are making their first trip down this summer," Shelia explains, wrapping up their conversation. "I can't wait to show them the pool. They all love to swim."

Before Ellie steps back around to leave, she poses one final question. "Forgive me," she says, "if this is an impolite thing to ask. But, by chance, are you Catholic?"

Shelia nods, suddenly as excited as a child. "Yes! Yes, I am. Why do you ask?"

In the privacy of her mind, Ellie sees her mother in that ER bed, asking Jack—Shelia's son—the same question.

"We are, too," Ellie tells her, acknowledging that Shelia is not terrible like Bunny thinks. She is just a mother in grief. As if there is any other kind. "My mom goes to church most weekdays. Maybe you two can go together sometime," she suggests.

"Oh, I'd love that!" Shelia announces, continuing to perk back up. "I'll be sure to pop by to talk to Bunny about it this week!"

All around the neighborhood, the lampposts light up.

"It was nice to meet you, Shelia," Ellie says.

"It was nice to meet you, too, Ellie," Shelia responds. "Enjoy the cream puffs." She offers a smile, one with so many stories hidden behind it. "They were always my Johnnie's favorite."

I know, Ellie thinks.

THIRTY-SIX

Sunday

Ellie wakes up on her parents' couch, the condo and world outside it still dark. On the far end of the sectional, Jonah sleeps soundly. Across from them, the muted television—the one they fell asleep watching together—is still tuned to the Game Show Network, where a handsomely dressed Richard Dawson, apparently preserved in time, continues to strut around on set.

"You're awake," Bunny observes when Ellie steps into the kitchen. She's seated, just as Ellie knew she would be, at the table, her light hair tousled from sleep. Nearby, the coffeepot already sputters out the morning brew.

"I can never sleep on days when I know I have to travel," Ellie explains.

Bunny, dressed in her Florida-inspired bathrobe, stands and pours them each a steaming mug. "Why did you two sleep on the couch? Why is Maggie in the front room?"

"She's slept on a bad dorm mattress for months." Ellie shrugs. "She needs her rest."

Bunny sets the mugs on the table, reclaims her seat. "There's a storm back at home," she explains, the bearer of happy morning headlines. "You'll be flying right into it."

Ellie sits, too. "We'll be all right, Mom." She pours a splash of white cream into her black coffee. "I'm sure that, at some point, we've flown through worse."

Beyond Bunny, Ellie can see through the window that the sun is rising. Strokes of yellow—determined to bring about this new day— begin to wash out the charcoal of night.

"I had a terrible feeling when you told me the three of you were coming," Bunny admits. She holds up her mug, takes a sip. "I don't know why, but I kept thinking you had bad news."

"And now?" Ellie asks.

Bunny sets down her mug. "I suppose even a mother's intuition is wrong sometimes."

In the living room, the sounds of hushed morning voices. Frank and Jonah are awake.

"When do you think the three of you will be back?" Bunny asks, her words outlined with a sense of sadness.

"Soon, Mom," Ellie reassures her. "Once Maggie gets home and settled in a few weeks, and we start to figure out her next steps, we'll make a plan. Okay?"

Bunny nods her agreement. "Okay."

Beyond the glass, the blackness in the sky is almost fully washed out with new light.

"You doing okay, Mom?" Ellie asks. "Are you and Dad all right?"

Bunny pulls her bathrobe tighter around her aging body. She tilts her head, briefly considering what she'd like to say next. "We're fine, sweetie," she tells her daughter. "Our life here is everything we've always wanted," she says and then gently touches her cross necklace. "Except for one thing."

"What's that?" Ellie hesitantly asks, not entirely sure she wants to know.

Bunny locks eyes with her daughter. "I miss you terribly," she admits.

Ellie reaches her hand across the table and squeezes her mother's aging fingers. "I miss you, too, Mom," she tells her. "But I know you and Dad are exactly where you're meant to be."

~

Their car—and their same old driver—arrives exactly on time. Their bags packed, the Baker family steps back outside and into the swampy heat. Jonah loads their luggage into the trunk right before they all say goodbye.

Once Jonah and Maggie are in the air-conditioned car, Ellie steals one last private moment with her parents.

"Thank you both for everything," she says, even though they could never possibly understand all that she means. "Really." She pulls them both close to her for an embrace. "I can't tell you how much it means to me."

Ellie slides into the back seat beside Maggie and closes her door. Her seat belt not even on yet, their driver is already throwing the gear-shift into reverse.

"Everyone okay back there?" Jonah asks from the front seat, just like always, and pulls his sunglasses onto his face.

Maggie dips her head onto her mother's shoulder. Ellie turns and looks through the rear windshield. Her parents, dressed in their colorful, tropical retirement wear, stand side by side and wave as Bunny makes the sign of the cross—a prayer, or a wish, before her family leaves.

"We're fine," Ellie says, and this time, she means it. She swivels back around to face forward, clicks her seat belt into place. "Everyone is fine."

THIRTY-SEVEN

Their flight is canceled.

This part, to Ellie, makes exactly zero sense. The last time, despite the storm and several delays, they still took off together. How, Ellie wonders, could her single choice—to modify the purpose of her family's weekend getaway—somehow change entire flight patterns? It seems improbable. Impossible. But then again, no one ever really knows the vast ripple effects that are sent out into the larger world due to the decisions she makes in her own singular life.

"This doesn't make sense," Maggie announces before crunching her way through the package of cookies she picked up at a nearby newsstand. They're standing at her gate as she prepares to board. "How is my flight still taking off on time?"

Through the wall of windows is a straight-shot view of the tarmac. The bold sun shines down on the runway, one final taste of the tropics for every traveler to enjoy before she jets away from this place.

"You'll be fine, Mags," Ellie reassures her daughter, and then pulls her own hair back into a low bun, securing it with the rubber band at her wrist. "I promise they wouldn't let you take off if it wasn't safe."

Overhead, the gate's speakers come to life. "We now welcome groups two and three to begin the boarding process," a member of Maggie's flight crew announces. A handful of travelers—with their book bags and their wheeled carry-ons, all full of the assorted contents each respective person believed she needed to feel at home while she was away—begin to stand.

"So, what's the game plan?" Jonah asks, his eyes down on his phone screen while he searches for a new return flight. "You'll come home after finals in a few weeks, and then . . ."

"I was thinking I'd apply to some schools a bit closer to home for the fall semester," Maggie explains as she nibbles through her last cookie. She wears her hunter-green crewneck sweatshirt, the one with the word *Vermont* emblazoned across the chest. "And, in the meantime, I thought I'd look for some part-time work in town. Maybe I can pick up a waitressing gig at one of the restaurants. Or get a few shifts at the bookstore or something."

Ellie can't help it. Her lips lift themselves into a wide U shape.

"What?" Maggie asks, her eyes narrowing at her mother's facial expression.

"Funny story," Ellie tells her. "But, as it turns out, I was thinking about picking up a few shifts there for myself, too."

"You were?" Jonah and Maggie both ask.

"I was," Ellie informs them. "Just a little something," she explains. "Start getting my feet wet again, you know?"

Jonah taps a finger to his screen, slides his phone away. "You'd better hurry, then, and get over there before the new owner takes over."

"New owner?" Ellie asks as more travelers move around them and join the boarding line.

"You didn't hear?" Jonah says, the curves of his arms evident beneath his T-shirt's sleeves. "That old couple recently sold it. They've had a sign about it in the window for weeks."

"Oh." Ellie tightens the knot on her cardigan, which she's tied around her waist. "I guess I've been in a bit of a fog," she admits. "I never noticed."

Above them, the speakers boom to life once again. "All remaining passengers are now invited to begin the boarding process."

Maggie balls her sweatshirt sleeves into her fists, an old nervous habit dating back to her childhood. "Well, I guess that's me."

Ellie pulls her daughter in for a hug. "You'll be back home soon," she reminds her. "Until then, try to enjoy it, all right?"

Maggie nods her face against her mother's shoulder. "All right."

"Come here, kiddo!" Jonah announces and wraps his arms around them both. "We'll see you soon, okay?" he says and playfully rumples Maggie's head of long hair. "I'll pull out some of our old board games for when you get back."

Maggie, wearing a half smile, joins the line. Ellie and Jonah watch as she hands the woman at the check-in desk her credentials. Before she steps into the passenger bridge, she turns back to face her parents one more time. "I'll see you guys soon," she tells them and tugs at a strand of her long, straight hair. "I promise to text you both when I land."

Maggie joins the remaining travelers then and moves forward toward her plane.

Back at the gate, Jonah reaches down and squeezes Ellie's hand.

"You okay?" he asks as Maggie disappears into the tunnel.

Sometimes, Ellie acknowledges now, letting go doesn't always have to mean saying goodbye. It can also mean giving someone the space she needs to discover something for and about herself.

"I am," Ellie says.

~

A little while later, Ellie sits in a turquoise-colored chair in the center of the terminal. All around her are fast-food booths and clusters of potted palm trees—what's real and what's artificial coexisting together in this place. Above her, the ceiling is made of glass. Sunlight filters through it and casts a series of long, illuminated rectangles across the airport's green patterned carpet. Ellie glances around her current surroundings and takes it all in. Throughout the well-lit seating area, this in-between space meant for both travelers who are coming and others who are going, the line between who's arriving and who's departing, whose journey has just ended and whose is about to begin, all blends together here.

While she waits, Ellie reaches toward the floor and pulls her phone out from the side pocket of her book bag, the one she's hardly used in days. On the top right of the screen, she sees that the device is still holding on with one last bit of power. Ellie swipes it open, hoping there's enough still there for her to do one final thing before this journey is over and she returns home.

Ellie is not someone who spends much time on social media. Even so, she cannot deny the fact that it is vastly impressive. It takes only seconds for Ellie to locate her. Gabby—in her real, present-day life—stares back at her through the screen. It's a photo of her in front of a wall of books, her fingernails still as purple as ever and pressed to her chin, her wild hair clipped back from her face with a colorful jeweled barrette. Based on her profile description, she now lives in another, different part of their shared home state.

The message Ellie sends is brief.

Hey, Gabby. Hopefully you remember me! It's been a while, huh? Anyway, I thought of you the other day and wondered how you're doing. I hope you're well. If you're ever in town (yes, I'm still here), feel free to reach out. It'd be nice to see you and have a coffee or something.

She slides her phone back into her bag. No sooner than she does, it pings.

Ellie! What a weird coincidence, Gabby almost immediately replies. I was thinking about you the other day, too! This is so random, but I'm moving back to the area this summer. You'll never believe this, but I actually just bought the bookstore in town, the one where you used to work! I'm heading there next week to take measurements. I'll contact you. I'd love to catch up!

Before Ellie can respond, her phone dies. She zips it away inside her bag and then leans back in her tropical-hued vinyl chair. Nearby, a little girl dressed in a Cinderella costume and light-up sneakers races past.

"We're here!" the child shouts, over and over, like the chorus to a song. "We're heeeeere!"

The girl's mother laughs at her daughter's enthusiasm and quickly snaps a photo. She turns to Ellie and shrugs. "What can I say?" the woman announces, never once apologizing. "She's waited a long time for this." She smiles. "We both have."

Ellie nods her understanding and watches the family race to the airport's monorail, the one that will bring them to the baggage claim.

"Here," a voice says behind her.

She turns and finds that Jonah, who'd gone off to the bathroom, has returned.

"Oh, dear God," she says and blinks wildly, just to be sure she's seeing things correctly. "What—what are you *wearing*?" she gasps.

"What?" Jonah tugs the bottom hem of his neon-orange T-shirt—the word *Florida* boldly emblazoned across its front in equally bright block letters—which he must have slipped on while in the restroom. "You don't like it?" He tosses a small bag at Ellie. "That's too bad, since I picked up a matching one for you, too."

Ellie can't help but laugh. The shirt is awful. Her father, she privately acknowledges, would love it. "I'm not wearing that!"

"Come on," he says. "You always wanted us to wear matching shirts when Maggie was little, but we never did." He raises a brow, challenging her. "Why not start now?"

Still smirking, Ellie slips hers on over her white T-shirt. "This is hideous," she says with a smile.

"I know," Jonah agrees. "It really is."

Above them, the airport's vast speaker system buzzes with a new announcement.

"So, listen," Jonah begins, his tone shifting into a different, more subdued gear. "I tried, but I couldn't get us on any flight out today. The earliest available isn't until late tomorrow afternoon."

Ellie feels her shoulders slump.

"But, in the meantime," he continues, "I came up with a good plan B."

Her head tilted, Ellie feels her face curl into a question.

"I found us a room at a hotel nearby," he explains. "There's a nice pool with one of those lazy rivers, a few good restaurants. Before we head back home, let's go spend some time together. Just us."

Thirty-five thousand choices. There are so many opportunities every single day to open new doors and to close old ones. To walk the tightrope that divides free will and fate. To choose which version of your life you want to live.

"Okay," Ellie says and then collects her things. "Yes. Let's do that."

Together, they walk toward the monorail with a sea of other travelers. Through the windows, Ellie observes the train pulling into the terminal's tube. The electronic doors slide open. A group of happy families, all ready to embark on whatever new memories await them, flood out.

Ellie and Jonah take a few steps. Before they make it far, a new expression molds itself across his face. She tilts her chin and, as if he's a good book, tries to analyze him.

"What?" Ellie's heartbeat flutters in her neck. "What is it?"

Jonah smiles, though it's curious—equal parts joy and sadness. "I just—" He cuts himself off, shakes his head. "It's nothing," he decides. "Really. It's silly."

A feeling. The one she's felt more than once in recent days, every time she's stood at the precipice of another unexpected something. Everything inside her chest—her breath, her heart—quickens. "Tell me," she says, already prepared for one last unwanted twist.

Jonah pulls in a deep breath. "I don't know why, but I haven't been able to shake this memory all weekend."

"A memory?" Ellie asks, surprised. "Of what?"

He laughs. "Of this silly drawing Maggie used to make when she was a kid." His gaze is suddenly far away, as if lost in another time. "It was this little sun wearing sunglasses." A trace of grief hangs along his smile. "For a while there, it was the only thing she ever drew." He pauses, remembering. "Do you know which one I mean?"

Ellie laughs, too. *Do you know which one I mean?* As if she could ever forget.

"I do," she says.

"Anyway, I don't know why that popped into my head." He flips up his hands. "Now and again, memories like that just sort of come back at random times, don't they?"

Ellie nods. "All the time, actually." Her heartbeat slows. There are no more unexpected turns in this story. Not now. Not ever, hopefully. "I remember things like that constantly."

Ahead of them, the crowd moves forward.

"Come on," Jonah says with a smirk. "Enough about the past." He takes her hand. When he does, it feels like home. *He* feels like home. "We don't want to miss this train."

As they filter inside, Ellie sees the large electronic departures board beyond the monorail's windows, and the clock displayed on its upper corner.

1:11 p.m.

Not quite the right time, though it's close enough.

"Please stand clear of doors and hold on to handrails," an automated voice announces overhead. "The doors are now closing."

Briefly, she shuts her eyes and makes her wish, knowing there's no reason left for her to wait. When she's done, she reopens them and then turns to face the train's glass front side. Outside, the world is all blue sky and concrete and palm trees. She smiles, thinking of where they've been and where they're headed.

"The doors are now closed," the voice says as they slide shut.

She considers asking him more about that memory, and others, but decides some stories are best left untold. Instead, Ellie keeps her gaze straight ahead. She wants to see what destiny awaits them.

This time, whatever it is, she knows that she's ready for it.

ACKNOWLEDGMENTS

They say it takes a village to raise a child. In many ways, it takes a village to get a book out into the world, too. It is with infinite gratitude that I thank the following people for the many ways they continue to support me and my work.

First and foremost, thank you to my agent, Eve Attermann, for always standing in my corner, cheering me on, and helping me to grow my writing career. You're the person who took that initial chance on me and set everything into motion. I'll never be able to thank you enough for all you've done (but I'll try). Thank you, Eve. Really. You've changed my whole world.

I'm so fortunate to continue to have Carmen Johnson as an editor. She always shares and understands my vision for my stories and provides the perfect balance of helping me see which parts of a manuscript will benefit from further development, while also letting my creative ideas shine through on the page. Her enthusiasm for my work means so much to me. I feel incredibly lucky to work with her.

Thank you to Faith Black Ross. Your attention to detail and thoughtful suggestions for how to strengthen this story have made such an enormous difference in the final product.

I am forever grateful for the many talented people at William Morris Endeavor, including Rikki Bergman and everyone involved in Business and International Affairs, as well as Nicole Weinroth. Thank you all for championing my work.

I owe so much to everyone at Little A for the magical ways they transform a simple document on my laptop into a beautiful, edited book, especially all those people in production, marketing, and the many steps in between, for all the great work they do. I'd also like to thank my publicist, Suzanne Williams, for getting my writing into so many hands.

I've had the good fortune to meet and become friends with many wonderful fellow authors in recent years, all of whom have been so supportive and kind. I'm especially grateful to Zibby Owens and her team for creating such an important community of readers and writers and, more so, for welcoming me into it with open arms. Thank you for all you've done for me.

I'd also like to thank my friends—those near and far, old and new—who have rallied around me and my writing in such an authentic way. Your ability to make me laugh and smile and to avoid judging me for bailing on things when I'm too deep into my editing to peel myself away is a blessing I do not take for granted.

To my parents: I imagine you'll see a lot of settings you recognize in this book. Thank you for providing me with so many sun-drenched memories throughout my life. We really are very good travel companions. It's never too early to plan our next trip. I love you both.

To my children: watching the two of you grow up is truly the greatest gift of my life. I have cherished every minute, every stage, every season. I hope that when you're old enough to read this book one day, you'll feel my love for you written all over it.

To Jay, my forever travel partner: I didn't set out to write a love story, but I guess I accidentally wrote one anyway. It's your fault. Writing a second book is very different from writing a first one. Perhaps you've picked up on that? Thank you for helping me (dealing with me?) while I worked on this novel and for constantly letting me bounce ideas off you. I'm so glad that fourteen-year-old Jay whispered hello to me in the back row of our freshman English class that first day of high school and asked if I wanted to play cards together instead of taking notes. Who knows where either of us might have landed if you'd changed that one small thing.

Lastly, to my readers: thank you so very much for reading my work and for allowing me to live out my dream. I put my whole heart into this book. I hope you can feel that on every page.

ABOUT THE AUTHOR

Photo © 2023 Sylvie Rosokoff

Angela Brown is the author of *Olivia Strauss Is Running Out of Time*. Her writing has appeared in the *New York Times*, *Real Simple*, and other publications. She holds an MFA from Fairleigh Dickinson University. Angela lives with her husband and two young children in New Jersey, where she is currently at work on her next novel. For more information, visit www.angelabrownbooks.com.